# THE CORPSE-RAT KING

"Lee Battersby's *The Corpse-Rat King* is rugged, muscular fantasy, sure to please those who like their adventures rough around the edges, with wit and style to burn."

*Karen Miller, author of* The Innocent Mage *and the* Godspeaker *trilogy*

"A stunning debut novel, well-crafted and grotesquely inventive. With its madcap story, unforgettable characters and fine balance between humour and pathos, *The Corpse-Rat King* ticks all the boxes. Fans of Joe Abercrombie will love this."

*Juliet Marillier, award-winning author of the* Sevenwater *series and* Bridei's Chronicles

"One of the best books of 2012, nailed on. Brilliant."

*Steven Savile, author of* Silver

# LEE BATTERSBY

# THE CORPSE-RAT KING

ANGRY
ROBOT

**ANGRY ROBOT**
A member of the Osprey Group

Lace Market House,
54-56 High Pavement,
Nottingham,
NG1 1HW, UK

4402 23rd St., Ste 219,
Long Island City,
NY 11101
USA

www.angryrobotbooks.com
Down among the dead men

An Angry Robot paperback original 2012.

ISBN 978-0-85766-287-3
eBook ISBN 978-0-85766-288-0

Printed in the United States of America

9 8 7 6 5 4 3 2

*To my beautiful wife Lyn, for her belief, her
unwavering support, and her constant love.*

*To Aiden, with faith that the huge steps he is
about to take carry him wherever he wishes to go.*

*And to Erin and Connor, who keep telling me
how much they want to be older so they can read
this book.*

*If I catch you using any of the rude words in
here, I'll ground you.*

# ONE

The battle was over.

The Jezel valley had been a place of gently rolling farmlands, with a series of short, steep hills at one end where sheep had jostled for grass under the shade of hardy, wind-swept trees. It was a perfect location for two armies to clash. In two hours, the valley had been transformed from a sleepy green nowhere into a madman's finger painting of mud, metal and ruptured flesh lying beneath a swathe of early morning mist. The lower reaches of the hills lay bare, denuded of handholds by soldiers grabbing at whatever foliage might help them climb above the carnage, only to be dragged back under, fingers curled around snapping branches. Two hours of pre-dawn chaos was over. Now the silence was broken only by the cawing of crows and an occasional cry of disbelief as one of the soldiers left behind to pick through the carpet of corpses saw the face of a friend, or comrade, or brother.

The dead lay across each other like so many stalks of threshed wheat. It was impossible for a man to step in any direction without sliding his foot across someone's flesh. Men lay embraced in poses at once familiar and obscene, metal-clad parodies of lust turned to stone and forgotten. Loyalties were impossible to discern. Scraps of standards were wrapped around necks or half-buried in the mud that fifty thousand feet had churned to a strength-sapping soup. A careful census might discover who had drowned rather than been beaten into eternity, but no such census would occur. The dead were dead. Those who had decided the need for conflict would move on, to gather more troops and seek further opportunities for warfare. Men can be recruited, but lands are limited.

Not all those on the field were dead, however. Here and there, members of the opposing armies wandered back and forth, bending to turn over a body here, removing a chest plate or shield there. In the aftermath of the battle, the need to identify those lords who had fallen, to ascertain blood payments and send tokens back to estates for identification and enshrinement, had brought down a practical kind of truce. Every now and again, soldiers from opposing sides would pass each other and stop to tell their stories and swap whatever items they had found on their wanderings. To count the fallen was a sad business. With so many thousands of corpses, there were enough deceased gentry that it would take two full days to drag the bodies away from the area. Only after that could the commoners be gathered up like so much kindling and put to the torch.

Minor nobility had been herded toward the far fringes of the battle, in order to blood them in inconsequential clashes. Should they rise in their king's favour before battles to come, they would have at least *some* sort of experience in their favour.

At the farthest corner, where the ground had become stony and unworkable, ending in a copse of ancient, gnarled trees, two men in the colours of the Kingdom of Scorby tiptoed cautiously through the fallen. A casual observer would see nothing to separate them from the soldiery concentrated on the more profitable slopes towards the centre of the battlefield. They were thin and darkened by the sun. The young one was taller, a little on the burly side, perhaps even barrel-chested. Close-cropped hair sat above an open face framed by ears as large as jug handles. His companion – older, smaller – walked with smooth grace between the corpses, seemingly less troubled by the proximity to death. His hair was longer, brushed back off his sharp features and tied back with a simple leather headband. He was, perhaps, a touch too slight for the military, but the quickness and deftness of his movements marked him out against his lumbering young companion. There was nothing to cause alarm or distrust, no reason to let the gaze linger before moving on.

But watch long enough, and the observer would see how they made pains to avoid their fellow soldiers, how they stooped and scuttled rather than strode with solemn grace, how they shied from any glance and how whatever it was they tore from finger and neck was quickly secreted so that, to all intents and purposes, their task seemed fruitless.

Marius Helles watched his apprentice turn over a corpse and bend to remove the chain gloves from its hands. He tutted. No sense, this boy. It was obvious to Marius, even from several feet away, that the dead man was no noble. Nobody of gentility would grip a smithing hammer so tightly in their cold fist, nor wear a leather jerkin with so many patches. The helmet clinging to the dead man's head was of poor manufacture, which accounted for the massive dent that had crushed the corpse's head into such an ovoid shape. Despite all his teachings, the youngster still could not see the obvious and move on to more profitable prospects. Marius hissed, and the young man looked up from his task.

"Not that one, Gerd. There." He jerked his head towards a splash of burgundy cloth waving above a tangle of bodies. "Check that one out."

"But this one…" Marius had picked Gerd up whilst on the run from a disastrous money-printing venture in the Tallian foothills. Gerd's accent bore the thickness of the mountains. Weeks of roadside elocution practice had done nothing to thin his tongue or round his vowels. An accent is a way to be tracked, Marius had told him, over and over, to no avail. He glared, and Gerd, thick as he was, took the hint.

"Stupid boy," Marius muttered, and picked his way across the dead soldiers towards the possible prize. Best to get there before the boy, in case Gerd mistook a ring for a wart and did him out of a week's eating. He scanned the corpses to either side as he walked. There, just a few steps away, a flash of chequered cloth that Marius immediately recognised as belonging to the house of the Duke of Lypes, a rich province. He hunched over, close enough to identify the body. One of the Duke's younger sons, sent to this end of the battle to keep him away from the battle-hardened mercenaries of the Tallian Empire who had borne the brunt of the main fighting. Marius smiled.

"Bet some princess cries when you don't turn up at her bedchamber tomorrow," he said to the young man's staring eyes. He traced the red slash that separated most of the young heir's jaw from his lower face. His gaze travelled down the boy's armoured body, hands patting and prodding until they discovered a small bag of coins at the waist. He undid it, and poured several silver coins into his palm.

"Nice," he said, nodding. Within half a minute, three rings and a gold charm joined them. Marius glanced towards the distant soldiers. When he was sure nobody was looking in his direction he rolled his tongue around, generating as much spit as his mouth could hold. One after the other, he began swallowing his prizes. When the last had been forced down his throat he gasped, then looked to where Gerd was standing over the body to which Marius had directed him.

"Gerd!"

Gerd made no response. He stood above the corpse, eyes wide, his hands raised to his mouth. Marius glanced at the nearest soldiers. No stare met his. He hissed again.

"Gerd! Get down to it, boy."

Still Gerd did not move. He began to whimper, each inhalation drawing out a slightly louder noise. Marius shook his head in frustration. This was the last straw. A corpse rat who could not stand the sight of the dead was too much of a liability. If Marius managed to survive this, despite the boy's best attempts to have them caught and strung, he would drop Gerd off at the nearest brothel with a handful of pennies, tell him to enjoy himself, and make for the border on the fastest horse an hour's straining at the privy could shake loose. He closed the distance between them in three long strides and shook Gerd by his arm.

"Do you want us to get caught, you idiot? What the hell…?"

Gerd pointed to the corpse at their feet. Marius followed his finger. A face stared back at him: one Marius had swallowed on any number of occasions, every time he had lifted a purse from a careless Scorban passer-by. The velvet overcoat and the thin gold crown that topped the dead man's helmet were only accessories to recognition. Even when caked with dirt and blood, the King of Scorby was unmistakeable. Marius reached out and grabbed Gerd's coat sleeve.

"Down in the presence of your King, boy."

"But…"

Marius yanked and sent Gerd sprawling over the King's body. He knelt upon one knee, and when Gerd made to rise, pushed him back down.

"Marius, he's dead."

"I know that, you idiot." Marius busied himself about the corpse, testing the welds of his fine plate armour. His gaze flitted about restlessly. Should anyone look their way, the stillness of his bent head would reveal nothing but concentration. "Do I look pious to you?"

"No, but then why…?"

"Because your goggling act has caught the attention of at least two of the soldiers, stupid, which means our day is over unless we can get away before they come within shouting distance."

Gerd raised his head, and Marius' fingers ceased their exploration long enough to flick him on the bridge of his nose.

"Stay down."

Gerd flinched and dropped forward. His face hit the mud with a soft squelch, and Marius suppressed a smile. Gerd whispered from the side of his muddy mouth.

"Are they coming?"

"Not yet." Marius separated a signet ring from the King's hand with a tug, then tore a bracelet from his wrist with a practiced twist of his fingers. "They're conferring. Shit!"

"What? What?"

"They've separated. One of them is coming." He palmed his booty and slid it up a sleeve, then redoubled his efforts, reaching forward to snatch at the crown around the top of the King's helm.

"Marius?"

"What?" The soldier was almost close enough to shout. He yanked at the crown, praying to gods whose names he couldn't remember that it was only placed upon the helmet, rather than welded. Kings did not normally wear such obvious identifying marks in battle: it encouraged enemy soldiers, rapacious for the largest ransoms possible, to make a beeline. But Tanspar, the young Scorban monarch, had been a man under siege in his own kingdom, and grandiose, crowd-pleasing gestures such as this one had become a signature. In this case, it had backfired in more than one way: the crown slid off the helmet with a soft scrape and disappeared inside Marius' jerkin.

"What are you doing?"

"Shut up, boy. This is our fortune."

"But you said… only steal what you can swallow, you said."

"Shush."

"But it's not fair…" Gerd struggled to raise his head.

"Hey!" the soldier called out in a broad Scorban accent. "You!"

"Shit." Both thieves froze, panicked eyes fixed upon each other. If the soldier had seen Marius slip the crown into his shirt front, all was lost. There was only one penalty for looting.

"You see?" Gerd wriggled one arm free, voice rising in panic. "See?"

"Gerd!" Through his lowered eyelashes, Marius watched the soldier stop and draw his weapon halfway from its sheath. There was no escape now. They were discovered. Gerd pushed against his restraining grip, trying to rise.

"Get off me," he said. "Get off." He drew his feet underneath him. Marius started to protest. Running was futile. Soldiers were everywhere, and where there were soldiers, archers would flank them in case a sudden flare-up between opposing parties occurred. The only way for a corpse rat to stay alive was through stealth. Slow movement, invisible progress across the field, sliding into woods or high grass when attention was diverted. That was the way to survive. Running from *anything* was an admission of guilt.

The soldier had drawn his sword now, and was

striding towards the two thieves, calling for his com-
patriots. Gerd pushed up, drawing his back out of the
mud, his arms straight and stiff. Marius' eyes shifted
from one figure to the other. They were caught, unless… He gritted his teeth. The timing would have to
be perfect. Gerd was still out of the soldier's view. He
let go of the younger man's tunic, and as he pushed
himself up from the ground, Marius crumpled. He
slid his head under the half-raised arm of the soldier
to the side of the King and pressed his face into the
mud, breath held. Gerd reached his feet and turned
to run. Marius slid his face sideways until it lodged
painfully against the edge of the dead soldier's
cuirass, so that he had half a view of the events as
they unfolded.

"I'm sorry, son," he whispered into the mud. There
was no other way. Marius wanted to live. There really was no other way.

The soldier closed in on Gerd, weapon held out in
front of him like a horn protruding from his midriff.

"I said stop and identify yourself, boy!"

Gerd threw his meagre booty into the air, squealed,
and ran two steps before the soldier was upon him.
The soldier lunged, and the sword slid into Gerd's
back and through him without the slightest impediment. Gerd stopped, impaled. His head fell forward,
his eyes taking in the foot of metal protruding from
his stomach. He opened his hand, and a glitter of
jewellery fell to Earth. Marius stilled his breath.
Please, he prayed, do not turn. Do not speak my
name. Gerd opened his mouth. His head lolled towards Marius. His lips moved in spasms. Marius saw

the beginning of his name: once; twice. Then Gerd's lips lost their strength, his neck gave up its fight to hold his head upright, and the dead thief slumped off the sword and hit the ground. The soldier turned towards Marius, and Marius unfocussed his eyes, staring into infinity.

"Oh, gods," the soldier whispered. His face swam into Marius' vision, blurred outline filling his sight. Marius fought the natural urge to blink it into focus. A metal-gloved hand reached out towards him, then beyond.

"Oh, gods. Oh, no." The soldier said again, then turned his head to shout. "Garion! Ektar! Here, for pity's sake. The King! The King is fallen!"

Shouts answered him, and the squelch of several sets of footprints sounded from all sides of Marius' head. A weight was lifted from across his shoulder. The soldier spoke briskly to his comrades.

"Take him, quickly. Get him to the camp."

"What about the others?"

"For gods' sake, man. I'll deal with them later. Take the King. I'll bring the thief in. Lord Bellux will want the body for burning. Go."

The light above Marius changed as the bodies moved, unblocking the morning sun. The King had been taken from the battlefield. Only common meat remained. Marius counted to forty, then let out a single, slow breath. He blinked once to clear the stinging from his eyes, then focussed his sight upon his immediate surroundings.

Less than a foot from him, a dead soldier stared back. A gash ran across the bridge of his nose from the left corner of his lip up into his forehead. A black pit gaped where his right eye had been destroyed by the killing stroke. Whoever had struck the blow had done so with strength, or desperation – most likely both. Marius could see jagged edges where the weapon had shattered the bones of the soldier's face. The socket had half-collapsed under the blow and white shards peeked out from between the ruptured flesh like a hard-boiled egg dropped from a great height. Marius, used to death, gulped back a sudden rush of bile. Already, flies were congregating in the shattered orb. Soon, prompted by the rising sun and the increasing heat of the day, more would come, until the eye that had once shone white would become a crawling mass of tiny black insects, writhing and mating, then flying away to die, leaving maggots in their place. Marius closed his eyes upon the thought. When he opened them, it was to stare directly at the hole once more, unmoving and directly in his line of sight.

As he watched, the empty eye socket blinked once.

Marius' head shot back involuntarily, striking the edge of someone's helm behind him. He let out a tiny scream, then resisted the urge to look around to see who might have heard. He blinked and slowly raised a hand to rub at his face. No sounds disrupted the stillness. Whatever soldiers remained were, he hoped, on the far side of the battlefield. If he were to raise his head and scan the area, he would find himself alone. How quickly he reached the sanctuary of the nearby grove would be a matter of how much caution he wished to forsake. From there, it was a matter of divesting himself of his stolen uniform, dressing in the simple village clothes he had stashed in a roll under the oak tree at the centre of the grove, and making his way out of the area along any of the merchants' paths leading to Vernus, or Qued, or one of the major cities of Tal where his prizes could be broken apart, melted and sold.

It would do him good. It had been two days since he had eaten, two days of forced marching through the wilderness to get to the battle just as it was ending, with poor dead stupid Gerd dragging along behind him so that he missed every open farmhouse window at every mealtime along the way. It was obviously affecting him. He needed to eat: something solid, with *real* meat, and an ale of heroic proportions to wash it down. Then sleep, and however many girls he could afford. Marius exhaled, and steeled himself to raise his head. It was time to lay down the corpse-rat and be a man for a while. All he needed was a slice of fortune, a space in which to make his dash.

He placed his hand flat on the ground in front of him, wriggled it to get firm purchase upon the shifting mud, and tensed. Slowly he lent into his arm, pushing upwards so that his shoulder slid out from underneath the soldier's embrace. His head followed it, inch by inch. Once it was clear he stopped, and waited. Only the sound of crows reached his ears. He smiled. Just a little further...

"I wouldn't do that," a voice like a rusted gate whispered from just in front of him. Marius froze. His head seemed to twist around of its own accord, until he was once more staring at the sword-blighted corpse.

While his eyes widened in sudden terror, the corpse smiled. Marius swallowed, once, twice. His voice, when it emerged, was little more than a choked cough.

"I'm sorry?"

"Get up like that," the corpse said. "I really wouldn't, if I were you."

"But…"

The corpse blinked, dislodging a cloud of flies. "A fellow like you, wandering around, it'll cause more than suspicion, don't you think?"

"But… but you're dead."

The corpse ran its tongue over cracked lips. "Well, that's all a matter of perspective, wouldn't you say?"

"No!"

"Heh. Well, perhaps you're right." It hacked, and spat a red globule onto the ground in front of it. "Still, I think you're missing the point."

"What?" Despite himself, Marius couldn't help but be drawn into the exchange. After weeks of Gerd's inability to hold down two consecutive thoughts, even a dead man made for stimulating conversation.

"Come here." The corpse tilted its head in invitation. Marius glanced about him, then quickly lowered his head back towards the grinning face.

"What?"

"You know how I'm dead and all?"

"Yes."

The corpse shot out an arm and grabbed Marius around the back of the neck. Marius pulled away, but the soldier held on with a dead man's strength. Slowly he pulled Marius down until no more than a centimetre separated them, and Marius' vision was dominated by the corpse's eyes: one black and endless, the other staring through him to a point so far in the future Marius was terrified to think of it. With surprising speed the corpse pushed its face forward and kissed Marius on the lips, then pulled him back to his former position. It smiled, as Marius drew breath to scream.

"So are you."

# TWO

Marius fell, far longer than the half-second it should have taken for his head to travel from the corpse's grasp to the mud. The mud let him go and he slid downwards, through the slippery scurf of the battle-field, into a warm, gritty embrace that held him briefly before he scraped past it and into an open space with neither light, not air, nor any sensation of movement or life. He simply moved away from life, receding from it at a slow pace that was all the more terrifying for its lack of urgency, and his complete inability to alter the rate of his journey, or indeed, bring it to a halt.

Just as he became convinced that he was destined to fall into the unending blackness forever, he burst through into a cone of dim, brown light. Before he could register the change he landed flat on his back, knocking the wind from his lungs. He lay stunned for long moments, lost in the sensation of airlessness, and the closed-in feeling of something deeply buried.

Gradually, as his senses returned, he was able to focus upon a ceiling several feet above him. It was dirt, rough and un-worked, as if Marius were observing a

21

garden bed from the underside. Here and there roots poked through the surface, hairy points hanging in the air like warts clinging to the face of a beggar. Occasionally, a drop of muck fell as some disturbance or other sent tremors along its surface. No hole existed to prove Marius' passage, yet he knew without doubt that it was from *that* ceiling that he had fallen, and were he able to penetrate its solid surface, he would find himself back at the battlefield, however many unknown miles above his head.

"How...?"

It was then that he became aware of tiny sounds around him, creaks and groans as of a large body of men standing quietly, expectantly. He stiffened, and fixed his eyes upon the ceiling.

"I don't suppose this is the new ale room at the *Axe and Raven*, is it?"

Someone giggled. Marius' bladder twitched in response.

"No. I didn't think so."

Marius decided to leap to his feet, to gather his legs underneath him like steel coils and lunge through whoever surrounded him in a mad dash for the nearest exit. Assuming there *were* exits. Assuming he could gather the strength to move. Assuming his body would let him. He considered it. His body declined to comment. He willed his legs to drive him upwards, and his arms to begin the motions necessary to propel him into a crouch. Nothing. Marius sighed. Ah well.

"I don't suppose anyone fancies giving me a hand up, do they?"

For a moment there was no response. Marius began to entertain the notion that something heavy had fallen from the sky and hit him on the head, resulting in a somewhat strange and vivid hallucination. Then rough fingers gripped the fabric at his shoulder, capturing a fair amount of flesh underneath, and hauled him to his feet. And beyond. Marius dangled from the grip of his hidden helper, too terrified to turn his head and see the face of whatever giant held him aloft. If it was anything like the ones before him, he didn't want to know.

Not a single face was whole. Countless strangers stared back at Marius – every age, size and ethnic grouping, and not a single one of them was complete. Skin had peeled back to reveal the underlying bone; eyes were absent from sockets; dirt trickled from all the usual orifices and ones that looked like they had been created by teeth long after death. Beyond them, in the darkness, the glint of unseen eyes winked at him, so many and to such a distance that Marius did not bother trying to count them. He scanned the crowd in soundless fear, taking in the hue and age of each tattered body. Soldier and peasant stood arm to rotting arm. Women eyed him with as much baleful energy as the few cats and dogs who crouched without panting at their feet. Children, most terrible of all, stood silently amongst their taller counterparts. A scream rose within Marius' throat like bile, and he calmed the temptation with the only words he could summon enough sense to utter.

"So you're all dead then?"

A little laughter, even from one of the children, would have helped his state of mind. He received nothing, not even a whisper of movement as a young woman raised a hand to cover a shy smile. The dead ranks simply stared. Marius' own laughter lurked behind his teeth. If it were to escape, he knew, it would never stop. He swallowed, then did so again, forcing it away down his throat.

"Is there someone I could talk to?"

At his words, the crowd parted. A corpse, no different to the others as far as Marius could establish, tottered on stiff legs to stand less than a foot before him. Marius sniffed, then wished he hadn't. It opened its mouth. A fine shower of earth fell from the open hole. A small snake broke cover to glide across its face and under a scrap of shroud still clinging to the dead man's shoulder.

"You wish to talk?" he said, without the corresponding movement from his jaw. Despite his fear, Marius frowned in surprise.

"How did you do that?" he asked, leaning forward to examine the corpse's jaw more closely.

"We are the dead," the corpse replied. "We are freed from many limitations." His voice, Marius noted, seemed to come from *within* him, as if someone were utilising a speaking tube from the other side of a wall, or some hole deep inside the dead man's chest.

"Remarkable," he muttered, then aloud, "I hate to be a bother, but there seems to be some sort of terrible mistake. I… what am I saying? What the hell is going on here?"

"There has been a battle."

Marius swallowed. "Um, yes."

"A king was killed."

"Ah. Well. You see–"

"We are in need of a king."

"We didn't know it was him, of course. And even if we did, we wouldn't… I beg your pardon?"

The dead do not breathe. It could only have been in Marius' imagination that the corpse sighed in irritation.

"We need a king."

"Um," Marius squinted at the rows of implacable dead. "Would it be impertinent to ask why?"

"He is the sovereign, anointed by divine right."

"Okay."

"He is placed upon the throne by the Lord God himself."

"Uh huh." Marius had dined with several kings. On the basis of that evidence, divinity came at the end of a thief's knife. Still, he wasn't going to debate that with someone who could hold him aloft with no apparent effort. "And?"

"We are the dead."

"Established that."

"We lie here in wait," The corpse swung about on one stiff leg, an arm raised to indicate the grimy expanse of the cavern. "Alone. Unheeded. Forgotten."

"And this means…?" The exertion of keeping this conversation going was beginning to tell on Marius. He couldn't imagine where it was leading, but he could taste the pint of ale he should be drinking at *Saucy Kat's House of Welcome* right about now. It didn't help.

"God has forgotten us."

"God."

"Yes."

"Oh." A single penny dropped against the stone floor of Marius' understanding. "And a king is God's representative."

"He is."

"A conduit to God. To remind him you are here, waiting."

"That is so."

"I see." Marius frowned. "Well, it's very interesting, but I don't see how I..."

"You are the King."

Marius blinked. He *knew* he hadn't heard that properly.

"I beg your pardon?"

"You are the King. Of an earthly realm. You were smote, and laid your life aside, and a warrior who had commenced the journey to join us observed you, and so you came."

"You *what*? Are you kidding me?

"It is as was seen."

The crowd behind the corpse parted, and a warrior, fresh killed and bearing only the injuries of weapons, not time, stepped forward. Marius saw the grin, and the scar that ran from low down the side of his face to the top, and the hole where an eye had been destroyed. The soldier stepped in front of the corpse and lowered himself upon one flesh-bearing knee.

"Your Majesty," he said. The rest of the assemblage followed suit, as well as their dead and rotting limbs would allow them. Marius shook his head, half in dis-belief, half in protest.

"Oh no," he said. "Oh, no. You have the wrong man. I'm telling you. You really, really..."

He struggled against the grip of his warder, twisting to release himself. Something shifted under his shirt.

Before he could lower his arms to grab it, a circle of gold fell out and rolled across the floor, to fetch up against the foot of the dead warrior. He gripped it between stiffened fingers, and raised it up so all could see. Then slowly, with great deliberation, he stepped forward until he stood in front of Marius, their faces separated by mere inches. He raised his arms, and with great care, placed the crown of Scorby upon Marius' brow.

"Your crown, Your Majesty."

Marius closed his eyes, and uttered his first words as King of the Dead.

"Oh, fuck."

# THREE

The throne room was nothing more than a cavern carved out of the earth by dead hands, no more or less square than any other hole and no more or less careful in its construction than any other burrow. The throne itself was a wattle and daub frame that resembled a chair in the way a corn doll resembled a full-grown human, and really, what else could he expect when the only resources available were roots, earth and the shit of the world? And kingly robes. Good God, they had even found him raiment. They smelled of dirt and worms, and lay stiff as old blood against his body, but they were his kingly robes, and Marius was too numb to ask where they had come from, or who might have possessed them before him. The Ruler of the Dead, in his dead man's clothes, sitting upon his throne of dead man's shit. It was all so perfect.

Around him milled an obscene parody of a court. The dead, dust for voices, emptiness for eyes, facing him in impatient rows, waiting for his first proclamation. Expecting the word of God made flesh for confirmation that they were no longer alone. Marius stared above their heads, at the crowded entrance to what he now thought of as the main hall. There was no escape, he knew, no exit in that direction. Still, it was the only bearing he had left, and so he stared at it. And waited.

The figures in his "court" shuffled about aimlessly, conversing about who knew what, sparing him an occasional glance, hiding behind bowed heads if he attempted to match their gaze. Marius slumped in his throne. A bubble of fear and panic sat at the base of his throat, and unless it was released, he would choke to death upon it before long. Which would be ironic, he thought, and very carefully did not laugh.

A figure appeared at his elbow, silent and respectful. Marius ignored it. Eventually it offered the politest of coughs. Marius sighed, and glanced up. It was the soldier who had crowned him. Marius snorted, and returned his chin to the fist upon which it had been resting.

"What do you want?"

"Your Majesty—"

"Sod off."

"Majesty, the people are waiting. They need to hear you speak."

"Fine. Tell them to sod off."

"Your Majesty, Please. Can you not see how they wait upon your word?"

Marius looked at the crowd. They glanced at him, he realised, not from awe, or fear. They waited in anticipation, and with more than a little unrest. He frowned.

"That's another thing. How the hell can I see so much, anyway? We're underground. I haven't seen any shafts, or torches."

"We are the–"

"Yeah, yeah. You are the dead. That's your reason for everything, isn't it? That still doesn't explain why *I* can see."

"You are our leader, Your Majesty. Our King. Whatever we can do, you can do. We are your subjects and servants. Of all the dead, you are the greatest."

"Yes, but I keep telling you. I'm not... dead?"

"Of course, Your Majesty."

Marius scowled. Bad enough to be amongst the dead, worse to be patronised by them.

"Look," he said, rising from his seat before his tormentor could react. "I am *not* dead. I swear to you. I keep trying to tell you. You picked the wrong man. Hand on my..." He placed his hand against his heart, and paused, gaze slipping from the corpse's face to stare at a point somewhere far beyond the walls. A smile spread across his face, and he looked back at the soldier in triumph.

"Let me feel your chest."

"Your Majesty?"

"Your chest." Marius reached forward and placed his hand flat against the left side of the soldier's torso. "Ha! Give me your hand."

The soldier complied. Marius laid it in the same spot. "There. You feel? Feel it? Nothing. No heartbeat. That's because you're dead!"

"Of course. We are the–"

"No, no, no. Here." He placed the soldier's hand above his own heart. "Feel that? Feel it?"

"Your heart..."

"Strong as a whale!"

"Beating."

"Like the pounding of a thrupenny whore!"

"That means you're–"

"Alive."

"An imposter!" The soldier stepped back, and drew a battered sword. Marius became very aware of the bodies around him, all of whom were staring in his direction.

"That's not strictly true," he said, backing away. Half a step and he fetched up against the edge of the throne. He toppled backwards, landing in an undignified heap on the seat. His robe swept up and across his face, and the too-large crown slipped down. By the time he untangled himself he was hemmed in by the mass of corpses, and the blood-rusted tip of the sword was pressed hard against the joint between his throat and shoulder. Marius swallowed, and the sword pushed further into his flesh.

"Hang on," he managed to croak. "I tried to tell you."

The soldier leaned into his sword. A trickle of warmth ran down the outside of Marius' throat.

"Told. You. Not dead," he managed, before the pressure against his throat became too much, and he escaped into darkness.

# FOUR

He would not have expected to wake, or to still be alive. Or to find his hands unbound, and a hole in the ceiling above his head, with the glint of daylight shining bright blue at the far end. The crowd of corpses standing above his supine body; rusted axes, sickles and swords in their hands – that was closer to what he had expected. Being forcibly hauled to his feet and dragged to the nearest wall – that was definitely what he expected. Having the crown of the late King of Scorby thrust into his hands, well, he wouldn't have expected *that* if he'd been given three guesses.

"Is there something going on?" he asked, trying his best to frame an innocent smile. For all the reaction he engendered, he may as well have kept his mouth closed. The corpses holding his arms simply pressed him harder against the coarse earth wall until he gasped with pain, ending any further attempt at conversation. Marius struggled, but soon gave up. The dead don't tire as easily as an exhausted and beaten thief. Even if he could have freed himself, where would he have run? Up the chimney towards daylight? Marius tipped his head back. The hole taunted him from at least forty feet away. Maybe the dead need sunlight every now and again, he thought, then stifled a giggle. It was too close to hysteria.

From somewhere in front of him came the rustle of leather. He delayed lowering his gaze, straining to feel the breeze of the upper world on his skin. After long seconds he closed his eyes and sighed. No such luck. The real world was out of reach.

"It is very far away."

"Yes." Reluctantly, Marius' eyes met the soldier's one remaining orb.

"Farther for us than you."

"What do you mean?"

"Once the dead travel below, we do not leave."

"Oh." Marius surveyed their mean surroundings. "Well, you know, a drape here or there…"

"Perhaps you will bring some back with you."

"I'm sorry?"

But the soldier had turned away, and gestured to the corpses holding Marius. They extended their arms, and Marius slid further up the wall. When he was dangling at the height of their reach, two more bodies detached themselves from the crowd and grabbed at Marius' kicking ankles. Before he could voice his objections, he was hoisted onto his back, limbs spread wide, high above the heads of the crowd.

"What are you doing? Let me down."

The arms lowered him slightly, until he was at eye level. Marius was just about to issue further orders when bone-strong fingers grasped his jaw and turned his head towards their owner.

"Don't forget to hold on," the soldier said, and let him go. Marius' bearers heaved, and he flew up into the chimney. Reflexes did his thinking for him. His hands and feet dove for the chimney walls, finding sanctuary in the soft earth and clinging, leaving him wedged in the narrow space like a spider between the rough edges of a pub's corner walls. For long seconds, the only sound was that of his panicked gasping. When he could trust himself to do so without fainting, he looked back down, and saw the soldier staring up at him. Marius had the overwhelming impression that his stiff, immobile face was smiling.

"Find us a king," the corpse called out.

"What? Why?"

"You stole his place. You are in our debt."

With the benefit of distance, Marius felt a small spark of courage return.

"And if I don't?"

"We will come for you."

"And if I never come back this way?"

The soldier shook his head, slowly, a movement of deliberate malice.

"You will come back."

"What makes you so sure?"

"Feel your heart."

The two men stared at each other for long seconds. The soldier placed his hand over his chest, and nodded to Marius to do the same. Marius inched around until he could wedge one shoulder into the crumbling wall, then slowly, carefully, did the same. He held it there for half a minute, eyes fixed upon the dead face below him.

"We have your heartbeat."

Marius felt life draining away, leaking from his body and dissipating in the heavy air. The soldier waved a hand in dismissal.

"You cannot escape us. The entire world is home to the dead. Now climb."

"Wait."

"What?"

Marius risked a glance at the journey above him, closed his eyes in sudden dizziness, and glanced back down.

"How will I contact you? Do I call out, or sacrifice a cat or something? I don't even know your name."

"We will know," the soldier returned. "Now go."

"Wait!"

"No more." The soldier stepped back, out of Marius' circle of vision. "The path to the world above is closing. Unless you want to drown, leave."

As if summoned by his voice, a spray of fine earth fell on Marius. As he watched, the circle of air below him filled in, the earth rising upwards as if intent upon capturing him. With nowhere else to go, he dug his fingers and toes into the chimney walls and began to climb.

The most wonderful smell in the world is that of fresh air. It hit Marius as his fingers crested the rim of the hole and clawed at handfuls of rough grass. After the heat and fetid air of the underground realms, the swirling breeze felt like an orgasm. Marius closed his eyes and almost lost his grip, until the pressure of earth against the soles of his feet reminded him of the urgency of his mission, and he scrambled over the lip of the closing hole and lay upon undisturbed ground for the first time in an eternity. Marius wasn't ashamed to weep. Indeed, he had done so many times as the situation warranted it: to escape a bar room beating; to entice a sensitive woman into his bed; at the sight of a gold riner between his fingers when the purse he snatched had weighed for pennies. Now he engaged in a different type of sob – that which comes from unexpected and blessed freedom.

He exhausted himself against the warm grass, pressing his face into the ground and letting his tears and snot soak the grass, until an itching sensation against his cheeks and forehead caused him to stop and twitch his head away. The irritation spread to his neck and round to his throat, then down to his chest. Marius frowned, and wiped his hand across his forehead. It came away with passengers – tiny red multi-legged invaders, crawling over every inch of his exposed hand, biting him with every step.

"Shit!"

He pushed himself away, swatting at the angry ants. Their greater numbers prevailed. Marius was forced into a shambling dance, pulling his shirt over his head and using the cloth to beat at torso and legs as he hopped and swung himself about. The ants fought back, moving across his chest and down onto his stomach, heading inexorably south.

"Oh no, no you don't!" Marius fell to the ground and rolled, crushing untold assailants beneath his weight. He felt a tickle at his waistband.

"No, no, no!" A boot flew in one direction, its twin in the other. His trousers fluttered after them, then his underpants. Naked and angry, Marius rolled and swiped, jumped and danced, cursed and swore and threatened undying enmity, until at last he stood above the anthill, waving a fist at what lay below.

"Funny!" he yelled. "Very fucking funny!"

He may have heard a laugh, or it may have been his imagination. He kicked at the tiny hole in the grass, bending his toe back and uttering a yelp.

"I see you're as in command as always," a voice behind him said. Marius stiffened in shock, hands automatically cupping his groin. Slowly, eyes wide, he tilted his head to look back over his shoulder. He felt his rectum tighten, and winced.

"Gerd?"

Gerd stared at him in impassive silence, his big jug-face grey and still. Marius smiled uncertainly, and sidled over to his undergarments. Slowly, he bent at the knees until he could risk snaking a hand out to recapture them. He flicked his wrist, and slipped the underpants over his ankles in one swift movement, then shimmied into them, eyes fixed upon his former charge. Only once his most essential parts lay under cloth did he turn and face the younger man.

"How did you get here? You were–"

"Dead?"

"Well–"

"Being carried away to be posthumously tried for treason and sentenced to cremation and dumping in unhallowed ground?"

"Yes, well, that was what I–"

"Impaled on a sword because of the betrayal of my teacher and supposed friend?"

"Well, I wouldn't call myself–"

Gerd stepped forward, quicker than he had ever

managed in life, and had Marius' genitals in his hand before the older man could so much as flinch.

"The dead called me, as I lay in the courtyard waiting to be viewed by Lord Bellux. Do you know how difficult it is for a dead man to sneak away undetected? Particularly when you have to come to terms with being dead in the first place?"

"No, I–" Gerd tightened his grip, just enough so that Marius' breath stayed where it was rather then leave him.

"The only place to hide was in the stables."

Marius managed a croak. His forehead knotted. Gerd's fingers tightened again.

"Under the hay."

"Uhhhh."

"The horses shit in their hay."

Marius' eyes crossed.

"I lay there for two days."

Marius' hands made little flapping motions, quite independent of his desire to have them grasp Gerd's hand and tear it away from the crushed remnants of his genitals. He tried to look down, to at least say goodbye to them, but Gerd squeezed again, and Marius' legs deserted their post.

"That wasn't even the worst part. Do you know what the worst part was?"

Marius must have made some sort of movement to indicate that no, he *didn't* know what that was, because Gerd gave him one last agonising squeeze. Marius swore the dead man's fingertips touched each other, before he let go and Marius slipped to the ground.

"Being fucking *dead*!" Gerd shouted, and walked

away. Marius decided to vomit, and what little bile remained in his body sprayed onto the grass around him. When he found the strength to raise his head, Gerd stood a foot away from him, watching him with arms crossed. Marius' clothes lay in a neat pile in front of him, folded and waiting to be put on.

"I'm to assist you in your task," Gerd said, his voice utterly joyless. "So get your arse up and dressed before I decide I'd rather be cremated and drag you back to the castle to join me."

Marius dragged himself over to the clothes and reached for a boot. He croaked once, and Gerd cocked his head.

"What?"

Marius beckoned him closer. Gerd crouched so that his ear was a few inches from his former master's trembling lips. When he could focus on his stupid yokel's face without his eyes crossing, Marius swung the boot as hard as he could against the side of Gerd's head. The young watchdog fell backwards, and Marius collapsed onto his pile of clothes.

"Get me," he managed on his third attempt, "some fucking water."

# FIVE

According to some, the castle of the Scorban King was the largest building in the world. It sprawled across the range of hills that marked the highest point of Scorby City, the capital of the Scorban Empire, and therefore, according to those self-same people, the world itself. Scorbans called it the Radican, as if giving it a name might imbue it with its own culture, its own personality, its own existence separate to the whims of those who occupied its dwellings. In truth, it was more like a small, glorious and self-important village – a maze of buildings and compulsively washed streets that glowed in the sun like a reflection of the King's magnificence.

Of course, this was its owner's intent. The light at the heart of the world, some called it, although those who called it *that* were as intent upon smarming their way into the King's favour as they were of preventing anyone from measuring the dimensions of any other palace, just in case. It was the glory of glories, the most exalted set of buildings in the cutlery-bearing world, the point around which all activity, interest and gossip flowed. It was the alpha, the omega, and the north point of all compasses. It was in *exactly* the opposite direction to that which Marius was shuffling with determined steps. By the time they reached the hillock that marked the outer limit of the village of Terfin, Gerd had pointed out this anomaly on no less than a dozen occasions.

"May I remind you," he said again as they crouched behind a hedge and gazed down at the ramshackle gathering of huts and ditches that some farmer in more prosperous times had dared to call a town, "that we have a mission to accomplish?"

Marius reached out without looking and clamped a hand over his companion's mouth. His finger and thumb pinched Gerd's nostrils shut. It would make no difference to the dead man, but it helped him feel better.

"*You* have a mission, dead boy." He waggled Gerd's head from side to side. "I have a thirst, and a need to bathe."

In truth, he wasn't sure it was worth the effort to do either in *this* village. The ragged collection of wooden round houses looked as if a spray of water might cause them to crash onto each other like so many sticks. Marius had seen better constructions in a school for the blind. The only direction not represented in their construction was vertical. Every other point of the world was fair game, and, it seemed, the inability of the builders to collect or manufacture a single straight piece of wood had bordered on the perverse.

It wasn't that the village was badly constructed, Marius thought. He had seen badly constructed buildings before. It was just that, if he was feeling cruel, he could imagine the builders falling over whilst holding a bundle of sticks and being too knackered to do anything other than live in whatever arrangement the sticks fell in. Down on what could optimistically be dubbed the main street, a motley collection of farmers dragged themselves out of their front doors and towards the building farthest from Marius' perch. Each time the door opened to admit another weary soul, an undertone of conversation leaked out. Marius waited, watching the trickle of men slow, and stop. When no more appeared on the street he let go his grip on Gerd and stood, brushing himself down and shrugging his shoulders in anticipation.

"Don't wait up," he said, stepping onto the hillock. Gerd grabbed his ankle.

"I could stop you."

Marius licked his lips. The first cold ale of the evening slid down the throat of his imagination. The first warm barmaid was already in his lap.

"Boy," he said, slowly sliding his other boot down his leg so that it fetched up against Gerd's fingers and crushed them into the ground. "You and all the armies of the dead couldn't stop me."

He stepped from the hillock and strode along the centre of the road into the village. At every step he expected to hear Gerd's leaden footsteps behind him, or at least a hissed curse from where the stupid boy cowered in the bushes. But nothing was forthcoming, not even a whispered insult. Marius laughed silently. Even dead, Gerd was a coward. The difference between the two men, Marius decided, was that *he* was a man of intent. And his intent was to get drunk, washed and bedded. Tonight. Tomorrow, he and whomever passed for a smith in this mud hill would strike a deal over the melting of the crown. Then he would buy himself a horse with which to ride to the nearest port, and set sail for somewhere where the dead were left out for the birds to scatter. Hell, he thought as stepped up to the tavern's entrance, I'll settle for a mule if that's all they have.

The door swung open onto a scene Marius had encountered countless times. He had spent a lot of time in piddling little hinter towns, where the poor rubbed up against the edges of whatever kingdom claimed dominion over their scrubby fields. After a while, the tiny poteen taverns all began to resemble each other: a few rickety hand-assembled stools gathered around one or two even more rickety tables; a bar, if the villagers were lucky, made from the largest logs that the fit amongst them could haul into town and hew into some shape with their axes, and if they weren't lucky, just a set of shelves with a woman in front to dole out the potato spirits and keep track of who owed how many pennies; if it were cold, some sort of fire, and if they'd thought ahead, a chimney. If not, a fire anyway, and walls black from the soot. Marius had spent long enough running from one petty crime to the next that even such grimy and depressing surroundings counted as some sort of welcome. He'd spent too many wet nights cowering under hedges and in hollows, alert for the sound of angry footsteps, not to appreciate a roof – any roof – over his head. He slapped his hands together in anticipation of the sour burn of rotgut, and stepped inside.

"Good evening, friends," he said into the meagre light within.

Country people are a notorious mix of hail-fellow and

close-mouthed partisanship. Marius wasn't sure what would greet his arrival. Singing, perhaps. The murmur of conversation. Perhaps even the convivial clink of earthenware mugs as simple folk toasted each other's work in the fields. He wasn't prepared for the sudden stoppage of all sound, or the way the woman behind the rough-hewn bar dropped a bottle to smash unheeded upon the floor. He was particularly surprised by the screaming.

"Is there a problem?" he managed, before the first villager threw himself from his stool and dove behind the bar. The rest of the patrons followed in short order. Soon, the only noise louder than their pleas to God was made by bottles shattering as each figure crashed over the bar top to land amongst his fellows in the small space beyond. Marius watched in amazement, his hand still on the rough wood door. Slowly, he let it swing closed behind him, and took a step forward.

"Um, hello?"

The prayers became a touch louder, a smidgeon more desperate. Marius frowned.

"Excuse me?"

Now several older gods were being called into play, possibly the first time their names had been uttered outside the penitents' bedrooms since the King had standardised religion. Marius reached the bar, and leaned over it.

"Look, what is going on here?"

The denizens of the serving area screamed as one, and scrabbled to get away. Realisation struck Marius. They were trying to get away from *him*. He raised his hands in what he hoped was a friendly gesture.

"It's okay," he said. "I don't want to hurt anyone. I just want a drink."

"Demon!" one farmer gibbered. Another rolled his eyes back into his head and fainted. Marius jerked his head back as if slapped.

"Steady on. That's a bit…"

His eye caught a stray bottle on the shelves, the last whole vessel teetering on the edge, ready to plunge towards the floor. Within its depths, a nameless liquid sloshed from side to side, helping to clarify the face reflected in the dull green glass. Marius stared at it for almost a full minute. Then, without thought for the bodies underneath him, he vaulted the bar and landed in front of the shelf. The villagers raced each other around the edge of the bar and banged through the door, screaming into the night.

Marius didn't notice. He reached out and drew down the bottle. It was a typical hand-blown affair, dull of hue, riven with runnels and faults from a too-cool fire. Marius buffed it as best he could with his sleeve, then walked on unsteady legs to stand before the fireplace. He knelt down, and held the glass so that the guttering flames illuminated the liquid within. A face stared back at him from the shining surface. His face, if he concentrated, and added life and animation to it. But not the face he knew, not the face that had grinned back at him from the surface of morning ponds, not the rakish smile and brown skin that had inhabited the looking glasses of whores from a dozen or more towns along the Meskin River.

The face that stared back at him, *his* face, was that of a man dead and buried. Grey skin hung loose from his bones. His eyes, so alert and aware of the world, stared dull and uncomprehending. His chapped and darkened lips, the teeth that protruded from between them, the rents and tears across his flesh from how many months spent in the company of shifting rocks and hungry insects… every angle showed the ravages of the ground. Marius blinked, and the lids in the bottle closed and opened with dull slowness. He licked his lips, and the tongue that parodied his movement emerged dried and black.

Very slowly, with deliberate purpose, Marius drew the cork from the bottle and placed the open mouth against his lips. He tilted his head back and let the liquor fill his mouth. He swallowed, and waited for the pain of badly-distilled alcohol to send him into paroxysms of coughing. Instead, he felt nothing, not even a slow burn spreading from his gut to his extremities. He emptied the contents in two long pulls, then, as the sounds of weapon-bearing life came to him from further down the street, he placed the bottle carefully upon the floor and stood. He nodded, as if reaching a decision after long debate.

"Gerd," he said, and that one syllable contained all the fury and violence of an avenging army.

The noise was coming closer. The village men, courage fortified by whatever hooch they kept in their houses, and the logic that comes to any man when trying to explain the unbelievable to a sceptical wife. Marius had seen this kind of anger before – shameful anger; from men persuading themselves that it was not *they* who had cowered earlier, that *they* were protectors and fighters. They would be carrying mattocks and hammers, pitchforks and sickles. Deadly weapons, in the hands of the scared. Marius made for the door and risked a peek out into the street. The villagers were no more than a dozen feet away. Were he to make his exit that way, they would be on him before he could reach the corner of the building. Despite his appearance, Marius felt very much alive. He was in no mood to decide on which side of the divide his life force rested. He closed the door, and surveyed his surroundings.

Apart from the sad wreckage of furniture, bar and shelves, the room was bare. Not even a wall hanging livened up the shit-and-mud decor. The fireplace was no more than a foot wide and constituted a shallow depression in the wall with a flue leading up and out. Marius leaned in, risking a burned face to see whether the flue might be wide enough to wriggle up, but it was no use. As far as he could tell, it was no wider than his doubled fists. For a moment he considered using a lit branch to set fire to the walls, but no more than a few flames licked the blackened coals. By the time it caught on, he'd be on the end of a pitchfork. A doorway on the other side of the room held more promise. Marius pushed through the simple bead curtain and stepped into the living quarters of the proprietress.

"Business was booming," he muttered, surveying the few items within the room. A bundle of cloths lay over a bed of hay in one corner, and next to it, side by side, two earthen pots saw duty as washbasin and piss pot. Another block of wood, fashioned in much the same way as the bar, served as table, strewn with the minutiae of a village woman: combs, daubs and pins abounded. Marius scanned them but found nothing useful.

By now he could hear the crowd just outside the front door, shouting and rattling their weapons. It would not be long before they felt brave enough to open the door and confront him. Marius sighed in defeat. There was no escape. He collapsed onto the crude bed.

"Fucking hell!"

He sprang to his feet, hands clutching the base of his spine. There was something *hard* in that bed, and sharp as well. He squeezed his eyes shut, and shook his head to banish the pain. When he could trust himself to open his eyes without tearing up, he ventured more slowly onto the pile of cloth and lifted it to reveal the hay below. A thick wooden pole lay underneath, a knotted dowel sticking out at an odd angle. Marius swept aside the hay to get a closer look at it. When he saw what it was, he could not help but laugh out loud in relief.

"Of course," he shouted to the walls, smiling when his outburst caused the crowd outside to fall into momentary silence.

The end of a pipe lay exposed, the dowel proving to be a spigot. It was that, Marius realised, upon which he had sat. The pipe disappeared under the hay towards the wall.

"Of course, she would," Marius muttered this time, grabbing handfuls of straw and flinging them aside to reveal more of the pipe. Alcohol was this woman's trade, but nowhere, in his panic, had he seen the source of it. A village such as this would be too poor to trade with merchants, not for the finished product. A smart woman, a *crafty* woman, would have a still secreted, away from the prying eyes of the populace. And where better to hide it than in a place no man would seek to invite himself? He cleared the last of the straw and tracked the pipe up to the base of the wall.

"Well, well."

He knocked against the wall, and was rewarded with the sound of a hollow space beyond. Marius smiled. No tired farmer would stop to measure the outer walls of a hovel against its inner dimensions. Nobody would come into this room and wonder why it seemed smaller than it should. If Marius had money to lay a bet, and someone to accept it, he would wager that the outer wall beyond this one held a door to freedom. All he had to do was find a way through.

Outside, he heard the front door creak open. Marius turned quickly, and grasped the end of the pipe. He heaved, and two feet of hefty wood tore free. Alcohol poured out of the broken end, soaking the straw beneath and spreading out onto the dirt floor. Marius hefted his makeshift weapon.

"Right," he muttered, then ran through the beaded curtain, screaming and whirling the pipe around his head.

Three villagers peeked through the open doorway. At Marius' approach they departed, and he heard the sound of bodies falling over each other in panicked retreat. He laughed and dealt the door a massive blow, yelling gibberish at the top of his voice. The crowd outside withdrew in consternation. Marius smiled, and snuck back into the bedroom. His manic act would buy him some time – enough, perhaps, to break through the wall and into the space beyond.

His foot came down upon the straw, and he grimaced as the wet grass squelched beneath his feet. Then his expression cleared, and he began to gather up great handfuls of it, dragging most of the bed into the main room and against the front door. When he was finished he rolled up one of the cloth blankets and dipped a corner into the pool of alcohol. He carried it into the main room and held it over the fire. Within moments the flame had caught the cloth and was racing up toward his arm. Marius flung the cloth towards the door. It hit the straw, and before he could track the movement, the entire pile was engulfed in flame.

"That should do it," he said, before racing back into the bedroom. The fire would hold off the villagers, but unless he could get through the wall before the flames ran round the room and found the pool of alcohol at his feet, it would only serve as his funeral pyre.

He lunged at the wall, pipe raised above his head like an axe. He swung, and the pipe broke through with such ease that Marius fell forward, balance destroyed by the lack of resistance, and slammed his face into the wall. A piece the size of his head broke away, and smashed on the other side of the wall.

"Gods damn it!"

He sat backwards, losing his grip on his makeshift club. It fell the wrong side of the wall. Marius heard it clang against something in the darkened room. He rubbed his head and frowned.

"What the hell?"

Now that he was looking at it more closely, he realised that this wall was different in construction to the other three sides of the room. Whilst the others had the typical brushed look of traditional wattle and daub structures, and each wall was a single sheet of the stuff, this one was made up of more than a dozen sections, a criss-cross framework with only the lumpy runnels of thickened mud dried between them. The

hole his head had made was smack-bang in the middle
of one of these smaller frames, and Marius could see
that the edges were thin and brittle, as if there was no
internal structure holding the mud together. He
gripped the edge of the hole and pulled. A sheet of
daub the length of his forearm came away, shattering
against the floor. Marius looked at it in amazement.

"No wattle," he said to himself. "No damn wattle!
But how…?"

He pulled another sheet from out of its frame, then
another, kicking at the flimsy structure until his original hole was big enough to admit him. The flames from
the other room grew louder, and smoke poured into
the bedroom. Marius glanced towards them and covered his mouth and nose with his hand. He needed to
get out of here *now*, otherwise the villagers would not
need to find him to see his dead body. He pictured
them, standing down the street, watching their only
entertainment go to the flames. They would be angry,
devastated. They would be looking for a corpse after
all this was over. He had no intention of making it easy
for them.

There was enough flickering light from the confla-
gration for him to make out the dim outline of the
room beyond, and in the middle, a vague, humped
shape. He stepped through. He could make out almost
nothing in the uncertain light – a broad lessening in
the darkness signified the opposite wall, but he could
see nothing to show the location of a door to the outside. He took a step forward and reached out, satisfying
himself that the opposite wall was there. His fingers
found the rough surface, and he followed it round to

the right until he came back towards his entrance hole. The room was little more than a closet, a couple of steps in either direction.

There had to be an exit here. He just hoped it wasn't out into the street. He could not recall seeing a door as he walked along the frontage of the building, but then, this room was proof of how well things could be hidden. He turned away, and stepped towards the back of the house. His shin struck something hard. Marius yelped. The still! He had forgotten it. He grimaced, then his eyes widened in sudden understanding.

The still. The means by which the owner of the tiny bar made her alcohol. He stooped and ran fingers across it, defining its shape in the semi-darkness by touch. A wooden cask the width of a man's chest, banded by iron hoops, and full of alcohol that even now dripped onto the floor in an invitation for the fire to drink. The rest of it was pouring out of the broken pipe in the bedroom. Any moment now, the front edge of the fire would meet the pool of alcohol on the floor and come racing across the ground faster than any man could move. All the way back to the source. The still. The one he was standing next to.

Marius took a step away from the offending barrel, then checked himself. The heat from the fire was washing across him. There was no time to hide. There was nowhere *to* hide. Nothing to crouch behind. Nothing to raise in front of him as a shield. Moment by moment, the light from the approaching fire illuminated features of the room that he had not previously seen. He could now see, down at floor level, the flap by which the bar owner had slipped in and out from the bedroom. Marius stared at it in sudden comprehension. There was no need for an outside door. He was trapped.

Marius glanced up. The fire had spread to the walls now, eating away at the dried daub faster than he could track it. The bedroom was engulfed in flame. He dropped to his knees. He should be coughing, shouldn't he? The smoke that rolled around him should be choking him, forcing his eyes to weep as he squeezed them shut against the irritation. Instead, nothing. Marius bumped his head against the floor. Of course. He was dead, at least, his body bore all the signs. It would stay this way until he really *was* dead. Which meant that he would lack the blessed release of unconsciousness as the flames ate his up clothes, then his hair and flesh. Asphyxiation would provide no relief. He would feel every moment of his immolation.

Marius covered his face with his hands. A dull *whoompf* washed over him as the fire caught the edge of the alcohol and the bedroom became an inferno. Flames licked at the edges of the hole. A wall of heat buffeted the room. Marius pushed away from the approaching fire, screaming as he fell against the barrel. The damn thing was red hot, and the bands of metal around its girth pressed against the skin of his back. The pain forced his attention away from the fire and back onto himself.

The still.

It was the only object in the room. Marius reached out a hand and pushed against it, wincing as the hot wood seared his palm. The heavy cask refused to move. Marius closed his eyes. That much liquid, in a barrel that solid, must weigh almost two hundred pounds. It was his only recourse. There was no time to think about it. Marius frowned, recalling the ease with which the dead warrior had lifted him from the ground. He must weigh nearly as much as the barrel, yet the soldier had hefted him without an ounce of effort. The dead had their own strengths, the soldier had said. And he was dead, was he not? At least, his body was. It bore all the hallmarks of being so. Perhaps it had the same strengths.

Without thinking, he rose to his knees and drove his shoulder against the rough side of the cask. It gave not an inch. He wrapped his arms around it, ignoring the pain that seared his flesh, and heaved upwards, pushing one leg underneath him and the next. The still resisted, but slowly, as Marius screamed, it shuddered, just the merest of movements, but enough for him to rock back and drive his shoulder into it again. Somehow, from some combination of strength and the crazed energy of the desperate, it loosed its hold upon the floor. Marius drew it up onto his shoulder in one sweeping movement, alcohol spraying outwards as it tore free of the drainpipe. It fizzed out of the opening, and the fire roared in response.

Marius staggered under the sudden weight, the iron band scorching a line of pain across his cheek. The air was full of the smell of burned flesh, and mud that bubbled and charred under the all-consuming flame. He locked his knees, screamed again, lumbered forward at the wall. Two steps, three, and then the pain and effort became too much and he half-fell into the fire-laced structure of the outer wall. The wattle and daub split apart under his assault and he collapsed forward onto blackened, fire-eaten grass. Sharp stubble tore at his face. He lost his grip on the still. It fell away from him, bounced once, and rolled back against the wall. Marius stared at it in dazed incomprehension. The fire reached towards it, licked at the edge of the barrel, and then leaped upon it.

Marius blinked, then somehow found the strength to raise himself to his hands and knees and crawl five feet away, ten, every inch a victory through blackened earth that burned his skin as he touched it. A ditch ran across the back of the yard. He dipped his head over the edge. The combined effluent of the village trickled passed his eyes, a brown sludge barely held together by the dribbles of water that survived the journey past house, well and fields.

Marius retched as the fumes rose up around him, a miasma that stank like a million years of broken privies. He slid into it face first, just as the fire ate its way through the heavy wood of the still and the alcohol inside exploded. Marius had been wrong on one count, at least: he happily lost consciousness, oblivious to the sounds of screaming villagers, and the crash of the bar finally falling in upon itself.

# SIX

The sky was the deepest black a sky had ever been, and magical pixies flitted about – red and yellow and white – hopping and skipping this way and that in time to their own unknowable rhythms. Marius smiled as he watched them dance. They came close, only to disappear as he reached for them with a hand that wavered in and out of focus as he swung it. He giggled. The stars shone with white disapproval. One by one, a pixie floated up to cover them, until the whole sky twinkled with warm red stars, showering love and approval down upon him. Marius felt his skin bead with moisture. His very skin was crying with gratitude.

"Thank you," he sang. "Thank you thank you thang yew."

A pixie floated into his vision. Marius waved a finger in greeting. The pixie waved back, and came closer, closer, until it hung less than an inch from the bridge of his nose. Marius crossed his eyes as he tried to keep the beauteous creature in focus. Still it descended. Marius held his breath, hoping, hoping... land, little creature. Let my flesh join with yours. Just one touch… The pixie ended its descent, and touched down less than an inch from his eyes.

"Fucking hell!"

He leaped from the trench. The spark buried itself deeper into his flesh. He swatted at it, scraped with ineffectual fingernails, and finally, cross-eyed with the pain, flung himself back down, face first into the water. The pixie died with a hiss. Marius lay face down, hoping against hope that the soft thing gently bumping its way down the side of his face hadn't been someone's dinner twenty four hours ago. This was it, he decided. There could be no lower point in his life. Dead, face down in a ditch, with a suspicious by-product kissing his cheek. Nothing could make life worse.

"Enjoying your drink?"

Marius wasn't proud of his scream, but at least he didn't have time to feel ashamed. The scream was followed by an instinctive inhalation, drawing mud and water directly into his lungs. He reared up, choking, spraying gritty brown phlegm onto the grass, the speaker and himself. He lurched forward. His knees struck the edge of the trench and he pitched forward. His face struck the ground. His hands left his throat and clawed at the scraggly grass. Prickles sank into the soft flesh of his palms but he didn't care. A ton of silt was caught in his throat, a great mass of riverbed balled up, an impassable dam, denying the passage of water, air, life…

Something hard thumped the middle of his back. Marius shuddered. His head snapped forward. Something loosened itself from his throat and hit the ground with a wet slap. Marius dragged in great lungfuls of air, heaving about the blackened grass like a surprised fish.

When he had regained some semblance of control, he squinted past tears at the amused face leaning over him.

"Forgotten that you don't need to breathe, then?" Gerd asked, smiling. The smile disappeared as Marius drove a fist into his exposed groin. Gerd slid gently sidewise to lie in a foetal curl.

"Forgotten," Marius croaked, "that you don't need your balls?"

When both men were able to stand, they made their way to the edge of the smoking bar house, and peered around the corner at the main street.

"Where are they?"

"The lower edge of the village." Gerd pointed the way Marius had first come. "There's a grove down there, a little spring. It's where they draw their water."

"Bit late now, isn't it?"

"There's a patch of ground on the other side where they bury their dead."

Marius turned his stare onto his companion.

"What?"

"Look."

He pointed across the main lane of the village. At some point, while Marius had lain insensate in the trench, the fire had escaped the confines of the building and leaped the gap. There had been houses on that side of the village. Marius remembered sneering at them as he made his way towards the bar – rude structures, rough and basic, peasant dwellings of shit and sticks with patchy thatches for shelter. No glass in their windows, no symmetry in their designs, roundhouses in name but only because no name had been invented for the haphazard approximations of circles they described. Exactly the sort of hovels Marius expected from people who scratched sixteen hour days in the dirt, just to claw together enough grain and seeds to survive until morning.

Now they were gone. All that remained was a trail of black ash and soot that stretched the length of the road and down into the first line of trees beyond. A small fire, really, to look at the trail it had left. Marius could have walked around it, and would have, if he had been walking through the wilderness and been confronted by a blaze of that size. But for a village so small – catastrophe.

"How many?" he asked, staring at the ruins.

"Three," Gerd replied. "Two children. Their father, running in to save them."

"Two children."

"That doesn't matter, does it?" Gerd asked, turning away. "They were just peasants. You didn't even know them. What were they to you?"

"Nothing." Marius found himself gripping the hot corner post. He snatched his hand away, wiped it against his trouser leg, spreading soot across the fabric. "Nothing."

"Well then. Any more plans?"

"I..." Marius stared down the track, as if he could penetrate the line of trees and see the villagers in their grief. He bit at his lip, turned from the sight, and strode past Gerd quickly. Without looking to see if Gerd followed, he walked quickly up the rise away from the fire, away from the funeral gathering. There were only three standing houses left, spared destruction by the path of the blaze. He was past them and leaving the village behind before Gerd caught up to him.

"You're going the wrong way," he said.

Marius said nothing, simply kept moving, head

bowed, staring at the ground six inches in front of each step. The path rose, slightly but steadily. It would switch back more than once, he knew, but it would go up into the foothills and on through the Spinal Ranges. He could follow the line of hills and end up going towards the coastal towns. Or he could crest them, descend the far side, and enter the Fiefdom of Tallede, then go straight through and into the wider realms of Tal itself. He would make up his mind on the way. Gerd reached out and laid a hand on his arm.

"We need to go back. The capital…"

"Don't fucking *touch* me." Marius shook his hand off.

"Marius–"

Marius was not a fighting man. A thief does not enter the profession because he wants to fight. He was a slinker, a tip-toer. He lived for the time after the fight, when the victor had departed and all that remained were the easy rewards and sightless eyes. But his father had been a King's Man, tied to his place by loyalty and a seal of service over the door, and Marius had spent his childhood running the alleys in that part of town where addresses were known by what tavern was nearest, not by street names. Before Gerd could complete his thought, Marius had whirled around, nudged the young man's restraining arm up with one elbow and driven his fist into the flesh underneath his jaw. Gerd's legs deserted him, and he slumped to the ground to stare stupidly up at his assailant.

"Don't. *Fucking*. Touch me!"

Marius spun away, strode stiff-legged up the trail. After several moments, Gerd followed at a distance, in silence.

They walked that way for an hour. Then Marius stopped still, staring up at the ridge running along the side of the nearest hill. Gerd managed to stop before he crashed into the older man's back.

"Marius?"

"I don't need to sleep."

"Sorry?"

"I don't need to sleep. Do I?"

"Um… no."

Marius drew in a deep breath, released it through his nostrils.

"I need to sleep."

"But…"

"There."

He pointed further up the hillside. Off to one side of the path, set into the edge of a short defile, was a flaw: a cave, hollowed out by countless eons of falling rocks, rain and animals, a deep-lipped hole a few feet high. Gerd stared at the ground between them and the opening, and sighed. It was a climb of perhaps twenty feet in height, through gorse and rocks that looked specifically designed to snag and tear.

"Marius…"

"You do what you want."

Marius set off up the incline, quickly disappearing among the grasping branches. Gerd listened to the crash of his progress for a minute or so then, sighing once more, he followed.

# SEVEN

The cave was as bad as Marius had hoped: shallow and damp, with a thin layer of lichen over every surface. He had taken barely three steps inside when his foot slid out from under him and he almost tumbled over onto his backside. He allowed himself a tight smile, and called back over his shoulder.

"Find some wood."

"What?" Gerd stopped crashing through the under-brush long enough to reply. Marius smiled again, a hateful little thing that utterly failed to find his eyes.

"Get some wood. And something for tinder."

They remained silent for almost a minute before he heard Gerd lumber away, moving along the rise away from the cave. Marius slid towards a small protuberance at the rear of the cave, winced as he settled his backside down on the slick, wet rock, and settled in to wait.

Slowly, the pool of light outside the cave entrance grew dim, then dark. Night crept in slowly, as if delivering an apology. Already in shadow, the space became deeply gloomy, then black. Marius let his eyes adjust. Even in this utter darkness, with light only a memory, he retained some small measure of sight, just enough to make out shapes, blurred silhouettes slightly lighter than the air. A part of him noted it, filed it away for future reference. Being dead may have advantages, should he ever escape his present predicament. The part of him that was always searching for an advantage, always hoping for the one angle to set him on the road to luxury, paid attention for a moment, then receded into the background once more. Marius waited until the sounds of Gerd's clumsy passage drew closer.

"In here," he called out.

"Coming." Gerd huffed up the final incline and appeared in the cave opening, his profile deformed by the armful of branches he held before his chest. He took a step into the cave, then another. On the third step his leg slid a foot further than he intended. He wavered, attempted to right himself. The branches went one way. Gerd went the other. He hit the rock floor with a shout, scrabbled for purchase, managed to right himself. Marius waited in silence. Gerd drew his legs beneath himself, slowly tested his weight then, carefully, drew himself up to his full height.

"You dropped your bundle," Marius said, no trace of amusement in his voice.

"You could have warned me."

"Terribly sorry. I was sitting here, trying to come to terms with all that has happened, and my mind just plain slipped away from me. It's a symptom of old age. Only," he slapped his thighs, "I plumb forgot. I'm not going to have an old age, am I? Funny how some things don't occur to you until too late." He stood, slid one foot forward as if walking across a frozen lake.

"Pick up the branches. I want a fire."

"Then why don't you make it yourself?"

"Because," Marius slid another step forward, and another, "I've been entrusted with a holy task by the will of the dead community you call home now, whereas all you're good for is to be a camp follower." He slithered up to Gerd and placed a hand on his chest. "Now do it."

He pushed. Gerd took a step backwards to steady himself. His foot found purchase on the lichen, then half a moment later, betrayed him. With a look of shock, he fell to the rock floor. His head hit the stone with a hollow thud. Marius watched him slip about, trying to right himself, then slid back to his stone seat and sat.

It took him longer than Marius would have thought necessary, but eventually Gerd piled the branches in the centre of the cave and sparked a fire into life. Slowly the air in the cave began to dry out. Gerd crawled haltingly around on his hands and knees, scraping lichen away from the floor as best he could, until a dry circle was viewable, with the crackling fire at its centre. Only then did Marius leave his perch, stepping forward until he was between the fire and the cave opening.

"I'm going to sleep here," he said, sitting down. "You can have the other side."

Gerd edged away from him until he was as far away as he could be and still be within reach of the heat.

"How can you be trusted?"

Marius lay down, rolled over so the fire warmed his back. He gazed out of the entrance at the sky. A few stars were visible, but not as many as there should have been. As he watched, another blinked out of existence. Marius frowned in sudden alarm. What was going on? Another unnatural trick? Were the dead about to manifest some new, greater, way of controlling his existence? Then he saw the edge of the clouds, and heard the first roll of distant thunder, and relaxed.

"I like to sleep with the window open," he said. "Besides, where would I go?"

Gerd offered no answer. They lay in silence, listening to the night time sounds of the forest below. Somewhere in the distance, a stream of light smoke rose into the blackness. The villagers, Marius guessed as he watched the tiny thread rise. With no shelter against the night they would have to build a fire, sleep underneath the trees as best they could. The night was cold, he supposed. Now he paid attention to it, he couldn't actually tell. He could feel the heat of the fire but he *knew* that was there. If he didn't think about it, would he forget what that felt like, too? He drew his arms harder around himself, focusing upon the distant smoke. The night was no friend to humans. Too many predators hunted by night, too many creatures better equipped for the dark. Ironic, he thought, having to rely for protection upon the thing that destroyed your life.

No, something inside him replied. The fire did not destroy their lives. That was *you*.

Marius rolled away from the voice, but the fire was too close, hot and painful upon eyes that had grown used to the dark. He turned back, and the smoke was still there, like a finger thrust upwards, searching for something to point at, someone to blame. He watched it gesture aimlessly at the sky, blaming the Gods, then closed his eyes.

"Marius?"

Marius sighed, then opened his eyes again and stared out of the cave.

"What?"

Gerd was silent. Marius could feel him gathering his courage. Oh no, he thought. Don't ask.

"Why do you hate me so much?"

Marius wanted to slap the ground, or slap Gerd. Instead he settled for another long sigh. Outside, the wind picked up, rattling the close-crowded trees against each other. The sound of rain stalked closer. A flash of lightning illuminated the landscape for an instant. He gazed into the night, and saw images he'd long since shuffled to the back of his mind.

"When I was a child, maybe six or seven – we didn't count birthdays – my father came home one evening and announced that he'd had enough of my face, and he picked me up and carried me to the end of our street and threw me into the mud. And just to make sure I got the message, he kicked me until I lost consciousness. And when I woke up, he and my mother had gone. So I had to fend for myself. I stole what I could, begged what I could. When I was nine, I killed a man. I thought he was a man. He was probably fifteen or sixteen, really, but he *looked* like a man to me. Killed him for a tenpenny and a tankard of cider. After that, there was no turning back."

"Oh, my gods. You mean it?"

"No, of course not. I grew up in a loving family. I had five brothers and two sisters and my father was a silk trader."

"Oh."

"My parents live in a nice house in a nice district of V'Ellos. I visit them any time I'm near. They think I'm an actor. I even pay a printer in Tarek fifty riner every few months to print up fake play bills so I can take them home and show my parents how well I'm doing."

"But why…"

"Because you thought it would be true, didn't you?"

There was a long pause. The rain walked up to the front of the cave and over. Marius felt the spray against his face, but made no move to wipe his eyes. Let it wet him. Let it see what it could wash away. When Gerd spoke again it was in a voice rich with guilt, and Marius shook his head.

"Yes. I'm sorry."

"I choose to do what I do," Marius said to the dark. "I chose the life I live. And I was good at it. I made a living, and the living was sometimes bad, but it was sometimes good. I consorted with whomever I wanted, and wandered where the will took me, and all in all, I was about as free as any man might hope to be, apart from some fear and some discomfort, and the occasional run for the coast. And then I met you."

"But… you asked me…"

"Yes, I did, didn't I? Wandering around your little village, with your granny and your pigs and no idea what a diamond even looked like. And I thought there's a happy lad. There's someone who knows what his place is."

Gerd stayed silent, but the question hung between them.

"I couldn't believe it, I really couldn't," Marius said, answering the silence. "Nobody could be that happy with pig shit and wanking in the bushes."

"I don't…"

"Yes you did. Every bloody village boy does. Anyway, you could have said no. You could have said, 'No thank you, I'm happy where I am. I don't want to see the world and learn a trade and have adventures and be rich.' But you didn't, did you?"

"Well, it wasn't exactly like you promised, was it?"

"Because I'm a *liar*, you idiot." This time, Marius did slap the ground. "I lied to you, and you believed it, and then I had to actually try and teach you something and make us *both* rich and happy." He squeezed his eyes shut, biting back the images in front of them. "And you still fucked it up."

After that, there was nothing more to say. Marius closed his eyes and let the raindrops find their way down his face to the ground. They felt like little fingers across his skin, like Keth, the dancing girl at the *Hauled Keel*, a million tiny touches designed to simultaneously relax the skin and embolden the blood. Oh, the things that girl could do with her tiny, dancing fingers. If Marius concentrated, he could pretend….

"You could have just said you didn't hate me and left it at that." The sorrow in Gerd's voice banished all thoughts of pleasure. Marius opened his eyes. He was in a wet cave, in the rain, and he was still dead.

"Yes, well, now you know."

They lay on opposite sides of the fire, listening to the rain thunder against the rock shelf outside. Marius stared out the dimly-lit entrance, willing on a sleep he felt neither necessary nor welcome. Anything to avoid another conversation. Then Gerd spoke once more, and the hope was shattered.

"You know, this reminds me of home."

"What?"

"This. It reminds me of being at home."

Marius contemplated the hard rock beneath his hip, the wind and spray chilling him from outside.

"How? You grew up in a village."

"Exactly." Gerd shifted, scraping his bulk across the rock floor. "It's like… winter, you know. You live your whole life with the village. You know everyone, they know you. You're with each other every moment of every day. But then, at night, in winter, you're lying in bed, and the rain is coming down, and there's a wall of water between you and everybody else. And you just know that the whole village is like you, lying alone, wrapped up in a warm little bubble, with a wall of water between them and the world. And you're all together and alone at the same time, and it's comforting, you know? The sound of the rain, curving round you like a blanket. Really comforting."

He lapsed into silence. Marius shook his head.

"You know, last year I spent six weeks sleeping under hedges, and probably about the same amount of time sleeping with whatever whore I could afford."

"What's that supposed to mean?"

"Nothing. I'm just too polite to say fuck you and your homespun philosophies." He clenched, and sent a fart towards the fire. "Now go to sleep before I set fire to your arse hairs."

He experienced long seconds of happy silence before Gerd spoke again.

"You know we don't need sleep."

"For fuck's sake." Marius scrambled to his feet and stepped to the edge of the cave.

"Where are you going?"

"I need a shit."

"We don't need to…" But Marius was outside, the water battering against his head drowning out Gerd's voice. He waited long enough to be sure that his young watch dog was still paying attention, then ran as hard as he could, down the hillside, into the night.

It's no easy thing, to run headlong through strange country in the dark. Roots leap from the ground to trip you. Branches reach out to grab your clothes and scratch at your eyes. Marius crashed through the undergrowth without care for stealth, snapping twigs and branches as he lurched from tree to tree. When he had run this way for a minute or so, he stopped, and leaned against a nearby trunk.

Behind him, Gerd had finally realised what he was attempting. Marius smiled as he heard the sounds of pursuit. The youngster blundered about like a blind bear, cursing as he tripped over every obstacle before him, shouting Marius' name with increasing despair. Headlong flight in the full dark of night-time was a necessary survival skill for a man of Marius' profession. It was one of many skills he had not bothered to pass on to his dunderheaded apprentice. Gerd tripped and fell heavily, crashing through the underbrush for several seconds at a tangent to Marius' location. Marius listened to him sobbing in frustration. Then, with perfect stealth, he crept silently away from the cave, down the hill at an angle, aiming unerringly for the track upon which they had started their journey.

Within an hour, he was striding down the road to Borgho City in the rain, whistling.

The Spinal Ranges were mountains, once, long before men appeared in the world, when giants and monsters made of rock and starlight and spirit wandered the world without fear of persecution or autopsy. When the world was young, and everything was proud, they jutted into the sky like a proclamation, a challenge made of rock and ice that dared the sun to leap over them, and promised impalement should it fail. But they had grown old, and the sun had not, and eventually they gave up trying to catch it every morning. They shrank, as the elderly do, and grew bow-backed and flaccid, and now they lay across the landscape like an invalided grandfather without the strength to get up and face the day. Where once they had split the land with impassable and implacable fury, now they lay supine under a web of trails and tracks, conquered by the uncaring need of humans.

The track along which Marius strode was wide enough to accommodate a fully-laden city carriage, and flat enough to indicate regular traffic. To Marius it stood out against the night like a silver stream, pointed inexorably to freedom. Not even the steady rain could dilute his sudden joy: Borgho City was four days' walk from the ranges, but that was four days for the living, who needed to rest and could not see silver streams in the night. Marius could be there in less than two days, so long as he kept up a steady pace and didn't stop to chat. The clouds blotted out the stars, the steady drumming of the rain silenced the sounds of the surrounding forest, and Marius could imagine himself alone in the world. All else had gone, washed away by the endless deluge. Only he strode on, with the whole world to explore: the ruins of great cities, the vast plains, the great fields of ice along the Northern Walls, empty of man, the whole world washed clean and only he was left alive… Marius stopped and shook his head. Perhaps another daydream.

An hour into his journey the track rounded a great rock, jutting out from the hillside like a sealed-up plague house, and began a slow descent towards the first plateau on the journey to the great coastal plains. Marius stopped for a moment to enjoy the view. The rain was spectacular, a waving blanket that swept the low-lying hillside vegetation first one way then the other in a constant rhythm. For a moment he could almost believe himself underwater, adrift above a vast field of seaweed, alive with the sway of the tide above. All he needed was a cloud of some small, silver fish to dart out of the trees and the illusion would be complete. He could even see the light of a huntermouth, a strange fish he had seen once when working a con amongst the fishing vessels of the Scorby fleet, that hung a light above its saw-toothed mouth to lure fish towards it, then savaged them. Marius watched as the light bobbed towards him, shimmering in the dark rain, the sway and swerve of it entrancing and hypnotising, as if he were a whitefish and the huntermouth was closing in…

"Shit!" Marius threw himself off the track just as the cart began to climb towards his position. His headlong dive took him into the nearby brush. He landed face first in a stickleprick bush.

"Fuck!" He careened backwards, pulling stickers from his face and hands and flinging them away. His heel struck an exposed root and he tumbled back onto the track and across it in a mess of flailing arms and legs. His head struck the massive rock on the other side and he pitched forward, landing face first on the sandy track. He lay that way for perhaps half a minute, waiting for his eyes to catch up with the rest of him, then rolled over, expelling a spray of spit and sand into the air, and found himself staring into the barely-interested face of an underfed, aged mule. Marius scrambled out from under the animal's gaze and stood, eyes darting to either side of the track in the search for the best escape route. When no sound was forthcoming from the mule he stopped panicking and let his gaze settle on the driver of the cart the beast was pulling.

Marius was no great judge of age, but something *that* old should either be buried or a tree. Marius had once spent a torturous month impersonating the chief eunuch to the Caliphate of Taran's second best harem, in a fruitless attempt to discover the location of the Caliphate's second-best buried treasure. In Taran they bred a special type of dog whose face, if it could be described as such, was nothing more than a mass of folds and wrinkles. The more wrinkles the dog possessed, the more highly it was prized. Marius had seen dogs that resembled mobile scrotums, pressed to the bosoms of cooing concubines as if the most precious possession on Earth, while his own scrotum sat alone, underappreciated and never once held to the bosom of anybody. But even the most scrotal of puppies would retreat to the nearest concubine's cleavage in defeat when faced with the almost supernatural collection of wrinkles that stared at Marius now.

The driver of the cart looked like a relief map of the Broken Lands after a major land battle had taken place. He crouched in his seat like a blind man's drawing of a spider, a straw hat that looked like it might be hereditary crammed onto his head; arms and legs like knotted string poking out of a vague assemblage of clothing as if they'd been leant against them and forgotten. He stared at Marius, and Marius had the uneasy feeling that the old man had died of fright, and someone had better tell him before he forgot and drove off. He slowly raised a hand, and bent his fingers in a wave.

"Hello," he said, praying the old man wouldn't spook and drive over him. He was in luck. After an extended pause, in which Marius could imagine his single word searching across the wrinkled phizog in an attempt to distinguish his ear from the rest of him, the old man leant over to a lamp that hung from a pole at the side of the cart. He tilted it so the light swung directly into Marius' face. Marius smiled, and waved again.

It is entirely possible that the descendants of the old cart driver still tell stories of the night he met Marius. Blinded as he was by the sudden flash of light, Marius didn't see him leave the cart, but he did feel the breeze as he passed, moving across him at an angle towards the bushes at the track's edge.

"Hey, watch out for the stickle…" But it was too late. The old man cleaved the stickleprick bush without stopping, stick arms waving like a pair of spindly black machetes, cutting a path through the bushes at a pace that would have impressed a charging elephant.

Marius watched him disappear into the gloom of the forest. Within moments the man was out of sight, but the sound of breaking vegetation continued for several minutes. Marius listened to the crashes of destruction fade into the distance, then turned back to the mule. They stared at each other. Marius' gaze slipped down to the sand at his feet. No footprints spoiled the ground between the cart and the forest.

"Well," he said. "What do you make of that?"

The mule snorted, although whether in agreement or disdain, Marius couldn't tell. As there seemed no chance of consensus, he glanced back down the track, then down the path the old man had taken, then back at the mule.

"Can't leave you here, I guess," he said. He climbed onto the cart and twitched the reins. "I doubt I need to rest my legs, either, but let's not take the chance, hey?" He pulled on the reins, and slowly, with great reluctance, the mule wheeled about and began to pull the cart back down the track. Marius leaned back, and glanced at the seat beside him.

"Hey, what do you know?" he said, "The old chap left his hat behind." He placed it on his head, twitched the reins once more for emphasis, and let his new pet figure out the rest for itself.

For the first time since his travails had begun, Marius relaxed. The mule plodded onwards like a surly automaton, one step after another without a single change of pace or demeanour, the rise and fall of its haunches hypnotic in the gently swaying light of the lantern. Marius quickly fell into the rhythm of the journey, letting his body swing along with the back-and-forth motion of the cart. Now he understood the old man's posture – faced with the endless tiny adjustments necessary to maintain balance, his body quickly admitted defeat and slumped into the shape of least resistance.

Without the presence of another person to remind him, Marius quickly forgot about the stickers poking into his face. It was only when he reached up to adjust his hat, to stop the incessant rain falling into his eyes, that he brushed against them and remembered to pull them out. He stared at the first of them, and frowned. He had felt nothing as he pulled it out, not even the slight tug as it loosed its hold upon his skin. Yet he remembered the pain of falling into the bush, and how much his head had rung in the moments after he struck the rock.

Gerd had been adamant that the dead were beyond such mortal sensations, but Marius was not so removed from humanity that he could dismiss the things he had so recently felt. Something was not right. Some vital information was missing, some essential truth had been mislaid, or neglected. Marius had seen his reflection. It was not that of a living man. And yet he did not *feel* dead, which begged the question: was he alone in this, or was this deadening of skin and soul simply something that the dead were persuaded into believing, because nobody had the strength of purpose or character to deny the common belief? Or was it Gerd who did not feel things simply because he was Gerd? And if so…

Marius stared at the prickle as if he might find the truth written upon it, like the foreign conjurers in the markets who claimed to write your name on a grain of rice. As if you'd even be able to read it if they did, Marius snorted, and flicked the prickle out of the cart. No, something was not right. Perhaps a few more hours of pondering while the mule strode gently onwards would reveal the missing link. What the heck, it was as good a plan as any.

The mule, unaware of how good the plan was, chose that moment to stop. Marius blinked, then did so again when he saw the shaft of an arrow sticking out of the beast's neck. He stared stupidly at it for a moment, long enough for something to whizz out of the nearby brushes and thud into his chest. Marius rocked back in his seat, staring down at a matching shaft that now protruded from his torso.

"Oh, for gods' sakes," He pulled the arrow out and flung it over the edge of the cart, jumped down and knelt by the mule, placing a hand on its neck to feel for a pulse. There was nothing. The animal was definitely dead. Another arrow sped out of the dark and slammed into his back, just below the juncture of neck and shoulders. Before he was quite aware of doing so, Marius rose from his crouch, crossing the dozen feet between the cart and the bushes in no more than two heartbeats. He burst through the branches and into the tiny clearing beyond, grabbing the hidden archer by the throat and slamming him up against the bole of a tree before the man had time to notch another arrow.

"What the fuck," Marius snarled as the terrified archer struggled for breath, "did that mule ever do to *you*?"

From behind him, a second assailant rushed at Marius, a long dagger raised above his shoulder. Without loosening his grip upon the archer, Marius turned. The new attacker lunged. Marius took a small step to the side, drew his arm away from his body, and grabbed the attacker just above the elbow as his strike slid past Marius' ribs. He squeezed, and the second man screamed. As he pulled at his trapped arm Marius twisted his wrist, and a loud crack echoed across the clearing. The attacker stiffened in pain, and in that moment Marius lunged forward and butted him with all the strength in his dead neck muscles. There was another sharp crack and the swordsman slowly crumpled until only Marius' grip on his arm held him up. He let go, and the dead assailant slid to the ground, sightless eyes turned up into his head. Marius turned back to the archer, still pinned to the tree by his unflinching grip.

"Why?" he growled, shaking his whimpering prisoner, and then, when he received no response, shouting. "Why?"

The archer said nothing, indeed, seemed capable of no reply. His gaze was fixed upon the dead stare of his companion and only a terrified sob escaped his lips at regular intervals, like a clockwork baby winding down. Marius curled his lip in disgust, and leaned forward so that his mouth brushed against his victim's ear. The archer flinched, his gaze sliding round as far as it could towards Marius.

"Run," Marius whispered. "Don't stop. Ever. Not for cities, not for oceans, not for the edge of the world." Gently, he loosened his grip upon his captive's neck. "Go on," he said, his voice soft in the terrified man's ear. "Run."

The terrified archer prised himself away from the tree. With one last look at his fallen colleague he stumbled towards the edge of the clearing. By the time he entered the brush he was running. Marius listened to his passage for perhaps half a minute, then sighed and looked around at his surroundings for the first time.

It was a meagre campsite, to say the least. The two bandits had obviously been laying in wait for unwary travellers, hoping to strike lucky, or at least snaffle some decent food. A tripod of crooked branches stood over a tiny circle of rocks, and the few charred sticks within were ample evidence that the fools hadn't even possessed enough smarts to start a decent fire. A single battered plate perched on top of the branches. Marius wrinkled his nose at the contents. Whatever it was in life, the meagre meal inside had far too much gristle to have been in good health. He dropped the plate into the dirt, and scouted around.

Two thin, ripped blankets had been rolled up and placed against the base of a tree, and apart from the bow and knife at his feet, it seemed the only things his assailants owned were the threadbare clothes they wore. It was no wonder they were so eager to purloin the cart, Marius thought. Compared to their pathetic belongings it must have promised untold riches. Reminded of the attack, he reached up and pulled the arrow from his back, looked closely at it, then flung it from him in disgust. Even the arrows were old, the tip showing signs of re-carving and repeated hardenings in the fire. The arrow struck the corpse of the swordsman. Marius looked down at him for a few moments, then trudged back to the cart to rummage around in the back. Eventually, he withdrew a short-handled shovel and made his way back to the clearing. Picking a soft spot on the downhill side of a short incline, he dug a hole a few feet deep, then carried the dead man over and dropped him into it. He stood, staring down at the unmoving corpse.

"Come on," he said eventually, then again, as the corpse in the hole made no attempt to rise, "Come on!"

Soon he was screaming it, tears streaming down his cheeks, his hands clenched into fists on his thighs as he crouched over and expelled his fear into the roughly dug hole.

"Come on, come on, come on you bastard. Get up. Get up. Please." He sank to his knees, shoulders slumped, arms hanging loosely at his sides. "Please," he whimpered, "Not just me." The bandit stayed where he was, neck bent at an unnatural angle, eyes staring through the dirt wall into infinity.

Then Marius heard something – a scratching; the tiniest of movements from the bottom of the hole. He leaned forward, gripped the edge of the grave, eyes searching for animation in the swordsman's corpse. The sound grew louder. Marius frowned. It sounded like digging. Dirt moved under the dead man, then a hole opened, tiny at first but growing larger and larger until it filled the bottom of the grave and the dead man was no longer held by the earth but supported by a dozen hands reaching up from below. As Marius watched he was slowly borne downwards into the dark, then passed beyond the edge of the grave to arms waiting just out of sight. Six faces peered up at Marius, their dead visages fixed in anger.

"The king," six voices sounded in the dark, whilst dead eyes met his, "Where is our king?"

Marius fell back as the dead reached up and began to pull the walls of the grave in after them. He scrabbled backwards, beyond the line of trees at the clearing's edge, the dead voices following him, "Where is our king? Where is our king?" until they were cut off and all that he could see from his hiding place was an unbroken plane of sand where the hole had been. He stood, eyes fixed on the empty spot, took one step backwards, and another, then turned, and with no more thought in his head than a dead man, ran from the clearing as if the wolves of Hell were chasing.

# EIGHT

There are some objects in the universe so large, so *immense*, that they bend the laws of physics to suit themselves. Smaller things, even if they are themselves of such a size as to stagger the imagination, are caught within their gravitational pull, never to be released, and what does manage to escape is either too small to be noticed, or so broken and destroyed as to be useless. Philosophers in the King's palace had recently announced that the planets orbited the sun in this way, and that light, a substance so large and all-encompassing that it covered the Earth like a blanket, was actually held in thrall to the spinning of our own planetary surface. No matter how large, or powerful, there is always something bigger that will suck you in, enslave you to its movement and make you a mere satellite.

Borgho City was such a place.

It is said that wherever a king resides lies the governance of a country, but wherever the largest river meets the sea lies the true power. Borgho City squatted over the largest delta at the mouth of the largest river in the largest country on the continent, and whatever power was held within her massive stone walls was as twisted and incomprehensible as the street system that had grown up over the decades of occupation. Its walls, it was said, had exhausted quarries as far away as the Penate Mountains. In fact, most of the walls were made of rammed earth, deposited in vast hills when the first harbour had been dredged from the silt and sand of the delta mouth, but Borgho City had grown so big that truth and memory were only two of its satellites.

A mile from those city walls, the road Marius was on crested a rise, before plummeting down towards the nearest gate. Marius paused as he reached the top, found a nearby lump in the surrounding ground, and sat down to watch the traffic as it approached the entrance.

Foolish men, such as those who never have to leave a city, will tell you that the walls surrounding it, and the guards who man them, exist to defend the city from its enemies – to provide a barrier between the riches within and the covetous, barbarian masses without. Wise men know that this is nonsense. Walls exist to contain gates, and soldiers exist that they may stand next to those gates and demand tribute from anyone wishing to enter. Outsiders desire entrance, guards exact a levee, and then spend it on booze, women and gambling. If they're good, gods-fearing men. If not, well, there are a million ways to part a guard and his money, and not all of them have to be approved by a majority of the churches to be fun. Thus the economy is kept vibrant, money moves in the right directions, taxes are manageable, and the whole system runs along as smoothly as a slaughterhouse production line.

The *truly* wise, amongst whom you can count guards, guards' mistresses and those who didn't learn their lesson the first time they tried to get into a city, know the truth: there *are* a million ways to part a guard and his money, so to a guard, money is a useless and transitory thing. If you really want to get into a city unscathed – that is, with your belongings intact and all those special little items you've secreted about yourself in the hope the authorities won't go searching for them – you need to know what your gatekeepers *really* want. There are as many desires as there are guards to a gate, and the only way to know which one is the most appropriate is to find a good vantage point, pull up a piece of ground, and watch a while.

It is said that the dead are infinitely patient, although it is usually said by the living, and how would they know? Perhaps they are, but only if they have nowhere to be, and nothing to be running from. Marius knew how to be patient. It was part of his craft. Even so, the hours chafed. It was mid-morning when he took his seat. By the time those passing him drew lunches from capes and carts and settled in to eat, his eyes were itching.

Still he sat, eyes fixed upon the gate ahead. Carts arrived, arguments took place, and tolls were handed over. Marius paid no attention to them. What was important to him came afterwards, once each supplicant had passed through the gate and the guards were left with whatever bounty they had taken. He watched as lunch came and went, and the afternoon was spent one trudging step after another, one petulant transaction upon the next.

The sun began its lazy descent behind the spires and towers of the city, and still he did not move. Shadows became puddles of black, then pools, then one large ocean that stretched from city to hill and up into the sky. The city bells rang for day's end, then final prayer. Torches were lit along the final approach to the city and over each gate along the wall, and still Marius sat unmoving. On the road around him, groups of travellers, deciding that one more night could stand between them and the attempt to find lodgings, drew their carts to the edge of the road and climbed inside, or nestled in whatever hollow they could find in the gloom, and drew cloaks over their faces.

Marius watched a final few enter the city, and then, though the gates still stood open to receive guests, he watched the guards make ready for the long, empty hours of the night. Only then, when it was clear to him what the men at the gates prized most dearly, did he allow himself a small laugh. He stood and listened to the mumbling crowd along the road. Then he set off into the deep darkness, away from the campfires, to make ready.

It is commonly believed that an army marches on its stomach, like some million-headed snail. Marius had been in an army, once, for about six weeks. Long enough to learn the whereabouts of the regimental pay supplies, and separate them from those who expected to be paid. He had learned many things during that time, chief among them being how far into the mountains he needed to run before he was safe from execution. But he also knew that it is not the stomach which is the most important aspect of a soldier's existence. Any spear carrier with decent enough cunning and a sympathetic sergeant can find a meal.

What a soldier truly prizes, and considers the greatest skill to be acquired, is sleep. Not sleep as you and I understand it, in a bed, perhaps even in our own homestead, with a cuddly wife or acrobatic mistress besides us. But sleep in the rain, sleep on a mountain pass with hateful foreigners in the rocks above and a two hundred foot fall below, sleep while the legs still march and the ears still hear orders. Sleep, standing at an open gate with a rich, under-defended city at your back. Sleep, undiscovered.

A sergeant may be sympathetic to many things, but sleeping on duty will never be one of them.

An hour after Marius left his position on the hillock above the final approach he shuffled the last few steps to the mouth of the city gate.

"Hello, lads."

Twenty minutes amongst sleeping travellers had transformed him. Calfskin gloves covered his hands, and the worn-out shoes he had been wearing since the turn of the year were gone, replaced by a pair of sturdy leather hiking boots that looked as if they had only just embarked upon their first journey. His travel-worn clothes, and more importantly, the nature of his features, lay hidden deep in the folds of a hooded oil-skin cape. A thick knobkerrie completed the ensemble, and Marius leant upon it as if it were a cane, surveying the hooded eyes of the guards. He suppressed a smile. Nobody likes being disturbed from dozing, particularly if they're being disturbed in order to work.

"Gate's closed for the evening."

"Looks open to me," Behind the guards, two wooden doors, twice the height of a man, thick and unadorned and of rough construction, stood open. A corridor the thickness of the wall above, perhaps ten feet in all, led into a short square. Marius could see an open hole in the roof of the corridor. Breach the doors, and the pot that undoubtedly stood above them could pour boiling oil directly onto you before you made the open plaza. Nasty stuff, but a city will do whatever it can to protect the dignity of its gods-fearing mothers and pure virgin daughters, even if nobody can remember having met one. He tilted his head to indicate the open passage, grunting slightly as he did so, and leaned further onto his support, shuffling forward a step in the process.

"I said it's closed, old man." The guards looked at each other over the top of Marius' head. "That is, unless you can pay the toll."

This time, Marius couldn't help but grin. "Oh, yes. And what that might be?"

"Well," the older, heavier guard said, resting his hands on his hips and squaring himself up between Marius and the doorway. "That all depends on what you've got, doesn't it?"

Some things never fail, Marius thought. The old teach the young all the mistakes they've spent years perfecting, the strong never stop to look closely at the weak, and the prepared always vanquish the stupid.

"Got?" he replied, cheerily. "Oh, lads, I haven't got a blessed thing."

"Oh, dear," the older guard said. "Oh, dear, oh dear. You hear that Jeltho? Not a thing, he says."

"Yeah, Ej, not a thing." The younger fellow laughed, a thick, hopeful sound.

"I find that hard to believe, don't you, Jeltho?"

"Yeah, Ej, yeah."

Big Ej stepped forward, looming over Marius. "I wonder if you're not trying to hold out on us, old man. I wonder if I'd not be better off searching you for contraband, and see just what you're hiding."

"Is Sergeant Olling still patrol master of these gates?" Marius asked softly. Ej stopped, and glanced at his young offsider. "Only, I remember him being patrol master when I was in the guard."

Ej leaned back, and narrowed his gaze. "What about it?"

Marius waved his hand airily. "Oh, it's nothing, really. It's just, I can't believe old Olling would be in charge and tolerate any, well, *tithing*, shall we say?"

The two soldiers shared another glance, and Marius pressed harder into the silence. "Does he know about the Maria Hole yet?"

"What?"

"Oh, you know, the Maria Hole. Down the wall there, twenty feet or so? Base of the wall, hole like the shape of old Maria Fellaini's front entrance? I don't suppose you remember old Maria. Too young, you are. But oh, when she danced the peekaboo, a strong man would have to see the doctor, get a salve to help with the bruises, you know what I mean, hey?" Marius chuckled. "But I can't believe old Olling's in charge, and one of you isn't down there having a kip, out of sight, in the warm. Must be someone else, now."

The silence between the two men deepened. Marius waited, head tilted, watching their uncertainty with a smile. Slowly, without talking, the guards reached the right decision, as he knew they would.

"You served?" Ej asked.

"Oh, yes. Was here for the Whores Uprising. *That* was a weekend, let me tell you."

Ej nodded. "What's your name, brother?"

It was all Marius could do not to cackle. "Ebbel. Ebbel Samming. Sorry I don't have anything to offer a former brother-in-arms. Should have known better. You have a good night, lads." He turned his back to the gate, began to take a shuffling step away.

"Wait on, now."

"Sorry?"

There was a hurried exchange of whispers. When Marius turned back, young Jeltho was absent, but the sound of rapidly moving footsteps could be heard, heading off down the outside of the wall.

"No charge for a brother-in-arms," Ej said. "You go on in. You've earned the right."

"You're sure?"

"Of course," Ej said. "Only… if you do catch up with the patrol master…."

"When did he last stand at a gate, hey?" Marius shuffled forward, leaned into Ej so that they stood, shoulder pressed to shoulder. He patted the bigger man on the arm. "I'm not one to rat out a brother guardsman, my friend. You have a good night."

"You too, Ebbel." They parted and Marius limped through the gateway. When he was ten feet or so past the gate, Ej called out.

"Oh, Ebbel."

Marius froze. He turned slowly, every muscle in his body preparing for flight. "Yes?"

"Try the *Mandrake Root*. Tell Dettsie I sent you. They'll have a room for you."

Marius waved the knobkerrie in salutation. "Thank you, friend. Thank you."

He shuffled away as fast as his charade would allow. As soon as he rounded the first corner he dispensed with the knobkerrie and the limp, and began to stride down through a maze of interconnecting alleyways away from the gate. He *had* spent a time in the Borgho City guard, or at least, as their prisoner. And there *was* a hole down the wall from the southern gate, but it neither resembled nor smelled like anyone's *front* entrance. It was, however, the reason he wasn't still under the guard's stewardship. It had taken him three months to become trustee of the gaolers' toilets, and another week to tunnel through the accumulated shit of the city's sump holes. There wasn't a bath strong enough to help those two guards tonight.

And, he thought, patting his breeches pocket, gods help "brother" Ej if he mentioned to anyone that he'd just been speaking to his old companion Ebbel Samming. At least, gods help him if he mentioned it to anyone who knew how to curse in Feltish. There are worse insults, but it takes one man to mouth them and another to mime the actions.

An open doorway beckoned, and Marius ducked

into it, taking a moment to transfer Ej's coin purse from his breeches to a hidden pocket sewn into the lining of his jerkin. At least three Riner in "tolls", judging by the weight. Enough to start the evening.

Out in the street again, Marius took a moment to get his bearings, before choosing a side lane and setting off at a quick clip. The *Mandrake's Root* was a soldier's haunt, a sturdy old building in the backstreets of the merchant's quarter: close enough to the food stalls and the prostitutes to be convenient but far enough from the foot traffic for a bit of peace and quiet, so that no casual passerby would interrupt the soldiers in their drinking, and no local would make the detour because they knew better. It was the perfect place for a former soldier to rest, have a tankard or two, and catch up on the gossip and rumours that made up the majority of a serviceman's conversational skill set. From where he was, Marius estimated it to be no more than a dozen streets to the east. He set his back towards it and headed towards the docks.

Despite the hour, the streets were packed. Like all harbor cities, Borgho never really closed down. Come the night, it merely swapped one set of merchants for another, one form of trade for the next, one class of clientele for the lower. There may be less velvet in the clothing, and the manners may be easier to understand, but the transactions were no less urgent than those conducted in daylight, and the streets no less vibrant with the movements of a big city at work. The streets themselves changed character. Where Marius had entered, they were reasonably broad – enough room to turn a cart, at least – and the buildings that flanked them were white-painted and open-fronted, a hearty "hello" to the travellers who entered.

But turn left and start moving down the hill towards the docks and the true nature of the city exerted itself. The streets became narrower, more winding; the buildings leaned in more, cutting the sunlight off before it could illuminate the dirt and graffiti that made up the city's natural colouring. Signs were smaller, the writing upon them more crabbed, the spelling simpler and more often incorrect. Even the language changed. Up high, the Scorban was clear cut and elegant, and words of as many as four syllables could be heard through poured-glass windows by anyone who crouched outside them at night. Down here, though, all languages intertwined in a dance of commerce and aggression, a patois that welcomed all comers and gave each one the opportunity to be dunned in the pidgin of their choice. The world was a darker, dirtier, more openly dishonest place. Marius felt perfectly at home.

He strolled along the cobbles with the grace of one who had been born to the streets. In truth, he had spent so long plying his trade among the night crawlers of cities from the Bone Coast to the Western Spires that it was part of his nature now. It was the daylight hours where he needed to remind himself of the mores and rituals. Only during the day could he not afford the luxury of relaxing as he walked, and merely taking in the sights, the smells and the sounds of the city. Here, surrounded by the filth of window-emptied chamber pots, with darkened faces peering out of equally dark alleyways, and with the press of unwashed bodies nudging him and hustling him off his natural stride, he was as relaxed as he had been since before the Jezel Valley had called to him, and Marius Helles had become Marius the Dead. At the thought of his current predicament he shook his head, and lengthened his stride. He had things to do. There would be time for sightseeing later.

It was no more than fifteen minutes' walk, to someone who knew the back streets and cut-throughs as intimately as Marius, between the Southern Gate and the *Hauled Keel*, nestled between a dozen identical taverns at the drinking end of the Borgho docks. Sailors resemble guardsmen in any number of ways, except that they don't give a damn who else drinks in their pubs, and their gossip has less to do with who's rumpling whose bed sheets and more to do with who has the run of the waves, and who went out and never came back. In that time, Marius' pockets were dipped no less than eight occasions, for a net loss of a dozen rivets, six flat stones, and two small bags of what he hoped were toy knucklebones. Sightseeing he may have been, but only with one eye. Thanks to those same dippers, however, he arrived at the tavern somewhere in the region of nine riner to the good. It would have been more, but dipping a dipper is tricky enough without the impediment of gloves, or dead fingers. Anyone can make a living in the big city, assuming you're quick enough. The only way to make a living in Borgho City is not to get caught, or if you're going to get caught, to only get caught by the right type of people.

Marius heard the taverns long before he saw them. The docks are a noisy, twenty-four-hours-in-the-day area. But the taverns seem to find an extra hour, and an extra layer of noise, as if those who work outside desire, rather than seek respite from the endless walls of sound around them; something to block the sounds out. Fights are rare in these pubs – the men have spent all day proving how hard they are. They've no need to do it in their down time, and besides, there are better ways to go about it than something that might result in spilled booze. The *Hauled Keel*'s Krehmlager is one of the best. Hard men drink Krehmlager. The suicidal drink two.

Marius pushed open the door and found a booth towards the back of the smoky, badly lit room, just as it was being emptied of drunken, snoozing bodies. He slid in, and signalled to a passing serving girl.

"A tankard of Krehmlager, a spice roll, and something for your break." He laid a tenpenny on the table. "If there's any left, save it for your old age." Serving girls may not make the world go round, but they give it a much more interesting shape. The girl smiled her thanks and left to fill his order. The beer would come from the heavy end of the barrel, and the roll would be fresh.

She returned in short order and laid his repast before him. Marius placed another coin on the table. "Is Keth in tonight?"

The serving girl eyed him warily, taking in his gloves, the cape and hood that covered all features. "You been away, sir?"

"Why?"

"She, uh…" the girl looked over her shoulder. "She doesn't do that anymore."

Marius snorted. "I know. Just tell her... tell her Marius is here, could you?" He pushed the coin forward. The girl took it, and hurried away. Marius stared at his beer until he felt a body slip into the booth opposite him.

"You wanted to speak to me, sir?" Marius closed his eyes for a moment. Keth's voice was as warm as he remembered it: mulled wine, with just a hint of a massage later in the evening. He kept his head bowed, and indicated the tankard.

"I want to drink it, but I'm afraid of what'll happen."

Keth laughed, and it felt like a long, slow swallow of something wonderful on a cold evening. "You might be right, Mister. Krehmlager isn't for the foolhardy. I've seen bigger men than you made into crying children after a couple of tankards of that stuff, no offence."

That was an understatement. The *Hauled Keel*'s special brew had a reputation that far exceeded that of the city's heroes, and every awestruck whisper of it was deserved. Marius had seen grizzled veterans swearing they could see the gods, and not the right ones, after no more than three tankards. He himself could usually manage no more than half a draught before he either fell asleep or ran for the nearest exit to be violently sick. He stared at the mug in front of him.

"I'm worried about what'll happen. If it'll have any effect. If I'll even taste it. What'll I do if it doesn't, Keth? What if I don't?"

A tiny line of puzzlement dragged down the inside corners of Keth's eyebrows.

"There's only one way to find out, Mister. If you'll

excuse me, I thought Senni mentioned an old friend's name, but I think she was…"

"It's me, Keth."

"I'm sorry?"

"Me. Marius. It's me."

Keth stared at him, doubt in every angle. "You're Marius?"

Marius nodded. "Back of the left knee, about half an inch up, never fails."

"Oh, God." Keth sank into her seat, stretched out her arms across the table. Marius reached out gloved hands, and she squeezed them between her strong, warm fingers. "Marius. What happened?"

"You don't want to see the worst of it, Keth. I'm in real trouble this time."

"What is it, sweetheart? Is it fire? I've seen men after fires. Pox? Spear wounds? Come on, sweetie, I've seen it all. You can show me." With a quick movement she slipped the fingers of her left hand down to the end of his glove and tensed. Marius, realizing what she was about to do, pulled away. It was too late. His arm came backwards. The glove stayed where it was. He and Keth stared down at his exposed hand. Keth swallowed.

"Pull your hood back, sweetheart, won't you?"

"Keth…"

"Just do it, Marius. Please?"

Slowly, Marius reached up and touched the hem of his cloak.

"Please, Keth. I don't want you to scream, or be frightened. I don't want you to see this."

"I'll be fine, Marius. Please. I have to see it."

Marius pulled back his hood. Keth didn't scream, or faint, or beg him to stop. She simply took in his features, her face a mask of blankness, for five or six heartbeats. When she spoke, her voice was very careful, and calm, and very neutral, as if she were speaking to an intruder with a knife.

"Okay, then. Perhaps you'd better put it back over yourself, love. Just in case. Best not scare the customers."

Marius replaced his hood and sank further into his seat. They sat that way for long moments. Marius peered at Keth from the safety of the hood's depths. She stared at him, her teeth working hard against her upper lip, then her lower, and back to her upper. Finally she reached across, pulled the tankard towards her, and took a moderate-sized pull.

"So," she said when she had recovered her breath.

"So."

"This is why you haven't come back before now?" She giggled, then cut it off quickly. They could both hear the panic.

"I almost had it," Marius said, his gaze falling to the table. "One more time, maybe two." He shrugged, stared at the table. "Maybe three. Then I'd have enough, and I'd be back, and we'd have enough, and it would all be…" he trailed off, waved his hand limply at nowhere in particular.

"No, you wouldn't." Keth smiled sadly. "That's not you, is it? We've learned that."

"No. I guess not."

"It's bad, though, isn't it? Really bad."

"Keth." Marius held up his hand, turned it so she

could see both sides. "I think I'm dead." He picked up the glove and put it back on. "I need to get away."

"Sweetheart, how can you be dead? You're walking, and talking, and…" she stared at him, stared at his chest. "Oh, God. You're not breathing, are you?"

"I need passage, Keth. On a boat, a good sized one, headed to the Far Isles. Something big enough that I can rent a cabin with some privacy."

"But…"

"You know who's in and who's going out. You can find me one. Here." He reached into his pockets, pulled out his remaining coins. "Take it. That'll be enough to reserve the cabin. Get a price. I'll have the rest by the time we ship."

"Shit." Keth swept the money into her skirt, fumbled about under the table for a moment, then stood, the money nowhere in sight. "What are you trying to do, waving money about like that? Trying to get us both…" She stopped, raised her hand to her mouth. "I'll… I'll try." She turned away from him, took a step, turned back. "Have you a place?"

"No. Not yet. I…"

"I'm on the second floor. At the end." She fumbled in her apron, withdrew a key and tossed it on the table. "I'll be off in a couple of hours." She nodded at the tankard and the roll. "Take those. No sense in letting them go to waste. I've got… I've got to go." She backed away, and pushed through the crowd. In a moment, she was lost to view.

Marius stared at the spot where she had been for countless seconds. Then, slowly, he reached out and gathered the key. He stood, took the food from the

table, and sidled towards the staircase at the back of
the room.

At the top of the stairs, a short mezzanine led into a
dark, sweaty-smelling corridor that ran the length of
the building. Sconces lined the walls between anonymous, unnumbered doors. Most of them bore scorch
marks above – from where drunken tenants had stumbled and spat – or worse, upon them. Sailors,
especially drunk ones, aren't picky about their surroundings. A pillow to rest their head and a pot to piss
in on the floor is all they generally required, and as
long as they stayed sober enough to tell the difference,
they were happy. Marius had seen worse dockside
rents – at least these had their doors on. Anyone who
cared to complain about the dirt and the generally
seedy air was either a stranger or still sober.

There was one exception. At the far end, directly
facing him, a white-painted door with lit sconces at
either side stood out like a princess in a workhouse.
A garland of dried flowers hung from a nail, and a
circle of spotlessness surrounded it where the walls
had been washed and the wooden floor swept free
of dirt and dead insects. Marius snorted in recognition and strode towards it. The key fit on the first
attempt, and he noted the absence of scratch marks
around the hole. Whatever else may be said about
them, the clientele of the *Hauled Keel* had obviously
paid attention when warned to leave this room
alone. The door swung inwards on oiled hinges, and
Marius stepped through.

Inside, the room was clean, but little more. Marius

closed the door behind him, made his way across to the dim outline of the bed, and found a lamp sitting upon a table next to it, a pack of lucifers at its base. He lit the lamp, then picked it up and used it to light three others at strategic points around the room. Once a modicum of visibility had been established he made his way to the single chair beneath the window, moved the neatly folded clothes onto the bed, and sat, throwing back his hood and running his fingers through his hair in relief. Only then did he take the time to thoroughly examine his surroundings.

Keth had tried, Marius could see that. Somewhere along the line, for whatever reason, she had decided to really try to make a home here. Nothing around him was new. The single bed sagged in the middle and the wood frame was bowed and warped from years, maybe decades, of water-rich air. But she had piled pillows and blankets upon it, and perhaps the thickness of the padding made up for the shape. Those blankets, and the clothes he had moved from the chair, were clean. Perhaps not freshly laundered, but certainly more recently than the once-a-fortnight swish through a bathtub of cold water that most bedding received in an establishment like the *Hauled Keel*.

The trunk at the bed's end had been old and battered when Marius had given it to her, but the clasp and hinges were new, and the designs she had painted upon it, flowers and berries on a vine, had been carefully applied. The tiny table and mirror she used as a dresser were uneven, one leg straightened up with a piece of wood, and the mirror itself had a long stain down one side where the silvered backing had tarnished. But everything was neat and orderly, and such toiletries that lay alongside the metal trough in the corner were newly purchased. More dried flowers, siblings to the bunch on the front door, were nailed to the walls, and from somewhere, the Gods only knew where, she had found a small painting of the Berries Veldt and hung it above the bed head.

The overall impression was of care, and a determination to feel at home, and the whole thing saddened Marius more than he cared to admit. He felt out of place in his stolen cape and rotting skin, like leaves blown onto a freshly swept floor, just waiting for someone to notice and push him back out into the gutter. He got up, placed the tankard and spiced roll on the lid of the trunk, and returned to his seat to wait.

Taverns like the *Hauled Keel* never really close. At best, there is a short gap between one shift of clients reeling away to their beds or the street, and the next lot coming in from their boats or shift at the workhouses and piers to eat, drink, and raise the right level of noise to help forget their lives. The serving girls work long hours, longer than their customers can drink. Then they have to clean up afterwards, sweep away the butt ends and pipe tailings, mop up the spilled beer and vomit, push the last complaining drunkard out the door and point him in the direction of wherever he's calling home that day. Only then can the takings be tallied, wages apportioned, and each girl find her own way to bed.

Keth was luckier than most – a flight of stairs is a short journey compared to many. Even so, when she pushed the door open and slipped inside, the lines of her body were heavy with fatigue. Marius watched as she slipped off her slippers and knelt to splash water over her face. She glanced at him and he, taking the hint, vacated the chair.

"I spoke to a fellow just in off a trader," she said, settling into the chair and sighing. "It looks like the very job for you. Be a love." She pointed to the food on the trunk. Marius retrieved it and passed it over. She bit into the roll, followed it with a sip of Krehmlager, and sighed. "Fresh."

"What did he say?"

"He's serving on a seven hundred ton barque called the *Minerva*. They've been docked three days, taking on supplies for a run to the Faraway Islands. Reckons they'll be out three, maybe four months, then as many back, trading iron and cloth for the usual stuff. They're waiting for the right tides, but he's due back on board in the morning so he thinks they'll be off in no more than two days. They've got cabins."

"What type?"

"Are you fussy, now?"

Marius shrugged, abashed. "No, of course not. Just so long as they're private."

"They will be. As private as you'll get on a working boat." She bit into the roll again and swallowed. "When did you last eat?"

"I don't need to eat."

She looked at him for several seconds. "I don't need to cuddle, but it's still nice every now and again. Have some." She offered the tankard and roll. Marius hesitated, and she shook them slightly. "To be polite, if nothing else."

Marius took them, bit into the roll and followed it with a mouthful of the lager. They tasted... nice. He blinked, swallowed, and took another bite and drink.

"Hey! Save some for a worker."

Marius twitched, then handed them back. "Sorry. I... I don't understand. I could taste them."

"Don't look at me. It's your story." Keth eyed him up and down. "It's done you the world of good. You look better. Not, you know, you, but better."

Marius snuck a glance in the mirror. Keth was right. He did look better. Not himself, no, not alive, but less... deadish. A hint of animation around the eyes, maybe. A touch of colour at the edges of his lips. "I don't understand this at all. Gerd said–"

"Gerd?"

"A... companion. Guard dog, more like."

"And is he dead?"

Marius smiled. The face in the mirror drew its lips up into a rictus. "We're everywhere, don't you know?" He grabbed the tankard from Keth, took a swallow, handed it back. "So what now?"

"Well it's only a one person bed."

"That never bothered you before."

"You were a person."

He snorted. "Fair point. I don't need to sleep..." He caught himself. "Or cuddle."

Keth laughed, then levered herself out of the chair. "Well, I need to wash and lie down. You can go out into the hallway for five minutes or you can promise not to look. What will it be?"

Marius placed his hand over the still skin of his

heart. "I promise."

"Liar." She smiled and knelt down in front of the pail. "Go on. Turn around."

Marius turned and faced the simple drapes over the window. There was a slither of clothing, and then splashing as Keth performed her ablutions. Marius resisted peeking, and tried not to remember how she looked naked. Not that such thoughts would do him any good now, anyway, he thought. Better to stay away from them. He did not need to add a lack of reaction to a naked woman to all the other signs of his continuing death.

"Tell me about this place," he said in order to give himself something else to think about. "Why all the effort?"

"It's mine."

"I know that. But why go to all this trouble? Surely when you move on–"

"No." Marius heard Keth climb into bed, and risked turning round. Only her face was in view, her long hair brushed out of its braids and spread out over the blankets. If Marius could have cried, the lack of stirring in his groin would have driven him to it. "You're not listening. It's mine. I own this room."

"But…"

"I bought it from the Waldens six months ago. They're the managers. Everything in here." A long white arm emerged from the beneath the sheet and waved at their surroundings. Marius stared at the arm, and waited for a sign from below. Nothing. God damn it. "I own it."

"What? You mean forever?"

Keth giggled. "Maybe. Or maybe not. I don't know."

"But why...?" Marius looked around at the dismal collection of furniture, the sad little decorations, the desperate attempts to add dignity to what looked like nothing more than a collection of cast-offs.

"Because I *can*." Keth sat up, a flush of anger spreading across her skin. The blanket fell away, exposing her body down to the waist, but Keth was too angry to notice. Marius did, and almost smiled. Not so dead after all. But Keth was biting out words, and he realised there was nothing to smile about at all.

"Do you have any idea how hard it's been to get all this? To convince someone to sell me even this lot, never mind this fucking room? Because I'm a *woman*, in *this* city? Do you have any concept how precious it is to know I can finish my shift and come home, safely, to somewhere that belongs to me? A woman, in *this* city, owning *anything*? Do you have any idea how hard I've worked for this? Don't you dare look down on what I have, Marius don Hellespont."

"Helles."

"Don't you 'Helles' me, merchant's son. You don't *have* to scrabble for what you want. You've always had a choice."

"But... you could have–"

"Could have what?" Keth glanced down at how she was sitting, and gathered the blankets about her. "What, Marius? Waited for you? Been kept by you? How was that ever going to work?"

"But I..." Marius turned away from her in confusion, saw the tankard and picked it up. "I could have given you better than this."

"God damn it, you don't understand a thing. It's not the having, Marius. It's not even the money. Look at all this. Look at it." She gathered up a handful of blanket and shook it at him. "I own this. It doesn't matter what it looks like, or that it's not made of velvet or smells of lavender. It's mine. I have it, and nobody can take it away from me. Everything in this room. This room. Do you know how many women own even a *room* in this city, for themselves? It's not about money, Marius. It never was. I can work, and own things, and have my own life."

Marius stared at her, saw the pride in her eyes, and the anger. And the words came before he had time to regret them, and realise what he was placing between them.

"How much of it did you earn on your back?"

She stared at him for longer than he could bear. When she spoke, she did so quietly, and her voice was the deadest thing in the room.

"Get out, Marius. Get out of my home."

There was nothing he could say. Marius walked to the door, opened it, and made sure to shut it behind him. He stood a moment, waiting. She hadn't even cried. Marius hung his head and walked back down the hallway, away from Keth. He was at the top of the stairs before he remembered to pull his hood back over his head. It was only when it struck him on the face that he discovered he was still holding the tankard.

"Ow." He rubbed the spot where the tankard had hit, looked at it, and then took a long, deep draught. There was no taste at all. Marius stared at it, then let it drop to the floor. "Fuck."

He was halfway down the steps before he doubled over and threw up.

# NINE

Marius left the tavern at a flat run, burst out onto the street past startled onlookers, and just as suddenly as he had appeared, stopped, looking about himself in panic. The mouth of an alleyway stood between the corner of the tavern and the next building over. Marius couldn't go back inside, not after the reception his vomiting episode had received from the patrons. Besides, what would be the point? Keth had already ignored his entreaties from outside her door. Knocking would hardly change her mind. But her window had been open. Could she ignore his voice through it? At the very least, she would have to leave her bed to close it, and then… Marius wasn't sure what would happen then.

But something had happened in that room, something that had opened a gulf between them and left him vomiting in an undeniably *alive* way after half a tankard of Krehmlager. He could still taste his bile, even though he knew the dead could neither taste nor regurgitate. He raced for the corner, turned into the alley, and sloshed through ankle-deep mud until he stood below the window of Keth's room, staring up at the gap between the open shutters.

"Keth." He waited, but no response came. He looked about, back towards the busy street. Nobody had stopped to see what the solitary figure was doing, standing alone in an alley, shouting. "Keth." Louder now, a little more insistent, just a little panicked. "Keth, please!"

Again he waited, and again there was nothing. Marius began to worry. What if Keth held the solution to his dilemma? What if she was the key to everything, and he had thrown her away in his fit of pique? What if his only chance at life had lain in that room, and now, with a few words, he had placed it forever beyond his reach?

"Keth!" This time, the only sound that emerged was panic.

Then, behind the thin gauze curtains, something moved. Marius stiffened, thoughts frozen in hope. The curtains parted and Keth appeared, a bed sheet wrapped around her so that she stood above Marius like some ancient pagan deity, albeit one with ice in her eyes and her face an impassive mask. Marius held his arms out at waist height, palms upturned, offering penitence to his cold goddess.

"Keth…"

Slowly, eyes fixed upon Marius, Keth leaned out of the window. She opened her arms, and grasped the edges of the shutters. As Marius gazed on in despair she leaned back into the room, disappearing once more behind the curtains. The shutters banged closed, cutting in half the world between her and Marius.

A scene had been painted on the outside surface of the shutters. A field of yellow flowers, viewed through a framed window. A blue sky hung above, empty of clouds. A fat, tortoiseshell cat lay on the windowsill, staring down at Marius with the same impersonal disdain he had seen on Keth's features. Marius knew the cat's name. He was Alno, and he was the cat that Marius had promised to buy for Keth one day, when the grime and desperation of their lives grew too much to bear, and he had sequestered enough money to take them both away to an estate somewhere in the untroubled countryside. Nothing too big, he heard himself telling her as they lay cuddled together for warmth under the lodging house's thin blankets. Nothing too fancy. But a place just for us, with fields of yellow flowers for picking, and an uninterrupted view all the way to the horizon.

Marius closed his eyes. It was not the sudden knowledge of what he had lost that defeated him. It was the fact of the picture itself, that it was painted on the *outside* of the shutters, not the inside, that Keth had known his fantasy for what it was, had known this rift between them would open up, and had been so much more prepared for it than him.

Slowly, he raised one hand and laid it upon the opposite arm. He clenched, digging his nails deep into bicep. He felt nothing. And now, he could not even taste his bile. Marius nodded, head bowed, then turned away and walked slowly back into the street.

Keth had found him a ship, at least. With nowhere else to go, he turned towards the docks and began the slow walk down the thoroughfare. The *Minerva*, she had said, and if the size she mentioned was anything close to the truth it was more than large enough to take him to the end of any ocean he cared to name. Marius hunched deeper into his cape, thoughts tumbling around the image of Keth's face, and the frozen, dead look she had given him as they parted.

The crowds slid past him as he walked, oblivious to the myriad nudges and touches of close contact. His coins were well hidden, and should he have chosen to, he could have ignored the fluttering touch as a well-placed hand sought out his pocket, swiftly flitting in and out in the hope of dipping a coin or two. But Marius was not in the mood to play games with street rats. When the next casual bump arrived, and the bumper's hand flitted into the inner pocket of his cape he grabbed the offending wrist, spun the startled thief around, and pushed them both into the mouth of the nearest alley.

"What the hell is your game?" he snarled, leaning down so that his dead face filled the view of the child cowering in front of him. A girl, no more than eight or nine years old by the look of her. She looked just like any other street rat: dirty and dishevelled from a lifetime of begging scraps from whoever trod the cobbles upon which she slept. But Marius knew the signs. The dirt was just a little too carefully spread over her face, a little too effective at blurring distinguishing features. The scraps she wore were roomy rather than ragged, all the better for the multitude of hidden pockets they undoubtedly contained. The wrist he held had strength within it that spoke of at least semi-regular feeding.

"Whose are you?" he growled. He grabbed her other wrist, held them both in one hand, and used the other to roughly push her sleeves up to her shoulders. He twisted her arms this way and that, examining the wrists, the inside of the elbows, her armpits. Not finding anything he reached out and grabbed her jaw, turning her head back and forth until he located a tiny tattoo just below her ear – a small fish with a hook protruding from its mouth.

"A Salmon Streeter? Look!" He let go of her jaw and held his hand up, spreading his fingers so the webbing between thumb and first finger was visible. A tiny tattoo of a horse's head nestled within the space.

"Pony Lane boy from way back." In reality, Marius had tattooed it there himself three years previously, part of a failed scheme to embezzle the street gangs around the old market districts that had led very quickly to his last exit from the city. "Tell Old Gafna to teach his brats better. Trip, dip, flick. It's not that difficult."

He dragged the terrified girl down the alleyway and back into the street, stepping through the flow of human traffic until they stood equidistant from any path of escape. Marius let one wrist go, keeping a firm hold on the other, and let the girl strain to be free. People barged past on both sides. Marius stood still. Pedestrians stared as they passed, without bothering to intrude. Still Marius made no attempt to move. Then he saw a child across the way, indistinguishable at that distance from the masses of underage poor who choke the streets of any big city, except that this child most definitely did not glance at the unusual sight of the cowled immobile stranger and the urchin girl so obviously in conflict. He moved past, hugging tight to the wall, completely failing to notice Marius staring at him, before turning into an alleyway and disappearing into the darkness within. Marius pulled the girl towards him sharply, so that she stumbled and bumped her face into his hip.

"Get," he said, pushing her away so that she tripped and fell backwards into the stream of humanity passing them. As soon as she was hidden by the press of legs he stepped back towards the side of the road and strode swiftly away. Only when he had traversed several blocks did he stop, and step into a nearby doorway. He leaned against the doorframe, and slipped a hand into the inside pocket of his jerkin.

"Clever girl," he said with a smile. The thruppence he had placed there during their altercation in the street was missing. He reached into a pocket slightly further down, better hidden by the stitching, and removed a small pouch. He counted out three tenpennies worth of coins, dropped the pouch into the street, and returned the money to his pocket. Good girl, but not good enough to notice her own victimisation. Old Gafna would correct her mistakes.

Marius slipped into the street and continued on his way. Word spreads quickly, at street level. No more fingers troubled his journey.

The Borgho City docks ran for several miles along both sides of the Meskin River, a mile-wide brown snake that had long ago been domesticated by regular dredging, tide-breakers, and a profusion of weirs and

locks further upriver. The docks were a mini-city in
their own right, with their own culture, their own
language, and several customs that would appear
bizarre to anybody who wandered in from even a
mile outside the unofficial city limits, even if they had
been a Borghan their entire life. There was no logical
reason, for example, for a ship's captain to throw
overboard a corn dolly dressed like Severn Magnassity, the folkloric discoverer of the mythical port of
Haventide, but you'd never find a ship that sailed out
without having done so.

Generations of families had garnered a tidy living
from making dollies and selling them at dockside.
Each such family had their own particular tradition
when it came to folding the corn just so, cutting and
tying arms and legs one way and not the other,
sewing and folding Magnassity's uniform in one particular shade and not the next. As each distinctive
style of Magnassity became associated with this plen-
tiful fishing season or that devastating tornado, they
went in and out of fashion, became famous or infa-
mous in their turn. Fortunes waxed and waned, dolly
families climbed and fell within their own unique
caste system, marriages were made, alliances were
broken, and woe befall the outsider who uttered the
words "But they're just corn dollies" in the wrong
tavern.

So the culture of the Borgho wharfs progressed, and
drew the mismatched travellers and vagrants who occupied them closer together, until all who lived there
spoke the quayside patois, where knowing the difference between a topreeb and a jibreeb makes all the

difference, and no dictionary in the world can help you if you don't. The *Minerva* was a massive ship, if Keth was correct – over five hundred tons of wood and leather that would loom over the surrounding area like a war tower – but the docks were so large that Marius knew it could still take him the better part of a day to locate it, longer if he had to cross one of the bridges upriver and explore the north bank as well.

Marius had friends who worked the ships. People like Marius had friends everywhere. It's harder to do the kind of business Marius did without the right sort of introductions from the right sort of people, and Marius had been doing that kind of business for long enough to build up a significant web of contacts. The only problem, such as it was, was that Marius' kind of friends invariably didn't recognise him without money passing between them first. Thankfully, the streets were crowded. Within half an hour, he was able to stop in the shadow of a tenement at the western fringe and distribute several tenpennies worth of coins into various hidden pockets, as well as two wedding rings which had probably been on their way to a pawn shop.

By common consent, the docks did not tolerate dips. There were a million ways for a foreign sailor to lose his money in a city like Borgho. The most interesting ones were illegal, or at best, highly immoral, even by Lower Scorban standards. It was mutually agreed, in an unspoken pact going back centuries, that what the city guard did not see it could not close down. And too much money fed too many people in the area for anyone to want that arrangement to go bad because the wrong sailor got dipped before he could lose money to his satisfaction. It was not a case of one bad apple ruining a whole bunch, so much as the whole barrel being rotten but the customer not needing to know until they'd already bought it and carted it home. Besides, an off-duty guard's money was as good as a sailor's, and nobody wanted to dry up a regular source of revenue.

So: no dips; no footpads; no knives dug into ribs and sudden visits to side alleys. Marius knew the rules, and at what street corner they started to apply. As soon as he passed the end of Fishwife Lane and turned onto the wide street known to all as The Pipe Barrel, he left his fingers in his trouser pockets, and walked without caution past the crowds that milled about the endless stalls and displays of the city's most determinedly honest criminals.

Remmitt Paschar looked like a corn dolly made flesh, his sun-baked skin having been flogged so often for so many civic misdemeanours that it had taken on the scarred and wizened aspect of the dried corn husks. Like a true Borghan street man, however, he had turned this impediment to his advantage. Decked out in whichever style of blue uniform was in favour amongst the dolly families this year he paraded throughout the docks, offering the discerning new arrival slivers of the genuine decking of Severn Magnassity's sloop the *Tidy*, or lucky charms folded from the original pages of his map book, and even, should the sailor in question look especially noble or discerning, at a price that was killing Paschar. He wouldn't even be thinking of this if it weren't for his children not having eaten anything but dumcabbage broth for the last week, the complete sextant with which Severn Magnassity himself calculated the exact position of Haventide. As Paschar himself would tell you, it's not thievery if both sides receive something from the deal, even if one side doesn't always get *exactly* what they think they're getting.

He was just taking the weight off for five minutes, sitting on an upturned crate in the space at the back of a mussel-fryer's stall, trying to light a fresh snout from the butt of a dead one, when Marius slid past the stall and stood over him.

"Hello, Remmitt."

"Ach!" Paschar leaped backwards off the crate, banged the back of his head on the wall behind him, and fell back to Earth. "Gods damn it." He scrabbled across the grimy cobbles until he recovered the bent snout and jammed it into his mouth. "Look what you made me do." He looked up at Marius, letting his gaze travel his entire body before settling somewhere around the arc of jaw visible beneath the cloak's overhanging hood. "Are you in need of a genuine relic of the rich history of our city, friend? I can see you have a keen appreciation–"

"Your mouth."

Paschar raised a hand to his lips. "My mouth? What about it?"

"Close it."

"Hey, now friend. I'm a friendly fellow, but–"

Marius reached down with one hand, and grabbed Paschar's shoulder. He hauled the trader to his feet and slammed him against the wall in one strong, fluid movement. Paschar gasped, then began choking.

"My snout…" he managed. "Swallowed… Gods…"

Marius waited, effortlessly maintaining his grip. Paschar eventually subsided, drawing his breath in a heavy wheeze, his eyes streaming tears. When he was at last able to breathe without hacking gobs of tobacco-flecked spit onto the ground, Marius used his free hand to pull back his hood.

"Remember me?" he said, in a friendly tone that wouldn't have fooled a child. Paschar stared at his pallid, cracking face for several seconds. He made one attempt to swallow, then another. Finally, he gathered enough saliva into his mouth to attempt speech.

"Helles?"

"In the rotting flesh."

"What on Earth happ… You're looking… How are you?" Paschar smiled, a weak attempt that gave up and died instantly.

"You know something? I've been better."

"Shame." Paschar nodded in sympathy, stopping when it became apparent that if he didn't cease now, he'd probably not be able to stop it for at least several minutes. "I've always wished the best for you, Helles, you know that. Always felt–"

"Shush, now." Marius shook him gently, so that only his teeth rattled, and not his whole skeleton. Paschar shushed. "I'm glad you feel that way, Remmitt. I really am. Because I've got a way for you to prove it."

"I'd love to, Helles, really I would." Paschar found enough courage to reach up in an attempt to prise

Marius' fingers from his shoulder. Marius clenched. The fingers found flesh, and Paschar quickly gave it up as a bad idea. "It's just, I've got these kids to feed, see…?"

"You have two children, Remmitt. They live with their mother in Jarsik Way, you're allowed to see them once a month as long as you're accompanied by a special constable, and last I heard, the oldest one is training for the priesthood because he heard you're allergic to churches."

"Well, you know kids. Always playing tricks on their old man…"

"I need information, Remmitt." Marius reached into his pocket, and removed a tuppenny piece, which he held before Paschar's eyes.

"Ah, well, I'm sure I don't know anything about it, guv."

"You don't know what I want to know about yet."

"Yes, well," Paschar looked from the coin to Marius' face, swallowed, and decided it was better to focus on the coin. "I'm pretty sure I don't know anything. Not for that price, you know what I mean?" He devoted the last of his courage to another smile. It wasn't quite enough. Marius refrained from sighing. He drew out another penny.

"That's enough."

"I'm not sure–"

"It wasn't a question."

"Ah. Yes. Well, that'll do nicely." Paschar reached up and took possession of the coins. "How may I assist your enquiry?"

"The *Minerva*."

"Oh, yes. That's a lovely pub, that is. Other side of the city, I think you'll find. Next to an undertakers, not that I'm recommending–"

"It's a ship, Remmitt. A very big ship."

"Oh, *that Minerva*. Right." Paschar swallowed. "Got you."

"Over five hundred tons. Must have lots of crew. I'm sure some of them would have been interested in a genuine sliver from the *Tidy*. I bet some of them would even like to talk to the fellow that sold it to them. I bet they'd like to ask just how big the *Tidy* was to hold so many genuine slivers."

"Hey now, I offer only authentic... north west docks, over by Meanside," Remmitt squawked as Marius tightened his grip. Marius smiled, and let go. Paschar slumped to the ground. He shrank away, pressing the back of his head hard against the wall. Marius crouched in front of him and leaned forward so that their faces were inches apart.

"I'll remember how helpful you were, Remmitt," he said softly. "If you were helpful enough, I won't have to find you again, will I?"

Paschar nodded, shook his head, nodded again, and finally settled for remaining perfectly still.

"I'd say goodbye," Marius patted him on his shoulder. Paschar did his best not to wince as Marius' stone-hard hand struck. "But you ain't seen me, right?" He rose, and stepped quickly past the mussel fryer, who had resolutely faced streetward during the entire exchange. Only once he could no longer see Marius in his peripheral vision did Paschar draw a single, painful inhalation, and begin to curse his tormentor.

Half an hour later, as he was in the process of re-luctantly parting with Severn Magnassity's very own sextant, just so his poor children could eat some real meat for the first time in months, Paschar stopped and stared into the distance. All of a sudden, a realisation had hit him. At no time during his encounter with Marius – not when he was talking, not when he was holding him against the wall, not even when he leaned down and shoved his awful, awful face into his – could Paschar recall his assailant breathing. As his discerning client began to protest, Remmitt stepped away from his stall and slowly walked, then jogged, and finally *ran* up the Pipe Barrel towards a bag he kept under a loose floorboard in a rented room of the Lodger's Rest Hotel. Within a week he was knocking on the door of a monastery in the heart of Taslingham, begging for sanctuary.

# TEN

Meanside was a good half hour's walk from the southern bank of the river. Marius set off at a fast stride, slipping through the crowds without bothering to watch the unfolding life around him. He knew his way around Meanside like blood knows its way through veins, and he barely had time to plan his progress before he was climbing the road that led onto the Magister, the oldest, largest, and most famous of Borgho's "thousand bridges". The mad King Nandus had built his palace here, and parts of the walls had been preserved along the walkways at either side of the busy thoroughfare.

Marius had been little more than a teen when he'd stood side by side with soldiers, street mongers and wharfies, and defended the span from the forces of Tarem Bridge, a half mile down the water, the year the river froze over and the Battles of the Blade Gangs broke out. Ninety steps towards the far side the broken remnants of Nandus' Wizard Tower... Marius stopped, and leaned against the bridge wall, staring down into the muddy swirl of water flowing underneath.

"Hey there, Mischa," he said softly, "It's me."

The water flowed past, unheeding. Marius watched it, seeing patterns in the churn. He needed to get to the *Minerva*, but there was time enough for memories.

She had been crossing the bridge from the offices of the dock manager towards the villas of the richer merchants when the fighting had welled up along the river, and she was caught at the foot of the Wizard Tower. Marius was already there, crouched against the bricks, trying to squeeze himself into the cracks.

"What's happening?" She threw herself to the ground as a volley of crossbow bolts flew over the wall from below. "What's going on?"

Marius had said nothing, just peered up at her from between his fingers. He was terrified. Even so, looking up at her, hair falling loose from its bun and framing her long, oval face, her large green eyes wide with alarm, he felt something shift inside him. Without thinking, he peeled himself off the wall and buried his face in her chest, hands gripping her arms with terrified strength.

"Hey, hey." She lowered herself down next to him, her back to the wall. Carefully, she prised him away and altered her stance so that they sat, huddled together, while combatants tangled about them.

"What's your name, lad?"

"Marius," he stuttered. "Marius don Hellespont."

"Oh," she looked surprised. "Raife's son?"

"You know my father?"

She paused. "I'm aware of him. So what's all this, Marius? What's happening?"

Marius pointed further along the wall. "It's the other bridge, Miss."

"Call me Mischa." She smiled, brushed his hair back from his face. "I don't let just anybody call me that, you know."

Marius reddened at the sudden familiarity, but it did the trick. His fear forgotten for the moment, his words came out in an unbidden stream. "It's the Tarem Mob, Mischa. They're using the ice, skating across it. They can't get on the bridge at the ends, so this is their chance, see?"

"But why?" Two fighters stumbled against them. Mischa kicked out, and they wheeled away into the crowd.

"Tarem Bridge and Magister. It's like any other gang. They hate each other."

"But this? Crossbows? Machetes? People are getting hurt, Marius."

"I know." Marius crouched lower. "I never thought this would happen."

Mischa noticed the red rag tied around his upper arm. "Tarem or Magister?"

"Magister," he replied, fumbling at the knot. "I only wanted a bit of fun."

"Don't we all, lad? Don't we all?"

They hunkered down and watched the fighting. Mischa shook her head.

"We can't stay here, Marius. It's only a matter of time before we're noticed." She made to stand. Marius pulled desperately at her arm.

"Don't. They'll hurt you."

She stopped in mid-crouch, and placed her hand on his shoulder. "If we don't move we definitely *will* get hurt. We have to get to the end of the bridge. It's the only way to safety. Look." She reached into her sleeve, and withdrew a small square of lacework, tucking it into his hand. "For protection," she said, giving him a quick kiss on the cheek. Marius inhaled, smelling the sweet smell of her perfume, feeling the smoothness of her cheek and lips against his skin. He closed his eyes. Something inside him woke up and cried for life.

"Do you trust me?" she asked. Marius opened his eyes and looked straight into hers. He had never swum in a pool so beautiful. He gulped, and nodded.

"Then come on," she said, pulling him to his feet. Together they ran towards the end of the bridge, hand in hand, dodging combatants as they ran. Twice, someone loomed out of the chaos, and Mischa kicked out. Each time she hit their assailant in the groin, and he doubled over. She kicked them again in the face as she stepped past.

"Steel toes," she gasped as they ran on. "Every working girl should have them."

They almost made it. They were in sight of the lower gate house that marked the end of the bridge when the press of the crowd pushed them towards the edge of the walkway. Grappling hooks hung where Tarem combatants had climbed up from the ice below. Marius stumbled, and they fell, landing against the wall.

"Come on," Mischa said, pushing against the wall to regain her footing. Marius rose, and pulled at her hand. She gathered her legs beneath her, and at that moment, something heavy and dark reared over the wall and dug itself into her shoulder.

Mischa screamed as the two-pronged grappling hook bit deep. She reared up, scrabbling at the wound, letting go of Marius in the process. He leaped towards her, but in that instant, the combatants below them pulled on their rope. Mischa lurched backwards, hit the edge of the wall, and before either of them could do anything, was hauled up and over. Marius slammed into the brickwork, hardly feeling the impact against his nose and cheek. He pulled himself up on rubber legs, and hung over the top, oblivious to the fighting around him, and the snapping retorts of shot and crossbow bolts flying past.

It was thirty feet to the ice. Mischa had struck three of her assailants as she landed. They lay on the ice, broken bodies bent at angles they could not have achieved in life. She had landed on her back, facing upwards, her neck twisted impossibly far. Her eyes were open, and they stared up at him, large and green and beautiful, and quite, quite empty. The rest of her hair had shaken loose from its bun and lay like a halo around her head, stuck tight where the spreading pool of blood glued it to the surface.

"Mischa!" Marius screamed at her, battering his body against the unforgiving bricks. "Mischa!" She did not respond, did not move, simply lay like a discarded marionette. Marius leaned further, gauging the distance, preparing himself to jump down, looking for a safe landing, no idea in his head about what he would do other than that he had to be with her, to touch her one more time, and cradle her head into his chest the way she had done for him.

Then a body hit the wall next to him and tumbled past, and the spell was broken. Marius turned and ran, and fought his way out of the battle.

Somehow he found his way home, avoiding the pockets of fighting that had yet to be quelled by the guard. His father found him in the front courtyard: filthy; bleeding from half a dozen wounds; clutching a lady's kerchief to his eyes and sobbing a single name into it over and over. He had carried his weeping son into the house and ordered his wife to run a bath.

Later, after Marius had bathed and had his wounds dressed, his father persuaded him to remove the scrap of fabric from his clenched fist so that his hand could be wrapped in a fresh bandage. Then he sat before Marius in his study's deep leather armchair and requested an explanation. His mother came in from the parlour, and settled herself on the couch, her needlework lined up on the cushion next to her. She folded her hands into her lap, waiting. Marius stood before them, twisting the kerchief round and round his fingers, and slowly, hesitantly, told his story.

His mother had berated him for a thug and a visitor to whores. She had risen in a fury and snatched the kerchief from his grasp, throwing into the fire that roared in the hearth. His father had said nothing, merely shaking his head in disappointment. Marius had been banished from their presence, sent to his room to consider the behaviour, and the company, expected of the only son of an ambitious merchant. Marius had dried his tears and left them. It was not until he threw himself onto his bed that he gave his emotions full rein once more, promising unutterable things to the dark and to the memory of Mischa's fall.

His mother had come to him, later, after the evening meal, to apologise. Fear born of worry, and anger born of fear, and she had not meant the things she had said. He was her son, her good boy, and she knew he would have nothing to do with that type of person. She was just glad that he had escaped harm. She had kissed him, and held him in her arms, and left him to his sleep.

But harm *had* been done to him, and his mother was never again the hearth of his home.

The dead lay on the ice wherever they fell, and nobody made any move to collect the corpses and see them to a burial. After the dogs had eaten their fill, and the birds, and the lizards that crawled out of the sewers in search of easy meat, the spring had come. The ice had thawed, and the bodies slipped beneath the surface of the swollen river, to tumble out into the harbour and provide a bounty for any fish that had survived the winter. But Marius was already gone, apprenticed to a Tallian court scribe recruiting entertainments for the Emir's summer palace. As soon as it was safe to escape the scribe's clumsy attempts at seduction he had done so. Later, upon his first return to the city, he had asked around, and found out the truth about Mischa.

She'd been in her late thirties, at least as old as his mother, as far as anyone could tell. In the capital they'd have called her a courtesan, and confined her to the richest end of town so that she'd never have to sully her perfect white feet with the dirt of the common quarters. In Borgho she was known by a more prosaic title, and she worked where the most money resided, among the ambitious merchants and those who fancied themselves so important that a drab late thirtyish wife was no proper accompaniment when being seen among other ambitious merchants. Marius understood, then, exactly why his father's name had been so familiar. He did not think badly of her for it. People made worse compromises every day. He never discussed it with his father. No matter how often he had returned to Borgho in the intervening years, he had crossed the river by other bridges.

Marius would have cursed his subconscious for bringing him back to the spot, but in truth, it fit his mood perfectly. The tossing water mirrored his thoughts, and he stared at it as if it could provide some sort of answer. But the water was just water, and his thoughts remained turbulent, and no beautiful green eyes stared back for him to dive into, and in the end, all he could do was turn his back on the water, and take the ninety-first step across the bridge.

The wharfs on the north bank were a mirror to those on the south, although the overall impression was of, somehow, a better class of dockyard. It was cleaner, more orderly. The ships seemed in better condition, and the wharfies and navvies who bustled about wore the livery of whatever stock supply company they represented, rather than the dusty, careworn leathers favoured by their brothers over the bridge. Clear lines of progress could be seen through the crowds, as each individual ship was served by its own orderly queue of human worker ants.

Marius threaded his way through, an object of complete indifference to those around him. On the south bank he guarded his hidden money pouches with a combination of secret pockets, attitude, and careful scrutiny of his surrounds. Here he felt at ease enough to stride through the mass of bodies with his concentration solely devoted to identifying the ships he passed. It wasn't difficult – even from a distance, the *Minerva* stood out against the backdrop of hulls and masts, a hulking monster looming over its surroundings.

Marius had been no more than a child when Mad King Nandus had received possession of his flagship, the *Nancy Tulip*. The north side docks had been created to cope with the construction, and they maintained the gloss that comes with living under a monarch's auspices, even an insane one who built his castle on an ancient, crumbling bridge, and commissioned a five hundred-ton clinker-built warship for the sole purpose of waging war on the Gods of the ocean.

Marius remembered sitting on his father's shoulders at wharf-side, as the ship slowly made its way from its berth a mile away on the opposite shore to the Magister Bridge, where it pulled alongside the single door and balcony built onto the palace's outer side. As soon as it had pulled up, Nandus appeared and gave a great speech about liberty, equality, and the need for giant clam slaves, then stepped directly from the balcony to the poop deck of the great ship, thirty feet above the water. The *Nancy Tulip* and its four hundred-strong crew of sailors, soldiers, and gunners, as well as Littleboots, the horse he had appointed to the Borghan Senate – which had surprised most citizens, who weren't aware Borgho had a senate – wobbled its way down the river and out onto the open sea, where the horizon swallowed it for all time.

The *Nancy Tulip* had been a massive ship. No clinker-built vessel had been commissioned that even approached its measurements. Marius had heard estimates of one hundred and forty feet in length, and its height was part of folklore. It had been so large that available technology had been unable to complete the task. New ways of manufacture had been invented: the nails were eight times as large as previously necessary, necessitating a whole new way of manufacture; hull planks were longer, wider, heavier, needing new methods of harvesting and cutting; the sails alone weighed as much as some small ships, and hoisting them by traditional methods would have broken any normal winch. Marius remembered gazing up at the side of the ship as it had passed by on its way downriver, seeing a nail head the size of his father's fist go by a few feet from his face, feeling a sudden chill as the sheer bulk of the ship blocked out the sun and a wall of shade engulfed the wharf. In all his years of travel he had never felt so overwhelmed by a structure as that day, when the *Nancy Tulip* seemed like the biggest object in the entire world, and its movement made him sick with vertigo.

The *Minerva* was bigger.

Ship-building technology had advanced in the last thirty years. Clinker ships were a thing of the past – the *Nancy Tulip*, ironically, had seen to that. Ships could not be built big enough or stable enough for modern needs using the old methods. Cog-built ships like the *Minerva* were the order of the day – smooth-hulled, wider at the keel, safer and more stable in heavy seas and high winds. Ships were bigger, as a rule. Rarely as big as the *Nancy Tulip*, but on average, the cog-built ship was the way forward.

Even by the standards of the new technology, the *Minerva* was huge. Marius stood to one side as a stream of navvies climbed the steep gangway. A dozen barrels rolled their way upwards to disappear behind the gunwales, as did a constant stream of wrapped bales. Chickens in wicker cages were carried past. A navvie staggered under the weight of a dozen crossbows. As quickly as the labourers entered the ship they returned, jogging down to disappear inside a massive warehouse twenty yards further down the wharf.

Marius stepped back into the shade of the building and admired the industry with which the navvies climbed the sheer face of the walkway. The deck of the *Minerva* towered at least forty feet above the wharf, and the hull was a good one hundred and sixty five feet from prow to stern, if Marius was any judge of size. Where the *Nancy Tulip*, for all its master's lunacy, had been a fully-functioning warship, weighed down with cannon and armouries, the *Minerva* was built for trade. Marius swept his gaze across the vast expanse of wood, estimating how much of the ship's innards might be given over to empty holds. He whistled. With the kind of load the *Minerva* was capable of carrying, it was likely to be headed out on a long, long voyage. Exactly what Marius was seeking. He stepped out of the shade and made his way to the foot of the gangway.

"Hold your horses, pal." A massive, anvil-jawed man in shirtsleeves sat on a barrel at the walkway's base, ticking items off a sheaf of paper as they passed. Without looking up from his task he tilted his head in dismissal. "Unless you're carrying supplies you're in my way, so piss off."

Marius stared past him towards the deck of the ship. "I'm to speak to the captain."

"Captain's already seen the dock master. Papers are all in order. Now you're in my way *and* you're getting up my nose." The sailor stood, laying his sheaf on the barrel. The passing navvies immediately stopped, and laid down their burdens. "I hope you know how to fly, laddie."

"My name's Helles," Marius said, as the sailor raised fists the size of a small child's head. "My... friend saw him last night, regarding passage."

"The lady?" The sailor lowered his hands, looked Marius up and down in something approaching surprise. "Red-haired lass, built like a long night in the tropics?"

"Her name's Keth." Marius said, feeling a disconcerting stab of jealousy.

"Bloody hell, son." The big man stepped back, and nodded towards the top. "If you can keep her to yourself you're more energetic than you look." Marius stepped on to the gangway, and the sailor returned to his seat. "Captain's in his cabin at the rear castle. Tell him Spone passed you through." He glanced up at the resting workers, dismissing Marius from his attention. "Right, you horrible lot of lazy old whores, sleep time's over. Shift your arses!"

Marius scurried up the gangway ahead of the belaboured navvies. He turned sternward at the top, away from the stream of labourers, and made his way past teams of sailors as they made their way to various holds arrayed across the deck. Everywhere was industry, energy, and organised panic as the crew made the ship seaworthy. A set of steps led upwards to a poop deck above his head, dominated by an enormous wheel that looked over all the terrestrial endeavours below it like a god's unblinking eye. Marius stared up at it for a moment, wondering at the size and strength of the man who could turn that massive wooden circle.

The space between decks was closed off by a pair of doors. Two stained glass windows faced out onto the deck – Marius would need to pass multi-coloured impressions of the Old Gods Oceanus and Aequoris in order to speak to the captain. He drew no comfort from the knowledge that the man responsible for his safe escape was so superstitious. He tugged the brim of his hood further down over his face and knocked upon Oceanus' blood-red nose.

"Enter." The voice from within was imperious, clipped. Whoever was knocking was interrupting something far more important than their errand warranted, that much was made clear. Marius pushed open the door and stepped through.

A trading ship is a working ship. All available space is devoted solely to the making of money. The only room not devoted to that noble purpose is used to house the absolute minimum number of sailors it takes to make the journey possible. There is no room for frippery, for useless substance, for baggage or personal items not utterly necessary to the trader's only mission – to make as much money in as quick a time as possible. Everything is streamlined, cut back, minimalist, functional. This was not the case within the walls of the captain's cabin.

The moment Marius stepped through the door, his feet left bare wood. The cabin was floored with mosaic tiles, patterned so that he stood upon the lower paw of a puissant lion, whose roaring head poked out from under the oak four-poster bed underneath the starboard window. Heavy velvet drapes were parted to allow sunlight in, where they fell directly across the captain's desk, a slab of black wood so large the cabin must have been built around it, rather than try and fit the thing through the door.

The captain himself was sitting in a high backed chair that looked like a replica of the throne of Lenthus XIV, the so called Moon-King of Ureen. Marius hoped it was a replica – its cost would be merely breath-taking, instead of impossible to comprehend. Massive gold-framed paintings adorned the walls. Marius counted at least two Fermenis, and one Cabdur that, if genuine, was probably worth as much as the rest of the boat added up. Tables abounded, and shelves, piled high with ornaments collected from around the five oceans.

Marius frowned. How could any of this survive even the most moderate sea, never mind the massive swells such as those he had experienced crossing the lower equator? Either everything was glued down with the strongest adhesive known to man, or this captain must have a boy solely employed to pack and unpack the room depending on sailing conditions.

Marius caught movement in the shadows of the far side of the room. As if in answer to his thoughts a young lad emerged, no more than eight or nine years old, polishing a small picture frame and replacing it on a low shelf by the door to the captain's wash room. He looked up at Marius and nodded a greeting. Marius returned it, and took a small step to the side, positioning himself so he stood in front of a small table that bowed under a field of velvet-mounted brooches and pins. He stood with his hands behind his back, and willed his torso to stillness. The captain looked up from a spread of parchment, and raised his eyebrows.

"And you are?"

"Marius Helles." Marius gave the captain a good looking over. He was tall, thin, with a nose like a flamingo's beak and a chin to match. His hair was tied back in the style favoured by certain Scorban nobles who had the sense to know exactly how long their family was, and wished for it to continue. His uniform, while certainly conforming to the standards of the Scorban Trading Guild in cut and style, looked to have been hand-sewn by merchants who wished to keep all their fingers, and knew exactly which material would be most costly for the job. Almost every trader Marius had ever met dressed for comfort first, warmth and dryness second, and protocol last. This man looked as if none of these attributes rated quite as highly as dancing. He drew up a pince-nez on a chain, and stared down at Marius from a mental distance of many miles.

"And just what do you think you're doing on my ship, Mister Helles?"

"Spone sent me up."

"And?"

"I'm your passenger. My companion left a deposit to secure a cabin."

"Ah. Yes." The captain leaned back in his chair and folded long hands over his stomach. "Your strump... companion."

"Is there a problem?"

The captain stared at Marius for several seconds, taking in the hood pulled over his face, the guarded stance, the motley combination of mismatched clothing. He smiled, a tight little thing worn by anyone who negotiates from a position of complete strength, and who has made their final assumption long before the voices have run out.

"A small one," he said. "The amount she left with us. It was, shall we say–"

"A deposit."

"Yes. Quite so. Passage itself will take rather more remuneration, I'm afraid. A passenger takes up considerable space, particularly one who will contribute nothing to our trading mission."

"How much?" Marius had been expecting this sort of tactic. After all, when everyone can see the barrel, it's only the one stretched across it who has to worry about its size.

"Let me see..." The captain counted off on his fingers, silently staring at the ceiling. "Another eighty riner should cover our expenses. That is," he added as Marius became even stiller, "unless there's a problem."

"No." Marius sucked his teeth. He needed this man. "Not a problem. Eighty riner, food and board in a private cabin from here to your destination. You are travelling to the Faraway Isles?"

"Port Moubard, actually. Will that suffice?" The amusement in the captain's voice could have strangled a parrot. Marius resisted the temptation to think of the captain as a parrot.

"I'm not fussy."

"Evidently not." The captain indicated the desk. "Payment in advance, naturally."

"When do you sail?"

"I beg your pardon?"

"When do you sail?"

The captain stared at Marius. Marius stared back. Faced with the darkness under his unmoving hood, the captain blinked and made busy with his parchment.

"First tide tomorrow morning. I'll be battening up three hours before first light."

"You'll have your money by dusk."

"Good." The captain waved towards the door – Marius was dismissed. "Be here by then, with my money, and I'll have a space cleared for you among the men."

"I said a private cabin."

"That's not possible, I'm afraid. We simply do not have the room to–"

"Ninety five riner, for a room above decks."

"Fine, fine." The captain returned to his parchment. "Let it not be said that Ethamanel Bomthe was not an understanding man."

"Bomthe?"

The captain looked up.

"You're aware of me?"

"Not a bit." Marius swung about and pushed through the doors, leaving the captain blinking behind him.

• • • •

Ninety-five riner in just over fifteen hours. One thing
was certain – Marius wasn't going to make that kind
of money from honest work. Neither was he going to
be able to pick enough purses. That left few options.
Marius strolled down the gangway, deep in thought,
dodging the stream of navvies still loading the *Minerva*
with wares. At the bottom, the man called Spone gave
him a distracted wave.

"All right for the off, then?"

Marius waved back. "Just getting my stuff."

"Right you are. See you for embarkation. Don't get
in any trouble."

Trouble, Marius thought as he headed off down the
docks. That's just what I intend to get into.

# ELEVEN

North of the river, Borgho City takes on a different aspect. Whereas the south quadrants are closed in, warrens of alleyways and tenements, and progress is often marked as much by who decides to block off which alley mouth with their stall as by a traveller's memory of the streets, the northern quadrants are more spacious. The streets are wider, the guards who patrol them – and guards actually do patrol them, which is another distinct difference – are cleaner, and once you crest the first line of foothills and move onto the slopes of Varius' Folly, the hill that dominates this end of town, the houses begin to resemble small palaces rather than apartments, separated from each other by orchards and fences of ornate metalwork.

There is good reason for this. Back when Borgho City was the centre of its own little fiefdom – before King Nandus disappeared on his disastrous campaign against the ocean, and the Prince of the House of Scorby had swept down at the front of ten thousand men and announced that Borgho was now part of the new *Kingdom* of Scorby, much to the citizens' indifference – the hillside had been occupied by whatever nobles the King had anointed each week. Even Littleboots had lived there, towards the top, in gold-plated stables that stretched for half an acre, with his own liveried servants and a field of finest grass, imported from Feen. The gold-plating had lasted less than twenty-four hours after the servants realised their equine master wasn't coming back. But the stables still stood, as well as the warren of escape tunnels the King had built underneath, for Littleboots to use in the case of revolution. The whole thing had been claimed by the horse's neighbour, a duke of some renown who swapped killing foreigners for importing their artwork, and the stables now stood as a magnificent folly at the bottom of his extended gardens. Whether the Duke knew of the tunnels beneath the stables was a matter of conjecture. His son did, and addicted to gambling as he was, it provided the perfect locale for a gaming hall of no little grandeur and quite a lot of bankruptcies.

All Marius needed was a stake, and a table to join.

The stake was no problem. Marius had had very little opportunity to be thankful for the deadness of his flesh, but the gewgaws he had lifted from Captain Bomthe's side table made no impression on his pain receptors, even as the motion of walking caused them to dig into his back and buttocks. With a definite destination in mind, and a time frame to match, he wasted little time in extricating himself from the docks and striding through the peacock-coloured frontages of the fashion houses and lending men towards the gentle rise that marked the end of the commercial quarters and the beginning of their residential area.

No aspiring merchants here – the owners of these double and triple storied keeps, surrounded by as many square feet of lawn as could be placed between their bedrooms and the press of humanity beyond the stone walls and elaborate metal gates, were the unofficial rulers of Borgho City. The King of Scorby may be sovereign of every stone in the ground and man or woman who walked across them, but just try ruling the citizenry without first feeding them, or clothing them, or at the very least, letting them watch pretty women take their clothes off while getting smashed on a Saturday night. The higher up the slope, the larger the lawn, and the more powerful the resident. At the top, well, Marius had been close, and the men and women who lived there were as far removed from the ordinary citizens of the city as Marius was from his birthright, and with as little concern for it. Right now, however, as he did his best to saunter as unobtrusively as possible along the well-lit promenades, and avoid the attentions of the fit and alert guardsmen who strolled along in pairs, he had a residence of only middling intimidatory presence on his mind.

The fifth Duke of Milness had been, in his early youth, a powerful figure amongst the nobility of Borgho City. He was handsome, dashing, an astute commander in the tiny conflicts the Borghans had called wars in order to justify the cost of minting medals, and an even cleverer general of his family's money on the trading floors. A popular figure amongst the matriarchs of the nobility, they saw in him a fine match for their daughters and weren't above sampling the merchandise just to make sure. But a fall from his horse while playing a spirited round of whack-the-prisoner on his thirtieth birthday had changed all that. The duke had become withdrawn, reclusive, even – it was whispered amongst other nobles as they passed each other in the corridor on the way to swapping bedrooms – rather smelly. He withdrew to his estate halfway up the hillside, and it was presumed that only the endless procession of tradesmen who passed through the gates in the daylight hours could vouch for his wellbeing.

Even so, after he was found dead on the floor of his bedroom one morning by a plumber who had dared approach his living quarters in pursuit of an overdue payment, his funeral procession was attended by hundreds of well-wishers who remembered his early days, and wanted a final glimpse of a man of such notable lunacy, and *this* in a city with Nandus for a king. Having no children of his own, the estate passed into the hands of a distant nephew, and it was only when the sixth Duke of Milness took possession of his new house did it become known what the old duke had been doing on his own all those years.

In short, water closets. One for every room of the house, one behind every oak in the gardens, one on either side of every bed in all seventeen of the bedrooms. One inside each bath. All of them linked. None of them functional. The sixth duke opened every door and window in the place, and moved into an apartment in the centre of the city for over a year.

When at last he could enter the building without his eyes watering, he brought several labourers with sledgehammers and wrenches, who proceeded to demolish every toilette in the place. Which is when they discovered the tunnels that the pipes all linked to, and following them, found themselves in the stables of that most noble and exalted member of the senate, Littleboots.

Unkind gossips speculated that perhaps the fifth Duke of Milness hadn't been so celibate after all. Downright vicious gossips wondered whether his isolation had been the result of being knocked back by the horse in question. The young duke simply filled in the pipes, sold the estate to an olive oil trader, and moved back to Scorby. Had he realised how quickly the trader would re-open the tunnels, and how often he would use them to enter the never-ending gambling saloon that had grown up under Littleboots' stables, he would have asked a higher price.

Things had evolved little since Marius had last visited the area. Merchants, as a rule, abhor change, unless they can control its value, and their domestic surroundings reflect this. The frontages that Marius passed looked as they had since he was a child – the trees were taller, and the vines that clambered along walls and dripped out onto the road were more established, longer in their reach. But they were the same trees, the same creepers.

The gate he pushed through and the lawns he walked past were those originally put in by the fifth Duke of Milness, and the door he knocked on had a history only slightly shorter than that of his family. It swung open on the eleventh knock. A swarthy, middle-aged man emerged, dressed in nothing more than an expensive silk robe which hung loose, exposing everything to view, at least, those parts not covered by the white hand of the woman hanging from his shoulder. He stared at Marius with ill-concealed impatience.

"Well?" he demanded. Marius coughed, and stared over the other man's shoulder, deliberately ignoring the long, slow movements of the woman's hand.

"I've come for the game."

"Wrong house, friend."

"Marius Helles told me to ask for Vimineth Sangk." He reached into his jerkin and removed the trinkets he had accumulated on the ship. "The entrance fee is fifteen per cent of the stake, he said."

Sangk smiled, and held the door open. "Helles? Why didn't you say?" He relieved Marius of his burden and eyed them speculatively. "Three riner."

The gold frame alone was worth that much, but Marius said nothing. He'd been gifted something greater. Sangk didn't recognise him, and that gave him an advantage. When it comes to gambling of any kind, you take whatever assistance you can find.

"Where is it?" he asked, stepping inside and turning towards the double doors at his right.

"Not that way," his host replied. He removed his lady's hand and drew his robe closed. "Go take a bath." She slid away from him and shimmied down the hallway. Marius watched her go. When he looked back, Sangk was grinning at him like an Endtown pimp. "She moves like that all the time, friend. All the time." He grinned wider, revealing a mouth full of gold teeth. "Let's go."

He turned and made his way towards the rear of the house. Marius followed in his wake, doing his best to look like a gormless newcomer, even tripping over the dip in the floor he had made with a brass bust after a particularly drunken misadventure. He could have found his way in the dark, with his eyes closed and his legs tied together. But Sangk's ignorance was his greatest weapon, and he was happy to trail along behind him.

They reached the kitchen that ran the length of the house's rear. Sangk beckoned him over to a ceiling-high larder door, and swung it open with a flourish.

"It's a toilet."

"Appearances deceive, friend." Sangk reached in and pulled a hidden lever. The rear wall swung open, revealing a tunnel.

"They certainly do," Marius agreed, and followed him into the dark.

# TWELVE

The central ballroom of the duke's underground tunnel system would be counted one of the eleven wonders of the world, were anybody counting such things. They weren't, and as a consequence only gamblers, addicts and the desperate were aware of the place. Hewn from solid rock, it lay over forty feet from end to end, with a vaulted ceiling twenty feet high. Bas reliefs of great moments of Milness family history had been carved into its smooth walls, and if there were perhaps a few dozen extra enemies being smote, or the mountain lion being bested bare-handed was several touches larger than the mouldering skin in the upper library, who could argue with someone capable of commissioning such a place?

Perhaps the most remarkable aspect of the giant cavern was its colour – every surface was a bright retina-damaging pink. Tapers placed at head height filled the roof with a dingy black smoke which did little to dispel the feeling that the visitor had somehow managed to burrow his way through to the centre of a giant, petrified marshmallow. At the entrance, a fat man in greasy coveralls lounged on a chaise longue with a massive tray of fried entrails perched on his stomach. At Sangk and Marius' approach, he levered himself into an upright position and nodded at Sangk.

"Three riner," Sangk said, handing over Marius' stake. The fat man examined them without interest, then turned and rummaged in a large wooden trunk behind his seat.

"Split into tenpennies," Marius added. The fat man paused, then resumed rummaging. He straightened, and held out a purse. Marius took it, and emptied the contents into his palm, counting out the thirty coins within.

"You miscounted," he said, removing a coin and flipping it to the fat man, who caught it without comment and pocketed it. Marius might not need a friend should anything become unpleasant. But he might. And if he did, that tenpenny piece might become money well spent. His business done, the banker slid back into his former position and recovered his tray. Marius returned the remaining twenty-nine coins to the purse. He and Sangk stepped into the centre of the hall.

A dozen tables were set up equidistant from each other, close enough that a player could choose to move tables without too much concern, but far enough apart that each game could be played out in relative isolation. Professional teams had infiltrated the hall in the past, and in the wake of some disastrous losses, Sangk had refined his arrangements. It would be very hard indeed for a player at one table to signal another without being seen by the three heavies who circled constantly, following each game. One nodded to Sangk as he passed – all was well. The tables were sparsely occupied at this time of day – only three had a full complement of six players, whilst two were completely empty. Marius nodded towards a table with three empty seats.

"What's the game?"

"Kingdom." Sangk smiled. "What else would it be?"

Marius paused, as if deciding whether or not to play. After a minute, he raised his purse and shook it. "Care to join me?"

"Oh, I'm afraid the house cannot play at its own table, friend. That wouldn't be ethical."

Marius dipped into the bag and withdrew a riner's worth of coins. "My treat."

"Well, in that case." Sangk swept up the coins and led the way over. "My pleasure."

They dropped into chairs on opposite sides of the table, just as the previous hand was being concluded. Sangk nodded to the dealer, and a new hand was dealt.

Though certain passages of play and various combinations have gone in and out of style over the centuries – the game underwent somewhat of a revolution during the Reign of the Triplet Kings, for example – the basic rules of play have remained unchanged since long before Marius' day. Like any addiction, the rules seem simple on the surface, and it is only with repeated exposure that the full measure of their complexity becomes apparent.

Forty-five cards are arranged in eleven suits, from four king cards at the highest value to two dozen peasants at the lowest. A single wastrel acts as a most unpleasant type of joker, always feared and always unwelcome. Cards are dealt face down to each player until the full pack is distributed. Each player draws the top card from their pile, and places a bet based on the value of that card. Once the round had been completed, they take the next card and make another bet, and so on, until they hold the full pile in their hand. The aim of the game is to build the most powerful hand, politically – the hand that most resembles the current political environment.

So, in Scorby, a hand containing one king, one queen, two princes, no princesses, two bishops and more soldiers than peasants would be a winning hand, whereas a hand full of princesses and peasants, with the wastrel, will result in a massive haemorrhage of money. Likewise, when played in Tal, a king with two queens, all four mistresses, and all four soldiers will prove unbeatable. The winning hand during the Asceticism, had gambling been greeted with anything other than the cleansing fire of a very large stake and bonfire, would have consisted solely of peasants.

The trick is to avoid multiples – two kings cannot both rule Scorby, so as soon as a player draws a second king he must discard both, and the bets he has already made are wasted – and always avoid the wastrel, for once he is part of a player's hand he cannot be removed, and that player cannot win the hand.

Like any great card game, the cards themselves are almost irrelevant. A good player can read his opposition's position by following his betting patterns and the number of cards he discards, and by knowing the lie of the political landscape. It is a game built on deception, wherein bluffs, brinksmanship, and outright lies have the greatest value.

Society ladies love it.

It is also the game of choice amongst the thousands of gambling dens that litter the length and breadth of the continent, providing both a common language and a quick political summation for the numberless travellers who move from town to town in an endless procession of shifting loyalties and commercial opportunity. It has survived dynasties, revolutions, repressions, banishment, cult worship, and war. Official histories will never say so, because official histories are always written for the sole purpose of kissing up to the monarch who commissioned them, but Kingdom has done more to tie together the lands of the Four Continents than any motivating force outside of the pursuit of money, and for most of the last thousand years it's been rather hard to separate one from the other.

Marius' table held five players, which meant that all the cards would be distributed, and none would have to be discarded. Marius was pleased by that – it made keeping track of hands a lot easier, and much of the success of a good card player lies in being able to estimate what an opposing player holds, if not before they draw their cards, then as soon as possible after. Marius laid his pile of nineteen coins on the table, drew his first card, and flicked a single coin into the centre.

"Not confident, eh?" Sangk laughed, checked his card, and threw down three coins. "Or just a cautious man?"

Marius kept his head bowed over his card. "I'll warm to the task."

Sangk was a braggart, and flashy. But he was a good card player, using a combination of bluff and intimidation to overwhelm opponents who lacked his capacity to stare straight at ruin without flinching. On a level table, he was at least as good as Marius. When the number of hands grew long enough to even out any margin of luck, he was probably better. Marius had one advantage in his anonymity, but it was going to be a victory won by inches. He needed to stay small, and gain control slowly.

The hand quickly progressed round the other three players. None were talkers, and all had the sullen silence that accompanies the hard-nosed gambler. Win or lose, they would be back tomorrow, and every day after, if not to these tables then to any of the other hidden games throughout the city. Risk is a way of life for such men, if not of living. They had no need of chat, or bravado. They were too hungry. Marius drew his second card, stared at it for a moment, then threw down another coin.

"Better settle in, my friends," Sangk announced to their fellow players. "Our new friend looks ready to make it a long night. He must be jealous of his wealth." He laughed, and threw down two coins before he overturned his cards.

Marius repressed a smile. It was too early to be drawn into Sangk's game of bluff and counterbluff. It was impossible to tell what the others were holding until the cards were revealed. Only once they were face up could he watch the shuffle, try to pick out the small marks and imperfections that marked a well-used deck. For the moment, he had a prince and a peasant. A weak hand, but it could become something stronger if the deal fell his way. He remained silent, and let the hand play out.

Inevitably, he lost the first hand, drawing little better than peasants and soldiers. He sacrificed the second, folding a pair of princesses in order to monitor the betting patterns of his opponents unhindered by the desire to protect his own stake. The third hand he won, just enough to make back his money and a touch more, and in such a way that Sangk's jovial accusation of luck could be accepted with an acknowledging tilt of the head. Sangk won the next, drawing enough out of the other players to put himself well ahead of Marius' initial gift. One of the others retired, leaving only four around the table. From now until they were joined by a fifth player, one card would be discarded face down after each deal, making the game that much harder. But Marius had gained valuable information during the previous hands. He knew the wastrel and two of the kings, and more importantly, he knew what signs the other players could not avoid making when they bluffed. It was these "tells" that formed the most important part of any game.

Now, he decided, he was ready to start playing.

Four of the next five hands went his way. His stake slowly built until it rivalled Sangk's. Marius concentrated on slow playing – undervaluing each hand until he was sure he held the strongest combination, then suddenly plunging a large bet into the pot at the point where his opponents had already thrown so much wealth in that they were committed to matching him. Sangk's comments grew increasingly acerbic, and started to flow earlier and earlier in each hand.

Marius suppressed another smile. Sangk was a damn good player but was renowned for his short fuse. A great player against the mediocre, and mediocre against the greats, and he was beginning to become unsettled. Marius loosened his play up a little, throwing bluffs and picking up cheap pots. His image was so established now that the other players were afraid to match his bets in case they were throwing good money after bad. One of the nameless players was low on coins, and Marius held back for a couple of hands, letting him pick up a couple of small pots to re-establish his confidence. Sangk regained his good cheer almost immediately.

"The luck is flowing in a different direction now, my friend," he said. "Enkie looks ready to reclaim all the chips you stole from him earlier."

"Indeed he does," Marius replied, with a nod of respect towards the silent Enkie. Then he slow-played an unbeatable combination – no king, queen, two princesses, bishop, three soldiers, the rest peasants, a perfect representation of the current House of Scorby – drew Sangk into throwing his entire stack into the pot, and sent him from the table, broke. Sangk exploded.

"Gods damn!" he lurched up out of his chair, stormed around the room grabbing at his hair. "Outplayed by a northern Scorban idiot!" He appealed to his bouncer, standing silent and immobile at the foot of the stairs. "Slow playing the nuts. Gods damn. Beaten by a guy who can't even *spell* Kingdom!" He drew out a bag from his shirt and spilled its contents onto the table. "I'm buying back in."

"Is that allowed?" Marius asked, trying to keep the laughter from his voice. This was exactly what he had wanted. There wasn't enough money on the table to match Bomthe's price. He needed Sangk to dip into his pockets, to make a rash gesture out of frustration, and the Tallian had complied.

"My house." Sangk thumped the table as he sat back down. "My discretion."

"Of course." Marius nodded his acquiescence. "May we have a count, please?"

Grimacing, Sangk counted out his new stack. Forty riner. Not enough to match Bomthe's price, Marius thought, but it would go a long way towards it. Once he'd taken it all away from Sangk, and beaten the other two players he'd still be thirty riner short. Not to worry. There were other tables, and even if Sangk took umbrage and sent him on his way, there was one more game down the Bellish Quarter he could try. Harder to get into, but a hundred-plus riner was a good way to get through the door. The dealer dealt the next hand, and Marius bent back to his task.

Enkie was the first to go. Marius caught him in a bluff, enticed him all-in, and beat him with a miserable Bishop-high combination that beat his wastrel-burdened hand. He made a point of shaking the man's hand as he stood. He'd played well, and Marius might come across him again in some den of the future, in which case, he'd want the man to remember his courtesy, not the way Marius had controlled his game and busted him. Only three players remained, and Marius hoped another might be called across to make up the numbers, bringing his stack with him. He was disappointed. Sangk, bent low over his coins, merely motioned the dealer to burn two cards from each deal and keep going. Marius scowled. Three-handed Kingdom was substantially more difficult than four-handed, and luck played a much more central role. Sangk was scared, he realised, and limiting the table numbers went a long way towards tilting the odds in his favour.

Sure enough, the next two hands went Sangk's way, until he and Marius had roughly equal stacks. Marius risked a peek at the fat Tallian, and saw him sitting back in his chair, arms folded. A smug smile spread across the lower half of his face. Marius responded by winning the next two, losing the following big pot to Sangk, and then knocking out their silent short-stacked companion. Then there was just he and Sangk. His host smiled.

"Equal or thereabouts," he noted, nodding down at Marius' pile. "I feel I have done well from your gift, my friend. You have my thanks. But," he stretched back, yawned. "It has been a long night, and I am tired. I shall take my leave."

"A shame," Marius said, thinking quickly. "I've enjoyed our game. It feels like we are just starting. Still," he shrugged, a gesture of dismissal. "If you are unable to continue…"

"Well now, well now," Sangk had been gathering his winnings. Now he stopped. "It is not a matter of being incapable."

"I am sure," Marius answered, riffling his coins so they made a musical tinkling. "But perhaps it is for the best."

"Why do you say that?"

"Oh," Marius shrugged, continuing to play with his pile of gold. "It is late, as you say, and you have played well. Perhaps you are right. Best to cut out when you are ahead."

Sangk was staring at Marius' coins. Marius made to scoop them up. "I shall test somebody else's stamina."

Sangk laughed, and slapped the table. "Okay," he said, motioning Marius to stop. "You've made your point." He gestured to the dealer. Two-handed Kingdom was amongst the most difficult of card games. From now on, the majority of the deck would be discarded before they even started. No hand could be trusted. That, after all, was the point of the game. Now it was a test of the combatants' ability to read their opponent, follow the cards, and display the biggest set of balls. "Let's play."

"Yes," Marius nodded, grinning into his coins. "Let's."

Marius started slowly. Playing two-handed was a whole new card game: many more variables than five-handed, many more burnt cards, much more left to chance. It took a lot of patience, or a willingness to be reckless to the point of suicide, to make significant gains against a single opponent. He pecked away at his bets: a coin here; two there; slowly building up small pots and backing away if he was unsure of a win.

Sangk splashed coins about like a reformed miser, making massive over-bets, chipping away at Marius' stack until he held a lead of almost two to one. Marius didn't mind. He was watching the cards, stringing together sequences, letting Sangk's outrageous play disguise Marius' manoeuvring. The dealer was dealing low-heavy hands: a lot of peasants and soldiers were surviving the burns. After a dozen hands, Marius had the read of the deck, and made his move.

The next hand, Marius opened with a bishop. A weak card, but a good start, one he could build on in a number of ways. Marius threw three coins into the pot. Sangk raised an eyebrow and matched his bet without glancing at his first card. Two peasants followed, and Marius bet the minimum each time. Sangk matched him, then, when Marius drew a queen on his fourth card and bet twelve coins, raised him another dozen. Marius stared at the Tallian under the edge of his hood. Sangk sat back and smiled.

Marius switched his gaze to the fat man's stack, and his own, then at the backs of the cards in Sangk's grip. The third card along had a tiny, imperceptible split at the upper right corner. Marius kept his expression still. He'd picked out that mark two opponents ago. The wastrel. Nothing Sangk did would matter. With the wastrel in his hand he could not possibly win. Every card, every combination was invalidated. Marius rubbed his jaw as if confused.

"You have a big hand?" he asked, as if trying to elicit some response that might give him a clue.

"Oh, a big one," Sangk replied, leaning back and rechecking his cards, as if reassuring himself of his decks value.

"Why such a big bet?" Marius mused, almost to himself. "Four cards in. What have you got? King queen? Two princesses?" He riffled a small pillar of coins. "So many cards left."

"Confused?"

"Ahhhh." Marius rubbed his face. I should get an award for this, he thought. The Queen of Muses herself should place a laurel around my ears. "Why so big? You could still lose so many cards."

Sangk said nothing, simply crossed his hands and waited. Marius shook his head.

"Okay," he said, voice full of uncertainty. "I call."

Four more cards passed, each bet growing in size, until Marius had Sangk right where he wanted the fat man to think he had Marius – pot committed, with so many coins in the pot that when the second to last card was drawn he had no option but to throw the rest into the centre for fear of folding the hand and being crippled. Sure enough, as soon as he pulled the card from his deck, Sangk reached down and pushed his stack over, spilling his coins across the table.

"Everything," Sangk said. "All of it."

Marius laid his cards face down, placed his hands on top of it to signify that he was merely considering, not folding. He made a great show of examining the fallen money and comparing it against his own. To call Sangk's bet would cost him everything. Exactly what he wanted. Once he won this hand he would have his opponent out-coined by a factor of more than eleven to one. After that, it was only a matter of time – a very short time – before he had them all.

"Call," he said, and turned over his cards. "Two princesses." He stood up, and reached over for the coins.

Sangk smiled, and slowly fanned his hand on to the table.

"One queen, one bishop," he said, and laughed. "No wastrel."

"But… how…?"

"Did you mean this?" Sangk casually flipped over the peasant card next to the bishop, revealing the tiny split at the top corner.

"What…?"

"Please," Sangk sat back and held his arms wide open, appealing to the room around them. "Do you take me for a fool? Do you think I don't know the make-up of my own deck? Each little mark, each little signifier?" He clapped his hands together, and leaned forward, picking up a card at random and holding it in front of Marius. "Do you think I didn't learn to do this at my father's elbow when I was a child?" he asked, stroking the card with his thumb, opening a split almost identical to the one on the bishop. Marius stared at the fresh mark as the fat man rubbed it against the face of a second card, muddying the edges until they were almost indistinguishable from either the wastrel or the peasant.

"No."

"Oh, yes, I'm afraid so."

"No." Marius shook his head. "You can't do that."

"In my own house? I think I can." Sangk leaned over and began scooping coins towards himself. "I win, don Hellespont. Whatever your little game was, you're busted. It's time for you to get out."

"How the hell…?

"What?" he asked, laughing. "Did you think I didn't recognize you? The way you walk, or hold yourself? The way you always lead with a small bet and never commit yourself until the third card, time after time after time?" He rose from the table, and began to scoop the money towards him. "Did you really think covering yourself up and putting on a funny voice would hide you from me? You're as big a fool as your father, don Hellespont, if you think you can deceive me like that."

"It's Helles. I go by Helles." Marius scraped his chair back and stood.

"Like I care," Sangk nodded to the burly doorkeeper. "Escort this bankrupt out of my house."

The giant came over and grabbed Marius by each arm. Marius struggled, and gave up almost immediately. He may as well be trying to squirm through wood. Sangk stood before him, and grabbed the edge of his hood.

"Next time," he said, and flipped the hood back, "try a better.... Oh, gods!"

He stumbled backwards, arms rising to cover his face. Marius turned his head to look at his captor. The doorkeeper let him loose, and stepped back, fear and disgust written across his previously impassive features. Marius smiled, and the doorkeeper broke, and ran for the nearby staircase.

"Oh, gods," Sangk was crying, over and over. "He's dead. He's dead. Oh, gods." Players at other tables were looking at them. Marius stared back. As he turned to each startled patron they leaped from their chairs and join the crush at the stairs.

"They're coming back," Sangk cried. "They told me when I bought it, they told me. Oh, gods..." He began to pray in his native Tallian, a long stream of syllables punctuated only by a rising ululation. Marius stepped forward and grabbed his collar, drawing him up.

"What are you talking about?" he said, shaking the heavier man. "What?"

"The duke," Sangk babbled. "The men he killed. They're buried down here, in the walls, in the back cave..." He began praying again. Marius let him go and he fell to the floor, pressing his head against the cold stone, begging forgiveness from whatever gods he could rally to his cause. Marius turned away. The room was empty. Only he and the babbling man at his feet remained. He bent over the table, scooping the coins towards himself and counting them out. Eighty riner. He gathered them up, made his way to the next table and the next, gathering the abandoned winnings together. When he had finished he counted one hundred and fifty riner.

"Not a bad haul," he said to his terrified host. "I should come here dead more often." He separated out a hundred riner and placed it in various pockets, then picked up the first of the remaining coins and waved it at Sangk.

"Never steal what you can't swallow," he said. "First rule." He placed the coin in his mouth, and gulped it backwards. It stuck in the top of his throat. Marius gulped again, pushed and pulled at it with the base of his tongue until it jumped into his mouth. He tried again, with the same result.

"Shit."

There was no spit in his mouth, and, dead as he was, he could not summon any. He pondered the coin for a moment. Then he tilted his head back, opened his mouth as wide as he could, and dropped it back in. Gulping, and jerking his head back and forth like a baby bird, he managed to get it down.

"Like a lizard swallowing a mouse," he told the wailing Sangk. "I've spent a lot of time sleeping under bushes." One by one he gulped the remaining coins down his gullet, until the table was empty. He looked over at Sangk for one, last, smug comment, and stopped.

Deep within the unused rear of the cave, where a small corridor lead to a tiny antechamber, something stood. Had he been alive, Marius would not have seen it. But his dead eyes, able to distinguish shades of dark from each other with much keener facility, saw the shape, and the one behind it, and vaguely, the impression of several more.

"They're coming back," he whispered, as the features of a long-dead man became clearer, dressed in peasant garb, the remains of an earth-moving basket hanging from his skeletal hand. The corpse leaned forward to get a better look at Marius. He opened his jaw, and a fine trail of sand dribbled out.

"Kinnnggg..." he hissed.

Marius stepped backwards involuntarily.

"I... I'm on my way," he said, and ran for the stairs.

# THIRTEEN

Dusk was falling as Marius strode along the wharf and up the gangway onto the deck of the *Minerva*. The lines of navvies had departed, and the remaining activity was by way of making the ship ready to sail. Marius skirted the main activity and headed for the captain's cabin. Halfway along the deck, the giant form of Mister Spone emerged from the crowd and waved at him.

"Hola, Mister Helles! Got yourself packed then?"

Marius waved back and hurried on. He knocked sharply on the captain's door and entered without waiting for permission.

The cabin had changed immeasurably since Marius had left. No paintings hung on the walls. The tables of knick-knacks were gone. The velvet drapes had been packed away, replaced by two sheets of oiled canvas that looked older than the ship by some measure. The throne upon which Bomthe sat had been superseded by a simple wooden chair. The captain himself had changed – the frippery with which he was clothed upon their first meeting was no longer apparent, and a simpler, more functional uniform now adorned his sparse frame. The charts over which he pored, however, were the same. He glanced up as Marius entered, and a frown of annoyance flashed over his countenance.

"Mister…. Holes, isn't it?"

"Helles." Marius withdrew a heavy pouch from his jerkin and threw it onto the table. It landed with a dull *thunk*. "Ninety-five riner."

The captain gathered up the bag without removing his gaze from Marius. He tipped it over, and counted out the coins within. When he was finished he gazed down at the neat piles he had built, tapping his teeth with one stiff finger. Marius waited in silence, head bowed, hands tucked into his sleeves like a meditating monk.

"Well," the captain said at length. "That presents me with something of a problem, Mister Hailes. I'm afraid our preparations have left us with very little available space. We simply do not have a cabin to spare on a single passenger, paying or otherwise. The best I can offer…"

Marius barely seemed to move, but suddenly he was beside the table and sweeping the coins back into the bag. The captain curled an arm around them protectively, and held his other hand up to stop Marius' movement.

"I can offer you a private space, although it is not so big as a cabin. If it is not to your liking…" His shrug finished his argument. The docks were only a few feet down the gangway. Marius could leave any time he chose to do so. Marius straightened, and regained his monk-like pose.

"We sail without a second mate this trip. His room is on the top deck, behind and to the side of my own cabin. We're using it as a storeroom for blankets and sundry items of clothing. It's rather full, I'm afraid. No room for a cot. Still…" He smiled, and the curtains were no longer the oiliest things in the room. "I'm sure you could make yourself comfortable, if the need was great enough."

Marius stared at the pile of money, contemplating, for a moment, the possibility of recovering it, making his way off the crowded ship unharmed, and finding some alternative form of escape without Keth's assistance. Then, slowly, he nodded.

"Show me."

The captain deposited his payment in a drawer within his desk. He leaned back into his chair.

"Figgis!"

The boy emerged from the cabin's rear door, and stood a few feet from the two men, sketching a short bow towards his master. "Yes, sir?"

"Show our guest to his quarters, will you?"

"Yes, sir." The young lad moved to the door, and looked back at Marius. "This way, sir."

Marius turned to follow him, noting as he did so that Figgis had not been told where his quarters were located. No need to wonder how long ago the captain had decided on his berth – it had been his intention since the start. He followed Figgis out onto the deck, turned to the starboard side, and shuffled sternward along the thin space between the captain's window and the railing. Marius glanced through the glass as he passed. Bomthe was staring straight back, tracking his progress along the deck.

At the rear of the deck, thin enough that Marius would have mistaken it for a simple panel if not for the small semi-circular hole cut into it at waist height, stood the door to the second mate's room. Figgis indicated it with a short wave of his hand, then scurried past Marius and back up towards Bomthe's cabin. Marius tugged the door open. It was small enough that he had to turn sideways to fit through. He did so, and slipped into the tiny space beyond.

To call it a room was to sell a mule as a horse. Marius had seen larger closets in the boudoirs of Endtown brothels. It was a good thing he didn't need to sleep, he thought as he searched for footing amongst the waist-high piles of blankets. He had never like sleeping on his side, and the room was not wide enough that he could have done so on his back. Whoever the second mate had been, he had undoubtedly left Bomthe's service in order to undergo puberty – a grown man, surely, could not have fit within the room for any length of time.

Finally happy that he had attained sure footing, he reached behind him and closed the door, plunging the room into darkness. Marius waited for a moment or two to let his eyes adjust, then slowly sunk to his knees and crawled further into the space. A small window sat halfway along the rear wall, covered by a blanket indistinguishable from those on the floor. Marius pulled it down and let moonlight into the room. Bomthe hadn't lied. It was a cabin, it was private, and it was above decks. As to anything else, well, the dead were beyond discomfort. Or, at least, they made do with it. With nothing else to do before the ship set sail, he started to fold blankets into neat squares and pile them up in the farthest corner.

By the time the moon reached its zenith he had folded almost eighty blankets into neat columns of fabric against the rear wall. Much of the floor lay exposed, for all the good it did. Marius could, at least, stand without fear of tripping. A small shelf had appeared beneath the window. It would have been a bed, perhaps, for the resident, unless he was wider than a small snake, in which case the floor became even more important. It gave Marius somewhere to sit, but nothing more. He did so, turning to stare out of the tiny window. Whatever his privations, he was where he needed to be – on a ship, hidden, about to sail across an ocean so wide the dead would never find him. Motion. Any motion was a good one. Once the boat was underway he could relax, and make plans for landfall. The Faraway Isles would be a start. Once there, he could find an isolated village, somewhere where the dead were discarded in such a way that he wouldn't have to live with their conversation. Then… well, he didn't know what would happen then, but it was a start.

He emptied his pockets and laid his riches out on the narrow shelf. A handful of coins, enough to gain a whispered conversation with a knowledgeable local, at least; a variety of stones, washers, and buttons to stand in the place of coins and foil the flittering fingers of street dips; a cosh, small enough to sit in the palm of his hand, that he had used once and sworn never to use again once the swelling had gone down, but that he'd never really managed to dispense with. He laid them alongside the satchel the dead had bequeathed him; and the accursed crown. It sat at the end of his makeshift row, twinkling darkly in the weak light, taunting him with its presence. Marius backhanded it to the floor, and kicked the priceless artefact across the room. It bounced from the wall of blankets and spun round to face him. The emerald in its frontispiece blinked at him as the light hit its multi-faceted face.

Marius turned his attention to the satchel – he had ignored it in his constant flight across the country, without thought for its contents. It had simply been a weight to be carried. Only now, with nothing to do but wait for his freedom, did he think to open it and spill its contents onto the shelf.

At first glance, the scraps that slid out looked like dried autumn leaves, a filthy wash of dead vegetable matter crammed into the bag like so much stuffing. It was only when Marius picked up a handful and examined them closely did he see what they actually were – scraps of paper: torn, crumpled, stained with dirt and age and, in some cases, blood; gathered from the corpses of who-knew-how-many dead, written upon in a range of scrawls, some bearing the mark of culture and education, some barely legible, as if the hands that drew the words were controlled more by willpower than by any combination of withered and rotting muscles.

Marius read through the few whose words he could discern – they were letters, from the dead to their living relatives. Marius scanned them quickly, mouth open in surprise. They were mundane, for the most part, of interest only to those who wrote them and, perhaps, those who might receive; it was the sheer number that boggled him.

Each scrap was, he realized, a tiny plea for continuation, a need to reach out and reassure the author that the life they left behind had continued with some part of them remembered. Even if it were just the knowledge that Aunt Madge still complained of gout, or that young Roldo was still studying sail making at Ballico College, the dead needed *someone* to remember. But it was the simple notes, the ones written with large, clumsy letters, telling Mummy how much she was loved or Daddy how much he was missed, with strings of X's at the bottom like a line of illiterate signatures, that finally caused Marius to open his hand and let the brittle sheets fall to the floor.

What was he supposed to do, he silently asked? There were so many. Was he to deliver them, like some sort of travelling postmaster? When they could not be read, when so many of them lacked addresses, as if the dead authors could no longer remember that important part of their previous lives? When the reactions of those who might have received them could only be a combination of grief, and fear, and anger towards the man who had delivered them? Marius was not the man to perform the task. Not him. He gathered the papers back up and replaced them within the satchel. So many letters from children. He placed the satchel on the floor and leaned his head against the wall, closing his eyes. Concentrate on what can be done. Concentrate on escaping the sword hanging over him, on stepping onto the sandy beaches of the Faraway Isles and leaving dead children, and dead kings, and the continent of Lemk behind. For the first time since he had picked up the Scorban king's crown, Marius allowed himself to relax. He opened his eyes, and stared through the window at the land he was going to leave behind.

A figure stood upon the wharf, an island of stillness amidst the ceaseless stream of moving humanity. As Marius stared, the figure stepped forward until it stood on the edge of the wharf, back to the press of movement, facing the flat stern of the *Minerva*, head tilted so the hood covering its face was pointed directly at the Marius' window. Marius raised a hand to his mouth, slowly, as the figure reached up and pulled the hood back from its head, exposing his face. Marius bit down on his hand, oblivious to the sudden flare of pain that shot up where his teeth met the dead skin.

"Gerd?"

Marius slid his head backwards, away from the window, blinking in sudden fear. When he could trust himself to peek out the window again without panicking he did so. Gerd stood motionless at the edge of the wharf. As Marius watched he stepped forward, off the edge of the wharf, and dropped below the edge of Marius' vision. He heard a dull splash, and then he was up off his perch and barging through the door, racing along the deck to bang his fist against the captain's door. After an eternity, the door swung open, and Marius found his way blocked by the massive frame of Spone.

"What the hell is the… oh, my gods."

Marius stared up at the big man's face. Spone was staring at him with a mixture of shock and disgust splashed across his features. Marius blinked stupidly, then, realizing the cause of the first mate's shock, slowly reached up and pulled his hood over his exposed face.

"I need to speak to the captain," he said warily. Spone nodded, then backed into the room, keeping as much distance between himself and Marius as possible. Marius hurried into the room, moving past the giant mate with an apologetic nod, and stepped up to the captain's table. Bomthe sat before a bowl of stew, a chunk of bread in his hand. Another bowl sat in front of a smaller chair to one side. Marius glanced at it, then at the mate, pressed against the wall of the cabin some feet away.

"Captain," he said without preamble. "We must depart, immediately."

"I'm sorry, Mister Helpus–"

"Helles. It's Helles, damn it." Marius raised a fist to thump it on the table, recovered himself, and lowered it stiffly to his side.

"I'm sorry, Mister Helles," the captain smiled, aware of his victory. "But I'm not in the habit of altering my plans on account of an hysterical passenger. We will slip anchor with the first tide."

"But… I must insist–"

"You shall insist on nothing, Mister Helles." The captain took a bite of his bread, chewed, and swallowed. He laid the remaining chunk on the table and looked Marius squarely in the dark shadow of his hood. "I will do you the courtesy of explaining, Mister Helles, because you have paid the money I asked, and because it will make your journey much easier to understand me from the beginning. This is a trading ship, not a passenger ship. Its sole purpose is to trade goods. Moreover, it is *my* ship. I decide when we depart, where we depart for, when we eat, when we make landfall, with whom I wish to trade, and how long I wish to take to do so. I am answerable only to those who invest in my journey, and who require me to provide them with a return on that investment. You are not amongst their number." He returned his gaze to his stew. "Return to your cabin, or I shall have Mister Spone escort you there. I will send you some food shortly. I do not expect to be interrupted again."

"But... there's..." Marius shook a hand towards the water at the back of the ship. Bomthe's lips compressed into a tight little smile.

"I do not care what problems you are attempting to leave behind you, sirrah, so long as they do not accompany you on your journey. Your concerns are not mine. Now, leave my cabin, please, or shall I call on Mister Spone?"

Marius glanced at the giant ship's master. He stared back at Marius, his features a blank mask of fear. Marius sighed, and dropped his head. He turned without a word and left the cabin. He was halfway along the narrow walkway towards his cabin, desperately trying to decide how to reinforce his door with nothing more than blankets and scraps of paper, when two hands appeared at the railing. As Marius pressed up against the wall in shock, Gerd hauled himself over the railing to stand, dripping, before him.

"Hello, Marius," he said, a nasty smile spread across his features. "How was your shit?"

Marius said nothing. Gerd stepped forward. Marius slid a foot along the wall.

"What do you think you're doing? Running away? Where to, Marius?" Gerd laughed, a sound like falling gravel. "Haven't you heard the saying? 'The entire Earth is the grave of great men.' L'Liva said that. You know, the philosopher? I've met him." Gerd took another step forward. "You can't run away from me. You can't escape us."

Marius lunged forward, lowering his head and driving it into Gerd's chest. Gerd stumbled backwards, clawing at the older man's back. Marius heaved upwards, driving Gerd against the railing, once, and twice. He heaved, and tipped his tormenter over the side. The younger man held on a moment, then his weight betrayed him and he fell away from the hull, tumbling as he fell twenty-odd feet to hit the water. Marius leaned against the railing, watching the rings spread outwards from the impact. How deep was the harbour below the hull line? How deep the *Minerva's* draught?

No question of asking whether Gerd could have survived the fall. The only concern was how long it would take him to reappear, and whether Marius could continue to block the dead man's attempts to recapture him long enough for the ship to weigh anchor. He waited, and watched, stepping to the corner of the railing to keep his eye on the stern as well as the side, but Gerd did not resurface. Eventually, as dawn began to lighten the sky, and sailors emerged from below decks to make ready for departure, Marius retreated to his room and sat with his back pressed against the door, hoping his dead weight would be enough.

Out the window, where he could not see from his position on the floor, a figure hauled itself out of the water to stand on the dock, watching the *Minerva* as she slipped her moorings and made out of the harbour. Only once the massive ship was well out into the bay did the figure turn, and push through the crowds, away from the wharf.

Marius sat against the door for three days, afraid to move lest the past come crashing through his door and drag him beneath the surface of the world for judgment. True to his word, Bomthe sent Figgis down the narrow passageway three times a day, to knock on the door and leave a tray of food. Three times a day, Marius ignored the invitation, and the diminutive cabin boy snuck back an hour later to gulp down the rejected meal and report back to his master that all was well with the passenger. At lunch on the fourth day, however, he opened the door at Figgis' knock, and did his best not laugh at the youngster's look of disappointment. He tilted his head to Figgis to bring the tray in. Figgis laid the tray upon the thin shelf, and nervously eyed the closed door.

"Will that be all, sir?" he asked, shuffling his feet. Marius motioned him to sit, then nudged the tray closer.

"Tuck into that, lad," he said, leaning back and smiling as Figgis nervously broke off a corner of the hard bread. "I've no great appetite, these days, and you look like you don't get more than scraps for your tea." He nodded down at the thin stew and broken biscuits. "Get stuck in."

Thankfully, Figgis admitted that, indeed, he was the poor, hard-done-to soul he appeared to be, and that it was, indeed, almost impossible to survive on the pittance he was thrown by the captain. Marius clucked in sympathy, and begged him to try some of the stew.

If you want gossip, talk to the ruling classes. If you want the truth of things, speak to those who serve them, the ones who change the sheets in the morning, who carry the breakfast trays into bedrooms, who water the horses at the roadside inns and never, ever reveal how blue the stool of the monarch is this morning. Within half an hour, Marius and Figgis were firm friends, bound by shared experiences and an understanding of just how cruel a fate it was to serve under a master who swept a spoon through your stew before passing it to you, to remove the best bits of meat for his own plate.

The deal was ridiculously easy to strike – Marius would give the lad his food, and let him eat in the relative comfort of the tiny cabin, and in return, he would know all there was to know about the *Minerva*, her crew, and the countless feuds, arguments, love matches and working relationships that made up its society. And on his next visit, Marius would receive a bowl of hot water, a stick of soap, and a blade with which to shave.

"Tell me," he said, as Figgis was wiping up the last of his stew with the final ball of bread, "about Mister Spone…"

# FOURTEEN

No man makes captain without having served his share of dawn watches. The hours between three bells and seven are the loneliest in the world; the coldest; the wettest. It is reserved for those on misdemeanour charges, those whom the mates have come to dislike most, or like Mister Spone, those who have attained the highest working rank on the ship and need only the experience of commanding the worst men at the worst time of the day to complete their education. Such an education gives a master complete knowledge – only at the most miserable hour, with waves crashing across the bow deck and the wind making a mockery of the sails, can a man truly understand the paradise of a dry corner, away from the rain, where he can light a snout and smoke, undisturbed, for a few stray moments before the call of duty and danger requires him to re-enter the whirlpool outside.

There were no such conditions that morning, but such a corner serves as well in the dry as the wet. Spone was crammed in, half-turned into the angle, striking a lucifer against the wood, when Marius appeared out of the dark and stood before him.

"Mister Spone." He clung to a beam as the ship pitched and rolled across the pre-dawn swell. Spone, his body perfectly adjusted to life at sea, stared at him and raised his hands into half-fists, unconsciously shielding his exposed side. He waited, saying nothing. Marius gripped tighter as the ship listed, then righted itself. "May I speak with you?"

Slowly, warily, Spone nodded, his eyes darting to the left and the right, seeking out ways to get around the man before him. When none presented itself he let them fall upon Marius, suppressing a shudder as he did so.

"You are a religious man, Mister Spone? A Post-Necrotist, I understand?"

Again, Spone nodded. Marius sighed.

"In that case, I must apologise for my appearance. It must have startled you." Marius stared at the man for several seconds. "It must have terrified you," he said, so softly that Spone could barely hear him above the wind. Marius stepped closer, transferring his grip from one stanchion to another. Spone shrank back as far as the corner would allow.

"I am not the hallowed dead, come back to wreak havoc upon the world of the living," Marius said. "I am not dead at all. Give me your hand." He held out his. Spone stared at it. "Please, Mister Spone. Your hand." Haltingly, Spone gripped it. Marius pulled it against his chest.

"Can you feel that, Mister Spone?" he asked. Slowly, Spone nodded, eyes fixed upon Marius' chest. "My heart, sir, beating, the same as any man's."

Marius risked releasing the stanchion, reached up, and drew back his hood. Spone winced at the sight of his uncovered face.

"I know," Marius said. "It's awful. Totally ruined my chances with the ladies." He laughed, and despite his confusion, Spone managed a small one in return. "Truth is, Mister Spone, I have no idea what it is, only that it affects me alone. Those around me are safe, have no fear on that count." Marius let go Spone's hand, and gestured ahead of the ship. "I've travelled far and wide for a cure, but nobody can tell me what it is, only that my flesh rots and my eyes film over, and as to the smell, well," he shrugged, a comical, exaggerated movement. "Ruined with the ladies." He offered his hand once more. "Once more, I can only apologise."

This time, Spone shook it.

"Had I known of your beliefs, I would never have barged in upon you in such a manner," Marius said. "I hope I did not cause you too much grief."

Spone straightened out of his corner, and banished memories of four terror-filled nights awake in his tiny cabin, praying. "Think nothing of it," he managed to say. Marius dug into his jerkin, and produced a lucifer to replace the one Spone had dropped. He struck it, and leaned in, cupping it to protect it from the wind. Spone accepted the gift, and lit his snout.

"Thank you."

"My pleasure."

The two men stood and looked out at the grey sky, watching as the sun peeked hesitantly over the horizon.

"Tough watch," Marius said, and Spone nodded in

quiet acknowledgment.

"Makes you captain, in the end."

"Is that the plan?"

"Eventually."

Marius nodded. "A good place to learn, then?"

"I've served under worse," Spone said, and Marius nodded in agreement.

"I've seen worse, for certain. So…" he let the thought hang for a moment, "He's a fair man, this Captain Bomthe?"

They stood, side by side, and Spone talked about his captain, and Marius listened, as the sun rose and the new watch arrived to take up their posts. When they parted, with a handshake and a firm wish for a good morning, Marius returned to his cabin, to think upon what he had learned, and to lay some plans for his future.

He stayed in his cabin for five days, during which time the *Minerva* made fair progress. The weather was temperate, and fresh winds propelled them across the open ocean with no need to tack or bring the massive mainsails into play. Figgis visited three times a day, bringing bowls of the increasingly thin soup and leaving with the empty vessels and a smear of broth around his cheeks.

Marius listened to the gossip-filled reports he delivered, filtering out the important tidbits as they rose to the surface: Captain Bomthe wished to avoid the coast and head straight out into deep waters; Mister Spone was worried about several items of cargo that had come loose in the aft hold; Captain Bomthe and Mister

Spone had gone down to the hold personally to secure the cargo; nobody knew what was down there; rumours assigned it to everything from gold bullion, to magical arms to be traded to the Taran heathens, to women set aside solely for the officers' use; Mister Spone was angry about something, but would discuss it with nobody; Captain Bomthe kept drinking, and sending Figgis out to refill his brandy skein. Marius simply nodded and kept his head against his chest, telling the young lad to eat up.

At dinner on the fifth day, he interrupted his visitor's monologue with a short cough, and a raised hand.

"The aft hold you mentioned." Figgis looked up from his bowl, a dribble of broth wending its way down his chin. "Could you show me where it is?"

Figgis looked uncertain. "I'm not allowed down there, Mister Spone says. Nobody is, just him and the captain."

"Oh, don't worry about them." Marius leaned back on his nest of blankets, and folded his hands across his chest. "You don't need to take me all the way there. Just far enough so that I can find my own way. If the captain or Mister Spone find me after that, your name will never occur to me."

"I... I don't know."

"Does he beat you, this captain of yours?"

"No... I... well, yes... but only when I deserve it," Figgis corrected himself quickly. Marius nodded. Shipboard discipline was no mystery to him. It was a hard life, and it took hard men. The cabin boy's definition of "deserving it", and by extension the captain's, might not accord with Marius' feelings on the subject. But then, Marius was in *their* world. One of the first things he had learned whilst travelling – learn the rules of your destination, so that they do not surprise you.

"I give you my word," he said. "I'll not ask you to do anything to make you deserve it. Perhaps…" he paused, as if considering his options. "What if you came to me between the third and fourth watches? Would the captain know?"

Spone would not be on deck until a full watch later, and like all good sailors, would sleep right up until the bell sounded. And Bomthe would have fallen into a drunken stupor long before, if Figgis was even remotely accurate regarding the number of visits he was making to the brandy cask. The young boy frowned for a moment, considering Marius' proposal. Marius sat still, projecting innocence with every fibre.

"I suppose…" Figgis said. "Just as far as I want?"

"Not a step further," Marius said. "All I want is to see this hold. After all," he held his arms wide. "What else can I do?"

"But why?"

"I'm nobody's agent, if that's what's worrying you." Marius leaned forward, and teased at the fingers of one glove. "I want to show you something, but I need your promise before I do."

"My promise?"

"That you won't fear what you see."

"Okay." Figgis shrugged. "You have it."

"Are you sure?" Marius stopped worrying at the glove. "I don't ask this lightly, boy. I need your promise to be a man's promise, you understand? Unbreakable, inviolate. Nobody knows about this but you and I. Not the captain, not Mister Spone. Nobody."

Figgis looked solemn, his face a child's play-act of seriousness. "I promise."

"Okay." Marius grasped the glove's fingers and pulled, sliding it off in one swift movement. He held his hand before Figgis' face. "You see?"

"It's a hand."

"Yes. And?"

Figgis looked at it, then back at the shadow of Marius' hood. "It's a hand."

Marius looked at his hand. The boy was right. It was just a hand. His hand. Browned by the sun, the fingernails slightly ragged from too much time without attention, a maze of tiny scars and flaws from twenty years of living amongst the lower ends of society. His hand. He stared at it, and Figgis stared at him, a look of increasing worry on his young face.

"Are you all right?"

Slowly, Marius reached up and pulled back his hood. "What do you see?"

Figgis shrugged. "I don't know. You? Listen," he shifted impatiently. "What's any of this got to do with me taking you below decks?"

"I…" Marius thought furiously, "I… do you know what fear of spaces is?"

"What? Like, being outside and all?"

"Yes, exactly." Marius nodded. "I… I have it."

"But I seen you walking along the wharf, and about topside with Mister Spone and all."

"It's… it's difficult." Marius lowered his eyes, as if staring at the floor, taking care to make sure his hand stayed within his line of vision. If he only had a glass, or something in which to see his reflection. "I can do it, but it... exhausts me. I... If I could spend some time, in that room, away from the outside..." He flicked his hand towards the open window. "I feel it, all the time, all around me..." He peeked up at Figgis. "Even if I could spend just a short time in this hidden store, away from people, away from..." he shuddered, "the sky. It would help me. *You* could help me." He looked straight at the young boy. "I need a friend here, Figgis. Have I not been your friend?"

His eyes slid to the empty bowl at Figgis' feet. The cabin boy followed his gaze, and coloured.

"Between third and fourth watch," he said, scrambling to his feet and gathering up the bowl. "But only for a few minutes, mind?"

"You have my word."

"And Mister Spone and the captain never hear of it?"

"Never."

"And if you're caught..."

"On my own head be it."

"Okay, then." He opened the door, and half slid out. "Shouldn't we... have some sort of secret knock or something?"

"Don't worry," Marius smiled. "I'll know it's you."

"Okay." Figgis left without another word. Marius lay back on his makeshift nest and stared out at the sliver of sky visible through the window. After all, he thought, who else would come and visit? He held his hand up. As he watched, the skin dried out, grew pale, then grey. His nails darkened. Cracks appeared in their surface. Small flakes dropped from his skin, and the fingers withered until they were little more than desiccated claws. He stifled a cry of alarm, and scrambled in his lap for the discarded glove, pulling it back on with a shaking hand. He curled into a foetal ball, and slowly reached up to pull the hood down over his face.

Slowly, night suffused the cabin. Marius stifled a moan of despair as his eyesight adjusted to the darkness, picking out details in the room he knew he would be unable to see with living eyes. He heard bells sound to end the evening watch, and shortly thereafter, the muted barrage of feet thundering through the ship as weary sailors headed below to their hammocks for a few hours rest, and their replacements headed upwards to take up their stations. After that there was silence, other than the creaks and groans of a ship under sail, and the occasional sharp call as an order was relayed from mate to crew. A single toll of the bell marked off each hour. Then, just as midnight sounded, Marius heard a scratching outside his door. He sat up, suddenly alert. Three quick knocks rapped against his door, then a pause, and two more. He smiled. The never-changing nature of the boy child – a secret escapade must have a secret knock. Marius would almost lay money on being gifted a secret password by the end of tonight's jaunt. He opened the door a crack.

"What's the password?"

Figgis stood outside, a look of fear suddenly filling his features.

"You didn't give me one," he began. "Do you think we need–"

"I was just kidding." Marius stepped outside and crouched on the narrow walkway. "Are you ready?"

Figgis nodded. "The captain's sleeping at his desk, and Mister Spone's in his bunk. As soon as…" He stopped as running footsteps sounded across the top deck, and crouched down next to Marius, eyes wide.

"Don't worry," Marius whispered. "It's just the changing of the watch. Give it a minute."

They waited in silence until the footsteps died away, and normal sounds returned. Marius laid a hand on Figgis' shoulder. The cabin boy was shivering, whether from the cold or fear, Marius could not be certain. "Go on," he whispered.

"Mister Hongg is master of the watch," he said. "He likes to catch a wink in the lee of the mizzenmast. It looks like he's standing watching the crew…"

"Not likely to see us if we use the near stairs, then?"

Figgis shook his head. "As long as we're quick, and quiet."

"Oh, I'm good at quick and quiet," Marius said, then bit off the rest of his comment. Figgis lived amongst sailors, true, but there was no need to expose him to more bedroom wit than was absolutely necessary. "Let's go, shall we?" he said instead, and ushered the young boy ahead of him.

The space between decks is a gloomy place at the best of times: packed tight with sweating bodies; badly lit; piled high with supplies necessary to survive a long voyage. Whilst the top deck may be polished smooth and presentable to visiting investors and dignitaries, no such effort is wasted on the lower areas. The wood is rough, the angles tight, and what little room is left for movement is cramped, fetid, and jealously guarded by anyone who manages to carve out a tiny allocation of personal space.

As mindful as he was of the desire to hurry, Marius forced himself to step carefully through the maze of cargo. Far worse than missing out on the captain's treasure room would be the consequence of discovery should he upset some precariously balanced box of victuals and ruin the contents by crashing them onto the floor. He tested each creaking step before he committed his full weight to it, slowly slinking down until he and his companion crouched beneath the steps.

"Which way, Master Figgis?"

The young cabin boy pointed deeper into the bowels of the ship. "At the end of the corridor, sir. The mate's cabin is just down there, and the powder room, then the locked room before the rear food store."

Marius nodded, memorizing the layout as Figgis spoke. It was all fairly typical of a Scorban trader, a layout refined through several centuries of sea-borne trading. The mystery room would normally be reserved for assorted junk that fit nowhere else – spare weaponry, maps of regions not visited upon the particular voyage, whatever items of trade the captain wished to keep for his own personal collections. It was tiny, perhaps three feet in either direction, the perfect sized for a moderate haul of purloined gold, or valuables not originally belonging to the ship's owner. A ship is the same as a man, in certain ways. Never steal anything the ship cannot swallow. Marius nodded, and indicated the darkness before them.

"Lead on."

Figgis took an uncertain step forward. Marius followed, observing the space around them as they crept. The *Minerva* was a working ship. Every ounce of available space was crowded with spare ropes, tools, boxes of tallow and wicks, hides, baubles, whatever the captain might be able to trade to islanders for valuable works of art, fruit, and delicacies. Whatever benefits society might obtain in bulk for a pittance, without having to waste valuable powder and ball. Marius did not need to pry open any of the boxes around him to see the cheap glass beads, thin blankets, and cotton bolts within. He'd packed such boxes himself, and spent his profits like any other sailor. Figgis reached the alcove he had dubbed the mate's room, and stopped. Theatrically, he raised his finger to his lip, and peeked around the thin wall at the short wooden bunk inside. Marius followed his lead.

Mister Spone lay with his back to the world, his massive frame balanced precariously on the slim wooden bunk. Marius was impressed – the man appeared to be in a deep sleep, despite being crammed into a space far too small for his hulking body. Then he saw the familiar square bottle of Borgho Wharf brandy sitting empty on the floor, and raised an eyebrow in understanding. Medicinal purposes only, of course.

Figgis snuck past, and Marius followed, cocking an eye over the spare space. No personal effects crowded the single shelf, or poked out of the locked chest. No other items of furniture either. Unless he maintained an apartment somewhere onshore, and Marius had never known a sailor so sure of returning from any given voyage that he was willing to leave his possessions in the care of another, everything the big man owned lay inside that miserable alcove. Marius felt a wave of sympathy for the sleeping sailor. It was a long time at a hard life, to be able to carry everything you owned on your back, even if you had to be a giant of a man to pick it up. Figgis was already half a dozen footsteps ahead of him, and he quickly turned to catch up.

"Here," the cabin boy said, indicating a rough-hewn door a few yards further down the corridor. Marius nodded and slipped past his companion, testing the handle with a quick twist of his wrist. It was locked. Marius grunted in disappointment. He had known captains so hard that they left doors open, knowing that reputation alone would ensure no disobeying of an order not to enter. Bomthe was obviously no such captain. Marius knelt and eyed the lock mechanism, gently snorting as he reached into his jerkin and removed a set of picks. Bomthe might be no terror, but he was no spendthrift either. The lock was as basic as it could be and still be called by the name. Marius made sure Figgis was watching, then deliberately closed his eyes and sprung the mechanism.

"Magic," he said in answer to Figgis' gaping eyes. "And a cheapskate with no notion of security." He stood, and indicated the door with a flourish. "Care to do the honours?"

Figgis shook his head. Marius shrugged, and carefully lowered the handle. No good giving the game away with a squeaking handle, he supposed. He leaned gently against the door, and it swung open soundlessly. The two interlopers stepped inside quickly, and Marius drew the door shut behind them.

The stench was the first thing to hit them – like rotting meat, with shit and piss rolled through it – a miasma so thick that Figgis immediately gagged and pulled his shirt up to cover his mouth and nose. Marius had no such need, but he still pursed his lips in disgust. No windows lit the room. It was empty, except for a pile of rags in the far corner. Marius took a step towards them, then pulled up sharply as his foot slid across the slick floor. He crouched down, and examined the planking, frowning when he saw the irregular pattern of stains that covered the space. He ran a finger through the nearest, and smelled it, then wrinkled his nose and wiped his finger clean against the wall.

"What the hell is this?" he muttered, staring around at the empty, stinking room. Figgis made no answer. Marius glanced up at him, but the boy was staring out into the darkness, and it was obvious that his living eyes could make out no details. Marius turned his attention back to the empty space. There was no sign of treasure, or secrets, or indeed, any indication that any had been stored there. Only the pile of filthy rags, and the stains on the floor, and the overpowering reek of ordure. Marius remained kneeling, rubbing his fingers together and frowning at the lack of evidence. He held his position for over a minute before giving up.

"Ah, well," he said, standing and slapping his hands against his thighs. "Never mi–"

The bundle of rags groaned, and sat up.

"Holy hell." Marius stepped backwards in shock, then gathered himself and leaned forward for a closer look. The bundle resolved itself into three men, encrusted with grime and filth, their matted hair plastered to their faces and tangled so deeply into their beards that it was almost impossible to see the features beneath. One held his hand out with torturous slowness, and Marius saw the heavy manacle around his wrist, the red edges of skin beneath sealed over and risen so that the manacle no longer bit into the flesh but was enfolded beneath it by months of growth. The man grunted, and Marius felt his features harden in response. He had heard such a low and bubbling moan before, and knew what it meant – the prisoner's tongue had been removed, undoubtedly in tandem with his teeth.

"You poor bastards," he muttered, shuffling forward and grabbing the man's wrist to further examine the damage. "What the hell did you do to merit this?" It was as he had supposed. The manacles had been in place so long that the skin had simply incorporated the edges, like gravel sealed up within a wound. He dropped the arm, and raised his hand towards the captive's face. The man flinched, and scuttled away as far as his chain and the body of his neighbour would allow. Marius opened his hand and made gentle shushing sounds.

"Hey, hey now. No." He glanced down, and saw where the chains fell from the prisoner's wrists to bolts in the floor. There was no give. However long they had been in this cell, they had been unable to do more than sit and accept whatever beatings and torture had been meted out to them. The chains were too short to allow them to even kneel, much less shift to avoid sitting in their own excrement. Marius' eyes narrowed.

It took a slow ten count to remove the fury from his voice.

"It's okay," he said as gently as he could. "I won't hurt you. I'm not going to hurt you. I promise. I just want to…" He touched the prisoner's hair, pushed it aside to catch a glimpse of one maddened, terrified eye. "My name is Marius," he said, withdrawing his hand and placing it against his chest. "Marius. I'm going to help."

At the sound of his name, the captive to Marius' left sat up, and uttered a moan that may have been an attempt to repeat the word. He lunged forward the bare inch the chain allowed, and raised his hands with sudden urgency, before dissolving into a welter of bubbling sobs. Marius glanced back towards Figgis, who had retreated towards the door and now stood as far into the corner as he dared, peering into the darkness with fear.

"It's all right, lad," Marius said to him. "They're just men. Prisoners, I think. They've been treated… terribly." He turned back to the sobbing inmate. "Have you heard of me?" he asked gently. "Does my name mean something?" He reached out and placed his hand on the man's shoulder, gave it a small squeeze. "It's okay," he said. "It's okay."

The prisoner raised his head. Marius shifted so that he knelt directly in front of him. "You do know me, don't you?" he said. The man nodded, once, a shaking, faltering dip of the head.

"Who are you?" Marius reached out and drew the prisoner's hair back from his face. When he saw the face beneath he fell backwards, eyes wide, arms splayed out to stop him striking the deck with his head.

"Oh, fuck," he said. "Oh, gods. What did you do? What did you fucking do?"

"Sedition," said a voice from the doorway. Marius spun around. Two figures filled the open door. A hand opened the gate of a lantern. Light spilled out, revealing the massive frame of Mister Spone. Captain Bomthe stood just behind him, an empty bottle swinging from his hand. "Treason, rebellion, and attempted murder." He stepped into the room, his tread as steady and sober as a priest's, and stared down at the chained men. "Guilty as charged," he said, and passed the bottle behind him. Spone took it without a word and handed it to Figgis, cowering in the corner.

"Take that to my cabin," Bomthe said without removing his gaze from Marius, "and wait there. I'll deal with you later."

"It's not the boy's fault," Marius said automatically, "I forced him to bring me here."

"I'm sure you did," the captain replied. "But still, he came." He gestured to Spone to come forward. "I run a tight ship, Mister Helles. I expect compliance and nothing less. I don't care *why* my orders are disobeyed, or how, just that they are." He ran his eyes across the prisoners. "What is our position, Mister Spone?"

"Three hundred miles from port, Captain," the big man replied. "Nearing the Durah Straits."

"Hmm. Near enough. I doubt His Majesty will quibble over a few fathoms." He turned from his perusal and stepped towards the door. "Bring them up. And bring our guest with you."

"Wait. What is going–" Marius made to stand, but Spone was standing above him. The first mate reached down and yanked him up quickly enough to stop the question.

"This way, sir," he said. "Quietly now, if you please." He shoved Marius towards the door, and it was all he could do to catch himself before he clattered into the doorframe. Spone placed a heavy hand in his back and pushed him ahead. As they left the room, four armed sailors slipped past. The giant mate forced Marius up nearby stairs onto the open deck. The sound of cursing and loosed chains followed them.

The captain was waiting. Spone took Marius' arm and stood next to Bomthe. Marius tested his grip, then gave up.

"What the hell…" he tried again. Spone simply shook him until he stopped talking. Bomthe didn't even look in his direction. Marius waited until he could refocus his eyes, then stood silently. Slowly, the sailors came up the stairs, dragging the prisoners behind them. They hauled their charges to a spot a few feet in front of the captain and threw them to the deck. Bomthe made a small motion, and the captors beat at the prisoners, forcing them up to their knees.

"They won't go no farther, sir," one of the sailors reported.

"That's fine, Quig," the Captain replied. "No need for much more." The sailors slapped at the prisoners until they shuffled apart as far as the chains would let them – without the bolts to restrict them there was perhaps a foot between each man. They knelt back on their heels, drinking in the night and the fresh air.

Bomthe gave them a few moments, then coughed slightly. As one, the prisoners stiffened, and bent over themselves in attitudes of terror. Marius glanced up at the first mate. The big man was staring at the prisoners with an impassive gaze. Marius swallowed, and risked another attempt to speak.

"Captain," he began, and winced. When Spone made no move to shatter his bones he took a breath and continued. "Captain, what *is* this? What's going on?"

"What's going on, Mister Helles," Bomthe stepped forward and stood behind the prisoners, facing Marius, "is government business."

"What are you talking about? What did you mean about… these men have been tortured."

"These men," Bomthe pulled back the head of the middle prisoner and stared down at his terrified face, "are prisoners of His Imperial Majesty Tanspar the First, having plotted to murder the King and his family and seize control of the parliament. They have confessed, and are here for the carrying out of their sentence."

"But Tanspar is dead. You don't have to—"

"His Majesty's physical condition is of no interest to me. His payment is good either way."

"What? No. I mean, why do you…?"

Bomthe looked up, and smiled. "Why me? Out here, instead of the block at Justice Square?" He dropped the man's head, and moved to his left, grabbing the head of the next in line and staring at it in the same way as before. "I don't question His Majesty's commands," he said softly. "I just carry them out." He frowned, and glanced up at Marius. "Tell me, Mister Helles," he said, twisting the prisoner's head so that he and Marius stared directly at each other. "You seemed to know this man."

"What?"

"You heard me." Bomthe gave the unresisting head a gentle shake. "In the room, you recognized him, didn't you? It makes for a strange thought, does it not, that you would take board on my ship, through an intermediary, that you would pay an exorbitant fee in such short time without protest, that you would break into the one store on this ship that contains not a single item a petty lock pick might be expected to steal, and after all that, you and this traitor to the crown recognize each other. What do you say, Mister Helles?"

Marius stared at the prisoner. He slowly raised his head, matched Marius' gaze for long moments, then slowly, imperceptibly, shook his head. Marius echoed the movement, tearing his gaze away from the bloodied visage back to the captain.

"No," he managed to croak. "Not even slightly. I, uh…" He took a deep breath, then steadied his gaze. "I was simply shocked at the inhuman conditions in which I found them. You run a barbarous sort of prison, sir."

Bomthe matched his stare for half a dozen heartbeats, before tilting his head back and uttering a short bark of laughter. "Ha! Well said, sir, even if I don't believe a word of it." He entwined his fingers in the prisoner's hair and shook him vigorously. The weakened man made no effort to resist, simply toppled from one side to the other. "You do know this man, I am sure of it, but it makes no matter to me. It doesn't change his situation. Or yours," he added, his smile tightening.

Marius looked away. "And what has this wretch and his friends supposed to have done to warrant such cruelty?"

"Oh, I'm sure you know," Bomthe said, letting loose his grip and standing back. The captive slumped to one side. Spone quickly stepped forward and held him up with his leg. "Treason, sedition, attempted murder."

"And how?" Marius asked, not wishing to hear the answer but knowing all too well what it would be. Because he *did* recognize the beaten and bloodied wretch before him, and recognizing him, knew exactly what plan he had implemented and failed. Because Gereth vel Brinken had been a drinking buddy of Marius' since he first started sneaking out from his father's house to drink at the dockside taverns.

It was Marius who, when he reached the bottom of his cups and had brains more booze than substance, would rail at the King and his government, and talk of hiring the storerooms carved into the cliffs below the palace and filling them with gunpowder. And it was Gereth who would laugh, and buy him another pot, and question him endlessly on the how and the when, and the how much.

And suddenly, Marius was cramped by anger, and betrayal, and the most overwhelming flood of pity he had ever experienced, so that Bomthe's smug catalogue of events was little more than a buzzing around his head, and when he did, at last, raise his eyes from vel Brinken's bowed head it was with a look that caused Bomthe to stutter to a halt. The captain took a step back, then recovered himself. He nodded, once, as if confirming an inner suspicion.

"None of this is familiar to you, Mister Helles?"

Marius' lips worked furiously to contain his thoughts, and eventually he controlled them long enough to bite out a single word.

"No."

"Well, then." Bomthe nodded to Spone. The giant mate reached down and grasped the back of vel Brinken's hair. He hauled him upright, shifted his grip, and pulled the condemned man's head back until he stood on his tiptoes, back arched in an obscene parody of a court dancer. Vel Brinken's eyes stood out white against his bloodied face, fixed upon Marius as if begging him to do something, *anything*, to relieve his sudden terror. Marius closed his eyes, then slowly opened them again. Vel Brinken saw the deadness in his old friend's gaze, and his own eyes closed in defeat. Bomthe nodded again. Spone drew his left arm up, then across the line of his prisoner's taut throat in a single, swift arc.

For an instant, nothing happened. Then blood welled up along the cut that Spone's knife had drawn, and before Marius could draw breath, began to flood down vel Brinken's throat and into the hairs of his chest. He jerked once, then again, his legs and arms flapping spastically as his body fought to retain the life that flooded out of him. Spone held him effortlessly aloft until the last spasmodic movement ceased and he hung in the mate's grip like so much meat on a slaughterhouse hook.

Marius tore his gaze away from the dead man, and saw Bomthe staring at him, his face an expressionless mask. As they matched gazes, Bomthe smiled, a tiny creasing at the corner of his lips.

"First Mate Spone."

"Sir."

"Carry out sentence."

"Aye, sir."

The big man took a step towards the edge of the deck, dragging the two living prisoners, now screaming in uncontrolled terror, behind him. He lifted vel Brinken's corpse without apparent effort, dragging the next in line upwards as the short chain tightened. With one flick of his enormous arm, Spone threw the dead man overboard.

The chain between vel Brinken and the next prisoner tautened as his dead body went over the side, immediately pulling him hard against the railing. He stuck there a moment. Marius heard the crunch as the neck brace pulled up hard under the prisoner's jaw, stretching his neck and pulling him off balance so far that he held on to the railing only by the tips of his whitened fingers. He struggled against it for a moment, but the dead man's weight was too much. With a short, strangled cry, he was over the edge, his grip tight enough to pull a thin strip of wood from the railing. The last in line toppled over and screamed as he was dragged across the deck to the edge, hands feebly scratching at the floor beneath him. But the momentum ahead of him was too great. In one scrabbling, screaming pile of limbs he went up and over. Three splashes sounded in quick succession, and then there was only silence, and the thin trail of blood left behind by the final captive. Marius and Bomthe stared at each other across the spectacle. Then Bomthe turned, and motioned Marius to follow him. Still not speaking, they stood side by side at the ship's edge and peered down at the dark water below.

Where the prisoners had hit Marius could see the frothing passage of at least a dozen sharks, their bodies sliding around each other as they beat the sea to white foam. Gobbets of meat floated to the surface to be instantly snatched and swallowed by the writhing mass.

"They follow the ship wherever we go," Bomthe said. "Much easier to feed from the scraps we throw overboard than spend days in fruitless hunting." When Marius said nothing he tilted his head, and observed him from the corner of his eye. "Who suffered the worst punishment do you think?" He straightened, while his passenger continued to watch the feeding frenzy below. "Master Spone. Escort Mister Helles back to his cabin, please."

"Sir." Spone stepped forward, and laid a hand on Marius' shoulder. "This way, Mister Helles."

Marius turned away from the carnage and walked back to his cell in silence.

The Faraway Isles, according to those who have endured the eight month journey there and back and lived, is a veritable paradise on Earth. Long, sweeping beaches of golden sand edge forests of such startling beauty that syphilitic artists form orderly queues simply for the chance to paint them and shag the magnificent dark-skinned natives that populate the islands in a heavenly parade of innocence and sensual delight. Trees hang heavy with fruit in a rainbow's profusion of colours, the tastes and textures of which leave such ordinary repasts as rabbit stew and cabbage potage as ashes in the mouth, and the crystalline blue waters of the shallow bays provide swarms of soft-boned fish that swim straight into a fisherman's net, and whose flesh flakes so perfectly that once you have tasted it, the mere act of fishing resembles a desecration of gods will. Assuming the listener is not lost within thoughts of such beauty that questioning them becomes impossible, it is often tempting to ask why the storyteller returned to tell the tale, why, indeed, he isn't still lying on those golden sands, eating the perfect fish, and showing the beautiful native girls that little trick he picked up at Madame Mirabella's House of Relaxation. The answer is invariably the same: "The captain caught me."

By contrast, the Dog Crap Archipelago looks exactly how it sounds.

Discovered less than four hundred years ago by the famous Tallian adventurer "Literal" Edmund Bejeevers, the Dog Crap Archipelago lay like a giant turd across the passage between Borgho City and the Faraway isles. Early explorers found nothing there to recommend the place to anybody, and indeed, early maps show a simple ovoid outline with the words "Don't Bother" written inside. A long, dripping string of shallow volcanic outpourings, its only advantage lay in a number of tiny freshwater lakes, and its location, halfway between Borgho and the Isles. They were a perfect place to lie up and replenish water supplies, as well as discard the barrels of waste and refuse that accumulated on the long voyages between ports.

Those early explorers brought rats – which leaped ship at the sight of land – and chickens, which had occasionally escaped their ship-board pens. Pet dogs were thrown overboard by sailors who had tripped over the bloody mutts once too often. Sick cattle were disposed of on the basis that it's bad enough tripping over pet dogs all day without landing face first in liquid cow shit.

The cows shat, the rats ate the garbage, and the discarded pets ate the rats. Seeds fell from pelts, or flew in on the wind. The islands were home to no natural predators. In truth, they had no natural *anything* before those early explorers arrived.

Within three hundred years, the first natives arrived.

Refugees from who knows where, it was left to the idle to wonder at what kind of society they had fled that a shit-stained island full of feral dogs and rats seemed a better alternative. But arrive they did, and claimed the archipelago for themselves, and began trading with the, frankly, astonished traders who still stopped there and were more than happy to start charging for the things they had previously thrown away for free. In no time at all, the Dog Crap Archipelago enjoyed a status in trading circles that "Literal" Bejeevers could hardly have envisaged, and which had otherwise escaped his other major discoveries.

It was Captain Bomthe's intention to spend a week on the main island, to sell their waste and restock their stores with fresh water and fruit-gorged cattle carcasses. It was Marius' intention to stay in his cabin and ignore the entire escapade. As a plan it was foolproof, for all of seventy-two hours.

Marius was lying on the floor, concentrating on a most ingeniously drawn pamphlet he'd discovered wedged into the space between two loose wall planks regarding the Queen of Tal and various members of her palace guard, when the sound of arriving cattle was replaced by a much more urgent commotion. Marius closed the pamphlet and lay with it on his chest, listening to the drama outside. He was trying to decide whether to rise and see whether the change in atmosphere was worth his attention, when there came a thunderous banging on his door, and Figgis came barrelling in.

"Captain's compliments, sir," he said, drawing up short and averting his eyes, breathing heavily. "Your presence is required on the poop deck as soon as possible, if you please. Very important, sir."

Marius had rolled over and pulled his hood forward so that the young cabin boy could not see his face. He spoke round the corner of the hood. "Thank you, Figgis. I'll be along presently."

The young messenger shifted his feet nervously but kept his ground. He stared at the planking before him. Marius sighed.

"Should I apologise, Master Figgis?"

Still the boy said nothing. Marius counted to three, then pulled himself up and turned his back on the waiting figure. He peeked at the skin beneath the edge of his glove, and saw it was grey, and rotting.

"For what it's worth, I hope it wasn't too severe a

beating," he said, staring at his deadened flesh. "There will be worse once you're an adult." He smoothed down his glove, and straightened. "Away with you, now, and leave me to get ready."

In truth, he had nothing to do, but the less the crew knew of his particular habits, the safer he would feel. He *might* be able to survive a one way dip in the ocean, but he had no desire to walk all the way to the Far-away Isles underwater, or to discover how much of his flesh would survive the pursuing fish. Figgis silently left, closing the door gently behind him, and Marius sat on the edge of the ledge until he had estimated a sufficient time to wash and towel himself down. Only then did he stand, and emerge into the blast of the midday sun.

The deck of the *Minerva* looked like the aftermath of a particularly vicious bar fight. The planks were awash with blood, and teams of navvies swept it over the side with massive-headed brooms. Towards the prow, the cargo doors were open. Haunches of meat were being lowered on ropes to the lower deck, where they would be smoked and cured for the journey ahead. Natives from the island ran here and there, carrying baskets of fruit upon their head, sternward along the side of the deck to where Marius knew more open doors would lead to yet more storage decks. The ever-present es-caped chickens screeched as they careened across deck, the mate's boy and his cronies in hot pursuit. Every-thing was bedlam as a hundred or more bodies wove and ducked past each other, orders were shouted and acknowledged, and the casual brutality of the officers was played out with languid good nature upon the

straining backs of the crew. Overhead, the sun dominated yet another cloudless sky, adding its vindictive
heat to the sticky atmosphere on board. Marius shaded
his eyes with one gloved hand, and offered thanks to
no god at all that being dead absolved him from the
need to sweat. There was enough stench of unwashed
humanity already without him adding to it.

"Ah, Mister Helles. My thanks for joining us." Captain Bomthe swung down from the poop deck to stand
beside Marius. Marius glanced at him, and once again
marvelled at how a man could stand in the midst of
carnage and stink and yet look as if he had just
emerged from a leisurely tea with the nobility.

After a week of observing his ever-present starched
uniform and stainless shirts, Marius had formed a fantasy: a cupboard in the captain's quarters, with six
months' worth of identical uniforms on hangers, each
one bearing a tag describing the day of the week to be
worn, the exact time to be discarded, and the level of
smugness to which the captain was entitled. Today was
a day of high smug, judging by the tilt of the captain's
smoothly-shaved chin. At least I can match *that*, Marius thought, and I don't have to risk a cut to do so. He
nodded, and turned his attention back to the deck.

"Are you ready to depart, then?"

"I'm sorry?" Marius turned from the spectacle
below. "What do you mean, depart?"

"Didn't Figgis explain?" The captain frowned. "I told
him to fetch you." He tutted. "I'm going to grow weary
of beating that boy."

I doubt he'd say the same if the positions were
reversed, Marius thought, but kept silent.

"Perhaps you might fill in any missing details," he said instead. The captain tilted onto his toes, then brought his heels back onto the deck with a crisp thump and began to stride down stairs and across the deck. Marius hurried to keep pace.

"We're to go ashore," the captain said as they walked. "Big occasion for the natives, don't you know. Death of the high muckamuck. Honoured guests of the royal family. Observe the funeral, eat the meal, swear in the new head banana, that sort of thing."

"Dead king?" Marius stopped in his tracks. Behind him a cow mooed, and he jumped forward before it could butt him out of the way. He stared towards the shore, blinking in shock as a hundred different possibilities presented themselves for consideration.

"Yes. Quite sudden, apparently. Probably choked on a monkey or something." Bomthe chuckled, and Marius assumed that the comment passed for humour wherever he came from. "Anyway, we're for the off if we want to be presented to the wife and kids before teatime. I'll be representing the Kingdom of Scorby, naturally, and you…"

"Yes?"

"Well, you paid for the trip. Thought you might like a free feed into the bargain." Bomthe laughed again at his natural wit, and resumed his walk. "Come along now. Mustn't be late. They may not be real royalty but I still don't fancy a spear in the belly, yes?"

The belly wasn't the first part of Bomthe that Marius would stick a spear into, but he dogged the captain's heels and followed him across deck to a rope ladder and down into a rowboat tied alongside. He'd had no desire to set foot on the island, but this new development merited all sorts of investigation. He may not be a real king, Marius decided as they pulled away from the side of the *Minerva*, but he'd do.

# FIFTEEN

The island was not only as bad as it sounded, Marius thought as he stood ankle-deep in the scummy wash and watched sailors pull the longboat up the rocky beach, it was as bad as it could be made to sound. They had landed in the centre of a curving beach that provided the only stretch of sand on this side of the island, and now stood exposed on a wind-scoured strip of grey pebbles. Behind them lay a fringe of whitened, low-lying scrub and a few stunted trees that leaned over in the wind like pensioners at a soup kitchen. At the far end of the beach, in the dubious shelter of a small, twisted copse, a collection of huts marked the beginnings and end of human habitation at this end of the peninsula.

As far as Marius could tell, none of the pathetic flora of the island had been harmed in the construction of the village. Instead, it appeared as if the huts had been cobbled together from whatever flotsam had washed up on the shore over the last three hundred years, as well as a smattering of items that could only have been stolen from visiting ships. Surely, no captain would willingly let go of the map board that served as the window shutter of that hut there, for example, or the collection of hand mirrors that tinkled in the wind from their current duty as some sort of half-assed mobile in that hut over there's half-assed garden.

A group of barely-dressed natives lounged under the trees, watching with disinterest as the crew swore and strained to drag the boat above the water line. Marius stared back at them, a look of deeply-held pain scrawled across his features. Eventually, the sounds of cursing withered away, and Marius glanced over his shoulder to see Bomthe lining the sailors up into some sort of ragged double line. He turned, and nodded to Marius with a smile.

"Shall we proceed, Mister Helles?"

Marius raised a hand towards the village. "Where? There?"

"That's right. Stand *up*, Wellings!" He slapped at one of the slouching crew members, who responded by stiffening almost an entire centimetre. "The King's family will be expecting us."

"You're kidding me."

"Kidding?" Bomthe's smile was as nasty as the wind. "Why would I kid, Mister Helles? This village controls the only safe embarkation point on the entire southern peninsula. Any trade that comes, comes through here. In local terms, these people are the rich and noble. If we wish to continue trading with them, we need to make with the nicey-nicey. Adjust that scabbard, Pergess, or you'll be using it to carry your pego." From the speed with which the sailor in question complied, Marius was only half-sure the threat was idle. Finally satisfied with the comportment of his troops, Bomthe swung around and raised his hand. "Ready, men. Mister Helles?"

Grudgingly, Marius trudged out of the surf to stand at Bomthe's side.

"Forward!" As one, the detachment strode ahead, or rather, they shuffled and slid across the rolling pebbles beneath their feet, stifling whatever curses sprung to their chapped and bitten lips. The natives waited until the column was almost upon them. Then one of the older men leaned down and cuffed a boy sitting at his feet, who slowly rose and wandered down into the village, kicking at the ripples of sand that marked the short path.

"Halt!" Bomthe commanded. The column shuffled to a stop. Marius stared into the centre of the half dozen huts. A small trestle had been erected in front of the largest of them, a pile of foot-long strips of bark to one side. Arranged along the table's length were more strips. On top of them lay a range of unidentifiable lumps of various dull colours. Past the trestle, a spit turned over a small fire, staffed by a bare-breasted teenage girl who frowned with concentration as she pulled something from one nostril with an extended finger and flicked it into the fire. The creature on the spit could have been no more unmistakably a dog if it still wore its tags. Marius swallowed, and was answered by the taste of bile.

"Now what?" he muttered.

"Now we wait for the new King to make his appearance," Bomthe replied, "and invite us to join the splendour of his inauguration feast."

"You make a magnificent liar." Marius couldn't take his eyes from the slowly rotating dog. The young cook caught his eye, snorted, and spat something thick into the flames.

"I am a diplomat," Bomthe said, following Marius' gaze, "and a servant of the King. Such service has its occasional sacrifices."

In the moments before Marius could formulate a reply, the new King chose to make his entrance. To their credit, none of the sailors so much as smirked as the balding, pudgy monarch swept out of the largest hut, his crown of bark and nut casings sitting high on his round head, a cloak made from strips of what looked to Marius like a variety of old naval uniforms trailing behind his loin cloth-clad body. He paused to look over his shabby dominion, then stared with regal haughtiness at the assembled company. Bomthe stepped forward, removed his hat, and bowed low. He glared upwards at Marius, and with a sigh, Marius copied his action. There was a shuffle behind him as the sailors did likewise.

The King waited until even Marius was beginning to feel an uncomfortable stretching sensation in the small of his back, then issued a command in a voice that resembled a small child experiencing explosive di-arrhoea. Two natives armed with spears emerged from either side of the hut and tapped Bomthe on the shoulders. He straightened, and motioned his men to do the same. Two sailors from the rear of the cohort stepped forward, bearing between them a sea trunk that had seen better days. Better months, if truth be told, Marius thought as he gazed at it. The sailors laid it down before the King and opened the lid, stepping back quickly to their place closest to the point of escape. The monarch bent his portly frame down into the open trunk until he disappeared behind the open lid. Marius risked a glance at Bomthe.

"An inauguration gift," the captain muttered.

The King straightened and raised his hands. Hanging from them were several rows of brightly coloured bead necklaces. Marius bit his upper lip.

"From Manky Glenis in the Pudding Square markets more like," he mumbled back. "I'd recognise her tat anywhere."

"It is never unwise to be prudent in one's outlay," Bomthe replied as the King raised his booty high above his head and called to his people in a joyous voice. "Besides, one must tailor one's gifts to the expectations of the receiver. It would seem we have made the right estimation in this instance." Before them, the King was busy rummaging through the trunk, dispensing penny rings and five-for-a-thruppence bead bracelets to the stream of islanders who had appeared from nowhere at his call. He looked over to Bomthe and nodded with expansive humour, a gesture the captain accepted with a small incline of the head. "It would seem we are now welcome in His Majesty's realm."

"Oh, happy day."

"Don't underestimate the value of our trade here, Mister Helles," Bomthe said as he turned and dismissed the men, who quickly sought the shade of the nearby trees, and the company of the island girls who were keen to show off their new jewellery to the tanned sailors so admiring of their charms. "We do very well from our commercial endeavours here. The archipelago is a source of almost unending bleaching and heating elements."

Marius stared at him while understanding took long seconds to register. "Shit?" he finally asked. "You trade for shit?"

"I believe the commercial term is guano," Bomthe strode into the square and greeted the new ruler with a solid embrace and double-handshake. "And I have it on good authority that is it very high-grade shit indeed." The king let him go and turned to crush Marius in a similar embrace. "This end of the island alone is a veritable gold mine of commercial-grade heating and bleaching material. I'm sure you can see why."

The King let go of Marius and stepped into the centre of the village. He clapped his hands several times in quick succession. Immediately, each of the islanders turned their attention to him. He shot off a quick-fire speech and they leaped to their feet and began busying themselves in diving into huts and pulling out items of furniture. Young girls ran behind the huts and returned with large fruits of various descriptions balanced upon their heads. Bomthe took Marius by the elbow and ushered him toward the table.

"I believe we are invited to join the inauguration feast," he said, "where it would be considered advisable to eat everything that is put before us and drink anything we are offered, do I make myself clear?"

"Like good diplomats, eh?"

"It does involve sacrifices."

They sat at the King's right hand and the villagers

and sailors intermingled around a series of planks laid on the sand before the table. Four natives emerged from behind the largest hut, carrying a long bark platter between them, upon which rested a mound of cooked meat. They laid it before the King, who piled his own plate high then indicated to Bomthe and Marius to do the same. They complied, and once they had finished, the rest of the village paraded past the table to take a meagre share for themselves. Once everyone was seated, the King clapped his hands, and the village fell to eating. Teenage girls passed amongst them, handing out small quantities of stunted and burned vegetables. Between mouthfuls, Marius glanced over at the sullen child still turning the spit.

"What about that?" he asked Bomthe, indicating the turning meat. "I thought that was dinner."

Bomthe raised his eyebrows. "Hm. I'll ask." He leaned over to the king, and asked a quick question in the native tongue. The King replied, and looked over to Marius, laughing. Bomthe smiled in return. "That is for the children," he said. "The late monarch's favourite hunting dog, apparently. The natives hope the children will ingest its loyalty and cunning along with its flesh."

"Huh. Then what are we eating, his favourite horse?"

Bomthe stared down at his plate and blinked several times before leaning back to the King to ask another question. Upon the reply he straightened, and stared out beyond the huts to the distant sea. He swallowed, then nodded to himself as if confirming some long-held inner thought. Marius noticed the action and stopped scooping the greasy meat into his mouth.

"What?"

"We are not eating the late monarch's favourite horse," Bomthe said carefully.

"Well, no, I hardly expected…"

"We are, in fact, eating the late monarch."

Marius felt what little blood remained in his face drain into his boots. "What?" he asked in a voice suddenly devoid of moisture.

"The islanders believe that it will imbue them with his strength, his nobility, and his wisdom."

"You mean they're…"

Very deliberately, with the King's gaze firmly upon him, Bomthe reached down and scooped up a handful of meat. He placed it in his mouth, chewed several times and swallowed.

"Be a good fellow, Mister Helles," he said, eyes fixed upon the horizon. "Eat your wisdom."

Marius stared at Bomthe, then at the King, the islanders, the sailors lounging around the village square laughing and stuffing their faces with handfuls of dripping meat. "But…"

"Trade with this village is worth several times more than the lives of everyone on board my vessel. You and I included. We are guests at the most important occasion this archipelago has seen in more than thirty years. If we offer such a gross insult as to refuse to dine with the new King, what do you think would happen to that trade?" Bomthe scooped up another gobbet of meat and ate it, closing his eyes as he swallowed. "What do you think our lives would be worth then?"

"You'd be surprised," Marius muttered. He reached down, picked up a few strands of the stringy meat, and held it up in salute to the King, who was looking around Bomthe at Marius with a curious half-smile on his lips.

"Ah well," he said, smiling back, "let's hope they serve you with chips, mate."

"If you like your tongue," Bomthe said in the same equal tone he'd been using since discovering the identity of their meal, "I'd suggest you keep it still." He slid the last of his meat into his mouth and swallowed. "You're on a very thin plank as it is, Mister Helles."

Whilst Marius was considering how wise it would be to push the conversation any further the King rose, cleared his throat for attention, and phlegmed up another speech. Children scurried to clear away the meal, much to the relief of Marius. The King sat down, elbowing Bomthe with a dirty chuckle and pointing to the door of the largest hut. The curtains across its entrance swished open, half a dozen naked girls ran out, and the dancing began.

Being dead should have meant, as far as Marius had considered the matter, that blood ceased to flow throughout his body. Sure, Keth had shown him otherwise, but Keth was different, and besides, he hadn't really had a handle on the state of his being then, and after all, that was *Keth*. And yet, as the girls before him gyrated and folded their nubile, sweating bodies into shapes he'd only ever seen formed by clowns making balloon animals for children in the marketplace, at least one part of his body exhibited proof that blood was flowing into it at a furious rate indeed.

A dancer shimmied up to the table, bent back at an angle that intimated a loss of at least three vertebrae, breasts swinging from side to side like passengers on a running camel. The King whooped in a most unregal way and leaned forward to slap her on the stomach, indicating to Bomthe that he should do the same. Bomthe complied with nowhere near the reserved air he had displayed during the meal.

The girl slid along the table and presented the swaying vista of her body to Marius. He swallowed, remembering the first time he had seen Keth. He had been alone, a stranger to the city, and the tavern window had shown the only light along the whole posh side of the docks. He'd squeezed himself into a booth with a pint of bottom scrumpy, and watched as the dancing girls moved through the crowd, sliding from one dropped farthing to the next, displaying themselves for those who would pay only to imagine, and marking out those who would pay more, later, to touch. Keth had swayed out of the crowd, back arched, hips swinging in long, slow circles, and leaned over the table towards him, long hair gently tickling the sides of his face, ends dipping into his flagon. And with no money, and no contacts, he'd gone out that night and found a game of penny ante, and the next night a game of three card poke, and the next joined in a plot to rumble a distributor of fake Tallian art treasures… and every night, every penny he earned, he brought back to the tavern, and waited with his solitary pint of dregs, waited for Keth to come swaying out of the crowd…

"No!" He pushed himself back from the trestle,

knocking his stool to the sand and standing, shivering, under the shocked gazes of Bomthe and the King. The dancer worked a shrug into her movements, a little dip of her shoulders that said "Whatever. Your loss, pal," and slithered over to the first of the sailors laying on their mats. Bomthe raised his eyebrows.

"A problem, Mister Helles?"

"No. No, I…" Marius wiped a hand across his eyes.

"Not your type, sir?" Marius heard the insinuation in Bomthe's tone, saw the smile. "Shall I call Figgis?"

"No, that's not… To hell with you." Marius swung way and stalked out of the circle of light, into the dark at the edge of the village. He stopped once he was around the corner of a hut and leaned his head against the rough dirt wall. Only then did he let out the breath he had been holding.

"Gods damn it," he breathed. "What the hell is *wrong* with me? Why am I even breathing?"

He straightened himself, took several more. "Just get through this," he muttered. "Just get through this and get back. Get it sorted." He nodded his agreement to the small voice at the back of his mind that was whispering all the things he would do once he got through this and got back. Yes, make it all right. Yes, take her away. Yes, even that. Even settle down.

He stepped back towards the feast, his composure restored, ready to make his apologies and see out the rest of the evening, then stopped just outside the row of torches stuck in the sand. Bomthe and the King were standing, deep in conversation with the girl whose dancing had sent Marius into his reverie. She nodded, and Bomthe passed her something which she quickly tucked into the waistband of the tiny grass skirt she was now wearing. The King waved his fingers and she left them, ducking between two torches a few feet from Marius. She turned when she saw him lurking in the shadows and smiled, coming towards him with one arm held out as if to take his hand.

"I'm… I'm sorry," Marius said, taking a step backwards. "It's not that you're not… desirable. It's just that, well… I'm sort of…"

She laughed, and lunged forward, quickly grabbing his hand and gripping it with a strength that belied her tiny frame. She smiled in a way that was far too lascivious to be mistaken, and let go his hand, patting him gently on his undying erection, then stepping past him, away from the raucous party.

"But… I…" Marius glanced back into the light, saw Bomthe and the King staring at the shadows in which he stood, and pursed his lips. He felt his face crease in anger.

"All right," he said. "All right." One more thing to make right when he got back. Just one more wouldn't hurt.

The girl laughed, and skipped away along one of the myriad sandy paths that criss-crossed the edges of the village, leading into the hinterlands of the archipelago. Marius watched her rounded buttocks as they bounced away from him, and a feral grin split his lips.

"I will," he said, and took up the chase.

# SIXTEEN

The island sand was a curse, sent to torment Marius by a vengeful and sadistic god. It shifted underfoot with every step, twisting Marius' passage so that every inch of forward movement was a victory won against the odds. By the time he reached the top of the hill it was as if he had chosen the longest route on purpose. The native girl waited with one hand on her hip, a smile that was part sex, part derision, clear in the dark. Marius cursed under his breath and redoubled his effort. The sand fought him with a million fingers, until he stumbled and landed face first at her feet. At any other time he'd be happy with that position, but for once, he took no pleasure in the view.

"You're doing this deliberately," he said, and found confirmation in her laugh.

She tossed her head, indicating a random pile of branches and leaves at the edge of the track, bunched against the base of a giant tree. Marius stared at it until, slowly, he began to make out some order amongst the detritus. If he assumed that gap to be a door, and those smaller gaps as windows...

"Your hut?"

She nodded , and moved towards it. This time, Marius did take a moment to admire the view, before climbing to his feet and tottering after her. A heat haze hovered around the hut, a living thing that Marius could see shimmering in the falling dark. Ignoring the burning in his calves, and refusing to question why he should even feel such a burning in the first place, he clenched his jaw, and stalked towards the opening that now yawned wide amongst the leaves, awaiting his entrance. The girl slid inside. Marius paused at the opening, letting the stink of sweat, foreign skin, and thick cooking odours assail him. When he was sure he could enter without gagging, he covered his mouth and nose with one gloved hand and stuck his head inside.

"Are you in there?" he called, frowning at the uncertainty in his voice. Where else could she be? Marius decided he didn't want to know the answer. A chuckle rose from the darkness, startling him. He had heard similar sounds before. Animals caught in traps, recognising their fate as he walked toward them out of the bush, preparing for one last fight before death.

"Stay outside if the dark frightens you so," a voice said in perfect Scorbish. "Otherwise, come in and stop wasting my night."

Marius scowled in a flash of embarrassment. He ducked his head, counted to three, and stepped inside before pausing, nerves alive to the thought of attack. Slowly, details emerged from the murk. Marius gasped, stumbling forward in astonishment.

From the outside, the hovel was no larger than the types of shelter street children build from whatever refuse they can liberate from the back of fish stalls and printing houses in the bigger cities, and not quite as well constructed. Two adults of Marius' size would have grown far more intimate than polite society would accept just by squeezing themselves into the same space, a prospect Marius had found appealing and repulsive in equal measure.

Now that he was inside, Marius didn't know whether to be disappointed or terrified that such an outcome was so unlikely – this was no dirt-covered hole dug out between roots. It was a room. A proper room. Not large, not by the standards of normal rooms, but still, it was considerably larger than the bundle of branches that formed its outer walls. And it had walls, real walls, wattle and daub structures that reached up to a thatched roof overhead.

"How…?"

Again the laugh sounded out. Marius took another step forward, then another, until he stood in the centre of the hut. Slowly he turned in a complete circle, taking in his surroundings.

Captain Bomthe had complained, often enough that Marius could recite it verbatim as he lay on his cot listening to the man on the deck above, of the incessant thefts visited upon the *Minerva* by the natives. In the three days they had been at anchor, enough supplies were lost that they would barely be replaced by the gains made from their stopover. Proof of their losses crowded the space around Marius: countless items, small and large, worthless and valuable, piled one upon the other with no thought for order, fragility, or purpose.

Marius completed his circle, cataloguing the contents with practiced, mathematical precision: urns; coats; bags of flour; boxes overflowing with beads, brooches, and rings; even three of the new arbalests being trialled by the King of Scorby's personal guard; all lay heaped together like haphazard spoils of war, spreading out from the walls in an ankle-thick carpet. Whilst the new King paraded his gewgaws down upon the sand, a small fortune had bypassed his gaze on the way up to this hovel.

"It will all be gone by the time you return to your boat, dead man," the voice cackled, as if reading his mind. "Do not bother yourself with such trifles. You have something for me?" A dark lump in the far corner stirred, and unfolded from between the piles of refuse. Two stick-like arms emerged from either side of a bundle of rags, dragging the mass into the centre of the room.

Disturbed air flowed over Marius, and despite the deadness of his sense of smell he gagged. The pile of rags scuttled forward like an angry insect, the sharpness of its movement making him stumble backwards until his shoulders hit the wall. The hut shook from the impact. Marius threw his arms out, absurdly afraid of burial underneath whatever constituted the outer surface of the roof. The creature reared up, gripping the material of his jacket, using the leverage to pull itself upwards until it stood on hind legs, pinning him against its dry, fetid body. Slowly, like some sort of predatory tortoise, a vague approximation of a head emerged.

Marius tried to speak, to offer some protest, but his

voice has deserted him – the beast was an old woman, old beyond belief. If the scarring of her wrinkled face could be counted an accurate witness, then there were rock formations at the base of fissures inside the Ageless Mountains that had fewer candles on their birthday cake. What Marius had taken to be an animal's pelt was a thin blanket, which did nothing to lessen its filthy, bestial nature. A hand, more claw than flesh, waved about in short pecks, indicating a spot in the dirt by his feet.

Marius had never believed in witchcraft. Not really, at least, as much as an upbringing in a household with two Neopagan parents and an Old Godsman grandmother would allow. He had known too many wizards, and been a conjuror too many times himself, to count magic as anything more than a combination of herbalism, sleight of hand, and a need for money. But this was different, somehow. Marius was used to hungry conmen trying to ingratiate themselves with their chosen sucker. There was something wrong when a witch was properly creepy.

"Sit," the old woman commanded. Marius lowered himself, imitating her cross-legged hunch. Halfway down he realised what he was doing and coughed. Great, he thought. Now I look *and* sound like her. The crone crooked a finger, beckoning him closer. Unable to choose between myriad misgivings, Marius complied.

"What does a dead man want with me?" she asked, her breath washing over Marius like the plague. Ignoring the burning sensation at the back of his eyes, Marius replied.

"Well, actually, I was following..."

The crone chuckled, and Marius stopped, aware of how ludicrous his unformed desire had been. Even alive, he'd have needed gold of some description to bed a woman such as the one he followed. In fact, only Keth had ever… He stopped that line of thought before it could progress.

"You have gold?" the witch asked, her voice suddenly sharp. Marius blinked in surprise.

"How did you know I…?"

"Ishga would not bring you unless you had something to trade. And I do not want your clothes." She laughed again, a low, dirty sound that turned Marius' lips downward in prudish disapproval. "Well? What have you got for me?"

Marius reached into his jerkin and removed the two wedding rings he had lifted in Borgho City. He held them out on his palm.

"Are these enough?"

She viewed them with a curt "*Tch*", and he lapsed into an embarrassed silence. This woman was nearly an animal. And here he was, a man of the world: sophisticated, educated – well, knowledgeable, at any rate – at home in any city in the civilized world, holding out trinkets like a child hoping for approval. He almost closed his hand and removed the offering. He couldn't say why he didn't.

"Well, what does she normally charge?" As soon as the words were out of his mouth, he regretted them. The old woman tilted her head and glared out of the corners of her eyes at him, and he realised with sudden certainty that this transaction was no longer about buying the sex of an island stranger. There was something deeper being bargained for, and he was momentarily too afraid to continue the transaction. Before he could act on his fear, however, the old lady pointed an unreasonably long nail, and speared the rings, holding them up to her eye.

"What's wrong with them?"

Marius stammered, and half-rose before finding his composure. Good gods, he thought, what is wrong with me? This is simple market negotiation, nothing more. You're acting like a naughty grandchild. The normal course, under these circumstances, was to imagine your adversary naked. It had the effect of re- moving the silver from their words, revealing them as the same sweaty, greedy lump of flesh as the rest of us. Imagining this woman naked was the last thing Marius wanted. He sniffed, and gathered his wits.

"Nothing," he said, deepening his voice and speak- ing slower. An old trick: control the pace of the conversation, increase the gravitas of your words. "I inherited them from an aunt, a spinster who died be- fore she had the chance to wear them in commitment to a man."

"Hmm." The crone lifted them from his hand, cupped them in her palm, and closed her eyes. "An in- teresting man, your aunt. The beard suits him. Not easy, affording a suit on a butcher's wages." She opened her eyes, look straight at Marius. "She turned him down, when he could not present her with a ring. A lonely, broken man, your poor aunt."

The rings disappeared into her rags and she leaned forward, until their faces were separated by less than a foot. Her smoke-yellowed eyes captured his with a glare so piercing he glanced away in case she read something he didn't want revealed.

"Why are you here, dead man?"

"I…" Marius peered around the hut and wondered why himself, just for a moment. "The girl, the one that brought me here…"

She laughed at that, a raw cackle that took an eternity to dissolve into coughing. She hawked, and spat a gob of phlegm past his ear.

"Been that long, has it, boy? Can't get a girl from the village, not looking like you. Maybe even *they* have taste, eh?" She sniggered, and Marius felt the life leave his face. "No, it is not that. You know that yourself. If you had simply wanted her, you could have rolled her on the sand. You allowed yourself to be led here. Your soul recognises the purpose, even if your mind does not."

Marius closed his eyes and let her words sink into his skin. Finally, "No, you're right. Not that." His shoulders slumped. He had hoped to get through this without admitting his fear aloud. It seemed he had no choice. Whatever this old woman was, she knew his mind better than he did. No hope of escape, then, without the penalty of disclosure.

"Where I come from…" he waved a hand in the vague direction of "away". "They've charged me… this… this task. I can't do it. It's impossible, a ridiculous thing. And I don't think… I don't think I can escape. I need to know…"

He straightened himself again. Do this properly. Negotiate from strength, and if you don't have strength, fake it.

"I need to see my future. I need to know what path to take. I have to escape. But I need to know: can I get it back?"

The island woman stared at him for ageless seconds, her hand sneaking out of its wrap to juggle the rings between her fingers. Marius stilled himself, lest the noise of his fidgeting influence her decision. Finally she nodded once, and rose, bones popping. She scampered over, drew him to his feet by the simple expedient of grabbing his jaw with one claw and pulling him upwards. He loomed over her, his jaw several inches above the top of her head. Still, she didn't let go. She examined him, running an experienced eye along his height. He had the unpleasant sensation of being measured up for a pot.

"Undress."

"What?"

"Get out of your clothes."

"Hang on a tick…" For no reason he could think of, Marius was terrified at the idea of standing before her, naked and exposed to her judgement. "Is that really necessary? There's a time and a place, you know."

"Oh yes," the old crone laughed, "Any time and any place, as long as you can dive between our young girls' legs." She waved a claw at his clothes. "Clothes cover your true nature, dead man. Pretend to be what you are not, or learn what you really are. Your choice." She nodded toward the world outside, and he understood the implication. Either lose his modesty, and undress, or make his way back to the ship with questions unanswered. He drew himself up, and refusing to meet her gaze, began to remove the clasp of his cape.

She waited with arms crossed, eyeing him as he disrobed. He saw the speculation in her stare and turned away, ignoring the queasiness in the pit of his gut. She made no comment at the sight of his hairless chest, the thinness of his legs, the length of his manhood. Marius had never been at ease with his weaknesses. Without money, or beer, or any of the thousand other shields he could place between him and scorn, he was as exposed as he had ever been in front of a woman, and he did not like the sensation. He folded each piece of clothing as he removed it, laying it in a pile on the ground behind him. When he was finished he stood with arms crossed over his chest, shivering despite the oppressive heat. The crone nodded in approval.

"Now you look like a man, and not a shrouded corpse, hmm?"

He ignored the remark, staring past her at a cat-o-nine-tails folded like a sleeping snake against a far corner of the hut. The witch clucked her tongue, then shot out a hand and grabbed his testicles in a grip like old hardwood.

"Hey!" The reaction to pull away was automatic, and he immediately regretted it. Her hand did not move, and the pain forced his knees to lock together, lest he fall to the ground and be suspended from her hand by his balls.

"Stand still, boy," she whispered, her mouth at ear level as he curled over in pain. "Where else do you think your future springs from?"

She tightened her grip. With the other hand, she reached out to enfold his member. Despite her age, the warmth of her grip did the job. He felt his member rise.

"Oh, for the gods'–"

"Shush."

"I was kind of hoping that Ishga…"

"I said *shush*." She squeezed, and Marius shushed. In less than a minute he spurted up her arm. Marius kept his eyes closed, hating himself for wanting more of her knowing fingers. When finally he was able to trust himself to speak, his question was less sarcastic, and more pleading, than he hoped.

"Are you finished?"

"Almost."

She shifted her grip on his testicles. While Marius did his best not to whimper she drew a razor-sharp nail across the skin of his scrotum. Blood dripped, and she caught it in the palm of her hand. Just as Marius was deciding whether or not to faint she let go, and he slumped to both knees, head bowed, fighting the rise of bile. The witch slid her hand down her other arm, depositing his ejaculation onto the blood. She moved around the hut, rummaging amongst the detritus, pulling out earthenware jars and sniffing the contents. One by one she dropped a pinch of their contents into the mixture on her palm. Marius slowly cupped his ruined genitals in his hand.

"Why now?" he silently asked the gods. "All this time with no sensation at all, and you decide now is a good time to give it all back? What have I ever done to *you*?"

The crone crossed the room to squat in front of him. Her free hand grabbed his jaw. Marius lacked the strength to resist. She raised his head and wiped a finger across his wet cheek, transferring the tears of his pain into the goo.

"Good." She clapped her hands together, crushing the contents into a thick globe, kneading it in her palms until it became a round, muddy parcel no bigger than a sheep turd. Once she was finished she placed it in her mouth, and swallowed.

"Well?" Marius managed to croak.

"Wait."

She folded back into her blanket. It wrapped around her as if of its own volition. Within seconds she was once again the anonymous lump he had first seen. Marius knelt before her, uncertain, unwilling to move lest it should break whatever spell she had commenced. The ache in his balls intensified, and he swallowed, trying to keep down the sourness that threatened to fill his mouth. One dose of the old woman's special kind of love had been enough. He had no desire to repeat the dose.

The old woman remained still. Marius turned his head slowly, waiting for some sign to emerge from the gloom. An itch began between his shoulder blades. He ignored it. I am dead, he told himself. The dead don't itch.

The dead don't come either, a voice answered. He ignored that, too.

After an eternity of waiting, the witch raised her head. Marius opened his mouth to speak, then stopped, and simply stared. The old woman was looking through him, and her brow wrinkled in response to sights he could not hope to see. Her eyes had changed colour, he realised with a burst of fear. Where the outsides of her eyes had been a dully milky yellow, borne of years of malnutrition, now they flashed more intensely than the flowers adorning the island hills, and her irises had brightened, moving from dull brown to iridescent red. When she spoke, her voice was deep, and resonant. No longer the whisper of an ancient crone, it filled the hut with the lilt of the young island men who lay on the hillside above the beach each day, taunting the Scorbish sailors as they loaded the boats.

"Death," she said. "A wave of the dead, never ending. They are angry, and you stand at their head. And never peace, never to know the rest that does not end. Never to embrace that which you hold most dear."

"But…" Despite his uncertainty, Marius leaned forward, willing the crone to talk. "My family? My… my mother?" A thought struck him, and he was shocked at the pain it brought with it. "What about Keth?"

"You shall not see them again. And what you will become… it will be a mercy for them. Their memories will be of a man. You are dead to them, as you are to us all."

"But…"

"No more." She shook her head. Her eyes cleared, brown and white bleeding into the iridescent colours. Within seconds they viewed Marius with normal light, and terror.

"I have seen the devil," she breathed, and he was scared more by the way she shrank away from him than by anything he had experienced since he ascended the path to the hovel. "I have seen the ruin of the world." She extended a shaking finger towards the hole through which he had entered. "Leave. Leave me be."

Marius leaned forward, trying to pin her eyes with his own. She slid away, scuttling back into the darkness and raising her hands to cover her face.

"What?" he cried. "What was it? Please, what will I do? What did you see?" He reached out a hand towards her, but she screamed a little girl's scream and batted him away with outstretched claws. He fell back, clutching at where she had caught his wrist. Blood seeped between his fingers, turning sticky beneath his touch as it reached the air. Marius stared down at it. There should not be a flow, could not be.

For a moment he almost screamed as well.

Then he lurched to his feet and stumbled backwards towards the entrance. Eyes still fixed upon the screaming witch he leaned down, and reached to where he had placed his neatly folded clothes. His fingers closed on air. Marius swept his hand across the floor, but all his despairing fingertips met was dirt. He tore his eyes from the crone and looked down. Nothing. He slung his gaze further, slapping the floor in disbelief. His clothes were gone: his cape; his breeches; his jerkin; the multitude of coins he had hidden amongst them; everything *gone*, as if they had never been, stranding him naked in this hole in the ground with a terrified old woman.

"Where are they?" He turned back to her, but the old woman had disappeared as completely as his clothes. Marius leaped across the hut. Then he saw it – a flap, half the size of a normal door, tucked behind a mound of mouldering cow hides. Marius dove over the hides, sliding face first through the open door and onto the rough ground beyond. He scrambled to his feet, and looked about him.

The hillside was empty. No matter which way he turned, only the copse of trees surrounded him. No evidence of human passage greeted his sight. Marius stepped back, and surveyed the witch's hovel. Well, he thought; that explained the magical transformation. From this side, he could see it was just a normal village hut, built onto the rear of a tree of massive girth. The sheer weight of scrub surrounding the tree's base hid it from casual view, but from this side, it was clear.

Strangely, Marius found it a comfort – another instance of "magic" that turned out to be nothing more than sleight of hand and need for money. All of a sudden, free of the oppressive atmosphere inside and the heady mixture of lust and fear, he could slot the old woman into his pantheon of con artists. The normal world reasserted itself around him. He re-entered the hut, and gathered the uppermost cow hide around him like a blanket. Apparently, curing was a skill that had not yet made it to the Dog Crap Archipelago. He swiped a cloud of nipping fleas from his face, and fought his way round to the front of the tree. Then, methodically, and with great care, he kicked the hovel's camouflaging until it was no more than broken twigs underfoot, exposing the hole cut into the hut's wall. With any luck, it would rain before the old bitch could repair the damage.

His task accomplished, Marius strode with as much dignity as he could manage back down the hillside and into the village. No villagers lingered outside as he passed. No smiles greeted him, waiting for a reaction from the foreign visitor. Marius frowned. He had heard about this sort of island's funeral ceremonies. They went on for ages, each new round of gorging followed by another, the feast broken only by pauses to drink whatever noxious alcoholic brew the islanders had managed to ferment from their fruit. Women would dance between courses, men would fight; there would be some sort of manhood ritual involving beds of coal and people's feet. If you were lucky enough to find yourself on the right sort of island, the chances of bedding a nubile, intoxicated virgin girl got higher with every course you survived. At the very least, these things tended to rumble on for three or four days, until everyone was either too sick, too tired, or too shocked at finding themselves married to a teenage girl whose name they could barely remember to continue.

The village should be a repository for drunks, asleep in whatever corner they crawled to before consciousness deserted them. The sounds of coupling should echo from within huts. The words of filthy sailor songs about the King, the Lord of The Stool and a randomly agreed upon number of foreign princesses ought to ring out. There should be impromptu wrestling matches. Weird, foreign islander chants should weave through the night. Drinking, carousing, vomiting, fucking, fighting and eating – where was it all? Not a sound greeted Marius. There was only the wind blowing against the thatches of the huts as he passed. The village was silent, deserted. Something was very, very wrong.

Marius wound his way towards the long cane tables.

They stood empty, the platters of fruit and meat tipped over and lying forgotten on the sand. In the space between them, the King's funeral pyre had burnt down to a mound of glowing coals. Marius stared at it, spotting blackened and shrivelled bones amongst the embers. No chance of shanghaiing a monarch there. He grimaced, and looked beyond the fire to the water's edge.

The natives stood along the shoreline, staring out into the wide ocean. Marius gazed along the rows of immobile strangers. Where were the sailors? He couldn't see a single one amongst the multitude – no Captain Bomthe, no Master Spone, not even young Figgis stood amid the press of bodies. Marius took one involuntary step forward, then another. At the rear of the crowd, a child glanced his way and then shouted. As one, the natives followed the child's pointing arm. Marius stopped, ready to turn on his heel and run as best he could towards the forest. Perhaps, if he were lucky, he could live out the rest of his days as a cow, hidden amongst the roaming herds. But the villagers made no move towards him. They simply stared, emotionless, as he approached step by hesitant step.

The crowd was slightly thicker just down the beach from where he stood. Now it parted, and in the flickering fire light, Marius could make out the new king, surrounded by those who would spend the first days of his reign jockeying for the key advisory positions within what passed for his court. They were standing over a dark lump on the sand. The islanders stared impassively at Marius, then, as one, turned towards it. Marius drew up to the outer edge of the crowd, and glanced down at the child who had raised the alarm. The child stared back at him, no fear on his face at the sight of Marius' dead features. Marius raised his face towards the King. He stood, as expressionless as those around him, his feet planted firmly at either side of the lump's apex. Marius glanced down at it, and sighed.

"Oh, crap."

The witch lay face down, one arm emerging from her filthy robes. Two small rings glinted in her open palm, directly between the King's legs. Her face, what Marius could see of it above the line of the sand, was contorted in terror, her one visible eye wide open and staring. Something small and wet lay next to her mouth. In a certain light, if one were thinking of it in the right way, it might have been mistaken for the end of someone's tongue. Marius tore his gaze away from her face, and found the King staring directly at him.

"Um…" Marius looked around him for any chance of help. Nothing. He pointed at the rings in the witch's hand. "They're mine." Something inside him cringed, and disavowed all knowledge of the idiot who just said that. To make matters worse, his body now seemed to be acting independently of his thoughts, and was edging along the body to crouch and extend a cautious hand between the King's legs.

Marius checked in with his conscious mind, only to find it repeating the phrase "Please don't, please don't, please don't" in a small, frightened voice, so he let it be. To his immense relief, the only thing his hand deigned to touch was the witch's hand. Before he could protest his innocence, his hand snapped up the rings and slipped them onto his little finger. With nothing else to do, he straightened, and found himself face to face, inches from the King.

"I, um..." He smiled, a helpless, crazy thing that crawled across his lower face and refused to leave. He stepped back hurriedly, doing his best not to trip on the witch's body. Desperate to look anywhere but the blank, non-accusing stares of the villagers he glanced over the King's shoulder at the surf breaking on the sand. His jaw fall open, and without thinking he ran forward, bumping past the King and splashing into the surf.

"Where are the boats?" he cried, turning to face the natives. "Where's the captain? Where are the fucking boats?"

The natives were looking past him, out towards the horizon. Marius went very still. He turned to follow their gaze, knowing as he did so what he was about to see.

Out towards the curve of the Earth, barely visible even with Marius' dead sight, a small, muddy patch of white might just be a sail in full billow. As Marius watched, it grew smaller, and dimmer, and faded away completely. The cows hide slipped through Marius' suddenly unfeeling fingers, and fell into the surf with a soft splash. Marius followed it seconds later, his legs giving way beneath him as if cut through by an axe.

"They didn't do *that* by accident, did they?" he asked nobody in particular. Behind him, a multitude of feet shuffled, and slowly slithered across the sand, back towards the village. Within a minute he was alone, naked in the water.

# SEVENTEEN

Marius sat in the sea for two days. Behind him, life for the natives returned to normal. The new King took up residence in his roundhouse. The bones of the old King were recovered from the embers and loaded into a large cane basket, which was taken to a tree at the highest point of the island, overlooking the bay, and hung amongst the remains of all the previous island rulers – no matter what he might face in days to come, the new King would be comforted by the knowledge that his forebears watched over him. The cane tables were broken down and returned to their various huts. The spoiled food was buried where native pigs could root it out later and eat, safely away from the local children. Those who had travelled from outlying villages made their goodbyes and wandered back down the forest paths towards their own homes. The timeless struggle of life on the Dog Crap Archipelago went on, much the same as it had every day of the previous three hundred years.

Marius squatted in the surf, dead eyes staring blindly at the empty horizon. The sun crawled towards its peak, driving the villagers indoors as the relentless heat reached its apex. Marius reddened under the onslaught. The surf slowly deepened, covering his outstretched legs, rising over his waist. The islanders returned to their tasks as the sun began the long descent towards night, and still Marius remained unmoving. Towards dusk, a thousand tiny stirrings announced the arrival of mud crabs from their lairs beneath the sand. They crawled over Marius' immobile form, something in his flesh persuading them against an exploratory nibble.

Birds arrived, attracted by the crabs, and as the water deepened into the night, fish. Still, they ignored Marius and he ignored them. He had no thought for survival. He had no thoughts at all. With no escape, and no possibility of returning to Scorby with a ruler for the dead, he was finally, irrevocably trapped. There was nothing to do but wait. The dead would arrive in their own time. After that, whatever fate could be considered worse than death, well, it would be his.

As the sun rose on the third day, several men emerged from the King's round house and drew an outrigger from its berth amongst the dunes. They dragged it down the beach and into the water a foot or two to Marius' side. A minute or so later a hand fell on his shoulder. Marius shuddered. Slowly, as if having to remember how to do so, his head swivelled around to view the hand, then followed the arm upwards until his eyes met those of the new King. He blinked. The King tilted his head to indicate the boat behind him. Marius' gaze followed the movement. He stared at the boat, then back at the man standing over him. The King took a step backwards and offered his hand. Marius stared at it for several seconds, as if unable to work out what it was. Then, slowly, he reached out and took the hand in his. The King leaned back, and hauled Marius to his feet.

Together they sloshed through the surf towards the boat. The islanders held it steady as the King climbed in and took his seat in the prow, then two of them took Marius by the arms and hauled him inside, seating him halfway along the boat's length. The villagers clambered in behind him. The King barked a short command, and they leaned into their oars, driving the boat past the first line of breakers and out towards the ocean.

It took less than ten minutes to power their way clear of the bay. Marius sat in silence, watching the King's broad back as the waves sped by underneath the boat. He leaned forward into the spray like a pet dog leaning out of a carriage window, face extended high to catch as much of the breeze as possible. The rowers sat around Marius, impassively leaning forward and back with each stroke, looking neither left nor right as they concentrated on their rhythm.

Lulled by the regular pushing of the boat against the water, the heat, and the absence of human sound, Marius found his mind wandering to the journey ahead. There seemed little doubt that the King had decided to chase the *Minerva*. Understandable, really. A dead body on the beach and then Marius sitting in the water, all in the first few hours of his reign – these were the sort of things that could easily be seen as omens of bad things to come. Marius could admire the speed with which the King had arrived at a solution. When in doubt, make a decision, *any* decision, and deal with the consequences later. Any movement is better than none. Advice, he recognised with a rueful grin, he would have done well to follow instead of wasting two days in despair while the ship raced onwards.

The island men seemed indefatigable. Perhaps, if they took the task in shifts and the *Minerva* ran out of wind somewhere along the way, they could catch up. Then what? Wait until night, row silently under the view of the watch, a stealthy ascent of the outer hull? And then… well, then he would make a decision, and deal with whatever consequences arose. No matter the result, he decided, he would remember the King's kindness, and find a way to reward him in suitable fashion.

As Marius was pondering, the boat slowed and came to a stop. The rowers immediately fore and aft of Marius shipped their oars. Marius peered at the surrounding ocean. Featureless water rolled away on all sides. The King had turned in his seat, and was staring impassively at Marius. Marius raised his eyebrows in enquiry.

"Is something wrong?" he croaked, noting with surprise how thin and broken his voice sounded after almost three days of exposure. In response the King looked beyond him, and slowly nodded once.

Immediately, strong arms wrapped themselves around Marius, pinning his arms to his sides. The rower in front of him turned. In one fluid movement he swept up a net from the floor of the boat and jammed it over Marius' head. While Marius was still stunned into immobility, the sack was drawn tight. Hands gripped his ankles. Marius found his senses and began to struggle, but it was too late. He was hoisted from his perch, and swung into the air. The tension on the net ceased. He hit the water, and immediately began to sink.

Marius panicked as the water closed over him, the thrashing of his arms only serving to wrap the net tighter about his head. After a few moments the panic passed. He stilled his body, spread his arms and legs in an effort to retain some buoyancy. Slowly, he reached under the edge of the net and worked his fingers along the edge, lips tightening in rage as he felt the rocks tied onto it to add weight. He pulled it off, and watched it spiral into the dark below him, then flailed about until his head broke the ocean's surface.

The outrigger was already a hundred feet away, the islanders heading back to their beach with all possible speed. Marius spluttered as his head cleared the water and stared after them.

"Bastards!"

The effort of shouting unbalanced him. He slipped beneath the surface, then fought his way above once more.

"Come back, you traitorous…"

He gagged as he took in another mouthful. The islanders ploughed on, not one of them looking back at the spot where Marius floated. Marius watched them getting smaller. Make a decision, he thought. Well, the King had certainly done that. Now, all that was left to Marius was movement. Any movement was better than none. He fixed his eyes upon the slowly diminishing stern of the outrigger, and started to swim after it.

In thirty-eight years of life, Marius had seen cities at every edge of the continent, from the Borgho slums in the east to the great perfumed quarters of Tal in the west, from avenues carved into the cliff faces of the Northern Mountain Kings to the vast mobile tent markets of the caravanserai that endlessly circled the Southern Dry. He had served in more armies than there were countries; watched rebellions begin and be quashed; gulled coins; seduced princesses, whores, mothers and virgins; argued politics with students and talked philosophy with all three emperors; been imprisoned and escaped more times than he could remember; looted battlefields; hunted witches; swindled, lied, cheated, conned, duped, plotted, regretted, defrauded, deceived and always, *always*, stayed one step ahead.

He had never once learned to swim.

The next few minutes were full of movement. Unfortunately for Marius, most of it was downwards. He thrashed his arms with the best of intent, but no matter how he shovelled water behind him, slowly, inevitably, his head slipped below the waves. Still, being dead had its advantages. Removed from the need to breathe, the water around him was no impediment to his industry: he beat on, movements slowed by the weight of the water, and did manage to achieve some form of progress. For every foot of forward momentum he achieved he slipped seven lower, until he glanced down and was embarrassed to see the white sand of the ocean bottom only a foot or so below his dangling feet. Marius ceased his efforts and settled gently onto the sand.

For a moment or two he stood, stupidly staring at the ocean floor. Then he doubled over and placed his hands on his knees. His body shook, and only the tiny fish that darted this way and that around the ocean floor were witness to his fit of hysterical laughter. Eventually the laughter slowed. Marius straightened, and drew his hands across his eyes, which prompted another bout of laughter as he realised the futility of trying to wipe away tears whilst half a fathom below the sea.

When he had at last regained his composure, he set his shoulders, and offered silent thanks that he had not turned around during his landing. He lifted his foot and took a slow step forward, testing his balance against the underwater tides and the increase in pressure. When he had completed it safely he paused, made sure of himself, and took another step. Then he was off, taking sluggish, heavy steps, ignoring the alien life that swirled around him before flitting off on its own particular path. Sooner or later, at some point ahead, the land would begin to rise. He would emerge, like an Old God from the surf, and stride up a beach. And then he would find out where he was, and make plans, and see an end to the events that had taken his life so far out of his control.

Somewhere ahead of him, the King of Scorby lay in state, viewed by thousands of loyal subjects a day, guarded by the finest palace guards, counting down the days to his immolation and ascension to Heaven.

Marius pursed his lips, and began to hum an extremely dirty marching song he had learned in service to the King's father. After walking the length of an ocean, armed with nothing more than two wedding rings and a dirty song, stealing him and delivering him to the armies of the dead would be a doddle.

The dead do not tack. They do not lie becalmed, waiting for a stray wind to propel them. They have no need to turn into a storm, or pull into sheltered bays to effect running repairs. A dead man, finding himself under fifty feet of water, with nothing to do but trudge along in a straight line, mile after mile, stopping neither for sleep nor weather conditions, with only the task of following one foot after another and avoiding coral outcrops and the attentions of any stray predator that might wish to investigate his passage, can make thirty miles a day without conscious effort.

Marius did his best to take interest in his surroundings, but so far below the surface the world is a dark and gloomy one, and even with his dead vision he could see only a few feet in any direction. Tiny fish darted here and there, colourless and pale. Small, scuttling things ran across the sand at his feet, stirring up puffs of sediment that added to the general gloom. Once, something massive and slow slid overhead, announcing itself with a long wave of disturbed water. Everything around Marius stopped as it passed, and even he paused, aware of the sudden emptiness the giant, unseen shape caused. Only once it had passed by did life slowly return to the space around him, and he continue his plodding journey.

With nothing to capture his attention, Marius quickly fell into that form of fugue known to all long-distance travellers. Time lost its meaning, and any sense of motion disappeared within the rhythm of his walk. Marius needed to maintain his concentration – if he forgot his task, and strayed from the straight line he was following, he could spend the rest of his days wandering the sea-beds in circles. With no external stimulation, he turned inwards.

He tried singing, but there are only so many bottles of beer that can fall before the entire liquor industry goes on strike, and you find yourself fantasizing about a pint of Old Grumpy's Falling Down Water and a cuddle with that plump serving girl who works down the *Whale and Insect*. He tried to begin a game of Spotto, but there was no variation of colour in the pale, washed out creatures he passed, and nobody's arm to punch if he saw a red one. In the end, he settled for talking his way through imaginary meetings, setting in motion all the plans he had held over the years, while he plodded through the lightless, sound-less world of the water.

He crested a small rise as he was being shown around the perfect little country cottage, slid down the other side as he shook hands on the arrangement to buy and hit the bottom just as he was laughing about how he'd negotiated the seller down beyond his wildest expectations. He skirted an open cave where something large and unseen flickered dully about the entrance just as he was taking over his father's hold-ings using a fake company front, and he sold off the assets and used the money to establish his own businesses between the cave and a large rock a dozen feet away. A cloud of krill-like creatures witnessed him handing his father a broom and pointing out the size of the warehouse to be cleaned. He was standing at the edge of a forest pool, the priest wrapping the withy around his hand and his bride's as he skirted a massive outcropping of rocks. He looked down at his bride's hand. He recognized it, and looked up at the woman next to him, opened his mouth to speak her name... and saw the ship.

It lay on its side, stern pointing towards the sky, the gaping hole where its back had broken tilted down so that, at a casual glance, it looked to have rammed its prow deep into the sandy bottom. Marius leaned against a nearby rock and viewed the keel from what felt like a safe distance, although why he should feel safe when surrounded by open water rather than the ship's wooden hull was something he couldn't explain.

Even from a distance, it was massive. It was hard to gauge this far under water, with the silty bottom swirling about him in the dark, but what he could see seemed to be well over twenty feet wide, and the stern must have been sixty or seventy feet from the break. Growths covered the hulk, so that it might well have been mistaken for a natural outcropping from above.

From this angle, below and to one side, Marius could clearly see the planks along the ship's side, over-lapping too regularly and smoothly to be anything other than man-made.

The incline upon which the ship rested was a steep one, and Marius was faced with a quandary of sorts – to slip down beneath the vast mass and work his way inside via the open break, to risk his wellbeing against who knew what kind of creature that may have taken up residence, in the hope of some sort of loot to carry with him; or clamber up the slope and crest the obstacle at its uppermost point, which would result in less chance of booty but fewer opportunities of being eaten, theoretically, and he would at least learn the identity of the boat.

In the end, his own nakedness decided him: what was the point of carving out booty when he had precious little ability to carry it, and unless he found his way to land, what would there be to spend it on? Marius was not yet resigned to spending his remaining lifespan under the waves, a resolution which required him to bypass this monstrous obstacle and continue on his path. He turned to the rising gradient, and crabbed his way towards the top.

As he climbed, the slope took him nearer to the boat's hull, until he could clearly see the keel's clinker construction. Giant planks, several feet wide, overlaid and fastened together with nails whose heads looked like metal doors in the gloom. Marius raised a hand in front of his eye, and spread his fingers, trying to block one from view. Some small spark of recognition flared within him. He redoubled his efforts, stirring up great clouds of sediment as he scrambled up the slope. Eventually he cleared the hull and fought his way upwards, until only a dozen feet separated him and the surface of the water. Here the slope flattened out, forming a plateau that stretched away into the distance. Light bent differently this close to the surface. After so long in the depths, the world felt washed out, mirage-like, despite its proximity.

For a moment Marius felt a flush of revulsion, and quickly turned away, back towards the comforting dark. He knelt at the edge of the plateau, and gazed down upon the giant stern, trying to gauge its height by the size of the broken windows that ran in rows across the flat face. Thirty feet, forty, fifty... there was no need. Two words ran across the top of the uppermost rows, eight feet high, the bright red lettering he remembered from his youth faded with exposure and the endless motion of the sea, but clear enough that Marius sank back onto his buttocks and hugged himself with the shock of recognition.

He was staring at the long-lost wreck of the *Nancy Tulip*.

Marius stood under the massive stern and gazed at the wall of wood towering over his head. Even with much of the ship missing, and the rest barely visible beneath thirty years of underwater plant growth, the dimensions of it stretched his belief. In an instant he was a child again, staring up at the ship as it wobbled erratically out of the harbour and into the open ocean. He reached out, as he had done that day. This time, however, he made contact with the hull, sliding his hand over the thick slime and shaking it into the surrounding water. He stretched back, neck bones cracking as he examined the hull. He should be moving on. He had a quest to fulfil, a life to recover. He couldn't afford to get sidetracked, or to lose his sense of direction. And yet...

The adult Marius was dead, but the eight year-old reared up out of his memory with all the vitality of a child up past his bedtime to go and see something wonderful down at the docks. He had to know. Even if all he found were crumbling uprights, transparent squids, and rotting detritus, he had to see inside, to try and touch at least a fantasy of what it must have been like to embark on that mad, fatal, glorious voyage. Marius gained as firm a grip as possible on a nail head that protruded at head height, and hauled himself up. Feet slipping, lurching from one precarious handhold to another, he began to climb.

Twenty minutes later, he had his hands around the throat of his inner eight-year old and was giving him a damn good shaking. How someone so dead could possibly have heart palpitations so painful was beyond him, but there he was, half in and half out of a gun port, wondering whether it was possible to vomit when you haven't eaten for a week and a half. To make matters worse, he didn't have any breath to catch, and the one time he'd given in to instinct and gasped a lungful in, he'd ended up with a mouthful of slimy water that made him glad there was nothing in his stomach for it to react with. Something was seriously wrong with his death, he thought for the umpteenth time. If he ever made it back to a proper grave, he was going to have to speak to someone.

Eventually, the spinning stopped, and he was able to stare down into the cavernous interior of the *Nancy Tulip*. Frankly, it was a disappointment. He'd managed to climb as far as the cannon deck, a long, empty room designed for two things—the cannons that lay somewhere below, at the lower end of the tilted floor, and as much space as possible for the multitude of gunners, deck masters, powder boys, and medics to move without tripping over each other or getting in the way of the recoiling guns.

When the ship had sunk, and twisted against the slope, everything on the deck had slid away, below the limit of Marius' vision. All that remained was a vast emptiness, with the occasional rotting plank looming up like a peasant's tooth. Marius slowly scanned the space in front of him. He had half-expected it, of course, but still… He shrugged, then hurriedly grabbed the edges of the hole as the movement caused him to overbalance. A piece of wood broke off underneath him, and spiralled away into the darkness, clunking dully against hidden obstacles as it fell. Marius gathered his remaining strength, drew his legs underneath him so that he squatted on the edge of the hole, and continued his climb.

When at last Marius reached the top deck, it was like cresting the top of a mountain. Once there, what else was left do but gaze downwards in all directions, knowing with utter certainty that you sat at the top of the world, and that no moment, no matter what you might achieve, could ever match this one, perfect sensation? Marius had no flag to plant, and no commission to claim the rotting hulk in the name of anybody, yet could not escape the need to do *some-thing* to mark the occasion. He settled for sitting on a relatively sturdy piece of railing and picking the splinters out of his hands, knees and feet while he stared across the ruined deck.

In truth, there was very little left. The hills around Borgho City were not known for their hardwoods, and much of the upper decking had been crafted from the pine trees that littered the surrounding areas. The seas had eaten the soft wood: only the spars remained, and some of the support structures. The immense oak masts had snapped during the descent: their bases remained, so massive and imposing that Marius could only guess at how it must have been to stand below them or even more incredibly, climb up them to stand upon the cross beams and pull in the acres of material that had made up the sails. Much of the deck had gone, but surprisingly, the enormous round silhouette of the wheel could be seen, and behind it… Marius gasped, and sputtered as he drew in another mouthful of water.

Behind it, glinting dully in the wavering light, was a corner of the King's stateroom, a structure made entirely of gold. Marius remembered it passing in the afternoon sun, rearing from the poop deck like a bullion bar of the gods. Now he stared at the bulky shadow, his hand raised to his mouth. It was impossible to believe. A fortune in gold, literally a king's fortune, and all he had to do was climb down to it. Marius' lips pursed, and his fingers gained fresh splinters as they tightened upon the wood. Climb down to it, all right, and then what? Naked, a dozen feet underwater, and without a single tool or friend to help. Well, he thought, maybe if I lick hard enough I can carry some on my tongue.

But he had to know. He had to at least touch it. Carefully, testing every step before he took it, he tip-toed over the edge of the hull and onto the nearest spar. It creaked ominously, and trembled as it adjusted to his weight. Marius froze, then, with nobody to be embarrassed in front of, turned his belly to the wood and inched his way down it like a child too scared to slide down a banister the proper way. He reached a cross beam and took a moment to rest. When he was sure it wouldn't break and send him tumbling down into the dark below, he crept across it, resisting the urge to lunge at the next spar and hang for dear life. Slowly, footstep by quavering foot-step, he made his way towards the stateroom, until he could reach out one trembling hand, and let him-self fall onto the ice-cold metal of its port wall.

He lay against it for several minutes, eyes closed, feeling the smoothness beneath his cheek. A bed made of gold. Not since his nights of pretending to be the Emir's eunuch had he slept in a bed of gold, and this time, nobody was waiting to stick anything up his rectum should he try to carry any of it away. He ran a hand across it, fingers cupping the corner. A frown crossed his face. He ran his fingers back round the corner, then forward again, then opened his eyes and focused on the path the fingers had cleared in the ever-present algae.

Tacks. A line of tiny tacks, running along a seam just the other side of the corner. Marius focused, peered closer. He could just make out a seam. He picked at it with one finger, slowly worming his finger under until a flap opened up. He pulled harder, and the sheet peeled away, revealing the wooden upright to which it had been attached. Marius snorted. Tin plate! Tin plate, with the slimmest covering of gold foil, pinned to wood like any other structure. That cheap, lying, faking nutcase.

Marius lay back against the wall, shoulders slumped. All that effort. The eight year-old within him shrugged as if to say "Adults. What did you expect?" and went back to playing in his room. Marius stared at the broken corner, and contemplated the journey to the ocean floor.

After a while, though, he shook himself out of his malaise. He was still on the *Nancy Tulip*. He was still at the door of the stateroom. Gods, even if there were no walls of gold to be found, it was still the ship of Nandus. And, he reminded himself, Nandus was a king, even if he was mad as a ferret in a bucket of honey. The thought that had been clamouring to speak since he had seen the name etched onto the stern raised its hand for attention, and this time, Marius let it talk.

If he hadn't hatched some scheme about using the lifeboats to open a second front and left the ship before it sank; if he hadn't thrown himself over the side when the sea swamped the deck; if he hadn't been in the prow, on deck, anywhere else on top; then Nandus, mad as he was, but oh, most definitely a king, might be lying in whatever shape the sea had left him, on the other side of the wall. Marius stared at the open flap of metal, and began to laugh.

The dead had demanded a king. Nobody had said he had to be *animate*.

Marius slid over to the spar supporting the front of the structure. He made sure of his footing, dug his fingers under the flap of tin, and began to pull.

Marius ducked his head through the hole and peered into the black water. The water was stiller inside the stateroom than out, felt somehow thicker and more fetid against his skin. Slowly, he slipped inside, turning so he hung onto the edge of the framework with his fingers while his feet scrabbled for purchase. Something flapped at the limits of his vision and he stiffened, images of giant killer octopuses filling his imagination. Then he focused, and saw the tattered remnant of some type of tapestry, stirred by his kicking.

Marius frowned. Surely, thirty years below water would destroy any fabric that had once hung on the walls. Which meant that the tapestry below must be made of some other material. Metal, perhaps. Marius had seen shirts woven from thin strands of gold and silver, soft as silk and worn by the richest, most stylish nobles in Scorby. He'd almost won one, once, in a game of Kingdom, but had been foiled by a messenger arriving with news of a royal coup, just as he was laying down a hand filled with a now-dead royal family. He blinked, remembering how much the shirt had been worth. The tapestry must be eight feet high, he decided, perhaps three or four feet wide. He could wrap it around himself like a toga, wear it rather than carry it. A tapestry that size, even if it were only made of silver threads... Marius was good at math. All con men are. But the equation had too many zeroes to keep track of.

Suddenly, twelve feet below the surface seemed a lot warmer. Marius watched the bottom edge of the tapestry float into sight, then back again, counting the number of seconds in each ebb and flow. As soon as he was sure of the rhythm he held his breath, counted to the right number, aimed for the correct spot, and let go the beam.

And missed.

The trailing edge of the tapestry waved to him as he sank past, flailing in despair at the three inches of space between his fingertips and the fabric. The deck of the *Nancy Tulip* was thirty feet wide, and there was only a foot or so between each outer wall and the outer railing. Marius had launched himself at an angle, and his despairing movement caused him to tumble as he fell. He didn't see the wall that jutted out from the rear of the building, only felt the solid edge as he crashed against it. Something snapped, and Marius had time to hope it was the wood and not his hip as he spun away and collided, back first, with the lower wall.

He slid down until he lay in the crook of wall and floor, staring up at the gloom through which he had fallen. Slowly, details began to emerge – from this angle he was able to make more sense of the interior architecture than he had when hanging from the other wall. To his right, a massive sliding door hung loosely upon its frame, its control wheel clearly visible. A bas relief was carved into its inner surface.

Marius squinted, trying to make out details through the carpet of barnacles and plant life. A series of human figures. A procession of women, bearing whips and carrying saddles. Marius turned his attention to the rear wall. There were some aspects of kingly life that were better hidden, he decided. That was one side of Nandus he could live without understanding. He found the wall against which he had crashed, and smiled in relief as he saw where a chunk towards the end had been removed by his fall.

The wall protruded several feet into the room, and now that he was looking, Marius could see another one maybe four feet above it, and another above that. Huge, triangular hinges hung downwards from the front edge, and the remains of what appeared to be a gate hung from lowest wall. Marius tilted his head to take in the view from the right angle. The gate reached about halfway up the wall. In fact, if he pictured it closed, and another one over the space above, he could easily see the spaces as some sort of cubicle, like the brothels of Hayst, or…

Marius blinked in astonishment. Stables. They were stables. This entire stateroom, with tapestries of immeasurable wealth hanging from gold-plated walls, and floors, he realized as he attempted to stand, of the same slippery substance, turned over to horses. Well, one horse, he supposed. Littleboots, favoured friend of the King and the only four-legged member of the imaginary Scorban senate.

In a way, Marius was relieved, particularly when he considered the whip-wielding women on the interior of the doors. But if this was the horse's realm, one question remained. Unless he slept in the stables along with his horse, where were the King's quarters?

Marius slid along his perch until he reached the point where walls and floor coincided. A pile of bones lay in an untidy bundle. He grabbed an elongated femur and used it to lever himself upright, where he could raise his hands on either side and balance against the three surfaces. He glanced down, and saw a heavy, equine skull staring up at him.

"Evening, senator," he thought, and almost overbalanced as a fit of giggles took him. The horse's skull made no reply, so Marius put his foot against it and levered himself upwards. The lowest stable wall was out of reach. Marius leaped at it anyway, and floated gently down to lose his footing against the slick gold floor, landing in a heap amongst Littleboots' bones. He lay there, tapping his hand against Littleboots' forehead in frustration, ignoring the swirl of sediment.

You're underwater, you fool. Swim up.

Marius could not swim. But he could thrash his arms and legs about like someone trying to catch arrows shot at him by a thousand angry archers. He carefully placed one foot on either angled surface beneath him, crouched down to gather as much strength as possible into his legs, and leaped. He sailed forward in a graceless arc, whipping the water to a froth.

Miraculously, he began to rise. Marius kept his eyes fixed upon the prize – the wall, ten feet above him, but getting closer, closer. He beat the water with renewed urgency, until the muscles in his shoulders and thighs began to seize up from the exertion, and rose in a series of little gulps, his efforts growing more and more frog-like as he lost what little sense of rhythm he possessed. His fingers brushed the underside of the wall, then again. He gave one last, almighty effort, and with the sound of his shoulder popping echoing through his skull, wedged three fingers over the top of the wall.

And there he hung, a half-inflated parade puppet, while his muscles twitched and spasmed, and he realized with incredulity that he was gasping in pain. Barely had he time to register the sensation before his fingers began to lose their precarious grip. Marius heaved his other arm up, and found purchase for his hand. Legs pumping and kicking, he drew himself up until his arms were fully over the edge and he could lever his upper body up. He plumped forward like a seal leaving the ocean, until, at last, he swung his legs over and lay on his back, gasping, no longer caring that he drew in only water and microscopic particles of filth. If it was instinct, then so be it. He needed the release, needed to calm the fandango in his chest cavity and let die the painful thumping behind his eyes.

When he was able to open his eyes without seeing dancing purple blobs, he turned his head and gazed along the floor of his new haven. What he saw made him stifle a sob. The stable was empty. Thoroughly empty, without even a pile of mouse bones left behind after all the hay had rotted away. Marius swung his stare towards the other wall, wavering in and out of vision above his head. It was only four feet or so, a fraction of the distance he had already travelled. It just seemed such a very large fraction, that was all.

Marius raised himself to his hands and knees, and slid clumsily over to the lip. He leaned back, and raised his arms so his fingers curled against the upper wall. Such a little effort, to rear up and pull himself over the edge. Such a small thing, to have a heart attack and die, *again*, under the water where nobody would ever know what had become of him. Then Gerd could go about his dead man's business as it suited him, and Keth could find herself a nice, rich, gentleman and settle down and have a hundred babies and as many cats running about as many gardens as she liked. Marius closed his eyes. No. He'd be damned if he was going to let Gerd get away with things that easily. And as for Keth, if she was going to settle down and have a hundred babies with anybody…

Marius sank back onto his haunches, then his backside, staring dumbly out into the room. Across the way, sideways women beckoned to him with whips and smiles that still seemed a little too knowing for just a horse. Something small and very important inside him fell over and broke with a sound that may have been his subconscious slapping itself on the forehead.

Marius stared into the dark for a long time, the memory of everything he had ever done with Keth, and everything they had ever said, scrolling slowly past his internal eye. When he got to their last meeting, Marius winced. The broken thing inside him cramped, and stayed that way. Oh God, he thought. She already knew she loved *me*. He regained his knees, and reached for the wall above him. It was no longer a matter of visiting a mad practical joke upon those who had bestowed this death upon him. He had a real mission now, one that sank into his bones with an urgency he had never before experienced. Getting back to the dead was only the first part. After that, he had to get to Keth. After *that*, well, he would get what he deserved. His grasping fingers found the edge, and he pulled himself upwards with renewed strength.

The first thing he saw as he crested the wall were the bones. A small heap of them, tucked into the back of the stable, pushed into untidy confusion by the gentle movement of the water. Marius slid down towards them. There was no skull visible, nothing that could be identified as king or sailor, nor even, Marius noted, as human. From any sort of distance they were simply a confused jumble. Marius came to a stop and plunged his hands into the pile, pushing bones to either side as he rummaged amongst them. The eddies created by his movements brought the discarded bones nudging back against the pile, and Marius quelled the desire to pick them up and fling them away. If this was Nandus, he would need them to piece together the skeleton once he found a way to transport them all ashore.

He was almost at the bottom when his hands met with a smooth, round object just smaller than the ball he had owned as a child. He grasped it firmly, and slowly pulled it out: a hard sphere, shining dully yellow where it was not stained black by the rotting of flesh. Two dark orbs stared out over a small triangular opening, and a row of off-kilter teeth grinned at him from a multitude of angles below.

Marius felt a sudden surge of elation – ringing the top of the skull, glued on by a thin line of dark matter he chose not to examine too closely, was a corroded circlet of gold. A vertical wedge of metal rose from the spot between the eyes, containing a single, large emerald. Marius recognized Nandus' crown, and closed his eyes for a moment in thanks. He could have kissed the mad, dead bugger, if not for the fact that he was a rotting skull, and hanging from the circlet was something that very closely resembled a bridle and bit. Marius decided not to re-examine the look on the whip-lady carvings. He picked away at the clasps until he was able to peel away the bridle, holding it between forefinger and thumb and flicking it away behind him. Well, he thought, raising the skull so they faced each other eye to missing eye, hello, Your Majesty.

"Who are you?" a voice boomed inside Marius' head. "Why do you greet me in such a manner?"

Marius screamed and dropped the skull, reflexively pushing himself backwards until he teetered on the edge of the drop, and only saved himself by clenching every muscle below his navel *really* hard. The skull rolled to the edge of the pile of bones, and as Marius stared at it in terror, it slowly swung around until it faced him.

"Do you mind?" the voice asked indignantly. "How dare you come into my presence, and scream like some sort of madman? What kind of gaoler are you?"

Slowly, Marius raised his hand to his mouth. As he

stared, something shifted within the pile of bones. "Well?" the voice demanded. Marius opened his mouth, then closed it. This is impossible, he thought.

"What is impossible?"

Marius blinked.

"You can hear me?"

"Of course I can hear you. You're no more than four feet away from me, you idiot. Which damn god sent you to torment me? Oceanus? Is it him? Come out, damn you!" Marius winced at the volume inside his head. "Come out, Oceanus, you watery coward!"

While Nandus' skull ranted and shouted for Oceanus to show himself, Marius took the opportunity to think quietly for a moment. That the pile of bones was Nandus was plain, and equally plain was that the madness he bore in life had stayed on beyond his death, needing only the appearance of another soul to draw him into conversation. With no way to form words, it was his life force that spoke, burrowing directly from Nandus' bodiless consciousness to his. We can *talk*, Marius realized. We can converse. I don't have to simply carry him back to shore and dump him on the dead. I can persuade him that it's the right thing to do.

He snuck a peek at the raving King, and all thought stopped. The pile of bones was on the move. What's more, it had grown smaller, because a number of them had found their neighbours. A hand and forearm had risen from of the pile. As Marius watched, it drew out a socketed bone, which it fit on to its base, before finding another and fitting it alongside. A leg slid out from underneath, and a pelvis emerged to nestle against its upper end. Oh, my good gods, Marius thought. It seems I won't even have to carry him.

"Carry me where?" the voice intruded, and almost without thinking, Marius lowered the mental partition that separated his conscious and unconscious thoughts. Almost three decades of removing his facial features from his inner workings made such an action automatic. He counted to three, and projected what he hoped was a suitable air of secrecy.

"Not so loud, my liege," he projected. "They'll hear you."

"Hear me?" Marius was gratified to hear Nandus lower its voice. "Who?"

"Your tormenters." He made a great show of turning from side to side, as if seeking out approaching strangers. "We don't have much time."

"Who are you?"

Marius was fascinated by the sliding bones. As he and Nandus talked they slithered across each other like petrified snakes, fitting into each other soundlessly, almost absent-mindedly. Of course, the part of him that he had shielded from Nandus thought. He doesn't know he's dead. He doesn't see it, so therefore, it can't be. He sees a full body, so his body behaves in the right way. I could probably steal half his bones and the rest would simply compensate, and he'd never notice anything was wrong.

"Marius don Hellespont," he projected. "Son of Raife, Your Majesty. Seventh generation Scorban, loyal to the crown." That, at least, was mostly true. His father, like any good trader, was loyal to the crown, no matter who wore it, or which crown it was. Can't make a living in prison, he'd always said. He'd been wrong, but Marius did not treasure the ways in which he had found out. The skull swivelled on its axis, imitating his movement, and Marius did his best not to shiver.

"Why are you here, don Hellespont?"

"To… to rescue you, sire. Your loyal subjects need you." Again, that was mostly true, he thought. No need to define exactly *which* subjects they were. The skeleton's hands reached down and picked up the skull, gently lowering it into place atop the completed vertebrae and setting it in place with a quick twist. Moments later, the final ribs were in position, and the skeleton swung about until it knelt on hands and knees, its blank, empty face pushed next to Marius'.

"Lead on, don Hellespont", it said, and Marius nodded once, before turning his back upon it with a sense of relief and surveying the room. The corner from which he'd swum lay a dozen feet below him, barely visible through the gloom. Almost as far across lay the massive black opening of the doorway.

Marius measured the distance. If he could get that far, push off hard and swim for all he was worth, he should be able to avoid falling past the lower edge of the door, some four feet or so below his current level. As long as he could make that perch it should be a small matter to clamber through and make his way back on to the outer deck of the ship. From there, he could climb down the incline of the boat to the sand, and use the alignment of the hulk to get his bearings. Then all he had to do was keep Nandus on side until he could get back to shore and find a way to contact the dead. Simple. Memories of his effort to rise from the stable floor made him gulp. The hard part would come first. He pointed towards the door.

"Down there, sire," he said. "We make that opening, and put its bulk between us and your gaolers. Once outside, they'll never catch us. Uh," he glanced back at the skeleton. "Are you sure you can... uh... make it?"

The skeleton clapped a hand on his shoulder. Marius tried not to flinch. "Have no fear, brave peon," Nandus said. "There's good blood in this body. I've the strength of a horse, and the bravery of one, too."

"Right."

"Wait!"

"What?" Marius had tensed for the jump. Nandus' command caught him off-balance. It took an act of will to stop himself sliding forward onto his face and over the lip of their precarious perch.

"Littleboots!" Nandus' skull was rotating from left to right, scanning a view Marius could not begin to guess at. "My brave steed. I cannot leave without him."

Marius turned back, and made sure the lid of his subconscious was very tightly shut. He did not need Nandus to know what he was thinking right now.

"Waiting for us outside, I'm sure, sire. We must hurry, lest, uh, lest he be discovered."

"Yes, yes! Onward, my subject. Hold fast, darling!" Nandus' voice rang loud in Marius' head. "Daddy will be with you soon!"

Marius did a quick tour of his mental shutters, testing the locks and doubling the guard. Then he gathered his legs beneath him, made sure of his aim, and launched himself into space.

The journey was less painful this time, in part because he was far less successful in keeping himself afloat. Marius made no attempt to gain height, or even to keep himself on an even keel. He was falling, but this time, he was more in control of his motion. Who knows, he thought, I might even get used to this. There are baths in Borgho, and a club that swims the harbour in summer. I could join them. It could be a whole new lease of life for me. Images of himself, bronzed from the sun and muscular from all the swimming he was doing, flashed through his mind. He waved to the girls who had come to line the harbour wall, just to catch sight of him as he ploughed through the waves like a handsome, virile shark.

The door brought him back to the present by the simple expedient of striking him under the chin. Marius flailed for a moment, then grabbed the lower lip and hauled himself up. He twisted so that he sat facing the King's skeleton, standing with feet braced on the golden floor of the stable.

"See?" he projected, hoping the King wouldn't register the dull thumping in his jaw, or his wonderment at actually feeling pain. "Nothing to it." He waved the King onward. "Your turn."

The King looked right, then left, leaning out over the edge. "No sign of the enemy?"

Marius sighed. This was going to be a long pantomime. "No, my lord," he replied. "But be quick." He rolled his eyes, then stopped. No telling how good the King's vision was. If Marius could see better now that he was dead, Nandus might be able to see forever without any eyes at all. "They may be back at any time."

Nandus nodded. He stepped back, braced himself in an obscene parody of a runner about to leave his mark, then stepped forward and leaped from the stable wall.

Marius watched in shocked silence as the King sank a dozen feet to the bottom of the room, and gracefully broke apart. He closed his eyes, suddenly very alone on his perch.

"Fuck," he said. "Fucking *fuck*." He opened his eyes again and stared down into the blackness. Cruelly, Nandus' skull had rolled into a shaft of lighter water. Marius could see the crown, a million miles out of his reach. He ran one hand down his face. He wasn't prepared to contemplate the idea of climbing down to retrieve it, not just yet.

Something stirred across the floor below. Marius leaned forward. Something was moving across the pile of bones, crawling here and there with purpose, getting bigger as it moved.

"No," he said. "No."

The bones were sliding across each other as they had before, scuttling in larger and larger groups, joining together, slowly gaining form as Marius watched, his mouth agape. A hand reached out and plucked the skull from the floor, bending back to put it atop the spinal column. Marius frowned. There was something about the arm, something not quite right. He squinted, trying to get a clear view, then rocked back as Nandus rose to his feet and waved at Marius.

"Oh, good and most ancient gods save your humble servant."

Marius suddenly knew what was wrong with Nandus' arm. It was not that it had an extra elbow, or that one of them bent in entirely the wrong direction, although that was bad enough. What was really wrong was King Nandus, and the fact that he was suddenly seven feet taller than he had been, and that his ribcage ran the length of his body from his vastly elongated neck to the massive pelvis that anchored his long, multi-jointed legs.

Nandus had landed upon Littleboots' bones, and in his dead, mad state, had incorporated them into his own frame. He reached up an arm – fetlock, Marius tried not to scream, it's a fetlock – and grasped the lower lip of the door, pulling himself up to balance precariously over Marius. He leaned down, and placed his human head next to Marius' ear.

"Lead on," he whispered. Marius stared past his skull, to the equine eyes that gazed back at him from deep within the huge chest cavity. Somewhere at the back of his senses, he thought he could hear something whinny. He turned away, closing his eyes against a sudden case of vertigo.

"This way," he said, swallowed and tried again in a much less panicky tone. "Towards starboard."

He pushed away from the door, refusing to hear the rattle of joints from the monstrosity in his wake.

The journey across the deck was a nightmare of controlled revulsion. Twice, Marius slipped on the overgrown wood, and twice Nandus steadied him by reaching out a parody of an arm. Each time, it took a conscious act of will not to leap away in fear. The third time it happened, Nandus leaned his monstrous neck down past Marius' shoulder and tilted his head to look at him askance.

"Steady," he said. "We'll be free soon enough."

Marius nodded, unable to speak. He regained his balance and slid towards the railing at the ship's starboard edge. Nandus tiptoed after, his hoof-feet making dull double clicks against the wooden beams. Once they had achieved the railing, Marius leaned against it and looked over at the ocean floor, measuring the drop.

"We should be safe," he said. "I'll go first. Just… aim for a soft spot, or something." He braced himself against the rail, then swung himself over. The sand came towards him more slowly than it should, giving him plenty of time to regret his leap before he struck it at an angle and rolled down the short incline to fetch his head up against the hull. He staggered back, rubbing his head, and collapsed onto his back, looking up the side to the deck. Nandus waited a moment, then stepped over the edge and dropped lightly to the ground, a descent of no more than a couple of feet for his massively elongated legs. He bent down in an intricate motion of joints and bends, and offered a hand to Marius.

"Let's go, man," he said. Marius took the hand and began to pull himself up. Nandus snorted, and, Marius realized that assistance was not what his companion had in mind. Slowly, scarcely believing himself capable of the act, he tilted his face down and kissed the delicate arrangement of bones in Nandus' hand.

"Your Majesty," he replied, trying not to gag. Up close, the bones were pitted and scarred. Thirty years of providing meals for uncountable tiny ocean creatures were written upon their surface. He let go, and dragged himself to his feet.

"We'd best be quick," he said, glancing up at the hulk, gauging the correct direction from its alignment. "The, uh, the enemy won't be long. Once they discover your escape they'll be in pursuit." He made a great show of glancing around. "This way, Your Majesty." He regained his alignment and stepped away from the ship, then stopped. Nandus was shaking his head.

"I think not, soldier." the King said. "Look at my ship."

Marius looked. "Yes?"

"Look what they have done to it. Those devils. Those unutterable fiends." He raised a fist and shook it at the hulk. "My pride and joy. My greatest work. I cannot let such an insult go unpunished." He turned upon Marius, and Marius was taken aback at how quickly the King's skull was inches from his face. "What better time to strike? Strike, while the Ocean gods slumber, secure in the misplaced knowledge that their tormentor, their divine revenger, lies shackled and helpless before their demonic ministrations! Let them sleep, let them snore in their watery beds. Nandus, destroyer of oceans, is free. Let their resting places become their graves!" He reared upwards, and Marius could not help but picture statues he had seen of great war heroes on their steeds, rising up on their hind legs to herald some endless stone-cut charge. Again, just underneath the King's words, he could have sworn he heard a whinny.

"No... Your Majesty. No." Marius made a grab for Nandus as the King settled back into a more normal position. He missed, and almost tumbled over. Nandus stepped forward, his hand raised into a fist.

"Once more into the breach, servile minions," he shouted. "Once more, or close up this ship with our Scorban dead!"

"What?" Marius bunched his fists, and pressed them against his forehead. "What breach? What *minions*?" He jumped aside as Nandus took a step forward. "Wait. Stop. There's nobody... Woah!" he shouted in desperation, as Nandus reached out an arm to haul himself back onto the top deck.

To his amazement, the King stopped. This time, Marius was under no illusion as to the snort of air and low, breathy rumble he heard. He reached out, and patted the Nandus on the rump.

"Good boy," he said uncertainly. "There's a good fellow."

"You'd better have a damn good reason for this impertinence," Nandus said, his voice low with repressed anger. Unconsciously, his left foot pawed at the ground. His jaw dropped open, and Marius tried not to imagine a giant tongue lolling from the side of his mouth.

"You need to resign this field, Your Majesty." He stepped forward, placed a hand on the ship. "We are alone, in a land of enemies. Ask yourself: what glory have they claimed from imprisoning their greatest foe, and what more would be theirs for seeing him killed and held aloft as proof of their might? Think, Your Majesty. How better to diminish them, and to raise your own value, than an escape from under their watery noses, to return with yet greater numbers, and conquer the entire sea in the name of the great and eternal Nandus, King of Scorby, the world, and all the oceans?"

Gods, he thought in that isolated part of his brain. If an eatery served me a pudding this over-egged, I'd send it back.

Nandus considered his words for several moments, staring out into the depths at his immortal glory.

Then, "No," he said. "It is well said, loyal servant, but now is the time. We strike now." He raised his voice once more into a shout. "For Nandy-poos, Scorby, and the god of my choice!" He pushed off and made the deck in one swift movement, disappearing between decks before Marius could react. In quick succession, a series of massive thuds emerged from the bowels of the ship. Marius could hear, quite clearly, a cry of victory each time Nandus' tortured imagination conjured up another foe to vanquish. Marius tilted his head, following the King's progress through the empty vessel.

"Right, then," he said after fifteen minutes, as Nandus' assault showed no sign of abating. "I'll... I'll just go and wait over here, shall I?" He refused to consider the chances of getting this lunatic back to the shore. He simply refused.

Instead, he stepped away from the hull and found

a small rise where he could lay back and knit his hands behind his head, and pretend he was lying in a field somewhere to rest off a particularly good drink, instead of waiting at the bottom of the ocean for an insane centaur with delusions of grandeur to finish beating up a ship full of nothing. His father had often told him that life was a funny old thing, which was certainly true when you were a successful merchant with a string of mistresses long enough to tire out three healthy country boys. But when it came to sheer comic potential, Marius thought, life had nothing on being dead. I'd laugh right now, if not for the fact that I have no idea how I'd stop.

Eventually, the rate of violence within the ship slowed down, and then all that was left was the sound of Nandus' climbing back up to the deck. Marius stopped his contemplation of the tiny krill swirling before his eyes and padded over to his former place at the side of the hull. Nandus appeared at the railing.

"Victory!" he cried, leaping over the edge and landing before Marius. He spread his arms, and deposited a pile of small, black objects on the ground. Marius knelt, and picked one up.

"Barnacles?"

"Spoils of war!" Nandus leaned down and, without any sign that such a thing might be considered unusual, began packing his chest cavity with the tiny shellfish. "Stolen from the very heart of Oceanus' empire. Oh, how he'll shake his fist when he finds out what I've done. How the name of Nandus will stick in his throat!"

"Yes, he'll certainly be miffed when he realises how

many, uh, spoils you've got," Marius agreed. Absently, he patted Nandus on the rump. "Good boy." A proud neigh rumbled through him. Great, he thought. He likes me. "May I suggest we make haste, sire, before Oceanus and his cronies return and... drown us or something?"

"Good thinking, man. Yes. Let us proceed, post-haste." Nandus galloped a few steps away. "This way, I think."

Marius sighed. "Woah!" he shouted, and watched in amusement as Nandus stopped in his tracks. Marius raised two fingers to his lips, and projected the sound of a short, sharp whistle at the stationary King. Nandus turned in a wide-arsed loop, and came trotting back to him. He lowered his head, and bumped against Marius' shoulder.

"What is the meaning of this?" he said, rubbing his head against Marius' arm. "How dare you speak to me in such a manner?"

"Not you, Your Majesty" Marius said, quickly turning his head left and right to take in the ocean floor. "Our steeds. We need transport for our escape."

"Transport? Where?"

"Here, sire." Marius indicated an empty spot next to him. "Who else, sire, but your favourite, Little-boots?"

"Littleboots?" Oh, my poor baby," Nandus' hand snuck into his chest and began to stroke the horse's skull down the length of its forehead, between its eyes. "Daddy's missed you, you brave senator. Did you miss Daddy? Oh, I thought you did–"

"Yes, well..." Marius bit his lip. Oh, he thought, I

can't believe I'm going to try this. If I'm not right about this… "Are you ready to mount, Your Majesty?"

"To your own mount be, sirrah."

"Okay, then." He laid one hand on Nandus' bony shoulder, lodged his foot between two ribs, and hoisted himself up and onto his broad, bent back.

"Are you ready?" he shouted. Nandus brayed his assent.

Stifling a giggle, Marius reached back, and slapped the King on the haunch.

"Giddy up!"

# EIGHTEEN

Nandus galloped across the ocean floor, elongated legs tirelessly chewing through the miles as Marius tucked his hands and feet around protruding bones and held on for dear life. Fish scattered before them, silver flashes of light zigzagging away in panic to return in a more stately fashion once they had passed. They crested an outcropping in a bound, dislodging a small cuttlefish and sending it tumbling across the floor. Marius glanced back at it as they passed, and laughed at how its waving tentacle appeared very much like an extended middle digit. With every step, fistfuls of barnacles fell from Nandus' chest cavity and scattered across the ocean floor.

The redistribution of wealth begins at the top, Marius thought, and stifled a giggle. Miraculously, with the thought implanted in him that they rode side by side, Nandus had not the slightest objection to Marius seating himself upon his back. He simply turned his elongated neck towards him as they spoke, and Marius steered him as he would a horse, at least, a horse made entirely of bones. He simply grabbed whichever collarbone corresponded to the desired direction and pulled until Nandus turned appropriately.

Very quickly they left the hull in the distance, and were soon pushing into shallower waters. Marius noted the rise in the ocean floor, and slowed his mount. He did not want to reach landfall before he was certain as to where he was likely to land, although how he was going to do that from his current position he wasn't sure.

They proceeded at a walk through shoals of brightly coloured fish. Coral beds stretched away on either side. Life abounded here, unlike the colder depths through which they had been travelling. Clouds of tiny rainbow-coloured fish darted hither and thither, pursued by darker shapes as long as Marius' arm. Serpentine heads slunk out of gaps in the reef and perused them as they passed, jaws dropping open to reveals rows of dagger-like teeth that made Marius wince as he imagined them tearing flesh away from his bones. An octopus slithered out of a hole in the rocks and moved like sentient liquid up the face of the coral bed, legs slipping out and back in hypnotic patterns as it stalked some tiny creature visible only to its eyes. Marius stopped to watch, fascinated by the alien movement. He was so absorbed that, when he first felt the bump against his upper arm, he waved it away without concentrating.

"In a minute," he said absent-mindedly. "I want to watch."

"Sorry?" Nandus neighed. "I didn't say anything."

Marius frowned down at the line of gold circling the rear of Nandus' skull.

"Didn't you just… didn't you just bump me?"

"No."

"Then what…?" Marius glanced around just as a sleek, finned shape swum up from behind and thumped against his back with its rough skin. Marius spun around in time to see a double row of triangular teeth pass inches from his face, followed by six feet of grey-white skin and a high, whip-like tail.

"Shark," he muttered, and then, in a sudden explosion of fear he dove from Nandus' back and squeezed himself into a gap where bottom row of coral left sand. Nandus looked down at him, his skull tilted in surprise.

"What are you doing?"

"Shark!" Marius pointed behind the King's shoulder. "Shark!"

"And what is that, then?"

Marius stared up at the King for long seconds. Then he buried his face into the sand, counted to three, and tried again. "Big fish. Lots of teeth. Eats meat. Loves people." Nandus shrugged. Marius stared at him despairingly. Quite slowly, he realised just how much of the ocean he could see through his compatriot. He could see the shark quite clearly, for example, closing in towards the King's exposed back. This time, it was moving at speed. Marius knew that this was not just another pass. This was a proper attack.

"Oceanus' pet attack dog," he gasped, reaching forward and pulling at Nandus' leg. "If he sees us now, all will be lost. We must escape his surveillance. Get down!"

He yanked as hard as he could. Nandus stumbled,

then sat down on the sand as the shark sped across the spot where his neck had been, open mouth snapping on empty water. It spun impossibly fast, its elastic body bending in two as it kicked over and dove again. Marius reared up, threw his arms around Nandus' neck, and sent them both crashing to the floor just as the shark's body thudded against his shoulder. Marius tumbled away, fetching up hard against the razor-sharp coral. It scoured his back, and for a moment, he felt a thousand shards of glass rub across his nerves. Then he was face up on the sand, Nandus' long, bony arm across his chest, his skull inches from his ear.

"Steady, man," the King whispered. "Let not fear command you. The moment shall pass, and the dog be on his way, neigh."

Above them, the shark circled, long slow flicks of its tail sending it back and forth across Marius' field of vision as it searched them out. After several timeless minutes, he noticed that it took longer and longer for the shark to appear in his peripheral vision. Then, eventually, it moved away and did not return. Slowly he removed Nandus' arm from across his chest, and raised his head to look about them. The ocean bed, which had grown still and silent during the shark's attack, was slowly returning to life. He rose to his knees.

"I think we're safe," he said. "It's moved on."

Nandus stood, and reached up to adjust his crown where it had slipped down across his skull. "Let us not tarry. If Oceanus can track us so far from his centre of power, he must be fearful indeed of our escape."

"Yes. That'll be it." Marius resisted the temptation to wipe sand from his knees. He peered around in sudden alarm. "Oh, hell."

"What is it?"

"I've got turned around. During the fight… I don't know which way we should be heading."

"Have no fear." Nandus clapped him on the shoulder and stepped away. "It is this way."

"How can you be so sure?"

Nandus stared down at him from his lofty height. "I am King," he said simply, as if this could explain everything. And for him, Marius thought, it probably can. With no better option, he stood at his shoulder.

"Well, then. I guess we should crack on, hey?"

Together, they stepped around the coral outcropping and out into an open part of the ocean bed. Marius could not help but notice a sudden lack of urgency in their pace, and a much greater interest in their surroundings than either man had shown previously. Well, he decided. Sometimes it's nice to stop and smell the kelp. Nandus must have felt the same thing, because he waved a hand at their surroundings as they walked.

"It must be said," his neck craned around so that his skull rotated through a full circle, "Some of Oceanus' lands are quite extraordinary."

"Yes. I was just thinking that. Extraordinary." Marius peeked around a bed of seaweed, waving gently in the current. Pleased at how extraordinary the empty space beyond seemed, he stepped into it.

"It would be a shame, would it not, to spurn this opportunity to learn all one can about one's enemy.

Given this opportunity?"

"Oh, yes. A shame. Indeed."

"Indeed."

Side by side, the two escapees strolled across their enemy's seabed, taking particular care to learn as much as possible about the distances between them and anything that might resemble a returning shark. Eventually, however, as it became increasingly clear that the shark had gone on its way, and would not be returning, they relaxed.

With nothing else to do, and lulled by the sedate nature of their journey, they began to talk, not as King and perceived subject, or con artist and unwitting stooge, but simply as two travellers, marvelling at the unique nature of their surroundings. Marius even managed to forget the mutated state of the King's anatomy, and accepted the occasional snort or neigh as no more than a slight peccadillo of speech, no more harmful or annoying than a stutter or reliance on a particularly favourite swear word. Twice, he was forced to stop and wait as Nandus gave in to the need to roll around in a particularly sandy part of the floor, bony rump twitching as an imaginary tail flicked sand over his flanks. And he quickly grew accustomed to watching with amusement as the King broke off mid-conversation to romp across the sea floor in pursuit of some brightly coloured fish that had strayed too close to his sphere of attention. He even picked up the crown when it spilled unnoticed onto the ground, and held on to it, not with the intent to spirit it away, but simply with the idea of returning it.

The truth was, he realised, he was beginning to like the man. Sure, there was no denying that he was as insane as a spider-web salesman, and it was hard to ignore the fact that he had a couple of, well, *equine* habits. But once you looked past all that – and if he were honest with himself, Marius could list at least half a dozen perfectly sane and upstanding members of society with habits far more disturbing than the need to occasionally take a quick gallop around the nearby area – it became obvious that whatever garbled thought process might overcome Nandus' attention span, and however disastrous results might have been in the past, it had invariably been done for what he had thought was the good of his people.

Nandus had been four years old when soldiers had burst into the sleeping quarters of the unpopular King, his father, and brutally murdered him while the young prince watched from his bed in the corner of the room. There had been no such thing as a consort or guardian in Scorban law. Nandus was proclaimed King, and whilst still not yet old enough to sleep through the night without wetting, became the focal point of a government reeling from years of tyranny and abuse. His word was inviolate law, and if his word was that today was Pirate Day, then so be it. Any wonder, then, that he grew up with no concept of the complexities that came with living in the adult world? He had declared war on the ocean, yes, but it was his response to a year of bad fishing crops, and fleet losses that had cost the lives of over a hundred of his subjects.

And Marius remembered the summer of hopping,

when Nandus responded to an illness that decimated cows around the local countryside by ordering everyone to wear only one shoe at a time. It made sense, damn it, but you had to be exposed to Nandus in too personal a way in order to understand his reasoning. Marius watched the former King frolic across the ocean floor, and felt a sudden weight of sadness settle about him.

Then he remembered the autumn of his tenth year, when Nandus had ordered that the forests along the Borghan peninsula be set on fire so the squirrels wouldn't get cold, and seven thousand peasants had died in the winter snows. A slow, rolling rage spread outwards from his throat, not at Nandus but towards those men who knew the childish insensibility of his commands and slavishly followed them anyway. The men of power, with access to money, and lands and all that Borgho could provide, and who put into place whatever demand the King made with no care for others as long as it increased their money, or power, or both.

Men like my father, he thought, then checked the thought. No, he corrected himself, recalling all the times he had stood before such men, all the schemes and illusions and confidence tricks. Men like me. Something swirled in the pit of his stomach, and he swallowed to rid himself of the feeling of sickness.

Marius was standing on a gentle rise while Nandus ran back and forth below him, chasing a cloud of tiny bright-red fish, all the while telling Marius about his relationship with a stuffed toy called Trade Minister Tipsy in a voice more disturbing for its reasonable tone.

Marius turned the crown through his fingers as he gazed down at the bizarre creature the King had become. Perhaps, he thought, perhaps there was a way to give this man what he had never been allowed to possess – give him back a kingdom, yes, and get Marius off the meat hook, but give him the chance to rule as a *man*, and not just an uninhibited child god. If anyone could do it, perhaps it was Marius. After all, he thought, rubbing his thumb across the tarnished filigree, what use is twenty years of travelling, of seeing every court and every one-tap tavern the civilised world has to offer, if not to guide this man towards genuine nobility. After all, what did he really think he could offer Keth, apart from a friendly face when she did, finally, grow old and die? Time, perhaps, to give himself over to something bigger than the selfish desires of Marius don Hellespont. He raised the crown, and waved it at Nandus.

"Your Majesty," he called. "You dropped your..."

Nandus turned towards the sound of his voice. He raised his hand in acknowledgement, then froze, just as something long, and dark, and impossibly fast brushed past Marius and swept down the incline towards him. Marius went to ground, the crown slipping from his grasp and rolling down the slope. He landed on his chest, and barely raised his head to shout before the shark was on top of Nandus.

If Nandus had reacted as a human, he could have thrown himself to the seabed and survived. The shark's eyes were located towards the top of its wedge-shaped head, and it could not see beneath itself. It had saved them, last time. He had had Marius to think of, then, and the good side of his child-like nature had come to the fore.

This time, he was on his own, and no matter his nature, it was the part of him that was Littleboots that reacted faster. He ran, generations of instinct driving him towards flight. Marius heard his terrified whinny, saw him jink and turn as his fear drove him across the open sand. Then the shark struck him at the meeting point of neck and shoulder blades. Four hundred pounds of muscle, travelling at twenty-five miles per hour, it hit him and burst through him in an instant. Nandus exploded in a fountain of bones, and Marius was up and running towards him as quickly as he could through the water, the King's scream of terror and pain going on and on inside his head.

With no thought for his own safety, or the return of the monster, he fell to his knees and scrambled amongst the bones, pinning them together and sobbing as they fell apart. A voice was saying "No, no, no" over and over, and it *had* to be his, because he could still hear Nandus crying out. Then his hand pulled a bone towards him and it was smooth, and round, and he looked down and it was Nandus' skull. Marius knelt on the sand, and cradled it in his lap, and it was mad to say it, he *knew* it was mad, but he could see the King staring up at him in pain and confusion, and all Marius could think to say was "I'm sorry. I'm so sorry."

"Marius..."

"Yes, yes," not realising that Nandus knew his name, not caring, just holding him, just wishing he could make it all better.

"My people…"

"Your people…"

"Tell them…"

"Tell them? Tell them what?" And really paying attention now, really *listening*, because he knew that this was the end, and that Nandus knew, and this was all he could offer, this one moment, to hear his words.

"Tell them… I died in battle. Tell them I…"

"Yes? Tell them you what? Tell them you *what*?"

But there was no more. Marius was alone inside his head. He stared stupidly at the skull. How could it be dead, *properly* dead, when it had held Nandus' thoughts, his essence, for so long under the water? He rocked back on his heels, and cried. Marius had seen men die before, had held comrades in his arms as they breathed their last. But this was different. This was *different*. This death had required a level of belief. It had happened because not only the victim but Marius himself could not imagine it any differently.

Something hard and round swelled up inside Marius' chest. He squeezed his eyes shut, and opened his mouth to let it out. Water filled his throat, and he panicked. He couldn't breathe. His hands flew to his throat. He reared to his feet, stumbling backwards, other arm flailing. Nandus' skull fell to the sand. Marius didn't notice. He couldn't breathe. Blackness pressed against the back of his eyes. Blood crowded the edges of his vision. He fell to his knees. He caught sight of Nandus, lying in the sand, blank eye sockets staring up at him.

And just like that, the panic stopped. The heaviness

in his chest dissipated. Marius lowered his hand, and placed it against his chest. Nothing. No heartbeat, no respiration. He was still dead. He stared at the King's empty eyes, and frowned. He had been about to drown. He knew that without an ounce of doubt. But how, when he was already dead? Over and over, his former life kept breaking through the boundaries of his death, imposing itself upon him when he least expected it. There had to be some reason. Was it just memory? Instinct? Marius could not begin to know. But, he thought, I bet I know someone who does.

Gerd. Bloody Gerd. Marius leaned down, and began scooping out a hole in the sandy ocean floor. Once he had buried what parts of Nandus and Little-foot he could gather, he would leave this ocean and find Gerd. And then, he promised, he would have some answers.

# NINETEEN

The morning sun had crested the horizon, and slowly, the children were moving towards the beach from the nearby village, baskets on their heads. The echoes of the dawn chorus were dying away, and the daily routine of survival was about to begin for the denizens of the swamplands two hundred miles north of Borgho City. Each day, while the women raised whatever crops the dusty ground would allow, and the men stripped and cured hides to send down to the city's markets, the children travelled down to the beach to comb through the sands for crabs, driftwood, and any other treasure the ocean chose to provide. Life was hard, and often short, and most of the children had seen at least one dead body in their brief lives.

None of them had ever seen one walking about.

Marius stood knee-deep in the surf and watched the children run up the beach, screaming. He sighed. Somehow, after everything he'd been through in recent days, this was the most depressing. He couldn't really think why – if he'd been sitting on the beach and a naked, dead man had wandered up out of the water, he'd probably have reacted in a quite similar way – but there it was. He'd always liked children, at least, in theory. Seeing a group of them racing away from him in terror seemed, he didn't know, *typical*, in some way.

Slowly he trudged out of the water and almost absent-mindedly righted the nearest basket, dropping the few bits of falderal that had spilled out back into its base. He wasn't familiar with his surroundings, and after that greeting, there wasn't much of a chance that he'd head over to wherever the children came from and ask directions. Once a man has been attacked by a sixteen-foot long shark, being assaulted by a crowd of angry natives doesn't have quite the same allure.

The beach stretched about thirty feet to either side. To the north, a massive natural abutment stretched out into the water, its sheer face rising several feet above Marius. To the south, the sand reached a grove of stunted, wind-bleached trees and bent around it, disappearing behind the foliage. The level of background noise changed, and Marius looked up towards the path the children had run down – the rumbling of concerned voices had intruded upon the susurration of water and birdsong. Bodies were beating their way through the overhanging branches of trees. Marius had no desire to explain himself, even if the approaching villagers would let him. He had less desire to climb his way to safety, or return to his long, sodden underwater trek. South it was, then. He turned in that direction, and jogged towards the stand of trees.

A hundred feet past the dog-leg turn, he ran into the scrub that defined the top end of the beach. There were only two options for the villagers. Either they would dismiss the children's report as the product of an over-imaginative game, or they would come looking for the frightening stranger. In which case, they would quickly make the same decision he had, and follow him south. The sooner he was out of sight, the higher his chances of escape. Fifteen yards behind the scrub he found a path paralleling the beach. He turned away from the village, and began to walk, alert for any sound of pursuit. None came.

After a hundred yards, the track widened out into a clearing. The sandy floor had been stamped down in a rough circle, hardened by the concerted effort of countless feet. To the east, a small path led back towards the unseen beach. Waves crashing against the shore just beyond the screen of bushes. The birds which had sounded so clearly on the sand were muted here, dulled, as if afraid to disturb the tranquillity. In the centre stood a wooden platform, hewn from trees that could not have stood locally.

Marius had not seen a single copse containing wood that straight. Any tree he had sighted on his journey so far had been stunted, wizened, twisted by the wind and the sandy soil into an arthritic cripple. Someone had transported these logs, a massive undertaking for such a tiny, unimportant village. The tower stood eight feet high, and was equally as long. Marius circled it warily. It was four feet wide at either end, and the logs were stacked in such a way that the sides formed ladders. Clearly, people were meant to climb to the top, but for what purpose?

Marius set his foot on the lowest rung. If nothing

else, he should be able to see the surrounding countryside from the top, perhaps spot any pursuit, and
plan the next stage of his journey. He hauled himself
upwards. Once his head cleared the top he paused. A
body lay in repose upon the log shelf. His eyes were
closed, his hands crossed over his chest. He was
dressed in what were obviously his best clothes – a
simple shirt and trousers, with a dun cloak over one
shoulder. Frayed at the edges, worn thin by years of
wear, but clean and patched, and beaten smooth so
that they lay comfortably over his dead flesh.

Marius nodded. Of course. A funeral table. It made
sense now. The surrounding land was too sandy to
accord a decent burial, and what fertile land there was
could not be wasted for the task – the villagers needed
it to grow whatever poor crops they could. The body
before him would make perfect fertiliser, Marius
knew. But he wasn't about to climb back down and
educate the villagers. Exposure as a method of burial,
then, and the bones consigned to the nearby sea once
they had been picked clean. Which meant the clearing, and the beach beyond, were undoubtedly sacred
ground.

Marius relaxed. Sacred ground meant taboos, and
taboos meant that the villagers, even should they be
pursuing him, would not rush into the clearing without some form of permission, or preparation, or
prayer. He would have time to work things out. He
climbed to the top of the table, and sat on the edge,
laying Nandus' crown down next to him and flexing
his fingers. The view was really quite exhilarating. As
he surmised, a small, enclosed beach lay to the east,

waves crashing with some anger against a steeply rising stone slope. To the west, the scrub rose gently into a series of low-lying hills that Marius recognised as the tail end of the Spinal Ranges.

With a grin, he placed the world around him. South must lie Borgho City, and if he followed the mountains a day or two, and turned north, he'd wander into the outer fringes of Vernus. Which meant, he thought, turning his neck to peer to the southwest, the highway from Vernus to Scorby lay in that direction, maybe no more than two or three days' walk, especially if he had no need to sleep or rest. Which meant he could be in Scorby City itself in little over a week, assuming he could keep himself hidden, and avoid confrontations, and find a way to enter the city without arousing suspicion. Then all he had to do was spirit the King away before his entombment, and get him out of the city without being seen… That part of the plan could wait, he decided. He had plenty of time to consider his options as he walked. Any motion was better than none. He reached down to recover the crown.

A hand was wrapped around the thin band of gold. Marius stared down at it. The dead man's hand was gripping the crown. As Marius watched, the corpse raised it so it hung over his expressionless face. His eyes sprung open, focussing first upon the crown and then sliding over so that he gazed directly at Marius. A blackened tongue slid out from between his lips, licked them, and returned. He and Marius stared at each other for long seconds. Then the corpse sat up, and extended his hand.

"I am Vun," he said. "Tanning Master of the village of Ebthek."

"Marius Helles," Marius took his hand and shook it. Vun looked about himself.

"Ah," he said, taking in his perch. "It appears one of us is dead. Or perhaps," he looked himself over, and Marius, "both of us. Are you to be my guide?"

"Uh, no. No, I'm afraid not. I'm just passing through, actually." Marius indicated the circlet. "I have a… task, I have to complete."

"I see." Vun sat up fully, and swung his legs over the edge of the platform. "So I am dead, yes, but not yet in the land of the dead. How is this so?"

Marius shrugged. "I wish I knew. I'm in a similar position. It's… confusing, to say the least."

"Confusing? What is to be confused about? We are dead. It is a simple enough thing."

"I wish I had your confidence."

Vun indicated their surroundings. "Life is simple, friend Marius. Death more so. No need to complicate matters. Here." He handed the crown back. "Complete your task, and good luck to you. Then meet me in the land of the dead." He swung his feet back up and lay down again. "I will look for you."

"But… don't you know what's going to happen to you?"

"It already has, friend."

"No, I mean…" Marius pointed to the sky. "You're out here for the birds. They're going to peck at you until you're nothing but bones. And then your villagers are going to climb up here and throw those bones in the ocean. There's no land of the dead for you in that."

Vun laughed. If there was one sound he was never going to get used to, Marius decided, it was a dead man's laugh. "Have you no faith, friend? Do you not follow the Truthful Way?"

Marius sighed. When some people talked, you could just hear the capitals. "No."

"The body is a jar of clay, my friend, a vessel for the soul. The bird is a messenger from Heaven. He breaks the jar and sets the soul free. I shall walk through the Kingdom of the Dead as a transformed being. Higher, purer, more worthy of God. And I shall look for you, and hope to find you there." He closed his eyes, and Marius realised why there was no expression on his face. He was at peace. Marius sighed again.

"I envy you your faith," he said, and realised with a start that, just at this moment, he did. He looked up at the birdless sky. "But…"

"Yes?"

He glanced at Vun, then at his own nakedness., and shuddered. This, he thought, is about as low as I could possibly fall.

"If you're waiting for the birds to release your soul," he said carefully, "Surely those clothes you're wearing are going to get in the way?"

# TWENTY

Marius climbed down the final step and jumped onto the clearing floor. Above him, Vun peered over the edge and offered him a wave.

"Safe journey, my friend."

"And you," Marius waved back. "I hope the birds come soon."

He turned his back on the tower and made his way towards the track. He'd learned a lot from Vun as they sat atop the tower. The track led down to a major roadway a mile to the west. Every three months or so, men from the village carried cured hides down to the road where they were met by a trader from Borgho, who paid them a small price for each hide they delivered. The trader took the hides back to Borgho, for what purpose, Vun could not say. He had been born in the village, and had never left. Village men rarely did, and those who left never came back.

Marius was not surprised. Faced with a lifetime of rummaging around in the skins of dead animals, he wouldn't turn his back on the fleshpots of Borgho either. But Vun was made of sterner stuff: he'd grown up at the

tanning tables, and had died underneath one when a
rotten leg had given away and crushed his back as he
was reaching for a fallen rabbit pelt. If Vun's timing was
right, the Borghan trader would be along in a day or so
to pick up the quarterly payload. Marius pulled at the
seam of Vun's simple cotton shirt. If he could find something to cover his face, if he could find some method of
payment, if the trader agreed to give him space on the
cart, he could avoid a long and tedious walk to the outskirts of Borgho.

If not… Marius gazed south, towards the rise that
heralded the beginning of the Spinal Ranges If not, he
would cut along the trade route that ran parallel to the
range, swinging across the plains east of Borgho in a
giant loop to eventually arrive at Scorby City. It would
be a long journey, and it had already been almost a
month since he had seen Tanspar dead on the battlefield at Jezel. Traditionally, the King lay in state for a
full season, three months of the year, so that all his
mourning citizens could file past in tribute. Then he
was interred in the crypt of the great Bone Cathedral,
beneath a single stone of more than a ton in weight,
carved with scenes depicting his greatest triumphs. Lib-
erating him from that would be a severe test of Marius'
skills to say the least. To say the most, it would be impossible.

Far better to spirit him away whilst he lay in the
open. All Marius would have to contend with under
those circumstances were the thousands of loyal citizens shuffling through the viewing area each day, plus
the tense and wary honour guard, and the citizens of
Scorby, and the militia, not to mention dragging a

heavy and rather recognisable corpse across who-knew-how-many miles of open countryside before finding a way to bring him down to the land of the dead.

He quickly changed the subject. Things were not quite that bleak. He knew how to contact the dead – his conversations with Nandus and Vun had shown him that – and any motion was better than none. And right now, motion meant getting his dead backside to the main road to intercept the trader. He increased his pace. Do the job in front of you – another of his father's aphorisms, but one that held water in his present circumstance.

He arrived at the track within a few minutes, and turned down it, away from the village. A passer-by would not have noticed anything more than the tiniest gap in the undergrowth. It was only used to bring the revered dead down to their resting place, and four times a year by those carrying hides to the road. Any path the villagers beat through the branches quickly became overgrown again. Nature plays a longer waiting game than man. But Marius had spent half his life hiding from one person or another, and his experienced eye picked out the multitude of tiny clearances and footfalls that denoted the correct passage. He stole forward, senses alert for the first sign of approaching villagers. Having to explain his presence, not to mention his choice of clothing, was not something he relished. He made the road in short order, and waited, crouched behind a bush that offered a ready hiding place with a good view of both the roadway and the track.

For the rest of the day, he was alone with his thoughts. The sun reached its apex, paused to survey its domain, and beat a hasty retreat towards evening.

Marius shrunk back into the undergrowth in time with the shadows, reaching a level of stillness uninterrupted by the insects that came out to feast upon him and the little lizards that came to feed upon them. The world hung still within the universe.

Then, some time towards the latter part of the day, voices came to him from down the track. Marius hunkered down, laying on his side and peering through two fronds. Several villagers approached, carrying a long, low-slung stretcher between them. A heap of hides sat upon it. Marius counted thirty, and was even able to identify some of them as rabbits and martens, as well as one large one that must have belonged to some unwary traveller's horse. He watched as the villagers laid the pelts in a tidy pile by the junction of the track and road. Then they left, bar one, a tall, gangly youth with a skinning knife strapped to his hip, who settled his back against them and stared down the track past Marius' hiding place, his arms folded behind his head.

Less than an hour later, a cart bumped and rumbled its way down the track to stop in front of the young villager. A burly man in a travel-worn cloak jumped down from the driving bench and offered his hand in greeting. The young man took it, and began to show the newcomer his wares. Marius listened as they haggled, shaking his head at the way the young villager allowed himself to be conned out of a fair price. Nobody came back to villages like this, he remembered, which meant nobody passed on knowledge of big city practices, and big city prices. Generation after generation of rubes, dying young in conditions only slightly better than subsistence farming. By the time the two men had finished, and shaken hands on the deal, the villagers had given away eighty per cent of the price the unworked hides would fetch in the markets of Borgho.

Somebody should show them how to cut and sew, Marius thought. Surely, even this far from civilisation, people must understand that finished articles fetch a higher price than raw stock. Somebody should show them how to negotiate. Somebody should give them all a clip across the ear-hole. For half a second, he was ready to jump to his feet and intrude, and show the young fool how to deal with a merchant. Then he caught sight of the loose grey flesh on the back of his hands, and stilled the impulse. The merchant rounded his cart and pulled three hessian sacks from the back, presenting them to the youth. Vegetables, undoubtedly bartered from villages further down the merchant's route. He placed them at the youth's feet, and clapped him on the shoulder.

"Open them," Marius muttered, "Get your hand into them. Pull the bottom up, for God's sake." The oldest trick in the book – hide a small bag of rotten produce in the middle of the sack as you fill it, then remove the smaller bag as you reach the top, just before you tie up. Everything round the edges feels like good stock. It's only if you plunge your hand into the middle that you discover the softness, the rot that will overtake the rest of your purchase. Nobody in a city would buy a sack of food without giving it a good stir. These villagers probably just accepted the fact that a certain proportion of their hard-won goods would be spoiled.

Sure enough, the young man simply hefted the sacks on to his back, nodded his thanks to the merchant, and turned back up the track. Marius realised he was gripping his thighs with suppressed fury, and frowned in surprise. The smart take advantage of the naïve. It was the way of his world, the code by which he'd made his living for twenty years. Why should he be surprised to see it in action here, never mind angry? He let go the ground, flexed his fingers. He knew why. He was not the same Marius who had made his living that way. Death changes a man. He raised his eyes once more to the merchant as he threw the first armful of hides into the back of his cart. He could do something. But what?

In the end, he did nothing. The merchant loaded the last of the hides, climbed up behind his oxen, and cracked the reins against their rumps, while Marius lay behind his bush and watched. Only when the cart had disappeared around a bend did he rise and step out into the ruts before him, staring after the merchant with his hands on his hips, a frown creasing his features. Like it or not, and Marius didn't, the fellow was only making his living. Marius couldn't bring himself to deny him that. He'd already done that once, he realised. The old man on the mountain track, just after he had escaped from Gerd. He'd taken his cart, his mule, even his hat, and not thought twice about the old man's fate.

He stared at the empty road. As soon as he was free of this curse, he decided. As soon as he was human again. He would come back to this village, and show them the true value of their labours. Next trade, or the one after, would be more fair. It was a childish dream, but it was the best he could offer. He turned his back on them, and strode down the road towards distant Scorby.

Within a few hundred feet he found himself breaking into a trot, and then the slow lope he had learned while in the Emir's armies. The Emir's soldiers could cover fifteen miles a day utilising the long, energy-saving rhythm, and still be in a condition to fight at the end of the journey. Marius had been a fitter man in his youth, but dead muscles do not fatigue, and dead men do not need to stop and rest just because it is night, or because they need to eat, drink or shit. The miles disappeared as he ran onwards. Day slowed towards evening, and fell into the dark. Marius did not stop. He planned as he ran, mind turned inwards to circle his task, picking at it like a crow at a dead man's body. The road upon which he ran met another; then another; widening, smoothing out, becoming more formalised until, eventually, his feet left compacted dirt and stepped onto the cobbled surface of the highway between Borgho and Frems, the capital of Bollus, the tiny nation to the north. He crossed the highway without pausing, plunged into the fields beyond, and kept running.

Few travellers would be abroad at night. Those who had not found rest in a tavern or lodge would be pulled over to the side of the road, tucked into the backs of carts or curled up beneath a tree with a cloak wrapped around them for warmth. Still, Marius was not prepared to take the chance of an unexpected greeting. He could travel faster in a straight line, and avoid confrontation by sticking to the wilderness. Borgho was two hundred miles to his left, and he had another hundred beyond that to get to Scorby City. Even covering fifteen miles between dawns, it was a long way. He ran on, as the sky lightened and became day, as the sun rose and fell, as night reclaimed the world, across the open fields along the highway's edge, into the woods beyond, up and down the spider-web of animal tracks and clearings, keeping the hulking presence of the Spinal Ranges to his right.

After two days he began to angle left, away from the mountains. He burst out of the trees and entered the massive plains that swept across the central area of Scorby. A pride of leitts kept pace with him for a while, snapping at his heels in the hope of bringing him down, but he maintained his pace, outstripping the heavy-legged predators. They wheeled away, went back to the long grasses to wait for slower, more easily ambushed prey.

By the evening of the third day the land began to rise. The isolated trees began to bunch together. The going became heavier, the ground more uneven. Marius slogged his way up the rise, turning with the hills as they swung round to a more southerly aspect. From here they would swing down to pass thirty miles east of Scorby City, providing the city's natural defences with their high passes and deep ravines. Here the hills were more gradual: lower; rubbed down by time and, depending on how many legends you were prepared to believe, the arcane sexual practices of giants. Marius changed his stride, swapping the distance-eating lope of the army for a combination of climbing and sheer graft. It took him a further day to crest the hills, and only then, when he was at their peak, did he stop and take stock of his surroundings.

He sat on a high, flat rock and stared down at the valleys below, mouth pursed in disappointment at the knowledge that five days of solid running had left him without the need to draw a single breath, or wipe even a lone bead of sweat from his forehead. He knew this place. He had been here before, seen the world from this angle. He blanked his mind, took in the view: the massive bluffs falling down in helter-skelter order to the green floor below; the few wide-winged hunting birds hanging on the breezes above; the broken rocks scattered across the landscape like the rotting bones of long dead gods. Something important had happened here, if he could only remember what. Somehow, he knew that knowledge was crucial to what was to come. Further down the slope, beyond the next peak, something was tucked into the long, flat valley floor. Marius stared along the broken path that led from his seat to the next high point along the range, as if by some dint of concentration he could stare through the body of the mountain to what lay beyond. He conjured up a vision of the valley, populated it from memory and, at last, raised a hand to his forehead in surprise.

"Good gods."

Just over the rise, and down the split valley on the other side, lay a few acres of relatively flat and rock-free land. A thin mud track bisected the huddle of half a dozen huts providing the miserable farming village with its only connection to the wider world. Three mangy dogs, owned by nobody and everybody at once, ran between those huts, chased by the few children owned by exactly the same people, or not, as the dogs. The fields held squash and other wizened, barely-identifiable marrows, and if the summer were particularly dry and followed by a particularly temperate autumn, cabbages sprang up without anyone's attempt to tend them.

At the far end of the village someone had erected a loose collection of wood walls that served as sty, barn and shelter for the motley collection of pigs and the single horse the village owned. And several feet behind that, on the path down to the plain beyond, wherein the single most important battle of the last twenty years had taken the life of Scorby's King only a few weeks ago, was the spot where a stupid young swineherd had persuaded Marius that he really did, after all, need an apprentice to help him in his endeavours. Marius rose from his perch and took a few slow steps towards the nearby peak. If there was a spot on this Earth more accursed in his life, it certainly wasn't closer than this one. And even if this miserable stain of a village was the only place on Earth he could find what he needed, well, he was still going to look everywhere else first. He wouldn't step foot in that village for a king's fortune, for all the concubines in Tal, hell, if it meant the restoration of his life itself.

Within half an hour he began his descent towards the huts a hundred or so metres below.

He was skirting the village by sunrise, treading carefully through the rocks and runnels that marked the edge of the village lands and the beginning of the drop-off towards the valley floor. The villagers would not rise for another half hour or so, until the upper rim of the sun was showing across the horizon. To Marius' enhanced eyesight it was already day. All was silent. Only the normal pre-dawn sounds of animals at rest disturbed the peace.

As he neared the sty, however, the grunting of the pigs was underpinned by something more rhythmic – the scraping of metal across the ground, and the tuneless humming of a voice he recognised. He stepped out from behind the pen's wall. Someone had been busy since he was last here – at the far side of the enclosure, a rough plot had been laid out and fenced in with gnarled wooden posts and rusting wire. A dozen scrawny chickens rooted around in the dust, skittering out of the way of the hunched figure that moved from end to end, turning over the floor of the run with a rake. As it passed, the chickens returned to peck without hope at the turned-over ground. Marius watched the lone workman for a moment, shaking his head in disbelief. Then he stepped out of the shadow of the sty and leaned gingerly against the fence.

"Grubbing in the dirt," he said. "It suits you."

The figure made no response. Marius watched in silence as he finished his slow, methodical coverage of the run, then made his way back through a small gate. He leant the rake against a wall and picked up a hoe, bending his attention to the piles of mud and dung churned up by the pigs.

"Ah," Marius said in amusement. "I was mistaken. Now, now you've found your level."

Again he was ignored. He sighed.

"Come on, Gerd. You know it's me. At least say something."

Gerd flicked a glance at him, then bent his head back over his task. Marius stepped forward to peer over his shoulder, stepping carefully between the mounds of pig droppings that Gerd was collecting.

"Nope," he said. "It must be fascinating for you, I'm sure, but I can't see it."

"It's honest work," Gerd replied. "Good work."

"It speaks!" Marius clapped a hand on his shoulder. Gerd neither acknowledged it nor shrugged it off. It lay there, like a dead fish, until Marius coughed and removed it. "So why are you here, then? I thought you'd be tracking me to the ends of the Earth like a little dead bloodhound."

"Grandma needs me." Gerd swung the hoe towards another pile of shit, spraying wet refuse against Marius' legs. "Sty needs maintaining, chores need doing. She's getting old."

"And she's blind as a judge and crazy as a banana skin. It's a tragic tale." He leaned in, so that his mouth was less than a foot from Gerd's ear. "I recommend a pillow, placed over the face." He straightened. "Where are all your dead chums, then?"

"We had a difference of opinion."

"Oh, really?"

"They wanted to hunt you down, no matter where on the globe you ran to, and tear you limb from limb and scatter you to the four corners of the wind, so that every moment of your afterlife was spent in torturous agony, never to be reconstituted and find peace."

"I see. And you?"

Gerd swung the hoe upwards and brandished it like a pike.

"I wanted to do it myself."

"Oh, you have to be kidding."

Gerd wasn't kidding. Without so much as a change in expression, he swung at Marius' head.

Marius ducked, and skipped backwards, out of reach. The hoe is not a graceful weapon, and Gerd was a less than graceful wielder. Compared to him, Marius was a dancer, a prize fighter, a light-footed professional fencer. Then, just as quickly, compared to Gerd he was a man lying on his back in a slippery pile of pig shit. He rolled over and drew his hands underneath his chest, ready to push himself up. A cold weight pressed against the back of his neck, and pushed him down until he lay with his face deep in the warm, stinking manure. He squirmed until he could tilt part of his face out of the mess – an eye, and the corner of his mouth – and squinted upwards. Gerd stood above him, his weight pressing the hoe down onto Marius. Marius spat his lips free of dung.

"What are you going to do?" he managed to ask. "Kill me?"

Gerd reached for something just out of his field of vision. A moment later, a broad, heavy-bladed axe struck the dirt an inch from his free eye and sank an inch into the hard ground.

"Chop you up," Gerd said. "into different pieces. Feed your limbs to the pigs, throw your torso down the cliff face. Give your head to the dead."

The pigs squealed in excitement, as if the sound of the axe heralded a new meal. They butted against the wooden fence, giving Marius a new memory of fear to block in later days. He was fleetingly glad that his bowels had nothing to add to the already-covered ground.

"And what will that do?" Marius eyed the nicked and stained axe head. He had no doubt it would be capable of the task. "They won't get their king that way."

"It'll make me feel better." Gerd pulled the axe up, out of Marius' view. He braced, waiting for the first heavy impact. Instead, the pressure against his neck lessened. He rolled over, conscious of the wet, sticky, mess across his face and hair. Gerd had replaced the axe on its mount, just inside the sty door. Now he did the same with the hoe.

"Get up," he said without looking at Marius. "Wash yourself off. You stink."

Marius sat up. "So?"

"You're not meeting my grandmother smelling like pig shit." He stepped over to a barrel in the lee of the shed, plunged his hands into the top, and splashed water on his face and upper body. "Hurry up."

Marius stood. He edged over to the barrel and washed himself down, keeping one wary eye on Gerd.

"What makes you think I want to meet your grandmother again?" he asked. The last time he was in the village, he had met the old woman to explain why Gerd was leaving, and how he would look after the boy and see him safe. All the while he had been forced to swallow down the lumpiest, indigestible cabbage soups he had ever eaten. There were parts of it that still hadn't digested properly. Two more minutes with the axe and the pigs would have been pulling bits out of his intestines like truffles.

"Because," Gerd replied, turning his back on Marius and walking towards the village centre. "You obviously need me, or you wouldn't be here. And if you don't, I won't help you. And I'll take you apart with the axe."

"Compelling argument." Marius followed behind Gerd. Men were just beginning to exit the huts, yawning as the rays of the sun stretched the shadows across the open square. As they saw Gerd and Marius they nodded slightly, before averting their gazes and hurrying past, to their jobs. Marius watched them, and saw the cautious nods that Gerd gave back.

"They don't seem too bothered by your current state."

"I'm a hard worker," Gerd replied. "I'm honest. I keep to myself. I built the chicken run, and repaired the sty. I've almost cleared another six acres of field in the lower valley." He shrugged. "Dead isn't the same here as it is down on the plains. They may be a little spooked by it, but as long as I'm not lazy and I don't touch their daughters, they leave me alone." He paused at the entrance of a low-framed, ramshackle hut on the outskirts of the village. "Be nice." He stepped inside. "Grandma? There's someone to see you."

Marius sighed, and put one hand on the door frame.

"I'm going to regret this," he said to the wood, and followed Gerd into the hut.

# TWENTY-ONE

"More soup?" The old woman stood above Marius, a ladle held in front of her like a white walking stick. Hot lumps of something that may have started out as vegetable matter dripped from it onto the back of Marius' hand. He watched it slide off onto the table, wishing he had a cloth to wipe it away. There was no chance in hell he was going to lick his hand clean.

"Uh, no, no thank you," he said, eyeing the bowl in front of him. It overflowed with the greasy, viscous product, the colour and consistency of pus. "I couldn't eat another bite."

"Are you sure?" the old woman waved the ladle about like a weapon. Hot liquid sprayed the table, the floor, and Marius. He held up a hand to ward off the attacking droplets.

"Quite sure. Thank you."

"Well, if you're sure." She turned away, and filled hers and Gerd's bowls with uncanny accuracy, before returning the cooking pot to its station next to the fire, and gaining her seat. Gerd picked up his spoon, and the old woman slapped his hand.

"You know better than that," she said. Gerd dropped the spoon with a guilty look at Marius. Marius left his own cutlery where it lay. He had no intention of picking it up to begin with. The old woman intertwined her twig-like fingers and raised her hands before her face.

"We thank you, Lord Gods," she began, and Marius could not help the slight hiss of derision that escaped his teeth. The old woman tilted her head so that her unseeing eyes fixed upon him. Marius stared back, until her lack of blinking began to make him uncomfortable. The moment he looked away, she continued. "For this blessing of food, and for the comforts of life which you bestow upon us, your humble servants. To your glory be."

"To your glory be," Gerd said in a small voice.

"Let's eat." The old woman raised her spoon and began to scoop the warm goo into her toothless mouth at a rate of knots. As she slurped and slapped her lips together in appreciation, Marius took the opportunity to examine his surroundings. Nothing had changed since his last visit. The single room that served as kitchen, living quarters and, he sniffed in horror, bathroom, still resembled a giant game of pick-up-sticks that had somehow ended up on their ends. Dried garlands of something that may have started off as plant life hung from nails, and if there was a right angle to be had, he couldn't find it. The only thing more rickety than the furniture was the old woman herself, and Marius still wasn't sure which of the pigs outside were her pets and which were her direct relatives. He stared in horror at the thick dribbles that escaped her maw and ran slowly across her hairy chin.

"You don't pray," she said in a spray of beige liquid. "Are you a godless man?"

"I have my own beliefs." I believe you are disgusting, he thought. I believe I want to get the hell out of here. I believe I want to be ill.

"Hmph," the old woman's lip curled. "Too clever to need salvation, eh? Don't feel the need to protect your immortal soul?" She waved her spoon at him like a sergeant major's crop. "Too busy, too clever, to think about life everlasting?"

"Oh, no." Marius stared at the chipped spoon as it swished about, dangerously close to the bridge of his nose. "Everlasting life is very much in my thoughts. Very much." He twisted his gaze towards Gerd, head resolutely bent over his emptying bowl. "Life after death is of interest, and all its many wonders."

Gerd peeked up from his meal, saw the look on Marius' face, and quickly ducked back down.

"Gerd, darling?"

"Yes, Grandmamma?"

"I'm a silly old bissum, I know. But I've gone and left the gate to the upper field open. Would you be a dear and close it for me?" She turned a toothless smile upon her grandson. "Please?"

Gerd glanced from her to Marius and back.

"You'll be all right?"

"Of course, sweetheart. Mr... I'm sorry, what was your name again, dearie?"

"Spint. Mister Spint."

"Mister Spint and I will just chat while you're gone, dear. Be a good lad."

"Yes, Grandmamma." Gerd rose, wiped his mouth on his shirt sleeve, and made for the door. Marius watched him go, while the old woman kept her sightless gaze pinned to his chin. As soon as the door closed behind him, she coughed.

"Right, now. Let's cut the bullshit, shall we?"

"I'm sorry?"

"You heard me, sonny."

Marius blinked. The old woman was staring right at his eyes, her blank white orbs appearing to look right through his skin to the lies beneath. "Mister Spint indeed. You think I'm stupid? Like I never went to the theatre?"

Marius raised an eyebrow in acknowledgement. "Well, it didn't seem likely."

"And what am I then? Mistress Comiglia?"

Marius' eyes widened. Mister Spint and Mistress Comiglia were married, in the play from which he had taken the name. The play was bawdy, and their marriage was, depending on the production... explicit. "Wait a minute," he said hurriedly. "If you think that's why I chose..."

The old crone cackled. "Don't be stupid." She leaned forward, her cabbage breath washing over him. "I know who you are, boy. You think I don't recognise your voice? Lack of sight doesn't make a woman stupid. It sharpens the senses, and the memory."

"I–"

"Tell me what happened to my grandson."

"What?"

"You heard me." She leaned back, and crossed her arms. "You're the one who came here with stories of gold and adventure, and stole my boy away from me. I know that. He's changed, and I don't mean he's grown up."

"What do you mean?"

"I'm not stupid. I can hear. He doesn't sleep. He lies there, pretending, those nights he remembers to, but he can't fool me. He's not that bright."

"You've got that right," Marius muttered.

"Watch it."

"Sorry."

"So?"

Marius kept his gaze fixed on the door. He could feel the old woman's eyes looking through him, feel the muted heat of her dislike washing over him in waves. She sat, immobile as a weathered rock, as if she had all the time in the world for his answer.

Finally: "He's dead."

"What?"

Marius sighed. "He's dead. Down on the plain. A soldier. He's animated, he thinks and dreams and carries on like he always has, but he's not alive. He's been to the Kingdom of the Dead, and… he's dead."

The old woman should have exploded, called him a liar, or worse. She should have swung a gnarled hand at his head, tipped back her chair, spat in his face and accused him of sins innumerable for his falsehoods. Instead, she raised her hands to her face, and breathed deeply into them, once, twice.

"I knew it," she said as she lowered them to her lap. "I knew it."

"How? How could you possibly–"

"The villagers never talk to him." She swung out of

her chair and shuffled over to the single window, raising her face to the shaft of sunlight that came through as if basking in the early morning heat. "They show him respect, of course. He's a good worker. He pretty much rebuilt our corrals by himself, and re-ploughed the upper fields, since he came back. But they don't talk. Not to him."

She turned from the window, and tilted her chin towards Marius. "If you're old, and blind, people think you're deaf as well. They forget to stop talking when you come near." She sighed, and a fire seemed to dim inside her. "What did you do to him?"

"I didn't…"

"You took him away, and got him killed, and now… " she returned to her seat, slumped into it. "What is he going to do when I'm gone, eh? What then?"

"I… I don't know."

"No. I don't suppose you do."

They sat in silence for long minutes, until the door opened and Gerd stepped through. He looked from Marius to his grandmother, and back again, frowning.

"You told her," he said finally.

"Yes."

"You *told* her."

"Yes. I did."

"What on Earth did she–?"

"I'm in the room."

Both men turned towards the old woman, sitting upright at the table, staring at something immeasurably far away. In an instant, the anger left them.

"Sorry."

"Sorry."

"Right," she said, standing. She felt her way along the edge of the table towards the chopping block and cooking utensils stacked in the far corner. Marius realised that it was the first time he had seen her need assistance to move around the room. If Gerd noticed he said nothing, but it was obvious to Marius that something had left the old woman, some spark of resistance towards the fates. "Mister…"

"Spint."

"Spint, says you'll be going with him."

"Grandmamma, I don't want…"

"You'll be needing something to tide you over." She busied herself rummaging amongst the bags and baskets, emerging with a cobb loaf and small bag. "This should see you for the day."

"Grandmamma…"

"Take a good stick. You can't go wrong with a good stick." She coughed, a sound that was as much sob as anything, then steadied herself and made her way back to the chair. "Mister Spint says he needs to go straight away, so you'd best be on the hop now, boy. Give me a kiss."

"Grand… yes, Grandmamma." Gerd stepped forward and kissed her offered cheek. She grabbed his neck, and held him to her for a moment.

"You be careful now, boy. Just… be careful."

"Yes, Grandmamma." Gerd straightened, and took the bag and loaf. He stepped past Marius to the door. "I'll be back as soon as I can."

"Yes, yes, I know."

"I love you."

The old woman said nothing, then, finally, "Off with

you now, boy. Come home soon."

Gerd opened the door, and stepped through. Marius made to follow.

"Mister Spint?"

"Yes."

"See him right, you hear me?"

"I…" He saw her then: old, small, frightened; sitting alone at her table, with her only comfort standing outside, suddenly alien and terrifying to her. He stepped backwards, and silently put the door between them. Gerd was waiting a dozen steps away, head bowed. Without a word, Marius joined him.

They stopped long enough for Marius to wash the drying remains of the old woman's soup from his face and arms. Then they were outside the village and running down the mud track towards the plains at the base of the mountains. They ran in silence, avoiding each other's gaze, letting the lie of the land dictate their progress. The ravines closed in behind them, closing them off from sight of the village, until they ran between grey walls that pressed against their minds with solemn finality. It was not until they had left the mountains behind and were well into the long, slow undulations of the flatlands that Gerd finally spoke.

"Why?" he asked, as they crossed a trade road and leaped across the drainage ditch on the other side.

"Why what?"

"Why did you tell her?"

"Because…" Marius stared at the grasses around him, at the open horizons and the roads he could not follow, "I'm sick of lying. I mean, look at me. Look where it's gotten me. I'm just… I'm just sick of it."

He put his head down, ignoring the world and the sunshine and his own mind. The dead men ran on for several more minutes.

"She won't survive, you know."

"What?"

"Grandmamma. She won't be able to cope with it. Your truth." Gerd glanced at him. "You've killed her."

After that, there was nothing left to say. They ran on, through the rolling plains of the Scorban Flatlands, skirting the farmlets and freeholds that dotted the plains like breadcrumbs, maintaining their tireless pace through both day and night. They travelled for six days, swinging past the distant lights of Borgho City and passing through the wonders of the Grass Fields without pausing; crossing the battlefield where their deaths had occurred with nothing more than a glance at each other and a thin-lipped tightening of their jaws; finally pushing down towards the coast, altering their stride as the smooth plains gave way to the more broken lands of the coastal ridge, tying their path to the roads that criss-crossed the lands outside the capital, following the major highway between Scorby and Borgho, all the while keeping themselves hidden from view, a hundred metres or more from the road's edge, behind the fences and the first line of trees.

Finally, as night was falling and they were no more than a day's journey from the capital, Marius called a halt. They settled in a small clearing amongst the trees, gathered branches and leaves from the surrounding forest floor, and built a fire. They sat on either side, staring into the flames. Marius held his hands towards the fire, examining their backs in the flickering light.

"Funny," he said at last, surprised at how loud he sounded.

"What is?" Gerd looked through the fire at him, face clouded with suspicion.

"I shouldn't need a fire. But I do." He turned his hands, stared at his palms. "Once it's night, and I'm still, I feel the cold. My hands are freezing." He looked up, caught Gerd's look. "Why do you suppose that is?"

Gerd shrugged. Marius stared at him for several seconds. "You do too, don't you? Look at the way you're huddled around yourself. You've been shifting around ever since you sat down, warming one side then the other. Why is that, Gerd? Surely, surely we shouldn't feel it. We are dead. Aren't we?"

"Well, *I* am." Gerd raised a hand to his chest. "A Scorban soldier sliced me like a haunch of beef. I'm sure you remember." He ran his fingers across his chest, and Marius could imagine the scar he felt. "You let it happen, after all. Did you get a good view?"

"I… I'm sorry."

"I beg your pardon?"

"I'm *sorry*." Marius looked into the flames again, saw the battlefield laid out in its depths. "I am. I should never… it's been a long journey since then. I'm really sorry."

Gerd sighed. "You bloody well should be." He stood and rounded the fire to sit by Marius' side. "I should hate you."

"Why not?" Marius smiled, a short, bitter movement of his lips. "You'd hardly be alone."

"No, I imagine I wouldn't." Gerd held out a hand towards his companion. "I don't hate you. I did. But not anymore."

Hesitantly, Marius took the offered hand, and they shook. "Why not?"

"I've had a lot of time to think since we left Grandmamma." He poked at the flames with a stick, watched the sparks that swirled up into the darkness. "She's going to die, and when she does, there will be nobody there to look after her, to make sure she's okay, surrounded by all those dead strangers."

Marius had his own thoughts on who would need protecting from whom once Grandmamma made her journey below, but he kept them to himself. Gerd was staring off into the night, and he sensed another of his homespun soliloquies approaching.

"Maybe I died for a reason. Maybe it's so I can help her, once she's arrived. It's all I've ever done. I'm good at it. I like it. Besides, I've been thinking about it, and it's not like you ever lied to me."

"Sorry? What?" Marius' eyes widened.

Gerd smiled. "You promised me adventure and riches, and seeing the sights of the world. Well, you've given me those. Not the riches, admittedly." He laughed. "But adventure, sights, experiences?" He waved at the surrounding night. "You weren't joking, were you?"

Marius stared at him in shock. After a moment, he began to giggle. Their laughter grew, cutting away their tension, their fears, until they were leaning against each other, tears streaming down their faces, howling with unrestrained laughter. Eventually they leaned back, and wiped away the moisture on their cheeks.

"See?" Marius said, brandishing his wet fingers. "This is what I mean. How is this possible?"

"What? This?" Gerd displayed his own wet hand.

"Yes. I mean…" Marius stared at his hand, glistening in the light of the fire. "Every time I forget my situation, it's like… it's like my body does too. When I was with Keth it was like I was still alive. I could feel my heart beating, I could feel… blood in…" He glanced down at his groin, "Areas. And the way I looked…" Again, he held his hand up so Gerd could see. "How long have we been dead? A couple of months? Where's the decay? Where's the degradation? I look at myself at times, see my face in a glass, and it's there, all the ravages of death, and I have to turn away and hide myself from view. But other times, times like now…" He looked his companion full in the face. "It's not there, is it? Not on you. Not on me. Why is that, Gerd? Why?"

They stared at each other, taking in their faces, their exposed arms, the light and vitality in their eyes. Gerd raised a hand to his face, felt the health and firmness of his skin.

"I don't know," he said at last. "I… I don't know."

"No." Marius stared into the depths of the fire. "Neither do I."

They lapsed into silence again. Marius felt deadness seeping into his skin, brought on by his hopelessness, his bewilderment. He glanced down at the back of his hand, and saw the first tinges of grey as his skin dried and shrunk over his bones. Gerd noticed, and stirred.

"So, tomorrow," he said. "What do we do? What's the plan?"

"Plan?" Marius replied, holding his hand up and turning it this way and that in the light, watching death spread across it like cancer. "I haven't had a plan since this whole thing began."

# TWENTY-TWO

There are larger cities on the continent of Lenk. There are more grandiose cities. But nowhere is there one that oozes power the way that Scorby City does. At its heart is a single castle, melded together over centuries from a sprawling cascade of buildings clinging along the ridge of a single, low-lying mountain. The locals call it the Radican, and the buildings that crowd its base have taken on some of its majesty – nowhere in the Scorban empire will you find cottages more ornate, or a populace so assured of their place at the centre of world affairs.

The wall that surrounds Scorby City is over twenty feet thick, although nobody has tried to invade in over three hundred years. It isn't worth the effort. Any potential invader would be so quickly and effectively wrapped in red tape that signing the necessary permission forms just to rape and pillage – and those forms actually exist – would take up most of a season. Scorby City is an oasis of rules and regulations in a world that all too often gives itself over to lawlessness and chaos. Everything is planned, from the layout of its square-cobbled streets to the number of times the cathedral bells ring to signify prayer.

The guards wear uniforms of clean, pressed material. The fruit and vegetables for sale in the markets are free of blight and deformity. The children are polite, the maidens virtuous, the politicians truthful and well-meaning. There isn't anyone on the entire continent who doesn't hate the smug, supercilious lot of them. But it was exactly this type of regimentation and order that gave the kings of Scorby an empire – no matter how unoriginal and rigid an army's way of thinking might be, it was priceless when facing an army of drunken, wild-haired mountain dwellers who thought baring buttocks was an effective answer to a rain of exactly three thousand arrows released at twenty second intervals. The Scorban empire was rich in land, and materials, and men, and Scorby City was the clockwork that made it all run.

The Radican rose two hundred feet above the skyline, before ending in a cliff face that fell to the valley floor. Brightly coloured buildings ran along a central avenue all the way to the top, growing in height and grandeur until reaching the Royal Apartments, a six-story edifice that stared out across a massive square at the top. Flags hung every few feet up the length of buildings, and the cobbles gleamed from the daily washing that sent a torrent of muddy water down into the more mundane, working depths of the city. There were children who made a living from combing the mud left behind from those washes, and selling the rings and coins left behind by Radican-dwellers too distracted or proud to recover them.

At its apex, separated from the front of the Royal Apartments by thirty feet of cobbles, as if the buildings themselves wished to step no closer, stood the Bone Cathedral, the final resting place of the kings of Scorby since Scorbus the Conqueror had united the tribes below him and set out to rule the coastal plains. Eighty feet high and with a canopy sixty feet in diameter, it was constructed entirely from the bones of those who had resisted Scorbus and his successor, Thernik the Bone Collector. Those who had never seen the cathedral passed on stories of massive chandeliers made from thigh bones, sconces of hollowed-out skulls, mosaic floors patterned from countless tiny, stained, toe bones. Order is not built on humility. Nobody creates an empire out of politeness. Scholars had estimated that a hundred and twenty thousand skeletons had gone into the making of the cathedral. Scholars are known for being conservative. Had they been even remotely accurate in their calculations, Scorby City would be known as much for its haunted, drunken scholars as for anything else.

A line of people stretched from the massive front doors of the cathedral, past the Royal Apartments, and down the main boulevard of the Radican to the city floor. Every thirty seconds precisely, they took a step forward. Those who went through the doors reappeared at the side of the cathedral twelve minutes later. Then they dispersed, making their way back down the hillside to resume their lives: quiet, reflective, their eyes downcast in deep, sobered thought. Whatever occurred inside the building, for many of these supplicants, would be the defining moment of their lives.

Two robed figures joined the line in the early morning light. They had spent hours before dawn approaching those who came back down the mountain, asking each citizen what they had seen: was it the King? Was he still on display? They had received no reply other than a shake of the head. In the end, the strangers had no choice but to join up and see for themselves, one pace closer every thirty seconds.

"You think it's the King?" Gerd asked as they took their first step forward.

"Has to be." They waited, stepped, waited again. "Look around. These people aren't here because they're being forced." Step. "What do you think it'll take? Eight, ten hours, to climb all the way up?"

They considered the winding path before them, moved, gazed upwards to the looming bone monolith at the end of their journey, moved again. In front of them, and now behind as well, those in the line stepped in concert, a long, silent, solemn dance to inaudible dirge music.

"Ten hours at least."

"Exactly. And look at them." They stared about themselves. The citizens were of a single type – silent, patient, uncomplaining. They had the air of people undertaking a pilgrimage, as if they wished to breathe in every moment, roll it around their minds to draw out every sensation, to be able to gather their children and grandchildren to them in future days and say "I remember when–"

"Silent contemplation," Marius said. "Parishioners, off to see a saint."

"Their poor, dead King." Step.

"Yep."

"And we–"

"Quiet, now." Marius lowered his gaze, stepped, and stepped again.

It took two hours to move past the final row of houses. Then they began to climb the broad avenue that ran between under the arched wings of the Radican. Slowly they rose above the rooftops of the city so that they stood with only the twin rows of frontages on either side. Bored palace residents stared listlessly down at them from the rows of windows above. Tiny alleyways crossed their path at regular intervals, creating side streets whose dead ends opened out onto thin air. Marius found himself counting the steps between each sliver of horizon – the atmosphere on the boulevard, surrounded by the unthinking herd and the high, dull walls of brick and plaster, was oppressive. Another hour passed, then another, the simple procession of step, wait, step dulling his thoughts until his entire world consisted of the grey cloth covering the back of the man in front, his body so attuned to the tedious rhythm of their ascent that it was several seconds before he registered Gerd's elbow digging him in the ribs.

"What? What is it?"

"Your hands."

Marius glanced down.

"Gods damn it." His flesh hung grey and withered across the prominent bones beneath. He glanced up at Gerd. "My face?"

Gerd nodded.

"Fuck." Marius lowered his head so that the edges of the robe hid him from view. "Lesson learned, then. We can't afford to lose our concentration, fall into dead patterns." His hands tingled. He watched in wonder as the skin grew pink, swelling with life until they looked like any other man's. "I'm never going to get used to that." He raised his head. "All right, now?"

"Yes," Gerd pointed ahead. "Here's something to keep you occupied."

"What?"

A dozen feet in front of them, somebody had set up a stall at the side of the queue. Bright painted wood stood in contrasting shades to the equally bright stone behind. The stall was in three parts. As Marius and Gerd watched, people stepped up to the first part, a giant board listing menu items for sale. After thirty seconds they stepped on, and gave their order and money to a fat, bearded man in grease-stained shirt and apron. He shouted it over to the three youths who manned the final section of the stall, who, quick as oiled machinery, seared meat in a massive wok, cut salad, threw it together on flat bread, rolled, folded and wrapped the finished meal, and passed it to the customer before their thirty second journey took them past the stall. Marius nodded in appreciation.

"Clever," he said. "Nothing like a captive market for making good money. You hungry?"

Gerd blinked in surprise. "You know what? I am."

"Me too. And I wasn't a second ago. What do you think?" he smiled mirthlessly, "Is our attention to being alive paying dividends, or are we just patsies for good marketing?" He drew a small bag of coins from inside his robe. "What would you like?"

"Where did you get that?"

"Oh," he smiled, and waved his hand non-committally. "The big city helps those who help themselves."

"Help themselves to others' belongings," Gerd grumbled, but he turned to examine the approaching menu. "There, um," he said after several seconds, "there seems to be an awful lot of rodent on the menu."

Marius laughed. "Don't worry," he said. "Scorbans consider magrats a delicacy. They farm them."

"They what?"

"Sure. There are factory farms on the city outskirts. They raise them like chickens. Very clean, very nice," he said in a passable attempt at a local accent. "They don't just scoop them out of the gutter. Raised on corn and oats, clean water, no garbage. They're good eating, if your cook knows what he's doing." He turned his eyes towards the board, paused long enough to whistle. "These prices, he must know what he's doing, eh?"

Their thirty seconds were up. They stepped forward, within hailing distance of the stall owner.

"What will it be, gentlemen?" he called, rubbing massive, hairy hands down the front of his apron, an act that served merely to stir fresh paths into the layers of grease and grime already there. Marius raised a hand in greeting.

"Business good?" he said with a smile. The stall owner shrugged.

"We're lucky today," he replied.

"Lucky?"

"Another week and we'd have been out of luck, and then…" he turned his hands up in a gesture typical to Scorbans, a short, dismissive upwards chop that said "Just my luck, shit for dinner again". Marius nodded in sympathy.

"How so, friend?"

The fat man indicated the stall. "Not my stall, see? Government owned. We just buy spaces in the lottery. Got to admit, I was lucky. Nobody wanted to buy this end of the reign. Another week, some other bugger would have won the concession, and I'd still be down in Cackmarket square competing with everyone else for grandmothers and lunch shoppers."

"The government…" Gerd shook his head, tried again. "You auction off the chance to profit from the King's death?"

"Not auction," the stall owner grimaced. "Lottery. We're not *savages*."

"Absolutely not," Marius nodded in approval. "Purely business, right friend?"

"Right."

"Damn civilised, if you ask me."

"Well thank you for your approval," the fat man replied, only the slightest hint of sarcasm creeping into his tone. "Now, if you don't mind, you might want to order before you pass by."

"Of course, of course." Marius dipped into the pouch, drew out a few coins. "Let's live like there's no tomorrow, shall we? Two of your large rolls, with extra chilli. And do you have any Kessa Water?"

"No, but if you've got three more of those," the owner indicated the coins, "I'll send Ethren down into the markets to get two bottles and find you in line."

"Done." Marius paid his price. "A pleasure doing business."

"Yeah, sure, of course." The fat man nodded, called the order across to the youths, who began the process of assembly, then turned towards the rear of the stall. "Ethren!"

Marius and Gerd stepped on as he began issuing instructions to the young girl whose head had popped through the curtain at the rear of the stall. She gave the two customers a good look over, then disappeared. Marius took the two rolls as they were offered, gave one to Gerd, and they stepped away from the stall.

"Brilliant," Marius said as he bit into his roll.

"What?"

"Well, this for a start." Marius brandished his lunch. "Seriously, that is really good rat. "But this whole setup. It's a brilliant idea."

"I don't get you."

"Look." Marius indicated the line around them. "How long is this lot going to take to get to the head of the queue? Ten hours? How many do you think brought lunch with them? I bet it's the same for every function that occurs up here. People get excited, or they're ordered to come up here by bosses or wives or public acclamation. Then they're stuck in the queue, hungry, thirsty, and what are they going to do?" He laughed. "Captive audience."

"So?" Gerd's shrug was eloquent.

"So?" Marius shook his head. "How many people do you think there are in this city?"

"I don't know. Twenty, thirty thousand?"

"Ninety-three and a half thousand at last census. I know, I helped fudge the figures on the Tallian quarter."

"What? You altered census figures? Why on Earth would you do that?"

Marius smiled. "Do you think it's a good idea if the Scorban government knows how many of its traditional enemies *really* live in the heart of its base of power?"

Gerd shook his head slowly. "Gods. Have you ever done anything honest in your life?"

"I..." Marius stared into the distance for a moment. "That's not the point. What I'm saying is, there's ninety thousand people down there. That equates to, what, say a thousand food merchants, maybe? Any one of whom would kill for the chance to open up in a prime location like this, above the stink and the sweat, with a guaranteed clientele, quiet, orderly, in and out in under a minute with no arguments, no fights, no chance of some fat-headed thug with a cosh and an inflated sense of his own hardness coming round every month demanding protection..." Marius stopped, smiling, until the person behind them bumped forward, and he stepped back into his place. "So, run a lottery. Give every merchant a chance to buy in based on something immutable, something unchanging..."

"Like the King."

"Exactly. The King's alive, but he's going to die one day. Pick a day, pick a week, and if the big man cops his whack, you're in. It's so *simple*. Just limit the upper range to, say, what, every three years or so, that way the merchants have to keep reinvesting, but not so quickly that they think they're being conned. A thousand merchants. What would you charge? A day's take?" He stared into the distance, calculating. "Good Gods, the take must be… Good Gods." He shook his head, took a bite from his roll. "Mm, that is good rat, though. Eat up, don't let it get cold."

Gerd took a bite from his roll, swallowed, and erupted in a coughing fit.

"What… the hell… oh my Gods that's hot…"

"Don't you like chilli?" Marius clapped him on the back. "You have to eat rat with chilli. Here. Ethren! Here, girl!"

The young girl from the stall ran up past curious onlookers, spared Gerd a quick look of contempt, then handed two cheap-looking bottles to Marius. He uncapped one and handed it to his still-coughing companion. "Drink this, it'll help."

Gerd took a long swig, then sprayed it out again as another cough overtook him. "You… bastard," he managed between hacks. Ethren shook her head in derision.

"Country boy?" she asked.

Marius nodded. "I'm educating him. Here." He produced a coin from his sleeve and handed it to the girl. "That's for the speed of service. No commission for the old man, understand?"

Ethren smiled and slipped the coin into her shift. Marius nodded in satisfaction.

"Good girl. You'll know when I need you?"

"I've got lots of chores," Ethren slipped a stray strand of hair behind her ear and glanced down the slope towards the stand. "I can make detours without being noticed."

"Good girl." Marius held out his hand, third and fourth fingers folded down. Ethren took it in the same manner, bumping folded fingers together in three quick knocks – slum handshake, from gutter rat to gutter rat. Then she was away, racing back towards the stand to carry out another of the old man's orders.

"What was that all about?" Gerd had recovered enough to stand upright. He eyed the departing girl with a sour expression.

"Kids and servants," Marius said, raising his bottle and taking a long draught, sighing as the peppery Kessa Water burned his throat. "They're always worked too hard and they're never paid enough. Makes for an easy friendship. It might never pay off, but it never hurts to make friends." He turned back to face the distant cathedral. "Now, it's about time I showed you how to eat this stuff properly."

They progressed up the hill, one step every thirty seconds, as the sun reached its zenith and began the slow descent towards night. Twice more, in the hours of their journey, they came across stalls at the side of the avenue, selling meals of meat and bread to the passing visitants. Twice more, though they were no longer hungry, Marius chatted to the stallholders, gathered gossip about the city, bought food, and secured the loyalty of the child who brought them Kessa Water with gold coins and guttersnipe handshakes.

The cathedral loomed over them, a massive, brooding presence darkened by the sun hanging behind it.

Its shadow crept down the boulevard towards them, eating the light, until it reached out and covered them. The quality of the air changed, then: the countless little stirrings and shuffling of people in line stilled; the muttered conversations died away; the sense that each member of the queue was somehow together on their journey, a silent and unspoken camaraderie born of common intent, melted. The shadow devoured them, and each individual was left alone with the knowledge that the object of their journey was upon them.

Soon, the journey would be left behind, and they would face their King, lying dead on a stone pallet in the bowels of the great bone building. It squatted, waiting, only a thin slice of its vast bulk visible at the end of the avenue – its great bone doors, open. A mouth, waiting to devour the line that wound towards it in solemn silence. Only Marius seemed untouched, chewing enthusiastically upon his magrat kebab, slurping Kessa Water, pointing out items of interest to his young companion – the library that Vissel the Reader built with his bare hands, dragging the stones up from the river in the dead of night after the rest of the royal family were long asleep; the monument down a side alley in remembrance of Rackno's first, unsuccessful, experiments with manned flight; the hand-dug runnels down either side of the boulevard, scooped out by residents during the Blood Nights to divert the flow of ichor around their houses and down the hillside into the city. The Radican was a living museum, the depository of a thousand years of the Scorban people's most significant moments. Marius knew them all, and delighted in Gerd's silent astonishment. He ate, and talked, and only stopped when the boulevard ended, and they faced the full facade of the Bone Cathedral across the empty space of the Royal Parade Ground.

The Parade Ground itself would be enough to take a man's breath away. A massive clearing, gouged from the top of the cliff, flattened by the feet of ten thousand workmen. Cobbles the size of a man's head had been quarried from walls of black granite in the heart of the Brooth Mountains to cover it. It lay between the balconies of the Royal Apartments and the Bone Cathedral like a vast stone lake, its open sides exposing the city two hundred feet below, inspiring a sudden vertigo in those who looked sideways after travelling up the crowded building-sided channel of the main boulevard.

Nine thousand men had stood here, ranked in perfect squares, during the time of the Defence, when Trechyan nomads from the north had swept down out of the upper plains and threatened the city. Nine thousand soldiers had crowded the square, turning in perfect unison to hail the King as he stood on the balcony above them, wheeling off in utter synchronicity to march twelve abreast down the boulevard and out of the city gates, a thunderous cavalcade of boots on the stone streets, a mass of military might that had never before been seen within the city walls. Only after they had stormed out onto to the plains to confront the marauding nomads, and been slaughtered to a man, did the city learn: in open ground, nomads cannot be defeated.

But it is impossible to conquer city walls twenty feet thick with a pony and a short bow. The nomads moved on, Scorby City wiped the defeat from its collective memory, and the Parade Ground never again held such a concentration of men. Now it served as a silent reminder to all who crossed it – bigger things than you move the world, bigger moments exist than your life. No matter where the boundaries of the Square were viewed, from Royal Apartments to cathedral or vice versa, the vast space held the same message: bow your head, show humility, remember that you are worthless.

Marius looked around, and spat out the last of his Kessa Water.

"Fuck me," he said. "They could do with planting a tree or two, hey?" He ducked out of line, scurried to the front of the Royal Apartments, and looked over the edge of the cliff.

"Gerd! Come and see this! You can see right down into the Red Quarter." He waved, looked back over his shoulder. Gerd shook his head, and gazed down at his feet. Marius frowned, and ran back to grab his companion by the sleeve.

"Come on, you've got to see this. You can see right onto the roof garden of the Cat Tails. They do business up there too, you know. All dressed up. You should see…"

Gerd shook his head again.

"What? What's the matter? You're not–"

"I'm afraid of heights, okay?"

Marius frowned, puzzled.

"But… you live on the side of a mountain."

"It's not the same." Gerd waved his hand at their surroundings, his eyes firmly fixed on the ground. "This… it's…" He drew a deep breath, sighed. "It's closed in and open at the same time. Everything feels tall. And thin," he added, risking a glance to either side. "I don't like it."

Marius stared at him for several seconds, then laughed. "It's a hundred feet wide, you great girl's blouse. You couldn't fall off of here in an earthquake." He laughed again, then stopped at the look on Gerd's face. "There hasn't been an earthquake in Scorby in seven hundred years. You're not going to fall from this extremely large and stable flat place because of an earthquake." He sighed, and stepped back into line, casting a wistful glance over his shoulder at the hidden brothel roof. "So you're really struggling with the sudden height, hey?"

"Yes. I am."

"Well," he reached an arm around Gerd's shoulder and tugged him upright. "You're really going to drop your lunch when you see this."

Across the square, at the very tip of the Radican, stood the Bone Cathedral.

# TWENTY-THREE

Separated from its surroundings by the great square on one side and by cliffs on its others, it stood alone like a massive, yellowing judgment upon the city. Its size was impossible to gauge. There was no viewpoint from which it could be seen in comparison to any other structure. It stood in isolation, with only the sky and the sprawling, distant mass of the city roofs for backdrop, its immensity relegating both to mere details in the distance. Its sheer bulk swallowed the eye, leaving the viewer with no other sensation but that of the building itself. It was Scorby's crown of thorns – terrible and agonising, but with the promise that history would remember the wearer, that the sacrifices would be worth it.

Skulls leered out at visitors as they arrived, vast totem poles of the dead holding up cross beams made from countless femurs. Scapulas provided swooping curlicues underneath friezes picked out in the most delicate of phalanges and knuckles. Deformed gargoyles leaned out from ledges, twisted children pieced together by blind madmen staring down at passers by with hunger in their empty eye sockets. The cathedral was a shrine to war-like and vengeful gods, and it fulfilled its purpose well.

Other monuments inspired an industry of craftsmen, flooding the tourist centres of the city with plaster reproductions of Scorbus' Tower and watercolours of the Vista, slivers of the One True Stake and genuine parchments from the Entombed Library, guv, yours for only a riner seeing as you look like a connoisseur of true art to me. Not the Cathedral. It was the scary grandmother of the city: only acknowledged on special occasions, and even then, only with a kind of frightened reverence, as if somehow it could rise from its foundations and usurp the rule of law with a single choice phrase or sharply delivered backhander. Nobody ventured too close, nobody kept a picture on their mantelpiece. And people minded their bloody manners.

"Oh, gods," Gerd said, gazing up at the dome, "I'm going to be sick."

"You can't be," Marius smiled. "The dead don't puke."

"You did!"

"I'm special. I'm a King." He frowned. "Sort of. You're just a walking corpse."

"Oh yeah? Just watch me." Gerd staggered several steps away and bent over with his hands on his knees. His back bucked: once, twice, then after a short pause, several times in quick succession. After a minute or so, he lurched back and leant his forehead on Marius' upper arm.

"That," he said, between gulps for air, "is just fucking cruel."

"Never mind." Marius patted him on the shoulder and pointed ahead. "We're nearly there now."

The line of visitants disappeared into the gloom of the building's mouth. Marius and Gerd followed along, eyes wide. Marius had seen the cathedral a hundred times, inside and out, but there was no preparation for each viewing. No previous history could dim the sense of awe, the sheer sense of horror at approaching the yellowing structure. Two guards stood at either side of the entrance, fully armed and armoured. Marius nodded at them as they approached.

"Look," he said. "They're not comfortable."

The guards fidgeted. Proximity to the cathedral did that. No man likes to be reminded of his mortality, especially a soldier. To have that transience turned into a mere tool of architecture was a thought that nobody needed. The soldiers looked anywhere but their immediate surroundings, and shifted from foot to foot. They would need no encouragement once their watch was over – would be down the Radican and into a tavern in record time. The line wound through the massive doorway and up to a smaller door, recessed into a wall a dozen feet behind the ornate entrance way.

"The actual entrance," Marius said. "The outside walls are just for show."

"The work," Gerd replied. As they stepped up he reached out, and ran a hand down a thigh bone set at shoulder height into the doorframe. "Gods, it's so..."

"Smooth?"

"Yes."

"Umpteen years of being rubbed by gaping tourists will do that," Marius' smile was grim. "Nobody quite believes, until they've had that first touch."

"It's… it's just…"

"Yes." Marius stared around them, trying to calculate just how many bones per square feet, how many square feet per wall, how many walls, and arches, and sconces, and architraves. "Isn't it just?"

The queue proceeded through half a dozen galleries into the central chamber, a vaulted hall thirty feet wide that stretched upwards into the dome itself. Marius pointed out items of interest as they passed: the crypt of Polimis, the fabled Unknown Hero of Scorby; the hall of artists, where the great poets and philosophers of the realm found their rest; Traitor's Hole, where the mummified bodies of great turncoats were displayed so all could see the wages of treason.

"No building material there," Marius said as they passed. "There's not a single bone left whole in the lot of them."

Gerd shuddered and remained silent.

Their journey was lit by a trail of sconces set at head height, throwing out a smoky, yellow light that only added to the sense of gloom.

There was plenty of time to view the King as they approached. Once through the antechamber, the massive interior of the cathedral was revealed, a vast empty, tiled space underneath the vaulted curve of the cathedral's dome: thousands upon thousands of bones curving overhead in the single largest unsupported roof in the Scorban empire. Marius always glanced up as he entered, and always returned his gaze to the horizontal just as quickly. It made him queasy to contemplate the curves of the dome's interior, to calculate just how much it must weigh, and how it would shatter should the bones come loose and plummet towards him. Much easier to ignore it. Much better for his sense of equilibrium to contemplate the dead man in the centre of the chamber.

He lay upon a golden bier, raised so that he faced out above the heads of his subjects. His eyes were closed, and in his gloved hands he held his sword and the Scorban Book of Passing, that tome of rituals and passwords once believed to be indispensable in aiding one's passage into the Kingdom of the Dead. Marius snorted as he spied it.

"Well we know *that's* a load of bollocks."

"Oh, you never know," Gerd replied, smiling ferally, "Maybe they have an executive wing."

They laughed, and quickly stifled their sounds as those around them glanced at them in annoyance. From up ahead, they could hear the sound of someone murmuring.

"Who is that?" Gerd asked. "A priest?"

Marius frowned. "Could be. The rites should have been finished days ago, but you never know. Maybe they keep one going for the tourists, sort of adding to the value of the experience or something. Still," he craned his neck, staring past the shoulders of those in front of him. "I can't see anybody." They stepped closer. They were only ten or twenty minutes, fifty steps or so, from standing directly in front of the King. "Maybe he's kneeling at the back corner of the display or something."

Two guards stood to either side of the bier, resplen-
dent in golden mail. One of them glanced at the
talkative couple and frowned. Marius took note, and
bent his head.

"Better be quiet," he whispered. "Show respect and
all that."

Gerd nodded, and they concentrated on staring at
the display before them. Apart from the two guards,
the only adornments to the chamber were two large
torches in golden braziers at either side of the bier.
Marius was not surprised. Compared to the walls
around him, any great show would seem gaudy and
kitsch. Better to keep things simple, and let the cathedral itself do the work of inspiring the necessary awe.

The King himself had been laid out in his corona-
tion robes, with his ceremonial crown perched upon
his head.

"Helps to hide the wounds," Marius observed, indicating the gold and velvet cap. Gerd nodded, and
nodded towards the voluminous silk gown. "Can't see
the killing stroke." They stepped forward. "How are
we going to do this?"

Marius let his gaze drift to the guards and beyond
them towards the exit at the opposite side of the
chamber. The hall was well-lit, the soldiers attentive.
Behind them stood the twinned entrances to the Hall
of Kings, where King Tanspar's predecessors lay
within their marble crypts. Long velvet ropes blocked
the entrances. The only other possible escape route lay
back along the line of supplicants, or across another
fifty feet of open floor to the far exit. Three dozen or

more grieving subjects lay between them and either door. Marius eyed the guards – tall, athletic, the swords at their hips appearing superbly functional despite the gaudiness of their ceremonial costumes – then looked back to the King in his heavy, swirling robes, hemmed tightly into his resting place by cushions, and now that he paid attention, wires surreptitiously looped around ankles and wrists and tucked down behind the fabric. He bit his lip.

"Ah, hell." He ran a hand across his eyes. "We can't."

"But..."

"We can't." He waved a finger at the various facets of the diorama. "It's impossible. We can't even get close enough to touch him, never mind get him out. And even if we could, even if we could distract the guards, and untie him, and get him down, all without being noticed, what do you think this lot would do to us, hey?" He nodded towards those ahead of them in the line. As they passed his resting place, the King's subjects gave in to grief. There was crying, and wailing, and oaths of revenge. Gerd stared.

"They'd tear us apart."

"At the least."

They listened to the emotion running through the room. Marius frowned.

"Can you hear that?"

Underneath the expectant murmurs behind them, underneath the echoing sounds of grief ahead, a voice. Singular, uncertain, verging upon panic.

"Hello?" it said. "Please, hello? Is there anybody there? Hello? Help? Help. Please, I can't see. Help. I don't know what's happening. I can't move. Can anybody hear me?"

"I hear it," Gerd whispered. "But where? It sounds like… I can't pinpoint it."

"I know that voice." Marius replied. "It's… it sounds like it's coming from…"

They stepped forward, almost directly in front of the King.

"Please?" said the voice. "Please, can anyone hear me?"

As one, they turned towards the dead man.

"Oh, gods," Gerd whispered.

Marius stared at the immobile figure. "They've embalmed him," he said.

"Hello? Hello?"

"Embalmed… you mean…?"

Marius nodded. "I've seen them do this. They soak him in a solution, then they open him up… stuff him with… oh gods. He's still in there?"

"Hello? Can anyone hear me? I demand… I need to know what's going on."

"Should we… can we…?"

"I don't know." Marius stared helplessly at the unmoving King, while the voice questioned and pleaded inside their heads. "I just… I don't know."

"Hey!"

They jumped at the sound of the guard's voice. The guard waved a hand at the line behind them.

"Move along please, citizens. Let someone else pay their respects."

"But…" Gerd took a step towards Tanspar. Marius grabbed his arm.

"Yes, sir. Of course. Thank you." He moved away, dragging his protesting companion with him. The guard turned his attention back to the line, and Marius quickly dragged him to the shadows at the entrance to the Hall of Kings.

"What are you doing?" Gerd tore his arm free of Marius' grip. "We've got to help him."

"How?" Marius swung him around to stare back at the snaking line and the pool of light in which the King rested. "Tell me, go on."

"I don't know. You're the... the... thief!"

"Shhh." Marius gave him a gentle shake, just enough to rattle his teeth. "Keep it down, for gods' sake. Look." He let go, sank back against a pole and slid down until sitting. "Let's say we do it, okay? We somehow manage to distract the guards, liberate our man, and evade every loyal mourner between here and the City walls. What then?"

"What? What do you mean?"

"Look at him." Marius waved a hand at the tableau. "I mean, really *look*. And think. He's as stiff as a board. He can't see, or hear. What are we going to do, lean him against a wall and tell everyone that begging for help is a sign from God? How long do you think that'll satisfy them?" He shook his head. "That's after we get him all the way through the city, out the north wall to the burial fields, with every single soldier and citizen of the entire city baying after us. Too hard. It's too hard. There are just too many wrong elements."

Gerd sat down, eyes fixed on the passing mourners. "What then? I mean, this was the plan, wasn't it?"

"Yeah, yeah. This was the plan." Marius waved a

hand into the crypt behind them. "We may as well try to steal one of this lot with the chances we've got."

Gerd stared into the darkness of the hall for long minutes. Then, slowly, he squinted in thought.

"Why not?"

"What?"

"Why not?" He slid over, and kneeled in front of Marius. "Look." He pointed back into the darkness. "It's dark, it's deserted. The guards aren't there like they normally would be. Everyone's paying attention to the show out front. We could sneak in, open up one of the display cases and carry one of the old kings out through a back entrance before anyone notices."

Marius stared at his young accomplice. "You've not actually visited the Hall of Kings before, have you?" he said at last.

"Well, no. Not as such."

"No." Marius leaned back against the wall and closed his eyes. "Because if you had, you'd know that the dearly departed monarchs are 'displayed' inside stone vaults, the lids of which are carved from single blocks of granite or alabaster, and which probably weigh in the vicinity of several tons. And the only side entrance is the one that leads to the rather smaller and less enjoyable Hall of Queens, where Scorby's proud centuries-long tradition of treating your wife like a second class citizen can be seen at its most emphatic." He sighed. "Nice try, though."

Gerd sat back. "You're right. We should probably just wait for the dead to drag us back below ground so we can admit failure." He matched Marius' sigh with one of his own. "Wonder what they'll do to you?"

"What?" Marius opened one eye and squinted at his companion.

"Well, when you tell them you didn't get them a ruler. I wonder what they'll do to you for failing them."

"Don't you mean, what will they do to *us*?"

"No, no." Gerd leaned back, and knitted his fingers behind his head. They interlaced with the ribs of a cherub who stare malevolently at Marius over his head, but he didn't seem to notice. "My charge was to stay with you and keep an eye on you. I've done that to the best of my ability. You're the one who had to get them a king. It's a pity," He took a deep breath, exhaled, and shifted position to one of utter comfort. "But you're on your own on this one." He crossed one leg over the other, wriggled around a bit on the stone floor, and lapsed into silence. Marius stared at him through his one open eye. Slowly, his gaze slid towards the darkness of the nearby Hall. Then his head turned towards it. He frowned in concentration.

"I suppose…" he said at last. Gerd gave no sign that he'd heard. Marius lapsed into silence. "We could…" Again, his friend made no response, and again, he let the thought fall away. Marius stared into the blackness for long minutes, a frown creasing his features. Gerd lay on the floor at his feet, for all the world as if he were sunning himself on a Tallian beach. Eventually Marius nodded, checked himself, then a minute later, nodded again.

"Okay," he said. "This is what we do…"

Gerd smiled and sat up. "About bloody time."

# TWENTY-FOUR

Even in the full light of the day, the Hall of Kings was a gloomy sepulchre, a vast white circle filled with columns like knotted ropes, whose walls and ceiling were one long bas-relief of human carnage. Skeletons played out life-sized friezes of glorious battles, bloody victories, noble and wholly fictitious death scenes. Stone crypts lay side by side like fallen dominoes, the lid of each tomb carved with a list of the dead man's glories, each monarch quite literally weighed down by his achievements. Statues dotted the floor like twisted guardians, intermixing myth with reality – here, a depiction of Tessimus and the Snake, there a visualisation of Beldo holding up the Carlanian Wall, still further on the lover Malanar and his goddess wife Pheleon.

With all the sconces lit it became a procession of ghosts, each flickering light rebounding from a multitude of curved and warped surfaces until the whole area seemed a shadow play just beyond the scope of recognition. In the dead of night, without even a single clump of half-terrified schoolchildren and a droning docent to add a human touch, it felt like the throne room of ghouls. At least, it would to the *living*. The two men who snuck from pillar to pillar were, of course, corpses themselves, and had seen the way the dead live. To them, it was just creepy.

"So what's the plan?" Gerd whispered, eyeing a nearby battle scene with distaste. Marius pointed along the row of tombs before them.

"Twenty eight Kings of Scorby," he said. "From Scorbus the Conqueror to Wet Somnac, missing only Felis Twain, who went mad and fed himself to his bears, and Nandus, who I've met." He smiled. "A smorgasbord of monarchy, and all we have to do is move a one ton block of granite to get at it."

"Right. So. How?"

"First things first." He stepped from the shadow of a column and approached the first tomb. "We need to find a live one."

"You what?"

Marius placed his hand on the tomb. "Dethel of Alongia," he read. "Conquered Scorby in 1108, declared the entire Somarrian peninsula a possession of the Alongian Empire, and spent the next twenty years systematically murdering anyone who didn't fit the Alongian physical ideals. Still," he winked, "he made the coaches run on time." He knocked. "You in there, Dethel old son? Wakey wakey." Only an echo answered him. He returned Gerd's worried stare with a shrug. "Nothing in there but ashes, anyway. Alongians cremate their dead."

He moved across to the next one. "Ah. Veen the Liberator. Dethel's eldest son. Had gone completely native by time the old man kicked on, mobilised the army and re-established Scorban independence. Reintroduced the ale races, established trade with the Faraway Isles, and most importantly for *our* purposes, was entombed like a proper Scorban." Again he knocked on the wall. "Veen, calling Veen. Are you in there, Veen?" He paused, then knocked again. "Hey, anyone in there?"

After several silent seconds, Gerd coughed.

"We have a purpose in doing this?"

"Yes, of course." Marius stared at the vault thoughtfully. "I thought we'd get something from him at least. Maybe we're better off starting at one end. Come on!" He strode purposefully towards the crypt nearest the entrance then stopped, and came back. "Changed my mind," he said as he passed Gerd. "Begin at the beginning." He strode to the far end of the line, at the deepest part of the curved hall. The crypts here were smaller, the decorations that adorned them worn smoother by time. The first was little more than a stone box with a giant skull made from smaller skulls perched at the head.

"Scorbus," said Marius, pausing to read the inscriptions on the lid. He pulled a face. "Maybe not." He moved to the second. "Thernik, son of Scorbus. The Bone Collector. Builder of the cathedral of Tovis, established the University of Scorby, all-round nice guy and defender of the faith. Also collected bones." He gestured towards the walls. "Lots and lots of bones. He should fit right in, don't you think?" He knocked on the lid. "Hello? My Lord Thernik? Do you hear me?"

From within the crypt came a muffled sound, as if someone was quietly shifting their weight. The tomb robbers exchanged glances, and Marius leaned back over the lid.

"Hello?" he said again. Gerd clapped his hand against his forehead; "Of course," he said, then, "Use your dead voice."

Marius straightened. "Ah, of course." He took a deep breath, stilled himself, willed the life and vitality out of his flesh. He felt his skin tighten, the muscles of his jaw loosen and drop, looked down and saw the skin of his hands fade to grey and start to peel. His young partner nodded, and he spoke again, this time from the dead part inside himself.

"Thernik, son of Scorbus," he said. "Do you hear me now?"

There was a pause. If Marius had any breath left in his body he would have held it. Then, a voice returned his call, deep and resonant as only a voice produced by the mind, without the aid of breath or voice box, can be.

"Fuck off."

"I beg your pardon?"

The voice giggled. "Fuck off. Fuck off, fuck off, fuck off, fuck off, fuck off…"

"Oh, gods," a second voice intruded, from somewhere further down the line. "Who woke Thernik?"

"Fuck off, fuck off, fuck off…"

"What is it?" A third voice came upon them.

"Someone's woken Thernik up."

"Oh, what?"

"Fuck off, fuck off, fuck off…"

"Thernik, for god's sake, shut up would you?"

"Fuck off, fuck off…"

"Who the hell woke him up?"

Marius and Gerd stared at each other.

"What's going on?" Another voice, and another.

"Somebody woke Thernik up."

"Who the hell did that? Pelenus?"

"Not me."

"Fuck off, fuck off, fuck off…"

"Um," Marius leaned over the tomb, as if somehow his physical presence might be intruded into the conversation. "Excuse me?"

"Krenk?"

"No, Krenk's not talking, remember? He's still upset over the comment you made about the Finnite War."

"Oh, for Goddess' sake."

"Fuck off, fuck off…"

"And another thing. This whole Goddess thing–"

"Look I told you before–"

"Oh, do we have to hear this again?"

Another voice spoke up, and another, until a dozen voices were arguing back and forth to an undercurrent of fuck offs, while the two men outside stared at each other in helpless wonder.

"What the hell did you do?" Gerd whispered.

"I don't know. I just…"

"Silence!"

The voice that silenced those babbling was another beast. The Hall fell into a sudden quiet that made Marius' inner ear ring.

"Who disturbs us? Who pulls Thernik from his rest?'

"Fuck off."

"Enough, Thernik."

A pause, then "Fuck off, Daddy" in a tiny voice. There was the subtle clatter of bones rearranging themselves within Thernik's tomb, then silence.

"Um, excuse me?" Marius coughed, then realised that would do nothing for the squeak in his mental voice. He composed himself and tried again. "Your Majesty?"

"Who is this that speaks to me?"

"Am I speaking..." Marius paused, realised just whom it was he was conversing with. "Am I speaking with... Scorbus?"

"I am Scorbus."

He blinked. "Bloody hell." He turned to Gerd, who raised his hands in amazement.

"Who are you? Why do you prise us from our rest?" The magnificent voice sounded peeved, waspish rather than angry. "Do you know how long it took us to get Thernik to quieten down last time?"

"I, uh, I apologise for that." Marius said. "We... What's wrong with him, anyway?"

"Who are you that would know?"

"Ah, oh yes, of course." Quickly, Marius explained their presence, and the mission they hoped to accomplish. As he finished, an excited babble broke out amongst the dead kings, until Scorbus quietened it with another booming command.

"Enough!" The babble ceased. Marius had the impression of a great head turning towards him, eyes boring into him through the marble wall of the crypt. "You will take me."

"What?" Several voices cried out in concert.

"I'm sorry?" Marius said simultaneously.

"You will take me."

A chorus of protest broke out. Each former monarch loudly proclaimed his own right to rescue and to claim the throne that awaited them. Marius laughed, bringing the hubbub to a standstill.

"I'm sorry," he said, projecting an image of himself wiping tears from his eyes. "But I don't think any of you are in a position to make demands, do you? I rather think it's up to me to decide who to free, don't you all?"

"You will take me." Scorbus said.

"And if I don't?"

There was a pause, as if the King was reining in a great temper and trying to pick the calmest, most reasonable tone with which to address him. Then, in just that reasonable tone of voice, he said, "Because if you don't, you will lose the favour of so many of those you wish to appease that it will be as if you never delivered them a king at all, and everything you hope to gain from this exercise will be forfeit."

"What do you mean?"

"It is simple," the King explained. "I am the first king. All oaths of allegiance belong to me. All those dead of whom you talk. Any who lived in my time will not follow a king who came after me. None will follow a king who came after them, not on the assurance of you, and not once they recite the oath of allegiance. Once they hear the words, and realise who you could have brought them, they will follow none other."

"Oh, gods," Gerd said. "He's right."

"What?"

"I pledge allegiance to the land of Scorby," Gerd stood with his hand over his non-beating heart, staring into the darkness, "to its king, to the land created by the first and greatest, Scorbus of Scorby. I pledge my everlasting allegiance and obedience." He beat his chest three times. "To Scorby, Scorbus, and the King."

"In that order," Scorbus said in a soft voice.

"Oh, balls."

The others lay silent, beaten into submission by the knowledge that, no matter how great they may have been in life, they were no more than subordinates to him that stood at the head of their line.

"I never thought about that," Marius said softly.

"No," Scorbus replied, "I imagine that, in this room, you're not alone."

"Well." Marius looked about him: at the walls; at the crypts stretching around into the dark; at Gerd. "I guess that's that, then."

The other kings remained silent, except for one, final, clear statement.

"Fuck off, Daddy."

# TWENTY-FIVE

The great hall was silent except for the rustle of clothing as respectful mourners shuffled slowly past the King's display. Occasionally, someone would break down and be led away, sobbing, or denouncing the Tallian bastards who had done this to the beautiful young King in his coffin, but they were minor disruptions. Given the chance, Scorbans can be as dignified and sombre as the next race, especially if there's a chance to make some political capital out of it. At this time, when they felt the eyes of the continent upon them, an unprepared visitor to the Bone Cathedral might gag to death on the air of dignity. Still, common folk are common folk, and there was no power on Earth that would have kept them in an orderly queue once the young man in the robe came screaming out from the Hall of Kings, pointing back over his shoulder and gibbering about ghosts and demons and whatnots.

If there's one thing Scorbans love more than the chance to put on an air of injured decorum, it's a bloody good spectacle.

Within moments, the line dissolved, and a crowd surrounded the stranger, growing in numbers as those further down the queue pressed forward into the space suddenly left open, only to be captivated by the hubbub in the circle's centre. The guards, unable to maintain order and drawn into the ruckus by their own Scorban curiosity, pushed through the milling crowd, armoured elbows digging a path with abandon. As they broke into the centre space, the newcomer was drawing the breath to drive his gibbering to an even greater level.

"Right, right!" the elder of the guards announced, puffing his chest out as he caught sight of just how many young women were staring. "What's all this then?"

"Demons!" Gerd pointed back the way he had come. "Demons in the King's tomb!" He tore at his hair. "Demons and ghosts and ghouls, oh my!"

A chorus of raspberries sounded within his mind. He ignored the comments upon his acting ability and fell to his knees, wailing hysterically. The guards exchanged glances.

"Come on now, lad," the senior guard said. "How about you stand up?" He leaned over and placed a gentle, yet heavy, hand upon Gerd's arm. "Here, Ghaf. Grab his other arm."

"Right-oh, Yerniq." The younger guard did as he was bid, and they slowly raised Gerd up. The crowd pushed forward, and Yerniq pushed back. "Hey, hey! A bit of room here, please." Gerd turned slowly in their grip, and stared back towards the Hall of Kings.

"Voices," he moaned, in a voice that drew a chorus

of "Rubbish" and "Get off" from his unseen audience. Those directly in front of him, however, leaned forward. As pious and grief-stricken as they were, this beat a dead King any day. "Voices from the tomb of the King. Haunted!" He fell back into the guards' arms, scrabbled at Ghaf's breastplate for purchase, and hauled himself up. "Haunted! Unless…" He stared at the entrance. "No!" he breathed. "It couldn't be."

"What?" Yerniq turned him to face the older man's scowl. "What are you talking about, son? Come on." He gave Gerd a gentle shake. "You're interrupting a very important occasion, young man. This had better be good."

Gerd stared about him like a frightened rabbit. Slowly, slowly, he regained his composure. When he looked at Yerniq again, some of the wildness in his eyes had departed, and his acting was only moderately on the wrong side of ham.

"Voices," he repeated. "From the tomb of the great Scorbus. I was within the hall, contemplating the death of the young King and the line of great masters that have preceded him…" At that, the raspberries in his head grew even louder, until Scorbus ordered the other Kings quiet, and they settled down. "I was standing before the crypt, head bowed in quiet meditation, when… when…"

He bent his head and wept in his hands. A silent chorus sang "What a load of rubbish".

"What, lad?"

He looked up, and restrained an errant giggle. Tanspar lay a dozen feet away in full regal state, and not a single eye was upon him. Every face in the room was turned towards the ragged seer. "I heard a voice."

The crowd waited. Eventually someone at the back said, "What? Is that it?"

He pounced. "A voice," he cried, "from inside the tomb!"

Yerniq frowned. This was all getting a little repetitive. He was aware of the press of people around him, and the dead King behind, and that his job was supposed to be ensuring the peaceful passage of one before the other, not babysitting strangers of no fixed stability who were just as easily marched down to St Tred's Hospital and thrown into the nuttery. But the fool was speaking again, and Yerniq leaned in once more.

"'Help me', it said. 'Help me.'" Gerd sobbed once. "I leaned my ear against the cold stone…" He demonstrated on Yerniq's breastplate. "Hello?" He knocked on the guard's metal chest. "Hello? Who's there?" He pulled back and stared around at the crowd. "Help me. Please, oh please. Get me out. Get me out."

Again he pressed up against Yerniq's broad stomach, and this time, he could see the crowd lean forward, as if expecting an answer. "Hello?"

The mob stilled, as if everyone around him was holding their breath at once. Gerd closed his eyes, and held still so long that the guard began to wonder if he had fallen asleep against his gut. Suddenly, the young man jumped up straight, and Yerniq let out a little yelp of shock. He was thankful to realise that he was not alone – several peeps came from the surrounding crowd.

"The King!" Gerd yelled. "The King!"

"What? Where?"

"Inside the crypt! Trapped inside, the ghost of Scorbus is calling! Quickly!"

He grabbed Yerniq and Ghaf and dragged them forward. The crowd parted, and closed in behind. Yerniq wanted to stop, to dig his feet in and bring order to bear. This was a nonsense story, surely, delivered by a nutcase who needed more than a meal or two to bring him to his senses. But something had gripped the mob, and they, in turn, seemed to have the soldiers in their grasp. They surged forward, Gerd at their head, until suddenly they were in the Hall of Kings , and Yerniq stood at the foot of Scorbus' crypt, staring down at the cold marble.

"Right then," he said, swallowing and looking up at the madman. "Why don't you just show us…?"

"Sssh!" Gerd commanded. Despite himself, Yerniq quietened. Gerd leaned forward, and placed his head against the top of the crypt. The crowd, silent to a man, leaned forward.

"Hello?" he asked, in a high, wavering voice. "Hello?"

Nothing. The crowd stayed still, collective breath held, but still there was no answer. Eventually, Yerniq straightened. He blinked, and as his eyes opened his entire countenance changed. The soldier took over: his lips curled, his eyebrows rose, his eyes fixed upon Gerd with knowing cynicism. Somehow, without knowing it, his arms had risen to his chest. Now he lowered them, and placed his fists on his hips.

"Well, now," he began.

"Hellllp meee…"

Whatever air had been in the room left. Yerniq's eyes bugged. His arms fell. He leaned forward, jaw dropping as he stared at the lid of the crypt. Around him, nearly fifty bodies copied his movements.

"The King!" Gerd pronounced. "Hear the voice of the true King of Scorby!"

Three feet away, curled naked against the bas relief figures of the next crypt, Marius frowned. "Don't over-cook it," he projected, even as he swallowed and once more threw a "Help me" towards the crowd. Ten years of practice had gone into his ventriloquism act, and he'd only ever performed in public once – a disastrous night in front of an aging duke and his nymphomaniac underage foreign wife. It had been enough to learn that, no matter how skilled he may be, no woman is going to sleep with a novelty act when there are pages in the room. What's more, he had to concentrate to maintain his dead state, to keep his grey flesh blending closely enough with the granite to avoid casual notice, especially with everyone's attention firmly fixed upon his neighbour's tomb. Gerd's response to his order was to send back a mental giggle.

"I can see your peepee," his young offside mocked. "I'd complain to the sculptor, if I was you."

"The stone's cold, okay?" Even Marius had to stifle a laugh at his injured tone of voice. "Just don't lose them now, okay?"

"Don't worry," Gerd fell across the lid of the tomb, his fingers scrabbling at non-existent seams, "They're going nowhere." He raised his head, and howled at the crowd. "Get him out! We must release the King!"

"Now, wait a minute…" Yerniq began, but whatever note of caution he wished to sound was obliterated as a surge of bodies stepped forward to grip the edge of the massive stone vault. "Ghaf!"

The young guardsman looked at his superior from his point at the vault's far end. "You want to be responsible if it's him and we *don't* do this?"

Yerniq pondered the question for several moments, then carefully spat on his hands and took up position between two visitors.

"Right," he said, sweeping his gaze across the company. "If we're going to do this, we do it properly. On three, lift and slide towards the bottom. Ready?"

He paused. "Three!"

As one, those around the lid leaned into the job, grunting with effort. Gerd cavorted around them, urging them on. Marius' thrown voice pleaded with them to hurry. Slowly, almost imperceptibly, Yerniq felt the stone shift.

"Harder!"

He threw his weight against the stone with renewed zeal. The lid resisted for long seconds, then with a grinding noise loud enough to wake the already-waiting dead King, slipped forward. Men moved from the sides to the top, adding their weight to the line of momentum. The stone slid further forward. A line of black space opened up as the crypt was exposed. It grew wider as each shove from the company opened up more of the hole. Ghaf let go, slipped between two of the workers, and plunged his arm into the gap.

"I can feel him!" he yelled, then. "No, wait. No." He looked up at Yerniq, a puzzled expression flitting across his broad face. "No, that's a skellington. But it's... yaaah!" He tried to pull his arm out, but it was stuck fast. He pulled again, and again, growing more frantic as his efforts continued to yield no result. "He's got me! Yerniq! He's got me!"

"What?" Yerniq stared at the young guard thrashing about at the other end of the vault. "What are you playing at?"

"Help!" Ghaf pulled and pulled to no avail. The hole grew wider. "Let me go. Let go, you bastard." He reached down with his other hand, panicking all the harder when that, too, refused to come back.

"What is it?"

The gap was more than a foot wide. Men stopped pushing at the stone. Several of them moved towards Ghaf, grabbing him about the waist and adding their strength to his frenzied efforts.

"The skellington!" he yowled. "The skellington's got me!"

Slowly, the combined efforts of the rescuers began to have an effect. Ghaf's arms emerged from the vault. As his left elbow emerged, Yerniq gasped.

"What the hell?"

A bony hand grasped the young guard's arm just below the joint. Several of the rescuers noticed, and let go in shock. He shot forward, and they quickly grabbed him once more and pulled. Gerd danced in the shadows, laughing in his high-pitched voice.

"The King! The King comes!"

"Help me!" Marius' voice deepened, became more commanding. Men leaped to obey, overcome by the moment. Soon, a dozen were pulling at each other in a chain, Ghaf's body at its head. His arms re-emerged. As his elbow passed out of the crypt, the skeletal hand that gripped it let go. Fingers wrapped around the stone edge of the crypt wall. Only one arm remained. Yerniq ran round to the side and reached down into the hole to grip Ghaf's arm. His fingers brushed bones.

"Pull, men!"

"The King! The King comes!"

"Free me! Release me!"

"Yerniq! Make him let me go!"

"The King!"

Ghaf's arm finally emerged. The bony hand that gripped it let go to join its brother on the crypt wall. Suddenly released, the chain of straining men fell backwards into a heap. Marius peeked at them from his cramped perch.

"All right, Your Majesty," he broadcast. "Time to arise."

As the pile of rescuers sorted themselves out, Scorbus, first and greatest King of Scorby, rose from his tomb.

# TWENTY-SIX

The skeleton stood above the fallen rescuers and surveyed the Hall of Kings. For five seconds nobody moved, then, as if of one mind, the pile of men found their feet, backing away from Scorbus' gaze until the bony wall pressed into their backs. Scorbus raised one leg and stepped out of his tomb. Marius gazed up at him. The King was huge: six and a half feet if he was an inch, shoulders broad as a bear; the long arms that hung from his shoulder joints spoke of a physical power that had been used, and enjoyed, regularly. The massive skull swung from side to side as he regarded his freedom, and Marius was amazed at just how large the bones were, how thick, how they radiated such a sense of solidity. Add flesh to them, he realised, and the effect would be overpowering. At the wall, Ghaf raised a quavering arm.

"Skellington," he squeaked. The sound attracted Scorbus' attention. He leaned forward, peering at the guardsman with his empty sockets.

"Bow down!" Marius boomed. The rescuers yelped, and the smell of fresh urine slowly began to permeate the air. They disobeyed the order. Most of them were clinging to the bony outcroppings for support. Marius sighed. He couldn't believe it was going to take more than a giant ambulatory skeleton to get this lot moving. He closed his eyes for a moment, deadened his senses, then unfolded from his hiding place and stepped into their circle of vision.

"Bow down" he yelled again, showing off his dead face. On the other side of the crypt, Gerd threw back his hood and joined him. Marius noted, from the side of his eyes, that he too had deadened himself. He stalked forward until his rotting features were a handful of inches from Ghaf's sweating face.

"Run," he said.

Ghaf didn't need further persuasion. With a whimper, he peeled himself from the wall and made for the exit at a flat sprint. As if he were the plug holding back the flood, the others swept after him in a wailing, screaming torrent, out the exit and into the great hall. Marius watched them go, a satisfied smile on his face.

"Well," he said as the last back disappeared from view, "that was fun. Welcome, Your Majesty, to the first day of the rest of your death."

He turned to Scorbus, and sketched out a bow. The King looked at him for long seconds.

"For gods' sakes, man," he replied. "Get some clothes on."

"Oh, yes." Marius scurried to the pole behind which he had hidden his clothes and slipped them back on. He returned moments later, and held out a pale gold circlet in his hands.

"You might like this," he said. "It belonged to... a

friend of mine. A king, Majesty, not so majestic and notable as yourself, perhaps, but still…" He bit his lip for a moment, shocked at how much the memory of Nandus upset him. "A King of Scorby nonetheless."

Scorbus reached down and removed the crown from Marius' grip. He placed the circlet round his brow. It fit snugly, and Marius realised just how huge this man must have been, fully fleshed.

"Perfect," he said.

A flurry of voices broke out from the other crypts. Marius blinked. He had forgotten the other Kings in all the excitement. But now they impressed themselves onto the tableau. Demands for information from many, demands for their own freedom from the brighter amongst them, one long litany of "Fuck off" providing a backbeat.

"Majesties…" Marius stared helplessly at Scorbus. "Please…" The onslaught of protest drowned his voice. Scorbus shook his head.

"Enough!" he broadcast, loud enough that Marius and Gerd winced and grabbed at their heads. The hubbub died instantly. "*I* am the King, the original and greatest King."

"But…"

"You will lie here until I see fit to release you."

"Oh, I say…"

"Enough!"

The room fell into a silence so deep that Marius wondered if the King's bellow had broken something within him, and he was now deaf to the sounds of the dead. Then Scorbus spoke again, and to his great surprise, Marius was relieved to hear him.

"I will come back,' he said softly. "I *will* free you."
He stepped forward, and laid a hand gently upon the
lid of Thernik's crypt. "When the time is right, I will
free you all." He turned away and faced Marius. "But
for now you need stay a while longer, my friends,
whilst we make good our exit. Young man?"

"Ah, yes." Marius quickly eyed the door to the main
hall. "Down the back here, Your Majesty." He stepped
over to an alcove behind the crypt of Belathon, the
thirteenth King of Scorby. "During the reign of the
Robber Duchess, when the cathedral was locked to
outsiders, several of my... well, let's call them spiritual
ancestors, were sealed up in the walls of this chamber."

"Why?"

Leave it to Gerd to ask the questions I don't want to
answer, Marius thought as he ran his hands over the
alcove wall, fingers seeking out the minute gaps
between the bones.

"I assume it was an ironic punishment for attempting to loot our tombs." Scorbus' reply was laced with
humour.

"Yes, that would be about it."

"Really?"

"Yes," Marius frowned in concentration. "Really."

"Foolish fellows."

"Yes."

"Why foolish?" Gerd looked between the two older
men. Marius glanced back at him.

"Meet my spiritual ancestors," he said, indicating
the display of bones before him. Gerd stared at them
for long seconds.

"Oh."

"Oh indeed."

"Then why are we–?"

"The chamber is about three feet wide, but it tilts downwards for about eight feet. Underneath it is the first of a series of storage chambers. Break through the flooring, and we can... Aha!" Marius sunk two fingers into the eye sockets of a skull, and pulled. Slowly, a section of wall swung outwards. "This way, Your... What the hell?"

A wall of bricks stood where the secret crypt should be. Painted across it, in white bright enough to be read through the gloom by even living eyes, was the message "Secret passage closed due to repair works". Marius read it, then read it again.

"Oh, shit."

Gerd and Scorbus saw the sign over his shoulder. "What now?"

"We could break it down," Marius replied, looking the bricks over. "I mean, we're strong, aren't we?" He tapped the wall experimentally. "Dig down, meet workmen, get crushed under a falling eave... maybe not." He sighed, and looked back at the entrance to the Main Hall. "Everyone will have run off, surely?"

All three eyed the entrance.

"Unless you have any other options," the King said, "Then grasp the nettle and make our play."

"Yes," Marius slowly slid across the floor and peered around the corner. "Nettle grasping. Sure." He stared into the corridor. "It seems empty. Come on."

As one, the little group sidled out of the Hall of Kings and into the corridor. Marius stopped them behind a pillar, in the space before shadows gave way to the expanse of the main hallway. "I can't hear anything."

Gerd shook his head. Scorbus waited, his huge skull staring unblinkingly at Marius. Slowly, Marius stuck his head around the pillar and breathed a sigh of relief.

"Empty," he said. "Come on."

He scurried out into the open space, Gerd at his heels. Scorbus followed more slowly, head swivelling as he took in the massive splendour of the great hall.

"My word," he said at each new sight. "My word."

"You don't remember this, Your Majesty?"

"Oh no," Scorbus paused to run a bony hand across a balustrade made from thigh bones. "I built the nave and the central church, and the hallway we've just left. But this…" he gazed upwards, at the interior surface of the massive dome above. "How on Earth did they manage that?"

"Yes, well." Marius stared at each exit in turn, half expecting to see someone gazing back at him. "Perhaps we ought to leave sightseeing for another time. We really must–"

"Wait."

"What?"

Scorbus' gaze had fallen from the dome, and now rested upon the lone figure in the middle of the hall. Tanspar had long ago given up calling for help. The only sound that now emerged from the embalmed body was gentle, hopeless sobbing.

"Who is that?"

"That?"

"The King," Gerd interrupted. "Recently killed in battle. Bravely killed." Gerd's face was a mask, and Marius quickly turned away from it. Scorbus strode towards the bier, his heels clicking loudly on the stone floor.

"Tanspar," he broadcast softly.

"Oh, oh thank God," Tanspar replied, his voice breaking with relief. "You can hear me. You can hear me!"

"I can hear you."

"Where are you? I... I can't see. Who are you?"

"My name is Scorbus."

There was a long pause, while the young King digested the name.

"What?" he said, eventually.

"I am Scorbus."

"But... but you can't be."

"I am." Scorbus reached out and laid a hand on Tanspar's shoulder. "I am the first King, and I am honoured to meet you."

"But... this is a trick. I am captured, aren't I? This is some Tallian—"

"Tanspar. You will listen to me."

"But..."

"Listen!" Scorbus' command echoed through the hallways of Marius' mind. He winced, and shook his head. Tanspar fell silent.

"You are King of Scorby. Ruler of the coastal lands and all the seas, commander of the air, representative of the gods above all." Scorbus said. "You will comport yourself as such."

"I... yes. Of course." Tanspar's voice changed,

firmed up. "Of course. What is it you want?"

"You cannot see because you are dead, my Lord." Scorbus turned to Marius, who mouthed 'embalmed' at him. "You are embalmed, and while your life has ended, you will soon be amongst equals."

"I'm... Equals?"

"Those who ruled before you. You lie in state in the Bone Cathedral. You will soon be laid to rest in the Hall of Kings."

"Ah."

"They will expect a strong man to join them. One who accepts his lot."

"I see. And how is it you are here to tell me these things?"

"I have been liberated. I am to take up a new place, among the free dead. You will be laid to rest with your peers."

"I see." A long pause. "And my wife, my children. What news of them?"

"They grieve, Majesty," Gerd broke in. "Bravely, but they grieve."

"Who are you?"

"A dead man," Gerd replied. "And your servant."

"Listen to me, Tanspar." Scorbus spoke before the young monarch could contemplate the idea of his family living on without him. "I will return. I make that promise to you, as I have the others. I will free you. But for now, face your peers with grace. You are King of Scorby, and always will be. Death does not end that."

"But this blindness... this deafness... how is it I can hear you? Where are my senses?"

"Majesty, we have to go." Marius leaned into Scorbus' line of vision. "I'm sorry, Your Majesty, but we really have to go."

"I will return," Scorbus said. "I promise you." He turned away.

"Wait. Please. Wait!"

"Be strong, Tanspar. Await my return."

"Wait! Don't go! Please!"

Scorbus strode away, Marius and Gerd in his wake. Tanspar's voice accompanied them across the hall.

"Where now?" Scorbus demanded. Marius pointed to the far exit.

"That'll take us to the far side of the cathedral, away from the main square. We can follow the line of the building to the front, then cross to the shadow of the palace. After that, we either climb down the face of the Radican or try to steal some clothes from a ground floor room and take side streets to the northern gate. Then we find the nearest cemetery."

"Cemetery?"

Marius nodded, remembering the grave in the forest, and the dead men coming towards him out of the gloom in Sangk's cellar. "Gateway to the underworld." He smiled wryly. "You'll love it."

"I see. Well, let's not waste time."

The trio made their way towards the exit. Partway there, Marius called a halt, and bent to pick up two halberds lying where Yerniq and Ghaf had dropped them on their way in to help with Scorbus' rescue.

"We might need these," he said, handing one to Gerd. "Have you ever used one before?"

"No. Have you?"

Marius had, once, while training in the Caliphate of Orm's army. In half an hour he had smashed three helmets, gouged out a sergeant's eye, and turned the regimental mascot into Sunday dinner. He leaned the pole against a wall. "On second thought, let's rely on speed. Come on."

They made the exit without incident. Marius poked his head out of the open door.

"All clear." He waved them outside.

"What now?" Gerd asked as he ran across the square towards the great avenue.

"Soon as we're across we head for the alleyway we saw on the way up, remember?"

"Yeah, sure. Why that one?"

"There's a closed-up business at the far end. At the very least it'll give us a place to hide Scorbus while we find some clothes for him. Once he's covered up we get down into the city as quickly as possible. I know a few places we can hole up, wait for night, then we can get through the northern... uh oh."

"The what?"

Marius skidded to a stop, and pointed towards the boulevard. "Trouble."

From footpaths at either side of the street, figures approached. They caught sight of the three escapees, and paused. The dead men stared back. For a moment, nobody moved. Then the figures on the paths raised their arms. Marius had time to sight the long, steel weapons they held, before a cry rang out and the boulevard boiled over with running figures.

"Marius?"

"Run."

"Where?"

"Run!"

He took off, back the way they had came. Scorbus and Gerd tailed him. The mob, seeing them flee, let out a roar and took off in pursuit.

"What happened?" Gerd asked as they ran.

"They rallied, obviously." Marius risked a glance back over his shoulder. At the front of the surging crowd he saw two familiar figures: Yerniq and Ghaf, torches held aloft, their faces contorted with rage as they yelled encouragement to the lynch mob. "I'm guessing they had something to do with it."

"So what do we do now?"

"Back to the cathedral. No, wait." He veered away, towards the front wall of the Royal Apartments. "This way."

They stopped halfway along.

"No doors."

"No windows."

"What now?"

"Gentlemen." Scorbus had remained quiet during the pursuit. Now, with the crowd closing in, he stepped back from the wall and indicated a balcony several feet above them, jutting out over the square. "The Royal Box, I imagine."

Marius joined him. "Yes," he replied, quickly glancing over his shoulder at the crowd. "But can we…?"

Scorbus tilted his head down towards him, and Marius imagined he saw a feral grin flitting across the empty skull. The King backed up a few steps, ran forward and leaped, swinging himself over the railings and onto the balcony with ease. Marius and Gerd stared at each other.

"Right," Marius said. "Just like that, then."

Together, they backed up. The crowd surged towards them. Someone threw a metal pipe. It clanged off the stones no more than a foot from the dead pair. The lynch mob roared. Marius and Gerd swapped glances.

"Ready?"

"No."

"Good. Go!"

Together they ran, and leaped. And missed.

"Oh my gods." Marius swung towards the wall, crashed against it, then swayed back out, to hang gently in the grip of a massive, bone hand. He glanced down at the cobblestones several feet below, then across at Gerd, dangling from the King's other hand. Something ricocheted off the wall behind them, then something else. Marius peeked upwards. The King's skull poked out between the railings, where he had lain down to effect his capture.

"Would you be so kind, Your Majesty?" Marius asked in his most polite voice.

"Of course." The skull retreated. Marius and Gerd rose gracefully as the King pulled them up through the hail of missiles flung by the crowd below. Within moments they were gripping the edges of the railing and pulling themselves over.

"Agh, damn it!" Something pierced Marius' calf, and sent him tumbling to the floor. He rolled to the base of the wall, and stared down at the shaft of a dart sticking out of his flesh. Blood ran from the hole. "Gods damn it, that hurts!" He pulled the dart out and flicked it over the edge of the balcony. He looked at the blood trickling along his pink flesh, then at Gerd's equally pink and flushed face.

"Never felt so alive, huh?" he asked. Gerd grinned in reply. From below them a command for ladders rang out. Missiles continued to rain down. A brick smashed through the glass door at their backs, and shards tinkled down upon them.

"Time to leave, I think." Scorbus said. Marius nodded in reply.

"I couldn't agree more." He sat with his back against the middle of the wide double doors, and reached through the hole left by the brick. "I can't reach the handle."

"Allow me." Scorbus stood up, ignoring the renewed efforts from below that his appearance engendered. He raised one foot and kicked the door. It smashed open, and Scorbus indicated the room beyond. "As you please, gentlemen."

Gerd and Marius bundled themselves into the room beyond. A stray brick followed them, smashing a vase by Gerd's head and showering him with china. Marius viewed him from the shelter of a 12th Dynasty armoire.

"That's a genuine Bentel III," he sighed, mentally calculating the selling price he could have commanded if he'd rescued it. "You could have bought your entire village a hundred times over if you'd caught that brick."

Gerd shook slivers out of his hair. "Because escaping would be so much easier if I was carrying a big pot around."

"Big pot? You bloody ingrate, do you have any idea…"

"Gentleman," Scorbus stood above them both and helped them to their feet. "We have more important considerations."

"Yes, but… it was a Bentel III."

"Never heard of the man." Scorbus matched Marius' stare for several seconds, before the smaller man turned away.

"Yes, well, no. I don't suppose you have."

A door stood opposite. Marius crossed to it, and laid an ear against the wood panelling.

"I can't hear anything," he said eventually. "You'd have thought that ruckus would have bought people running if there was anyone here, wouldn't you?"

The others didn't answer. He shrugged. "Only one way to find out."

He grasped the handle, and swung the door open. An empty corridor stretched fifteen feet away to a blank wall. A single oil painting stared back at them from the far end.

"Processional corridor," Marius guessed. "Changing rooms on either side, probably, opening out onto a cross corridor, one for men and one for women."

"How do you know?"

Marius thought back to the sight of Nandus upon the balcony, commanding his assembled armies to go forth and conquer the invading crab armies of the Sea Kings. His adult logic filled in the gaps his childhood images presented. "The balcony is only used by the Royal family, for official occasions, when they're all kitted up in their regalia. That stuff is heavy. You don't think they wear it around the house, do you?" He snickered. "Last time I saw a princess up close, she wasn't wearing thirty pounds of ermine cape, I can tell you that." The last time he'd seen a princess she'd been wearing nothing more than a velvet mask and a pair of thigh-high sealskin boots, but that was a memory he'd dwell on when he had time to savour the image. He inhaled, then nodded down the corridor.

"Let's get a wriggle on, eh?"

As one they scurried down the hallway. At the junction, Marius stopped against the wall and ducked his head around the corner.

"Nothing either way," he announced. "I say we move towards the front of the building, see if we can find a side entrance or something we can get out of without attracting attention."

"Sounds good to me," Gerd replied.

"Right." They moved left down the cross hall. They'd gone a dozen steps before they realised they were missing something. Marius turned around. Scorbus stood in front of the portrait, staring up at it.

"Your Majesty?" Marius and Gerd exchanged glances. "Scorbus?"

The King made no move to acknowledge him. Marius edged back towards him and coughed gently.

"Your Majesty? We really do need to…" He glanced up at the portrait, then stopped, and looked at it properly. "You?"

"That is me," Scorbus replied, his voice low and heavy. Black eyes stared fiercely down at them from beneath heavy brows. Marius swallowed, taking in the long mane of grey hair, the heavy jaw half-hidden underneath a beard of truly impressive dimensions. Robes of bear fur sat heavy upon wide shoulders and the matching hat looked as if it had been completed from an entire cub. The picture was dark, completed in heavy swipes of black and russet: threatening, imposing; an image of a thunderous old monster. Scorbus reached one hand slowly up and laid his bones open upon the face.

"Scorbus," Marius' voice was gentle, awed.

"This is how they saw me," Scorbus said to nobody in particular. "This is how you remember me?"

"I…" Marius thought back to his tutor's lessons, to the bloodthirsty stories his parents didn't know he was being told. Scorbus and the conquest of the coastal lands, the establishment of Scorby: a creation myth baked in blood and mayhem. He glanced at the portrait, and the empty skeleton reaching mournfully towards it.

"Look where they hung it," he said, placing a hand upon the King's shoulder and turning him so that they gazed back down the way they had came. "The last image any King sees before going out to greet his people. A reminder of what a King represents." He looked up at the massive skull and realised, with a sudden burst of clarity, that what he was saying was the truth. "You are the mark they all have to aim for. The first and greatest King. That is not a product of fear, Majesty. It's worship."

"Do you…" Scorbus stared down the corridor at the broken doors. "Do you suppose…"

"Marius!" Gerd had wandered down to the far corner as the two talked. Now he ran towards them.

"What?"

"Time to go," he said, racing past them towards the rear of the building. Behind him, a soldier ran out into the corridor, saw Marius and Scorbus staring at him, and flung himself back around the corner. The dead men shared a look, then took off after Gerd.

"How many?" Marius asked as they reached the far corner and checked to see if the approach was empty.

"Lots."

The corridor was empty. They raced towards a door at the far end. "Lots and lots." They reached the door. It was locked. "What do we do?"

"What else?" Marius kicked at the handle. It smashed under his assault. The door swung open and the three fugitives piled into the room beyond.

It was obviously an office of some sort, Marius decided as he looked around. Bookcases dominated, lining each wall from floor to ceiling, leather spines standing erect along every shelf. Two small writing desks sat in alcoves, their backs to drape-less windows that stared out over the city a hundred metres or so below. From his vantage point, Marius could only see the docks, small and blue in the distance, betraying nothing of the squalor and violence visible at ground level. From this height, it looked like a painter's impression, or a king's ideal. A massive wood desk squatted in front of the window. Three maids sat around it, a deck of cards spread out before them. They stared at the little group, their expressions a mixture of fear, resignation, and sullen insolence.

"It's our break," one of them uttered, before the manner of the group's entrance sank in. Scorbus completed the tableau by standing up and revealing himself to the women. One fainted immediately. The other two abandoned their chairs and threw themselves behind the desk, where they took up wailing and asking a multitude of gods for salvation. Gerd ran to a door on the opposite wall and pulled it open.

"Nope," he said, and quickly shut it again. "Lots more, coming this way." He returned to the door through which they had come. "And here come the first lot." He turned to Marius. "Trapped."

"Right." Marius thought for a moment. "Help me with that writing desk." He indicated the one nearest the door. Together they pulled it over and blocked up the broken door with its bulk. "Now the other one." They moved that against the other entrance. "That should hold them for a minute or two, at least."

"So now we're trapped, and we're even more trapped."

"Ah, yes." Marius scanned the room. "Nothing. Nothing we can use." His gaze fell upon the window. "Oh," he said slowly. "Oh, no."

Gerd saw his gaze. "You must be kidding."

"Oh, I wish I was. I really wish I was."

"I told you I was afraid–"

"Yep. Remember that."

"And this is your–"

"Yep."

Marius looked out. Below the window a thin ledge, perhaps six inches wide, ran the length of the wall to a corner a dozen feet away. Below that, a sheer drop of a hundred feet led to broken alleyways and a line of rooftops. He undid the latch and swung the window open. A breeze grabbed it from him and slammed it back against the wall.

"See," he said, turning to his companions. "Our escape route. Easy."

Scorbus and Gerd joined him.

"Yes," Scorbus said, in a voice so polite it promised painful torture before death, "this should round off the rescue nicely."

"I'm open to ideas."

"I imagine you are." The King levered himself up and edged out of the window.

"Go that way," Marius pointed back the way they had come, towards the square and the far edge of the cathedral, just visible around the corner of the palace. "The crowd should have moved further down the hill by now. They'll be expecting us to go that way."

Scorbus glanced down at him, then very deliberately and with great purpose, began to move in the opposite direction.

"What is he... all right, out you go." He pointed Gerd out the window.

"Like hell."

"What? Look, we don't have time..."

A crash behind them caught their attention. One of the writing desks had shifted several inches away from its door. As they watched, another impact knocked it further away.

"I'm not going," Gerd said as a third impact shook the door.

"But..."

"Nope." He stepped away from the window. Another collision struck the door. This time it opened far enough that a leather-clad arm was able to slip through the gap and scrabble around for purchase. Marius stared at Gerd.

"Scorbus is just about gone by now," Gerd said. "It's not me that has to be sure he gets down."

"Oh, you bastard." Marius turned towards the window. From the corner of his eye, he spied the two conscious maids curled up in the corner. They were staring up at him with eyes full of terror. He winked.

"Marius Helles, ladies. If I had more time…" He blew them a quick kiss, closed his eyes, and thrust himself out of the window.

The wind clawed at him as he straightened and shuffled gingerly a few steps along the wall. A moment later, Gerd clambered out, swaying as he clumsily gathered his legs beneath him and stood. Marius reached out a hand and helped to steady his young companion.

"I thought you weren't coming."

"Changed my mind." As Gerd spoke, something whizzed past his shoulder. The two companions watched it fall towards the distant street.

"See?" Marius said to nobody in particular. "You don't get workmanship like that if you work for just any old King, you know. That is a perfectly balanced knife, that is—"

"Get moving!" Gerd risked his balance to give him a shove. Behind them, several people could be heard clambering over their barricade into the room. Within seconds a second crash announced the entry of the remaining pursuers. Marius began to shuffle along the tiny ledge, scouring his fingers across whatever miniscule purchase the worn stones accorded him.

"Son of a bitch!" Marius looked back at Gerd. Beyond the young man, a head had emerged from the window, and the arm it guided was swinging a sword towards him. As Marius watched it struck the wall an inch or so from Gerd's hip. Marius scuttled a few steps further, dragging Gerd with him.

"Keep moving!"

"They won't follow us," Marius replied. "They'd have to be insane!"

As he spoke, a soldier levered himself out on to the ledge.

"Wait a second!" Gerd turned towards the soldier and whistled. The young man looked up. Gerd back-handed him across the jaw. He slumped, and Gerd continued his swing, pushing him back into the arms of his colleagues. As they staggered under the unconscious soldier's weight he leaned down and stared at them through the window.

"Don't be insane," he shouted, then scooted back to Marius.

"I just want you to know," he yelled, enunciating carefully above the wind so that Marius caught every syllable, "in case this all goes wrong…"

"Yes?"

"Fuck you."

"Right." Marius nodded. "Thanks."

They shuffled on. Within a minute they turned the corner of the building. Three feet ahead of them, the ledge terminated against an abutment. It stuck far enough out that none of the three could have grasped its corner with outstretched arms. Scorbus leaned against it, arms folded, and regarded them as they approached.

"Oh, hell," Marius said

"Oh, hell indeed."

"What do we do now?" Gerd turned his face to the wall, and closed his eyes. Marius could see his fingers digging into the stone walls. Specks of dust coloured his fingertips. "There's not even any way to get back in."

"Funny you should mention that," Scorbus replied. "You see, I've been thinking while I waited."

"Yes?" Marius braced his rear foot, ready to make whatever run, or shuffle, for it he could.

"See down there?" Scorbus pointed past the edge of the abutment. A dozen feet away, and as many down, a rampart ran along the tops of the adjoining palace buildings, overlooking the cliff face. A clear line of sight ran from their current vantage point to the far edge of the palace building, a hundred yards distant, broken only by four doors built into the inner surface. Marius and Gerd stared at it.

"No," Marius said.

"I don't think we have much choice."

"We'll never make it."

"We certainly shall."

Marius stared at the gap between the two spots. Only the city floor was visible. Nothing would break his fall.

"We'll be smooshed."

"Bend your legs." Scorbus grabbed Marius' wrist, and before he had time to protest, braced his back against the abutment wall and heaved. Marius was launched, flailing and screaming, into thin air. "Roll when you land!"

Marius didn't so much roll as *flollop*. The ground slapped him like an angry parent, smashing the air from his chest and delivering a dizzying blow to the back of his head as the inner wall of the battlement refused to get out of the way of his loose-limbed, clattering approach. He lay face up, scrunched against the base of the wall. Gerd landed a foot away, bent-legged, rolling forward and springing to his feet like he'd been practising. As Marius attempted to remember which limbs belongs at the top of his body and which at the bottom, Scorbus hunkered down against the wall, bounced experimentally, and launched himself across the gap. He landed perfectly, rolled next to Marius, and finished on one knee, hand held out to help Marius to his feet.

"Nobody likes perfect people," Marius muttered. He creaked upwards and swayed as the dizziness hit him again. "You know that, don't you?"

"Let's hurry," Scorbus led them down the rampart, towards the far end of the palace. "Logic dictates that the troops will come this way."

"How do you know that?"

Scorbus jerked a phalange back at their perch. "They'll know that was a dead end. They'll send archers up here to pick us off."

"Oh." Marius doubled his step. "Nice."

"It's logical."

They trotted on. Marius took a moment to glance over the edge. The cliff began to fall away at this point of the Radican, becoming a high slope rather than the sheer face that it was further up. Even so, they were still dizzyingly high. A dozen feet ahead of him, a sluice opened up at the bottom of a building. A wave of effluent spewed out to land in a midden that covered the face of the hill, emptying into a small gully at the bottom of the cliff wall. As Marius watched, small figures emerged from the brush at the edges of the gully to pick amongst the new outpouring of castle waste. He frowned. He knew that place. It had a name, and a story behind it. It was important, too, a significant part of the castle's history. He shook his head. He couldn't quite remember, couldn't quite wrap his mind around the salient facts…

Then Gerd called out to him, and his reverie was broken. He'd fallen behind the other two, and Gerd was gesturing at him to catch up.

An arrow skittered across the ground next to him, and Marius realised that Gerd wasn't waving at *him*. He glanced over his shoulder. Troops were pouring from the uppermost exit.

"Run!"

Marius followed instructions. The three fugitives bolted towards the lower end of the rampart. They were twenty yards away when the bottom-most door opened, and soldiers emerged, blocking their escape.

"Back, back." They turned again, saw the first group closing in.

"What do we do?"

Marius turned between the closing troops, mind working furiously. Then he remembered the name of the midden, and what it meant to the castle.

"Quick!" He ran two dozen steps back towards the

first group of pursuers, head craned over the side of the battlement. "Here! Quick!"

Scorbus and Gerd joined him. "What are you doing?"

"Here. Right here."

"What are you on about?"

Marius glanced at the advancing soldiers, then back over the edge of the building.

"This is the spot."

"Spot? What spot?"

Marius pointed downwards. They stood above the great sluice, and its vomitous trail of garbage.

"The spot to jump."

"What?"

"Jump."

"Are you mad?" Gerd waved at the piles of rotting refuse forty feet below.

"What, are you afraid you'll be killed?"

"No, I'm afraid I'll spend all eternity with legs the consistency of warm lard."

Marius pointed back along the rampart. The King's Men were racing out of the towers. "You'll spend all of eternity in little bits and probably cooked to perfection to boot if they get hold of us." He gave Gerd a sharp shove in the chest. Gerd tottered backwards, waving his arms in circles to remain upright. His heels slipped over the edge. "Now jump."

He pushed again. Gerd had time to shout "You basta..." before he and his insult disappeared. Marius spared him one glance, then looked briefly at the skeleton next to him.

"Ready for this?"

Scorbus tilted his head towards him in a way that, had he borne any flesh at all, would have treated Marius to a blood-soaked manic smile. He nodded, and turned his gaze away.

"Oh, wait a minute." He reached out, and adjusted the band of gold around Scorbus' brow so that it sat straight. "You're going to want to make the right impression when we land, Your Majesty."

He bowed, and Scorbus returned the gesture, before briefly laying a hand on Marius' shoulder.

"Excelsior!" he cried, turned and leaped, leaving Marius alone to face the approaching guards. They were almost upon him. The air was thick with their roar. He could smell them, sense their sweat and fear and exhilaration. They would descend upon him like hungry dogs, tear him apart and feast upon his tattered flesh. He could see the blood in their eyes. He smiled.

This moment needed something special, a bon mot his pursuers would remember their whole lives, would talk about in bars and at family events forevermore. This was the moment when he entered the folklore of Scorby. He stepped forward, and raised both hands as if pushing against a wall.

"Stop!"

To his immense surprise, they did. He saw them, frozen in time: seventy-two soldiers surrounding one small, frail, dead human. Swords drawn, bloodlust in their veins, armour gleaming in the scorching sun.

"You idiots," he said, and jumped.

# TWENTY-SEVEN

A hundred feet is a long way to fall, long enough for a man to regret his decision to jump. Marius scanned the rapidly approaching ground for any sign of Gerd or Scorbus, and seeing none, closed his eyes. He probably wouldn't be killed by the fall. Probably. After all, could a dead man be killed? But even if he wasn't, he could break every bone in his body, and the idea of an eternity spent dragging around a fleshy sack of powdered bones was the least inviting thought he could come up with right at that moment. Not for the first time, he had cause to regret his facility for making plans *after* he put them into action. Then the ground rushed up and collided with his face.

Marius had expected an impact somewhat akin to a mountain dropping onto his chest. Instead, it was as if warm arms had reached out to grab him. His momentum slowed, gently at first, then with increasing pressure until he drifted lazily downwards through a warm sea of close-pressed dirt, tiny particles scratching against his cheeks with the intimacy of a kitten's paws. For three minutes he hung, suspended in the earthen solution, his thoughts growing still as a sensation of peace stole over him. Then the dirt receded. His eyes snapped open. He fell a dozen feet through open air to land face-first upon the hardened dirt of a well-trodden floor.

"Ow."

He sat up after a few moments and stared at the vaulted ceiling above him, stretching his jaw to remove the ache of his landing. No sign of his passage disturbed the ceiling's surface. He smiled, and stood. It appeared that he had landed in an underground cathedral, a tunnelled compatriot to the giant building above. Fully thirty feet round, and almost as high at its apex, it was impressive not for the sheer size and industry of its manufacture, unlike its above-ground cousin, but for the sheer fact of its existence. Whereas the halls of the dead Marius had experienced previously were rough-hewn things, reminiscent of man-sized mole burrows, this space spoke of care and purpose. The walls were smooth, the ceiling unbroken by root or fissure, and someone had even begun the first rudiments of decoration. Formless carvings ran away in both directions at waist height.

Marius followed their path, trying in vain to discern some method or pattern, then stopped, shaking his head. He wasn't sure, after all, that he wished to understand just what it was the dead might worship. A few feet away, Gerd and Scorbus were hauling themselves to their feet, heads turning to take in their surroundings. As Gerd looked over to him, Marius sketched a bow.

"How in the hell did you do that?" Gerd pointed

towards the ceiling. Marius smiled.

"History."

"What?"

"History. Well, folklore, really. A little nickname I discovered over the years." He stretched, feeling bones pop. "I'm rather glad it turned out to be true."

"What are you on about?" Gerd scowled at him in exasperation. Marius indicated the King behind him, standing at ease as if nothing about his situation was unexpected.

"The biggun there. That midden we just jumped into, a lot of the locals have a name for it. Scorbus' graveyard." Marius spied an opening at the far end of the space, and made towards it. "This way."

Gerd and Scorbus followed.

"Well?" Gerd asked as they entered the tunnel.

"Well," Marius replied. "Rumour has it that our friend Scorbus had a habit of disposing of those who he deemed, shall we say, irritating, Your Majesty?" Scorbus tilted his head in what Marius was sure was an attitude of amused acquiescence. "There are halls below the mountain, old places where political prisoners, or just people the King disliked, were done away with in private. Rumour has it that such people were thrown into the midden like so many cabbages, whether they were dead or not quite so dead. Of course, it was a long time ago, and you know how an historical figure's deeds are exaggerated. Pains me to say it, but I'm rather glad the rumour was true."

"But why?"

"Why throw them in the midden, or why was I hoping it was true?"

"Well… both."

"For the first, you'll have to ask him." Marius jerked a thumb at Scorbus, who stared back at it from his impassive skull. "As to the second, haven't you noticed the routes the dead use to climb back and forth into the real world? They're always gravesites, or a place where a dead body has lain." He smiled at Gerd's look of surprise. "Told you I pay attention. Anyway, I figured if the rumour was true, at least, in the quantities he's supposed to have gone through, the whole midden was likely one vast entrance. They don't call him Scorbus the Bloody for nothing, eh?"

"Actually," the King's voice seemed to emanate from somewhere slightly in front of him, as if his presence preceded his bones by half a step. Marius failed to control an involuntary jump, then grimaced. He had forgotten that Scorbus was *real*, not just an animated collection of bones. "I suffered nose bleeds a great deal, growing up. We just used the nickname to, hmm, embellish the truth somewhat. It was rather a difficult time to be King." A bony hand clapped Marius on the shoulder. "A bloodthirsty reputation helped when dealing with the barbarous Tallians."

"But…"

"Seems we struck lucky. Bold gambit, dear fellow, bold gambit." Scorbus laughed, and Marius felt the blood in his face freeze. "Bold gambit indeed."

"But…"

"Still, perhaps those who followed me perpetuated the myth, hmm? Vellus, Miglaine, Erejan and the like? I know 'Thernik the Bone Collector' is no exaggeration. Perhaps they were the bloody ones, living up to my myth with their actions? Perhaps you should instead be thanking *them* for their murderous ways?" Scorbus straightened and walked on in silence, while Marius gaped at him.

"How… how did you come up with that?" he eventually asked. Scorbus tilted his head as if surprised by the stupidity of the question.

"They told me, of course. Seven hundred years trapped in a box, you have to talk about something."

"Yes. Of course. How dim of me." He turned away, and shook his head. There was no way, he thought, even if it took *him* seven hundred years, that he would become used to the ways of the dead. What else would you do but sit in a box for the better part of a millennium, chatting amiably to your neighbours about bloodshed and murder? "Of course they did."

"Waste of perfectly good subjects."

"Pardon me?"

"All that murder and torture. I tried to tell them – subjects bring you closer to god. How can they do that when they're lying underneath a rubbish pile with their throats cut? Take away his subjects, and a King is no better than a merchant." Scorbus shuddered, his bones rattling in the dark. "No."

"I had a friend who thought the way you do," Marius said, pointing at the crown perched haphazardly on Scorbus' skull. "That was his. Of course, he turned himself into a horse."

"Really? I once knew a man who gave birth to a two-headed chicken, or so he claimed. I'd like to meet this friend of yours."

"Bit hard. He got blown apart by a shark."

Scorbus stared at Marius for long moments, his empty orbs staring into Marius' eyes until the latter blinked and glanced away. "What a curious fellow you are, young man," he said. "Curious indeed."

"Oh yeah," Marius answered sadly, "I'm just a bundle of surprises."

Gerd had strayed a couple of feet ahead of the conversing couple. Now he stopped, and raised a hand.

"Shh," he said. "There's someone ahead."

"This way." Marius grabbed Scorbus' upper arm and tried to pull him back down the corridor. The King planted his feet and pulled, and Marius stumbled. "Your Majesty—"

"No." Scorbus straightened, and just for a moment Marius had a vision of the man around the skeleton, the King as he must have been in his pomp: tall, massive in his strength, with a bearing that simply *demanded* obedience. Scorbus tilted his head backwards, and viewed his companions down the line of a long-missing nose. "Behind me, if you please."

Marius meekly obeyed, and found Gerd already there. They glanced at each other in mute embarrassment, then stood behind the King and waited silently for the first of his subjects to arrive.

It was all rather simple, in the end. After all, the throne was waiting, and the subjects were willing, and honestly, nobody could even look at Scorbus and not recognise him as lord and master of *something*. And somehow, in amongst the bowing and cheering, and the praising of the lord and the promises of brave new worlds and the procession towards the royal hall and the new King proclaiming himself to his adoring subjects, Marius and Gerd found themselves slowly filtered through the crowd until they stood at the very periphery. Nothing stood between them and freedom but an unwatched corridor leading away into the darkness. Marius didn't even have to motion. They might even have managed to sneak away unnoticed, if not for a familiar, grinning face, and hands as heavy as gravestones falling upon their shoulders.

"Now where," the dead soldier asked as he lifted them from the ground and turned them towards the suddenly silent multitudes, "do you think you're going?"

Marius searched desperately through a mind suddenly bereft of witty rejoinders, and settled for mute acceptance of his fate. He allowed himself to be dragged to the small space at the feet of the King and deposited in an untidy heap. He sat still, staring up at the ceiling, until a crowned skull leaned into his vision and tilted in polite enquiry.

"Care to join us?" Scorbus asked, in a voice so polite Marius could hear the sword swinging down towards the back of his neck. He rubbed at the tingling skin just under his hairline.

"Majesty," he managed.

Scorbus leaned back against his rude throne, and bid him rise with a languid wave of his hand. Marius stared at him. That's the difference, he thought. He's a skeleton, held together by gods know what, not an ounce of flesh or sinew to his name, with a bent gold bracelet around his forehead and rags on his back, sitting on a pile of shit that looks like it's been slapped together by a class of blind orphans, and still he looks like a king. He shook his head in mute amazement. No wonder he conquered the world before he was thirty.

"Gentlemen," Scorbus said, and Marius became aware of Gerd standing silently at his shoulder. "We are indebted to you. Our first act as lord of this realm is to grant you a boon." He interlaced his fingers, and placed them before his jaw. "Ask me one thing, and I shall grant it."

Marius blinked, stared around him. How many dead surrounded him? How much gold in their rotting teeth, how many grave goods filtering down through the soil to lie in piles in hidden chambers of this endless warren? How much could he carry with all his dead strength? He had barely begun to calculate when Gerd cleared his throat, and spoke.

"Please, sire," he said, in a voice that reminded Marius just how young the boy was. "I'd like to go home."

"Is that all?"

"Yes, please."

Marius closed his eyes, yet still, somehow, knew that Scorbus was nodding.

"I cannot restore your life to you, young master. I am but a conduit to the gods. I do not share their powers."

"I know sire. I just… I just want to go home."

"Very well. I release you from my service. Now…"

Marius kept his eyes closed, aware of the countless gazes fixed upon him, two ageless, empty sockets in particular.

"I was told I'd get my life back."

The room became very still. The dead can become unseemingly still when the need arises. Marius waited. After several long, uncomfortable seconds, he frowned, and nodded once.

"Fuckers," he whispered, very softly. He pictured the stupid boy beside him, with all the riches of the dead his for the asking and all he wanted was...

"Fuck you, then," he said at last, opened his eyes, and glanced angrily at his young companion. "I want the same."

"So be it." Scorbus stood, and clapped his bony hands together. "Clear a space!" he commanded. The crowd parted, leaving an empty circle around the throne. Scorbus stepped down from his makeshift throne and indicated the roof above.

"Go with our thanks," he said.

The soldier appeared once more at Marius' side.

"Need any help, sir?" he asked, sarcasm thick in his voice. Marius smiled, the nasty little smirk of someone who has won when he shouldn't have and knows the other side was robbed.

"Don't worry." He stepped away and looked up at the roof overhead. "I've learned a thing or two about being dead." He raised his hands above his head, palms outwards, closed his eyes and concentrated.

The earth above him remained still. Someone at the back of the crowd giggled. A small pebble fell from the roof and bounced from Marius' forehead. After another minute or so he opened one eye, then another, then dropped his arms and sighed.

"I don't suppose anyone wants to give me a hand up?"

Several volunteers stepped forward and thrust him overhead. Marius dug into the roof with his fingertips, and glanced back at the assemblage below.

"I'd say go to hell," he said, as those at the outer edge of the crowd began to drift off into the dark. "But, you know..."

Those still gathered made no response. Marius set his face forward and began to dig for the surface.

# TWENTY-EIGHT

The night was cold and still. The paupers' graveyard outside the walls of Scorby City was as empty as anywhere else that had nothing to steal and no chance of witnessing a good street fight. Only the sound of a passing owl on the hunt broke the silence. Toward the back of the graveyard, a mound of dirt without a headstone began to shiver.

A dirt-encrusted finger broke through, then another, and another. Soon, an entire hand cleared the grave's confines. A twin followed it, and they flapped around until slowly, with inexorable effort, they drew out the arms to which they were attached. It took another fifteen minutes of frantic activity before Marius pulled himself chest-deep out of his hole. When he was finally able to rest and look about, he was not amused.

"You could bloody help, you know."

Gerd smiled from his perch atop a nearby grave and leaned back against its simple stone.

"And deny you the satisfaction of your victorious exit?"

"Very… fucking… funny." Marius wiggled another inch closer to freedom. "I am going to slap the smartarse right out of you when I get out of here." He looked down at himself. "If I get out of here." He leant forward on one elbow and raised his other arm. "Please?"

"Ah well," Gerd rose and dusted himself off. "If you insist."

He grasped Marius' hand, and together they succeeded in hauling him out of his predicament. They fell onto the ground, rolling over to gaze up at the stars.

"How did you get here so fast, anyway?" Marius eventually asked. Gerd waved his hands in front of his face.

"I am the dead," he intoned in his best "scary ghost" voice.

"Ha ha. Seriously."

"Seriously." Gerd placed his hands behind his head and made himself comfortable. "It just comes to me, you know? Like a skill you get."

"A skill I could have used."

"I'm as surprised as you are."

Marius sighed. "I'm not, actually."

"What do you mean?"

Marius sat up, and examined the back of his hands as they hung loosely over his raised knees. "You are dead, and I'm sorry about that, I really am. But the thing is, I'm *not*. Oh, I know…" He raised one hand and waved it at Gerd, showing the white and withered flesh in the moonlight.

"But didn't they say…?" Gerd nodded at the open grave.

"Yeah. They did." Marius set his jaw. "I don't have to listen to *them*. It's like… Remember I told you I spent three months imitating a eunuch at the court of the Caliphate of Taran?"

"Um, yeah?"

"Well, the only way I could get away with it, the only way I could make anyone believe I was a eunuch, was if I believed it as well. It's something that Jemefie, my first acting master, told me. It's easy to take an audience along with you when you're on stage. But if you want them to have faith in you after they've left the tent then you have to believe yourself."

"So you believe you're dead, is that it?"

"No." Marius concentrated, and his hand filled out in response, growing more pink as blood rushed in to fill expanding capillaries. "But the mob down there," he tilted his head at the ground, "They have faith in their own deaths. They made me believe in mine, made me forget that I belong with the living. Thing is," he concentrated again, and watched his hand shrivel and die, then blossom once more into life. "Look what I can do now." He smiled, and even though his face was ruddy and in the bloom of health, Gerd saw something dead lurking just below the surface, and shuddered. "I can make myself believe *anything*, as long as I need to."

Gerd sat up. "What now, then?"

"What am I going to do with this?" Marius examined his hand, "I don't know."

"No, I mean, what are you going to do at all?"

Marius stared over the simple headstones, away

from the open earth at their backs.

"Good question. What about you? Back downstairs with our friends?"

Gerd grimaced. "I don't think so."

"You have a choice?"

"Well," Gerd smiled. "In all the excitement of the new king, and your hilarious exit, nobody thought to wonder about what my release from service actually meant. So I guess I can do as I will, hey?" He leaned back, and stared at the sky. "Granny's going to die, soon. She knows it, too, that's why she wants me with her. I'm the only family she's got. I'll be there when she goes, then I'll be ready. Meet her below, help her adjust, show her around. That sort of thing." He stood, and turned to get his bearings. "The mountains are that way."

Marius followed his finger, and nodded.

"The opposite direction to Borgho City."

"Yeah."

"Yeah." They sat, staring at the blue line of the horizon, until Gerd eventually stirred.

"So…"

Marius sighed. "Yeah. Keth. I should probably, you know…"

"Tell her you love her. Make things up to her."

"Yeah. You know…"

"Do the right thing."

"Yeah."

"Buy her that place you talked about."

"Yeah." Marius closed his eyes, pictured himself at the window of a little cabin, a big, fat ginger cat under his fingertips. Keth walked towards him across the open fields, her hair swinging loose in the breeze, smiling, arms full of fruit for dinner. "That actually sounds good."

"Get a job."

"Hey?" Marius' eyes snapped open. "Steady on," he said, clambering to his feet. "No need to go too far."

"Well," Gerd joined him. "How then?"

Marius threw his arm around Gerd's shoulder, and turned him towards the distant city. "There's a running game at Big Nessie's, just under the dock fronts. Guys who've been at sea for two years and big idiot merchants with more money than card sense. I can work up a stake on the way there. In fact," he took a few steps, guiding Gerd with his arm, "If I had an off-sider, a stooge, if you like…"

"Partner."

"Yeah, sidekick, who wanted to split the takings…"

"Partner."

"Yeah, like I said…"

Talking fit to wake the dead, Marius steered his partner down the long road to Borgho City.

# ACKNOWLEDGMENTS

My thanks to Lyn and the kids for understanding and allowing me the space and time to write, and not rolling their eyes when I was banging on and on and on about the damned book. To Marc, Lee and Amanda at Angry Robot for steering the book through to publication, and Darren for all the cool promo and web grooviness. To my agent Richard Henshaw, for making me rich and powerful so that I can kill minions by the millions without having to fill out a single tax form.

Big callout to the Anxious Appliances, and to Chuck McKenzie, with whom I struck a deal waaaaay back in 2002. Here it is, Chuck: How do you make a hormone? Put sawdust in her Vaseline!

To my beta-readers – Adam, Kim, Greg, Miffy and David. Can't wait to kill you in the sequel, guys! Big props to all those brilliant Oz SF people who have held my hands, patted my head, told me to shut the fuck up and write, and been friends every step of the way, especially Kate Eltham, Tehani Wessely, Stephen Dedman, Adrian and Michelle Bedford, Dave Luckett, and Paul Haines (miss you, buddy).

Lastly, to my wife, Lyn, and the kids. I know I've already mentioned them, but they're worth a second call out. Love you, my fambly. If you're still reading this, why not drop into the Battersblog and tell me your dirtiest joke. I need one for the sequel's acknowledgment page…

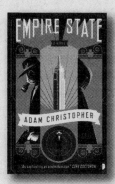

# TOO LATE TO STOP NOW

## Grab the complete Angry Robot catalog